FOUR THREADS OF FATE

BY KAYLEE CROSS

BOOK 1

FOUR THREADS OF FATE

Copyright © 2022 by Kaylee Cross

All rights reserved. No part of this publication may be reproduced, stored or transmitted in any form or by any means, electronic, mechanical, photocopying, recording, scanning, or otherwise without written permission from the publisher. It is illegal to copy this book, post it to a website, or distribute it by any other means without permission.

This novel is entirely a work of fiction. The names, characters and incidents portrayed in it are the work of the author's imagination. Any resemblance to actual persons, living or dead, events or localities is entirely coincidental.

Kaylee Cross asserts the moral right to be identified as the author of this work.

First edition

FOUR THREADS OF FATE

TRIGGER WARNINGS

This book contains a small part where rape is mentioned.

There is talking about abuse, physical and emotional, and torture, PTSD and death.

If you have any questions as to where exactly or how it is used/described, don't hesitate to reach out to me!

FOUR THREADS OF FATE

BOOKS BY KAYLEE CROSS

Four Threads of Fate series
Four Threads of Fate

FOUR THREADS OF FATE

I can and I will.

Don't let others tell you what to do. Make your own path and be happy.

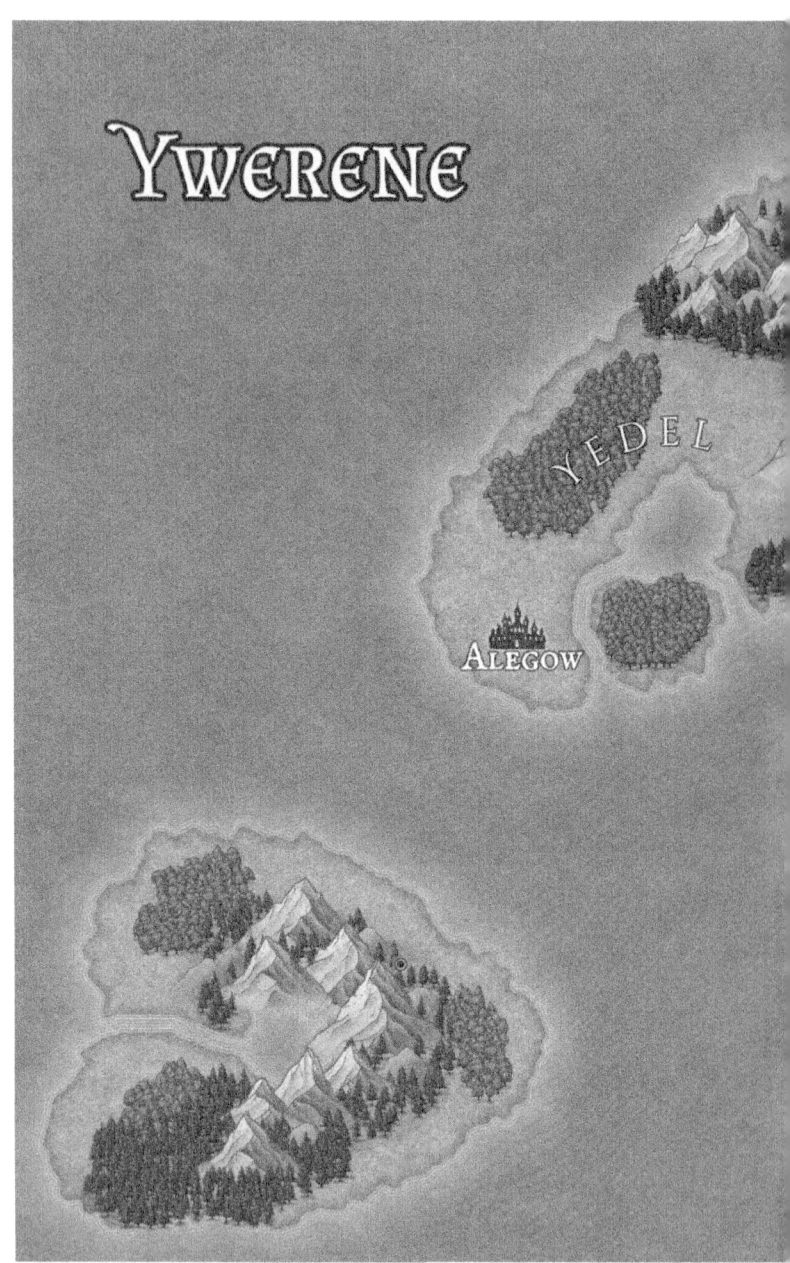

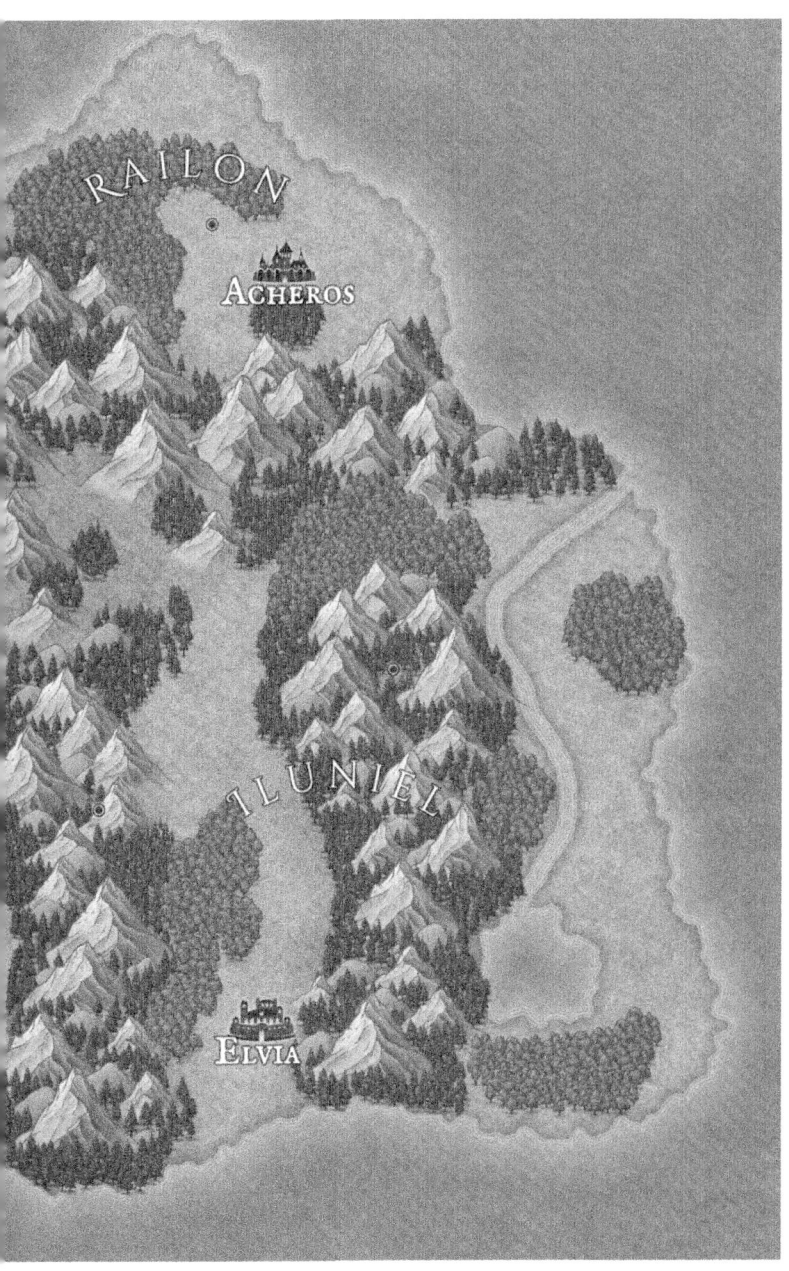

# FOUR THREADS OF FATE

CHAPTER 1

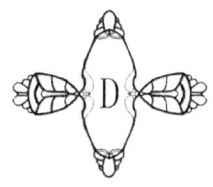

Four trials, four deadly trials, to give me the chance to reach my full potential. Four trials that will determine the fate of the entire kingdom.

I don't know what they do or what they will be, but I do know that they can change you.

Just like they changed my sister.

Leanne used to be this loving, sweet, righteous big sister. Until she reached the fourth trial. She completely turned on everyone. She became coldhearted, ruthless I might even say, which is not a good look for a queen. But since she is the eldest and our parents died, she had to step up.

Now I am about to take on these trials to gain my full magic potential.

That's the reason I'm here most of the time, just to clear my mind. This beautiful green landscape, surrounded by trees, flowers, and countless animals. It just makes me happy and feel at peace with myself and my surroundings. The creatures here differ from deer to gendrils, which are dog-like creatures. I even got one laying right beside me, called Yuno. She always comes to me when I'm here, as if she knows I need her company. We usually just lay in the grass, looking at the clouds moving through the sky, listening to the wind blowing through the field. It calms me and the humming magic beneath my skin down.

I have had two out of four elements since birth, earth, and air, and I know the first trial will release the other two, fire and water.

"Dawn!" someone suddenly shouts from behind me.

I turn over onto my stomach and peer between the trees. Not seeing anything at first sight, until a head with bright red hair walks out from behind a tree. "There you are," Madion says.

As usual, her hair is in a perfectly braided crown around her head, courtesy of her mate Jade.

They met about six years ago, after almost killing each other. Since Madion is our General, she had to go to Yedel, where she met Jade. And the rest of that story is complicated and quite triggering for both of them.

"What can I help you with, Madion?" I say with a smile before turning over onto my back again.

She lays down beside Yuno and me, softly running her hand over the fur of the former. "I wanted to see how you were doing after yesterday. You left in a hurry," she says quietly. Knowing all too well that I don't want to talk about the conversation I had with Leanne yesterday.

"I'm fine. We both should've walked away from that conversation before it had gotten out of hand. But it is what it is. I'm going to do these trials and I don't care whether she agrees or not," I say in response, still not in the best mood to talk about it.

"Okay." She turns on her side, facing me. "Changing the subject then. You need armor or at least clothing that'll survive the four trials. And Jade said she could help with that."

"I know. She came to my room last week," I state. "I assume she heard from you that I was planning on taking on the trials and offered to put together anything I need. I didn't accept yet."

"Dawn, we're your friends. Let us help," Madion immediately counters. I turn my head to look straight into her eyes and I can see that she means it. "You're not alone. Me, Jade, and Nate will always be here for you."

Ah yes, Nate. The apprentice of the best blacksmith of Iluniel. We met a couple years ago via that very blacksmith. The meeting was rough for him, but we became friends soon after.

"I know all of you support me. I just wish I had Leanne's support, too. She is always sitting on her golden throne, with a crown on her head, acting as if she is the only person who matters in this world." I take a deep breath. "I just want us to go back to the way things used to be. But that last trial, that very night, did something to her, and I want to know what."

And with that, I get up and walk towards the town. Madion hurries after me and Yuno retreats into the forest.

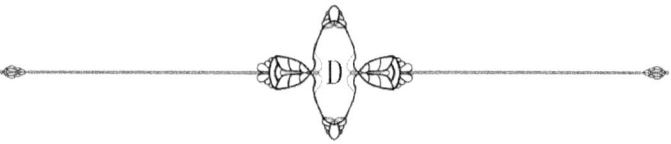

When I reach the gates, my guards, Adrian, with his shoulder-length blonde hair tied up, and Jake, his short black hair matching his dark eyes, eye my weapons that I always carry around first and then the rest of my body to see if I suffered any injuries. Once they see I don't have a scratch on me, they let me through. Madion and I walk into the town for a while before we reach a small wooden house, the front yard covered in fabric, ribbons, lace, and weapons. We're greeted by a black and red-haired, ebony-skinned woman.

"I see you've dyed your hair again, Jade. Looks better than the puke-green you chose last time," I say as an answer to her always changing appearance.

One month she has her natural black hair, the month after that she has gone completely blue, and another month later it has all the colors of the rainbow. You never know what to expect from the warrior, who is a seamstress by night.

"Thanks for pointing out my mistakes, Your Highness," she sneers back, but immediately after, sticks out her tongue. I return the gesture and Madion sighs.

"Shall we go inside? You said you already made sketches for Dawn's outfit," Madion says, crossing her arms and tapping her foot on the ground.

She's getting impatient again.

"I indeed have. Follow me." Jade lays down the dress she was working on and leads us inside. There she guides us towards the gigantic oak dinner table, which is also littered with fabrics, ribbons, lace, and weapons.

"I was playing around a bit with the cloak, but I think I came up with a pretty good concept," she says as she proudly hands over the sketch.

It shows a rough sketch of me with an outfit I've never seen before.

And holy heaven. It's amazing.

It consists of tight, black pants, with intricate golden embroidery of curls, flowers, and leaves on the side of the legs. A dark blue shirt with the same embroidery as the pants across the chest and the sleeves. Leather brown boots and a black cloak. And of course, the entire outfit has got hidden pockets and compartments for my weapons.

"Jade," I mumble, not taking my eyes off the paper. "I need this right now."

She beams at my words.

"It's amazing. You truly outdid yourself," I say as I hand her back the sketch. "And I'd be honored to wear it during the trials."

"Thank you," she says while slightly inclining her head.

Madion takes her trembling hand and squeezes, showing how proud she is of her mate.

"Well, I still need to prepare for my dinner with Leanne tomorrow, so I'll leave you to it." Mostly mentally, though. "We'll meet tomorrow at our usual spot. I've been meaning to try a new trick I came up with," I say, snapping them out of their staring.

"Of course. Take some time for yourself tonight. We'll see you tomorrow," Madion answers, steering Jade towards the back of the house, in the direction of the bedroom.

And that's my cue to go.

"Try to be your most charming self during dinner. Leanne loves that!" Jade calls after me, making Madion snort. I flip her off and exit the little cottage.

When I reach my room, I fall down on the bed and close my eyes. Thinking of everything that could happen tomorrow night, this week, this month.

The worst outcome would be that I don't survive the trials, but I won't lay down my life that easily.

Opening my eyes, I look around my room. Once you enter my room, you'll find a desk and several bookcases on your left. My bed and the bathroom are on the right. With that come the books that are spread all throughout my room.

However, the best part of this room is the balcony, where you can look across the enormous flower garden. As a child, I used to go there every day with my mom, smelling the flowers, making beautiful bouquets out of them, and giving those to my dad. He got one every day, but that didn't cease his excitement when I came into his office with yet another bouquet.

Now I usually slip out at night to peacefully sit with the flowers, trying to remember the days with my mom right there next to me.

After a while of daydreaming, I decide to let the bathtub fill with hot water. I need to clear my head and soothe my sore body.

Because I might've been injured without Adrian and Jake knowing.

And it might've happened because I tried a new move with my sword I have yet to perfect.

Luckily, my healing is quick, so it'll be all gone within an hour.

If the wound had been caused by Alk though, that would've left a scar, or it could've killed me.

Because Alk is the only substance that can kill a member of my family.

It might sound odd, but an ancestor of mine apparently angered someone. Up to a point that the man cursed our entire bloodline, giving us our only weakness.

But my dad tried to have every piece or drop of it destroyed, hoping to keep us all safe from then on.

He must have missed that last bit though because he would not have died if the dagger that went into his heart wasn't made of Alk.

I'm not going to rack my brain over that now. I need to clear my head for a bit with a book, while laying in piping hot water.

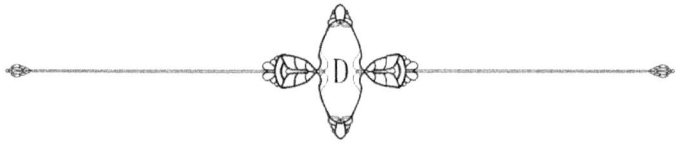

I'm awoken by the blinding sunlight coming through my window as someone yanks away the curtains. I let out a grunt and cover my head with my pillow, but it's immediately ripped away by someone. Then I cover my head under my blankets, but those are thrown across the room. Leaving me sprawled in bed, in my nightgown, still half asleep.

"Get out of bed. You were supposed to be at the training court an hour ago," Jade drawls as she leans against the wall, weapons strapped to her legs, arms, and waist. She even brought her bow and quiver.

Madion is on the other side of the bed, making her the person who pulled open the curtains. She is also covered in weapons. However, she has a sword strapped across her back instead of a quiver.

"Give me a minute. I barely slept last night," I mutter, sleep and terror still clouding my mind.

Madion lets out a sigh. "The same nightmare again?"

"Yes, my parents being murdered in front of me, me trying to save them but failing by mere inches, and then the murderer drives their blade straight through my heart. The exact same dream, every time, but I can never see the face of the killer." I say in response, still shivering.

The nightmare is identical every single night. I'm always too late to save my parents. I always die, my parents always die. It's a mess I can't seem to figure out.

"You two go ahead. I'll change really quick and meet you downstairs," I say before anyone else comes with their theories again.

Jade chuckles. "Do you really think we're just going to go? Not a chance. You go change. We're waiting right here for you."

I let out a long, low grunt before I haul myself out of bed. Shuffling towards the big chest at the end of my bed, which contains all of my clothes. I open it, grab the first pair of pants I come across, put them on, find a matching shirt, put that on too, pull out some socks, and then close the chest again. After shuffling back to my bed, Jade and Madion watching carefully so that I don't lay down and fall asleep again, I sit down and put on my socks and my boots. Jade hands me the daggers from my nightstand, and Madion gives me my sword from the other side of my bed. When I stand up, they both loop an arm around my elbow and lead me out of the room towards the training court.

The court is completely empty when we enter. No soldiers in sight, no guards, no one.

"Where is everyone?" I ask.

No response.

I spin around and find Jade and Madion are gone, too. I look around, searching for any kind of movement, but find none. I push out a wave of my magic, trying to pick up anything, still nothing.

Where the hell are they?

They've never done this before, so I unsheathe my sword, readying myself for anything. My magic hums beneath my skin in anticipation of what's coming.

The hairs on my neck stand up and my magic immediately responds, forming a shield of wind behind me as Madion brings down her sword. As soon as my shield drops, I bring my sword around to meet hers. Our swords clash, and Madion smiles at me. A wicked grin that would send people running for the hills, but not me. I know that grin. She has a back-up plan.

Jade.

She comes in from my right. I keep my sword against Madion's, keeping my eyes on her. And right before Jade is about to strike, I turn away, letting her clash with Madion.

This isn't their usual tactic in battle, I notice. They always circle the people they're fighting against. Yet they're not doing it now.

Jade and Madion are both back on their feet by the time I turn around to face them again.

"What the hell, Madion. You could've seriously injured me with that move." I heave.

"No, I couldn't. And you know it." Is her only response as they both attack again.

Though this time, I'm ready.

I quickly grab a dagger from my right thigh and block Jade's sword while I block Madion's blow with my sword. I push them back, but Jade immediately goes for my knees. I try to sidestep, but Madion is waiting for me. She sweeps my legs out from under me and they both jump at me.

Madion pins down my right leg and arm and Jade my left leg and arm. I try to get free, but they only squeeze my arms harder.

"Get off me," I sneer.

"No," Jade merely says. Waiting for something.

They want me to break free, although I can't use my arms and legs.

But she does not want me to use brute strength.

She wants to see magic.

"Why are you two even doing this?" I ask again, trying to rip my arms free while trying to mask the building of my magic inside me at the same time.

"What do you mean? We're just training, and you are losing," Madion says with a smirk.

"No, I'm not," I say and let my magic out.

They're both flung back a few feet. I get up as soon as they're both off of me. Searching for my weapons, but those seem to have been blown away, too.

Just my luck.

But I have two daggers left on me. I take one, leaving the other just in case. I look around, panting from the magic outburst, trying to see where Jade and Madion landed.

They're both slowly getting up, looking at each other. But as their attention snaps to me, I can see they're both angry, very angry.

I wonder why.

They do find their weapons, unfortunately, and start circling me. Using their standard, but successful, move. I position myself in a way that Madion is on my left and Jade on my right. Which is the best position for me to be in. Jade always goes for the legs and Madion for the chest. But not this time. The second they try to touch me, well, they'll be even more pissed when they find out what I'm about to do.

Madion throws a subtle nod in Jade's direction. Here we go. Let's hope I practiced this enough.

I raise my dagger, as if I'm going to fight them with steel. But at the same time, I close my eyes, take a deep breath, and relax my body.

Jade and Madion strike, but the blows never land. As I open my eyes, I'm greeted by growls from both sides of me.

I might've pinned them to the ground by using my magic with the earth. I look to my left and find Madion, feet buried in the ground, hands completely enveloped with earth and stone, anchored to the ground. She is glaring at me as I look higher. I give her a smile before turning to Jade.

She might be in an even worse position than Madion. Jade is sitting flat on her ass, legs in front of her, completely covered in earth and stone. Her hands are pinned behind her, anchored to the ground by more earth and stone. She's glaring at me, too.

They're both pissed I outsmarted them. They can't use their magic on the earth. Jade can control water and air, and Madion controls fire and air.

By the looks on their faces, I know they're going to take revenge soon. Very soon.

"I was losing, Madion?" I say, slightly taunting her, "It seems that you've both found yourself in a bind. Literally." I casually sit down in between them, leaving them stuck on the ground.

"Dawn, I swear to heaven, if you don't let us go right now," Jade breathes. "I will—"

I put my chin on my fist. "What will you do? You can't go anywhere. Which makes this a good time to talk about what's coming."

Madion looks curious, not angry, and asks, "You mean the trials or Leanne?"

"Both." Their faces turn grave. "I'm scared," I confess. "Scared of the trials, but also scared of what Leanne might do. She threatened me last night that if I dared to do the trials, she'd do everything in her power to stop me from completing them. What if she tries to sabotage me? The trials are already deadly on their own. Would Leanne sabotaging me be the thing that gets me killed?"

I wrap my arms around my knees and let my magic hold on Jade and Madion's restraints dissipate. As soon as the earth and stone are loose enough, they shake themselves free. Letting big chunks of earth fall on the ground. Then they make their way over to me. Jade sits down on my right and Madion on my left, taking the same position as me. And like that, we sit there.

"You'll be okay, Dawn. You already showed just now that you're resourceful. I wouldn't have thought about covering my enemies in dirt to keep them down," Jade says, which earns her a small smile from me.

She throws her arm around my shoulders and pulls me in close. Madion comes from the other side lays her head on my shoulder.

Silently telling me I'm not alone, I never will be.

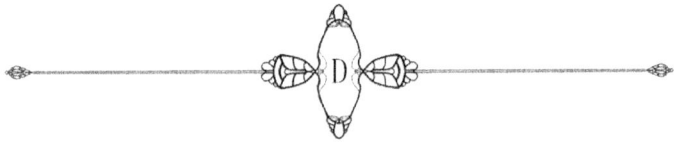

It's been hours since the three of us stopped training.

We talked for a while about how I should approach Leanne. In what ways she could sabotage me before, during, and even after the trials. And we came up with various ways she could do that. A lot of which could get me killed.

I also need to figure out what really happened to her. No one changes that much, going from the kindest princess you'll ever meet to a bloodthirsty queen.

How I should take on these trials was a point of discussion, too. I just need to stay calm. I'm strong, I can take it. Once the letter comes, I can start making my plans. Now I just need to keep my head straight.

As I approach my room, I notice my door is ajar. I draw my daggers, one in each hand, and slowly step closer.

Reaching the door, I push it open, ready for an attack. But nothing comes.

I sneak into my room and close the door. I do a quick search to see if anyone is here. Again, nothing.

Then my eyes fall on my bed. On my dark blue bed sheets lays an envelope. With my name on it.

I pick up the envelope and cut it open with my dagger.

Inside I find the letter I've been waiting for, what I've been training for.

~

Dawn Maria Rowena Sungust,
We hereby summon you for your first trial.
In one week, when the sun sets, be at the sacred dome.
Beware of the shadows. They are more dangerous than you might think.

~

CHAPTER 2

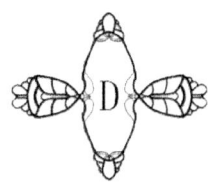

I drop the letter, not knowing whether I should be excited or terrified. I got what I wanted. I'm going to take on the trials and come out victorious. Hopefully.

Because, at this point, failing isn't an option for me. I want to make my parents proud, show Leanne that I can do it, but most of all, prove to myself that I am not weak. And I never will be.

I pick the letter back up, read it over and over, before deciding to take it to Jade and Madion right now.

I walk onto my balcony. Savoring the sweet smell of the flowers surrounding it, before lowering myself onto the pavement below.

As my feet touch the ground, I pick up noise from my right. The guards are doing their usual midnight check up of the grounds. If I get caught now, Leanne will have me locked in the dungeons again. So I retreat into the bushes behind me, leaves tickling my arms. I calm down my racing heartbeat and try to take slow and quiet breaths as the guards pass by.

I freeze as they both look in my direction. They squint their eyes as if they're seeing me.

I can't have them find me.

I dredge up the smallest bit of magic and direct some of the surrounding air to my left. Causing the bushes to rustle and the guards to run towards it.

Then I exit the bushes on the opposite side and sprint to the end of the garden, straight into town.

When I reach their house, it's already dark and silent inside. So they're already in bed. Great, I feel like pissing them off even more.

Creeping closer to the front door, I gather a bit of magic in my palm, press it against the door and let it spiderweb over it. Checking for any wards or spells to keep people out. When I find none, I have to say I'm slightly disappointed. I had expected them both to ward this house head to toe. Blowing up anyone who dared to touch it. Apparently not.

I pull my magic back in and enter the cabin. The dining table is still covered in fabric, weapons, and more fabric. And when I look to my left, I find a mannequin. With my suit on it. Not finished yet, but it already looks as breathtaking as the sketches Jade showed me.

The embroidery is amazing, consisting of little flowers, leaves, even small branches. I've known from the moment I got to know Jade, who is now one of the fiercest warriors in Iluniel, that she was an excellent seamstress. She could turn any piece of fabric into something amazing.

I make my way to the back of the cabin and let my magic spiderweb over their bedroom door, too. Finding nothing there either, I quietly open it.

As I peer into the room, I find Jade and Madion in bed, cuddling.

I stand at the end of the bed, seeing how peaceful they look as they sleep. I try to memorize their faces for when I wake them up, knowing they'll be pissed at me for the second time today.

I lift my right hand, ready to tie them down with air this time. But as I try to lower it, I find it stuck. Encircled by a small, but strong, air current. It pulls me back against the wall, and as I try to wrench it free with my left hand, it's pinned to the wall on the other side of my head.

And as I stare at my hands, I realize that Jade and Madion were awake and ready to strike.

When I look to the bed and find them both sitting up, each one has a hand outstretched.

"Good morning," I say, trying to break the tension.

"It's literally one in the morning. Why are you awake?" Jade says, sounding bored and tired. "We sent you back to your room hours ago."

"May I show you why I came?" I ask, gesturing to my jacket with my air-bound hands.

Jade lets out a sigh and gets out of bed, her shorts clinging to her waist and thighs. But she doesn't set me free as she approaches. She crosses the space between us, eyeing my jacket and my face.

"You better have a good reason for being here at this hour," she breathes in my ear.

I just grin at her, trying to hide my discomfort and the fact that my magic desperately wants me to break free.

I've been tied up many times, magically and with ropes or chains, mostly during combat training, but also by Leanne.

Almost every time I'd sneak out at night, she'd catch me and chain me up in the dungeons. Knowing very well that my magic doesn't appreciate that to put it lightly.

Jade pats down my jacket, trying to find the pocket I put the letter in. I can feel my magic getting more agitated by the minute, but I need to get a grip on it. I can't have it lash out every time I'm in a situation like this.

Eventually, Jade finds the envelope that contains the letter. She walks back to the bed, leaving me pinned against the wall.

Beads are forming on my temples now as Jade slowly opens the envelope.

They both read what's inside and then glance at me.

"That's soon," Madion says. "I thought you'd have at least another month to train."

I take a deep breath. "Apparently not." Trying to keep it all in. "But on another note, could you please let me go?"

"Now, why would we do that?" Jade says, challenging me.

But she falls silent when she looks me in the eye. As if she can see I'm about to explode. Madion follows Jade's line of sight and sees the strain, too.

They simultaneously release me, and I drop to the floor.

"Sorry," they whisper.

I wave a dismissive hand as I try to calm down. I'm shaking and sweating like crazy. So the gust of wind Madion sends over me is very appreciated.

"It's fine. I need to be able to keep myself in check. Even if my magic is trying to just explode to get me out." I swallow deeply, clenching my fists. "I need to get it under control."

"Dawn, you're twenty-one years old. You have at least another five hundred to go," Jade tries to reassure me, her eyes still filled with worry.

"I know," I say while slowly getting up, "but that's something to talk about another time. I came here for that." Pointing at the letter now in Madion's hands.

"Do you think you're ready for it?" Madion asks, reading the letter again.

I take a seat on the bed in between Madion and Jade. "Maybe. But since we do not know what the trial will be exactly. I can never be sure."

"What about this line?" Jade says, pointing at the ending line of the letter. "It looks like a clue to me."

I think on the line for a bit, rummaging through every single creature I know that is associated with shadows. The most obvious examples come up first. They often place shadow hounds and gendrils in the category of shadow creatures.

"I'd say the most obvious option might be the best one here. It's her first trial, so they won't go all in from the start, right?" Madion asks from my left. Carefully placing her hand on mine, I interlace our fingers and give her hand a squeeze. To tell her not to worry about what had just happened. I receive a small smile in return.

"I hope you're right. I can handle shadow hounds. Everything else I'm not sure about," I say in response.

I nestle myself between their pillows as I feel my eyelids closing on themselves.

I should really sleep.

"Dawn, you're sleeping here tonight. I don't give a damn about what Leanne has to say about it. You're not climbing your balcony in this state," Jade says, as she pulls off my shoes and covers me with a blanket. "First thing in the morning is us three going to Nate to get you a new sword. Since the last one didn't fare too well during practice."

We might've bent it with our magic in ways you can't unbend it again.

I wave her off as I roll over to my side and close my eyes.

I feel two kisses on my cheek before I fall asleep.

Hoping to sleep a whole night without nightmares.

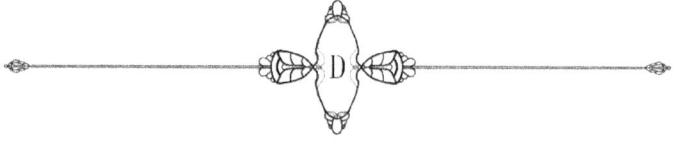

Six hours later, I'm awoken by an iron pot falling on the floor and a trail of swear words that would send the priest running. I'm guessing the pot fell on someone's toes.

I untangle myself from the blankets and shuffle over to the bathroom.

The hot water soothes the muscles and the magic strain beneath my skin. I figured that out a couple of years ago.

I sneaked out at night, but as expected, Leanne caught me. Immediately put me in shackles before leading me to the dungeons. Where she left me, for two days, to teach me not to sneak out at night without permission of the queen. She left me in the dungeons, burning up from the inside because of my magic being subdued.

When she finally let me out, I immediately ran to my room. My magic roared beneath my skin to get out, even though I had no safe place to do so. Then I turned on the shower and stood underneath the steady stream. And it helped. It calmed me down and my magic slowly retreated into my soul, calming itself down.

Now I've been doing it every time I need to. Just letting the water stream over my back, soothing every muscle and fiber in my body.

After standing under the running water for about ten minutes, my stomach growls at the lack of food. I change into the clothes Jade left on the bed for me while I was in the shower and exit the bedroom. I'm met by the amazing smell of Madion's baked potatoes. They're heavenly.

"You completely awake?" Madion asks me while serving me a large portion.

"Yes, of course. I always have a good night's sleep," I mumble, sounding as sarcastic as possible.

Jade and Madion both won't look at me when I say it. I can't blame them. They both can't do anything about it.

"We sent word to Nate that we'll be visiting later for your sword," Jade says from the other side of the table, shoving her mouth full of potatoes, trying to break the awkward silence.

I just nod. Shoving down potatoes myself too.

We eat in silence before heading out to the forge.

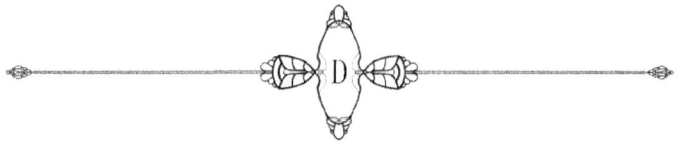

The forge is on the other side of the town. A big, round, black building. Only Nate and the head blacksmith work there. The blacksmith, Vergus, doesn't allow anybody besides customers inside. The three of us and Nate are exceptions and can come by any time we want.

Vergus has been like a father to us. His full, slightly greying beard, and short cropped, also greying, brown curls, already make him look like a dad.

He took Nate in when he was fourteen years old. Nate had been living on the streets for years, from what I heard. His parents died in the Great War when he was only eight years old. And everybody else was afraid of him, due to his rare power over three elements instead of only one or two. They just couldn't care less where he went.

As for me, he is always there when I need him.

He will listen to anything I need to say. He is my shoulder to cry on. He is the person who will let me ramble on and on, and when I am finished, he'll make the corniest jokes he can come up with.

As we enter the forge, we're greeted by no one. Typical.

We walk our usual way over to the workbenches, where we find two sweating men hammering on pieces of metal. The grey-haired male, Vergus, greets us with a wave of his hammer before continuing. The other male, dark brown hair stuck to his forehead from the sweating, lies down his hammer and comes our way.

"I heard you needed a sword, Dawn," Nate says as he takes off his dirty apron.

I walk over to him. "And I heard you could make me one, Nate."

We stare at each other for a moment before bursting out in laughter.

Nate then grabs my wrist and leads me towards an almost empty table. Only a sword lies on it.

"I already made you one," he says, crossing his arms.

I let my hand slide over the blade. It might look simple, like you'd expect a sword to look, but it feels like it's so much more. It feels powerful, yet ordinary.

"It looks like an ordinary sword. Shouldn't she have something spectacular for the trials?" Jade asks.

"It's already perfect, Jade. At least it looks better than that raggedy, five-year-old sword you use for practice," I say to her with a grin, earning me a sneer back.

"It looks amazing. I'm glad I get to use a sword made by your hands." I look up at Nate, earning me a smile.

"I'm glad you trusted me with it," he whispers back, earning him a grin from me.

We stare at each other for far too long. Madion clears her throat and says, "Okay, enough of that. We have work to do."

I glare at her before saying, "I don't complain about you and Jade sneaking off whenever you can for whatever you like to do in supply closets or empty rooms."

Now Madion and Jade look at me as if they could kill me right here on the spot. I just laugh at them. They storm towards me, both grabbing an elbow and start hauling me towards the entrance of the forge. I give Nate the small parting wave I can manage while trying to hold on to the sword with my other hand.

"Be gentle with her! She's very fragile," Nate calls out from the other end of the forge before returning to his work.

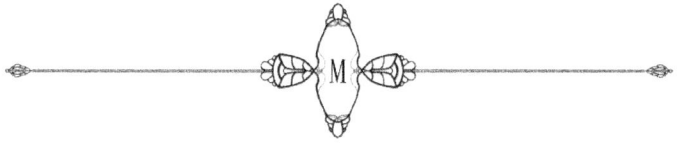

"Jade?" I call out. "What are you doing?"

She ventured into our bedroom about an hour ago, while I was getting started on our dinner, and she has yet to come out.

I could use some help with it as well, even though she isn't known to be very skilled at cooking to say it nicely.

She has almost burned down this house five times since she moved in. Luckily, I can control fire and air, so I could put it out each time before it got too big.

"I'll come help in a moment!" Jade suddenly shouts back.

I sigh. She's up to something again.

But she'll come out once she's ready to show off whatever she made now. Probably another dress, one of the ten she made the past month.

The door to our bedroom opens, and a giggle sounds behind me as Jade approaches the kitchen. I don't look over my shoulder, since the broth in front of me needs a good stir.

Silent footsteps come closer to my back, and I feel myself smiling before arms come around my waist and Jade presses her face against my back.

"Am I not allowed to turn around?" I ask her, still slowly stirring the pot in front of me.

"No, and you have to close your eyes while I do something."

"You realize I am the one making our dinner as usual, and we don't want it to overcook."

"It'll only take a few seconds," she mumbles.

I close my eyes at her request and raise my hands. "Fine, you have ten seconds."

Her arms immediately vanish from my waist, and a moment later, some fabric is brought in front of my chest and tied around my middle and neck.

Then Jade turns me around and takes my hands in hers.

"Now you can look," she whispers, sounding quite excited.

I slowly open my eyes to find her with a broad smile and a new apron. Her initials stitched right above the waistline.

She pulls on the fabric covering me, so I look down to find myself wearing a similar red apron, with my initials embroidered on it as well.

I let my hand glide over it, feeling the smooth fabric. "This is what you've been working on the whole day?"

"Yes," she answers, hesitantly.

I lean forward and press a kiss to her lips and cheek. "I love it."

"That makes me really happy," she whispers, kissing my hand.

"Now, shall I get back to our dinner before it overcooks?"

"Yes, please. Can I help in any way?"

I turn back to the stove and start stirring again while adding some more seasoning. "You could cut up the vegetables."

"On it," she says as she grabs a knife, cutting board, and the sack of vegetables I got earlier on the market.

Jade gets to cutting while I get to making the bread we'll be having with the soup.

We start humming a song while we do our tasks. The bread comes along nicely in our magic-fueled oven. I put a pinch of my magic in it and can now control it however I want.

Then I glance to my right and completely stop what I'm doing.

Jade is cutting the vegetables.

Neatly cut slices of carrots are on the corner of the cutting board, together with chopped up onion, leak, and celery.

But how she's working on the tomato.

And it's a massacre.

I step behind her and put my hands over hers, stopping her from murdering the tomato even further. It's a pile of mush. Seeds littered across the board.

"What did it do to you?" I ask,

She snorts and puts down the knife. "I don't even like tomatoes, so I might've gone a bit too far in chopping them up."

Putting my chin on her shoulder, I set our hands down on either side of the cutting board. "Shall we leave it be, then?"

Without an answer, she conjures a gust of wind, and every bit of the tomato goes in the bin.

"Now, let's get the rest of this in that pot and get everything done. I'm hungry," she says, reaching for the neatly cut vegetables.

I let go of her hands and help with getting the piles into the pot. Jade stirs while I check on the bread, which seems to be ready at any moment.

So I quickly plate the table for two and light the candles.

We always keep them on during dinner, to make it feel more intimate.

"Madion, I think the soup is done," Jade says.

"Coming," I respond as I straighten the coasters.

When I return to the kitchen, the soup and bread are both done, and we take them out of the kitchen to the table. Once it's all set, we take off our aprons and I head back to turn everything off before joining Jade, who has already taken her seat.

I sit down next to her, shuffling my chair a bit closer to hers. She serves us both to the soup and a piece of bread.

Then Jade puts her hand on the back of my neck, making me turn to her. She grips my chin and kisses me once before getting to her dinner.

I chuckle and do the same, knowing she'll have dessert ready once we're finished.

CHAPTER 3

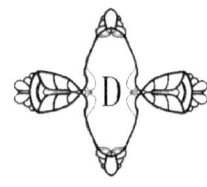

Yuno always attacks from my right and my body just automatically moves out of the way. She snarls at me, showing her long fangs and bright yellow eyes. I smirk, challenging her even more.

Her grey and white tail divides into three, showing that she is about to use her powers.

Gendrils are odd but fascinating creatures. They might look normal, mostly wolf-like, which means in size she comes up to my hip.

But gendrils have special features. Their bright yellow eyes, as bright as the sun, their fur varies from snow white to pitch black. Claws that, if used right, could rip you to shreds in seconds.

And then you have their magic over the earth, which is still not fully understood until this day. They divide their tail and let them connect with the earth. As if pulling the magic straight from the ground.

Yuno is doing the exact same thing right now, eyes still closed, tails on the ground. I can feel the power radiating from her, calling out my own in response. This is going to hurt, with or without protection.

I pull on my own magic, raising a shield of rocks.

But Yuno beats me to it. She crumbles my wall and fires her own magic at me.

I get flung back a few feet before landing on my back, knocking the wind out of me.

"And here I was thinking I was going to win this time," I wheeze, trying to get air back into my lungs.

Yuno pads over and starts licking my face. I smile at it since it's almost the only way for her to show any affection. And I don't mind it. She has been here. Always has been here. Just like Vergus, just like Jade and Madion, and just like Nate.

But it is different with Yuno, even though she's an animal.

She understands me. At least it seems like it. She doesn't judge me when I ramble on for hours and hours about anything. It's nice to have an animal companion, someone to curl up against when you're afraid, someone to have at your side at all times.

Unfortunately, Leanne doesn't allow Yuno to even enter the town. She has to stay in the forest, otherwise she is to be executed on the spot.

Another reason why I rather spend my time outside the walls.

Yuno finally stops licking my face, allowing me to get up. I survey the surrounding trees, swearing I heard something. But I don't see or hear anything now.

And since I have spare time before my dinner with Leanne, I decide to practice something. It might be a stupid move, but I need to control my magic sooner rather than later.

I take a deep breath. "Yuno?"

Her ears perk up, a questioning look in her eyes. As if she already knows what I'm about to ask.

"Can you restrain me with your magic?" I ask, very unsure.

Yuno growls at me. She knows it's not a good idea. But I still want to do it. I need to be able to restrain my magic, and myself.

Because once I finish the trials, my magic will be way stronger than before. And I am afraid of what might happen if I am restrained at my full magic potential.

I look pleadingly at Yuno, and it almost sounds as if she sighs before she nods towards a small hill.

We walk over, and she guides me to lie on top of the hill. I feel the grass beneath my fingertips as I lay down. Yuno takes her place at my feet.

She looks me in the eye one last time to ask for confirmation that I want to pull through with it. I give her a nod and take a deep breath.

I can feel her pulling on the earth at my sides. It slowly covers my arms, chest, and legs. Spreading further and further until only my head, neck, feet, and waist are left bare. The earth hardens in less than a second. And the second it snaps into its hardened state, my magic starts pushing. Pushing against those four layers that still cover my soul. Four layers that keep the full might of my magic contained until I finish all the trials. Every trial will make one layer break.

And it will change my features too. I don't know what because those changes differ from person to person. My father's eyes turned from green to almost white, with a circle of silver around his pupils. His hair went from black to white. And our healing factor also speeds up with every layer that breaks. Which means that we're almost immortal when we finish the four trials.

Yet with Leanne, I never really noticed much difference after the fourth trial. Her hair is mostly white, but she doesn't have the authentic full white hair, even though she finished all trials.

The magic is straining more and more beneath my skin. I need to control it to break free. I can't let it explode.

I take another deep breath and dig into that magic, pushing it to my will, taking the reins.

Slowly I feel it giving in, as if it knows I'm about to set us free. I keep pushing and tugging it in the right direction and I'm given more and more to take on these restraints.

I thread small tendrils of my magic through the dirt and stone covering my body. Weaving it through every gap and tear I come across. My magic hums in approval as it notices we're almost free. When I have filled every crack with my magic, I let it expand. Pushing against the insides of those cracks, widening them. Causing more cracks and tears in the ground.

I close my eyes and give one final push. Breaking the restraints around my arms, legs, and chest. The dirt and stone fall off of me with ease as I rise to my feet.

Yuno lets out a hum of approval as she walks over and sniffs at me.

She scrunches her nose, telling me I smell horrible. As if I didn't know that. I scratch her behind her ears, making her immediately drop to the floor. Rolling over onto her back, inviting me to scratch her belly, too.

I let out a laugh and give her the well-deserved belly scratches. A thank you for today.

All of the sudden her ears perch up, a sign of danger. I look around and find two armed men coming our way. I get up and palm a dagger, the only weapon I have on me at the moment. Yuno takes her spot beside me, growling at the upcoming threat.

But as the two figures come closer, I relax. I know those two figures all too well.

Adrian and Jake. My guards.

Yuno sees who they are too and relaxes.

They stop a few feet away from us and look me over.

Adrian gives me a smile as he says, "How fun, Dawn. Have you been playing in the dirt?" Jake snorts, and I give them both a glare.

"No, I was training," I say, crossing my arms over my chest. "You two could use some extra training, too. It seems as if you've gained some pounds." Now they glare at me, and I let out a chuckle.

Jake clears his throat. "We were sent to retrieve you for your dinner with Leanne."

And there goes my good mood. "That dinner is tonight." I look at the setting of the sun. "Not for another three hours."

"We are just here to retrieve you. We do not know why so early," Adrian states, taking a step towards me. Suggesting they will take me with them now. Conscious, unconscious, in chains, it doesn't matter. Ordered by the queen herself.

I raise my hands in surrender, not wanting to be dragged back unconscious. They both incline their head slightly.

I give Yuno one final scratch behind her ears before I take my place between Jake and Adrian.

Suddenly I feel something cold clasp around my wrist. When I look, I find a shackle, with a chain that leads to a shackle around Jake's wrist. I tug at it, but Adrian rests a hand on my other arm.

"Orders," he mutters with a sad smile. Knowing all too well what happens to me when I get locked up in the dungeons. He takes my hand in his and gives me a reassuring squeeze.

We make our way back to the castle, where a very nice evening with my sister awaits me.

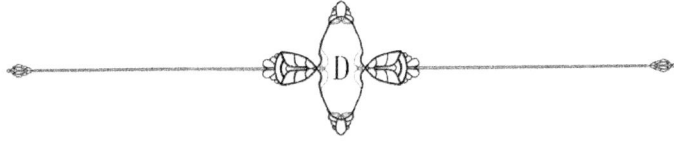

Back in my chambers, Jake finally unshackles me. They both give me a hug before leaving me to wash, dress, whatever I need to do to look presentable tonight.

I find a dark purple dress waiting for me on my bed. It involves a corset, so there will be servants helping me later.

But first, I need a bath.

With a small wisp of wind, I let the bath fill with hot water. I shake off all my clothes in front of the bath. Half of them stick to me because of the dirt that covers me from head to toe.

My whole body tingles because of the hot water as I let myself sink into the bath. I let out a hum of relief. Feeling the all too familiar strain in my muscles and soul subside by the water.

It always keeps me thinking. How my life would've looked if my parents didn't die that night.

They died the night of my seventeenth birthday.

We know they were murdered since I saw their final moments happen.

I was the one that saw it happen. Their bodies dropping to the floor when I reached them. Both of them stabbed through the heart.

The killer had an Alk dagger in their hand and came at me. I passed out soon after and remember barely anything else.

But there was no sign of struggle before, or after I arrived. So they knew the person who killed them. We just never found out who did it.

And I've had nightmares ever since.

What would they think of me taking on these trials? Would they be against it, like Leanne? Or would they be proud? Dad told me that his father was proud of him when he took them on. I hope, wherever they might be now, that they're proud of me too. I will try to make them proud every day for the rest of my life.

Leanne was always my biggest supporter. Until our parents died. I know it hit her hard, but I didn't expect her to shut me out like this.

By the time I have every last speck of dirt washed off, the water has turned cold.

I lift myself out of the bath and wrap myself in a fluffy towel that I laid out earlier.

As I enter my bedroom again, I'm almost scared to death. Two servants are waiting at the end of my bed. Remina and Calis. The usual pair that helps me. They've dressed me since I was little.

"Good afternoon, Your Highness. We came to help you prepare for your dinner," Remina says, giving me a strained smile, her apprehension shining in her brown eyes.

Everybody knows my relationship with Leanne isn't great. So, I'm expecting everybody to be preparing themselves for another loud night.

"Thank you," I say. "I'm guessing you have everything already thought out for me."

They both give me a genuine smile this time. "We most definitely do," Calis muses.

I let them do whatever they want to do over the course of an hour. They help me put on my dress, they pull on my hair, apply color to my lips and eyelids, and finish it by hanging my necklace around my neck.

I turn around to look in the mirror, and I look beautiful. I love dressing up, but not daily.

A dinner or a ball here and there is amazing. But to walk around each and every day in heels and a corset, barely able to breathe, that's not for me.

Calis and Remina both hum in approval, deeming me ready to face Leanne tonight.

Someone clears their throat behind me, and as I turn, I find Adrian and Jake waiting in the doorway. Ready to take me to dinner. I give Remina and Calis another thank you before walking over to Jake and Adrian.

They both extend their armored arms to me. I loop my arms through theirs and begin making my way towards the dining room.

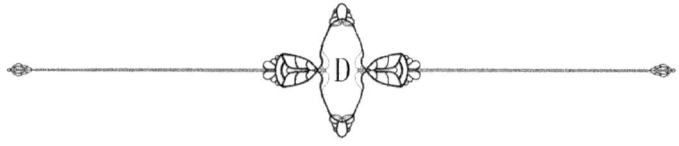

It almost feels as if I'm walking towards my execution. The entire castle is silent. Guards are at every corner.

They remember the last dinner we had and have taken precautions this time.

I notice some of them have shackles hanging from their belt. Glowing shackles, courtesy of Vergus, probably ordered by the council. They're made to suppress magic.

Speaking from experience, they work.

The council is a group of lords. They converse once a month about the current state of the kingdom. And they've had their fair share of opinions about Leanne and I.

We come to a stop in front of a big wooden door. Jake and Adrian free their arms from mine and take their spots behind me. The servant at the door pulls it open when I give him a nod.

I step inside the dining room and lock eyes with my sister.

She's sitting in her usual spot. At the head of the table on a big, carved out wooden chair. Vines and leaves made of wood cover the back and armrests, with a crimson red seating area. Leanne herself is wearing a similar crimson red gown, embroidered with golden and white thread. And, of course, on top of her head, the crown.

"Dawn," she says, "nice of you to join me. I heard you were out in the woods again."

I make my way over to my usual spot at the other end of the table.

"I was until these two dragged me back here," I say, jutting my thumb at the two men behind me. "In shackles, must I add." Showing her exactly how pissed I am at her for doing that.

"I apologize, but I couldn't have you running off and not have this dinner with me," she answers.

"You know I wouldn't run off. You just gave that order to taunt me," I sneer at her.

She just chuckles, taking a sip of her wine.

"What do you want to achieve with this dinner, Leanne?" I say, absently swirling the wine around in my glass. I'm going to need it tonight.

"I want to talk about several things. Starting with Draven," she explains with a sigh.

"What did the great kingdom of Railon do this time?" I empty my glass. "Send even more spies?" I wave over a servant, asking for a refill.

Leanne does the same. "They haven't done anything yet. But they are preparing for something."

The first course is brought in. Just a simple chicken broth with some bread on the side. Thank god. I was not in the mood for some fancy first course that comprises a small slice of bread with an even smaller slice of cheese or caviar on top.

"Then why are we discussing it, when I can't do a thing about it," I ask, swallowing a spoonful of the delicious broth.

"Because I want to discuss these things with you. We are sisters, after all." Averting her eyes and taking another sip of her wine as she says it.

"You haven't acted like it," I whisper to myself.

Leanne slams her palm on the table, causing several guards to reach for their weapons, some even touch the enhanced shackles. "If you have something to say, Dawn. Then speak," she snaps.

I don't give her the satisfaction of looking scared. I just sit there, sipping my wine.

Let her be angry for a minute.

I put down my glass after a minute and say, "I said, you haven't acted like it." I look her straight in the eyes. "Or am I wrong?"

Her nostrils flare. "What have I done that tells you I am not your sister?"

"What have you done?" I say, more calmly, "You lock me up in the dungeons if I don't listen to you. I have nightmares about you locking me up, you know." My voice gets louder. "You shackle me to the walls of a cell, knowing very well that my magic, and I, for that matter, panic even at the thought of being restrained. And for what? Because I go out at night?"

She thinks about her response for a minute before she answers with the most obvious answer she could give me. "I want to protect you. From things outside the gates, but also inside them."

She lowers her hand back to her lap, trying to look composed.

"Oh, come on, that is the most unoriginal reason you could give me. Protecting me doesn't involve restraining me when you feel like it." Now I get angry. "And what about the trials? How will you protect me there? Are you going to come with me? Are you going to send a dozen guards with me?"

"I have never given you my approval for taking on those trials, and I never will," she says, "But I have no other choice than to follow the rules. You are to do them alone. I will respect those rules, but don't think for one minute that I am happy about it."

Why can't she be happy for me for once, support me for once?

"You are never happy about something when it's not the way you want it to be." I take a deep breath before continuing. "Mom and dad would have supported me. They would have supported me the moment they heard I wanted to take it all on. They would have cheered me on at every trial. But they're gone." I blink back tears. "And as my big sister, I was hoping you'd support me like they would have."

One moment I'm in my seat. The next I'm on the floor, Leanne kneeling over me, her legs on either side of my hips.

"Don't bring them into this. They're gone. Move on." She extends a hand, magic pooling out of it, enveloping my wrists and chest. My magic immediately wraps around hers, trying to stop it. But she is stronger. She has completed the four trials while I haven't even started them.

Guards close in on us, swords drawn, shackles ready. But they don't move in yet, knowing we could both lash out at any moment.

My magic grows and grows inside me, readying for one massive push against hers.

"Move on?" I choke out as her magic reaches my neck. "I moved on a long time ago. It seems as if you have yet to move on. Lashing out every time I bring them up." My vision starts to blacken around the edges.

That gives my magic the final push.

I lash out with my full might, dissolving Leanne's hold on my body, filling my lungs with air again.

Then I lay on the ground for a short while, breathing heavily while coming back to my senses, until Jake looms over me, simultaneously feeling the all too familiar touch of shackles snap around my wrists. I see them snap around Leanne's wrists seconds later, too.

My magic immediately retreats deep inside me, back into my soul.

Jake and Adrian hoist me up. I'm shaky on my knees, so I almost drop back on the floor, but Adrian catches my elbow just in time to keep me upright.

I lock eyes with Leanne one last time, seeing disbelief and rage in them, before Adrian and Jake lead me back to my room.

Arriving there, they let me go. But don't unshackle me.

I turn around, looking expectantly at them. "Could you free me?"

"Are you going to lash out?" Jake asks, the keys dangling from his waist.

"No, that was only meant to stop me from being choked to death," I snap back.

Adrian doesn't want to look me in the eye while Jake just comes forward and undoes the chains. They bide me a good night before taking their places outside my room.

I undress and curl up in bed. Wishing I could have one dinner with Leanne, where we aren't at each other's throats.

CHAPTER 4

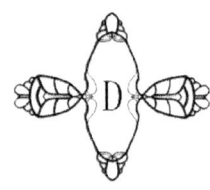

"Mom? Dad? Where are you?" I call out as I roam the castle halls. Not knowing what is waiting for me in one of those rooms.

All doors in the hallway are locked, except for one. The one door I never want to open again, but I have to. I need to know who did it.

I tiptoe over to the door, looking through the small gap into the room. My parents are both on their knees in front of a hooded and masked killer.

I accidentally bump into the door and falls into the room, right as the killer drives their dagger into mom's heart. She looks at me, tears sliding down her cheeks as she drops to the floor. Dad tries to lunge for her, or me. I've never figured out. But right as he touches my mom's cold hand, the killer drives their bloodied knife into my dad's heart. My dad lashes out with one final punch, a fist engulfed in flames, against the killer's throat, before he drops to the floor, too.

I became an orphan at seventeen years old.

The killer seems as if they are in some kind of trance, not responding to the grave injury my dad just dealt. They pull up a mask, covering their face up until right under their eyes. The killer turns around and stalks toward me, while I'm frozen in the doorway. Tears sliding down my cheeks as I take in my parents. Lying dead on the floor, almost hand in hand, looking into each other's eyes. The killer gets to their knees in front of me and stares into my eyes.

I suddenly feel lightheaded as the killer lifts their hands and starts to suck the air from my lungs, slowly suffocating me.

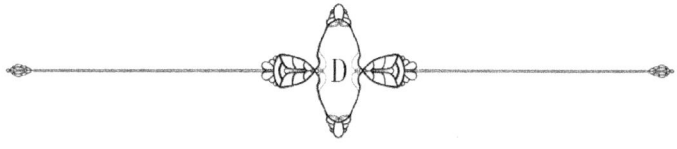

I jolt awake, drenched in sweat, stuck to my blanket.

The same repeating nightmare.

My parents are murdered in front of me and when the killer notices me, they try to get rid of me, too. Every single time, the dream ends there. The only thing I know for certain about the killer is that they used an Alk blade. Any of the other facial features I pick up might be my own imagination.

"I will find who did this. I promise you, mom and dad," I whisper as I clench my necklace in hand.

A golden moon, with a cage between its tips, containing a dark blue and a light blue stone.

My mom always wore it. The dark stone stood for my dad and the lighter stone for her. They were always very close. Always supporting each other.

That's what I expect a mate to be. Not only someone that loves you, but someone you can rely on, someone that makes you feel safe the moment he or she starts talking. Someone that can put back all those broken pieces inside of you and hold them there, for as long as needed until you're able to hold them on your own.

I let a small air current cross my blanket, drying it. When I deem it dry enough, I close my eyes, wipe away my tears, and sleep.

Ready for another day.

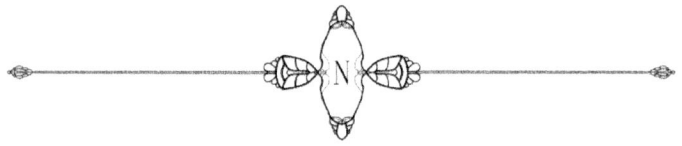

With his hands just below mine on the handle, Vergus helps me lift the mace from the bench.

How the person who ordered this is going to carry or even use it is beyond me.

Luckily, I have Vergus to help me. Because I might be strong, but this mace has to be at least five times my weight.

Together, we put the mace back in the fire.

The man that ordered it wants some more spikes.

If somebody gets killed with a mace in the next few weeks, I didn't make this thing.

Leaving it in the oven for now, we walk away from it and lean against my workbench. We've both been up before sunrise and still have a lot to do.

I have to meet Dawn before her trial to give her something.

Vergus has a pile of swords and daggers on his desk waiting to be fixed or remade into something else.

So we've got a lot to do in a short amount of time. We really need to make a schedule.

Vergus suddenly puts his hand on my shoulder and glances at me. "Do you remember the first dagger you made?"

"I do," I say, thinking of the memory that is very important to me.

"Never had I seen that bright of a smile, let alone on you." He gives my shoulder a squeeze. "After weeks, you finally managed to correctly bend the flames to your will so that the metal you had pressed together wouldn't shatter by the heat."

"And then you threw it at the wall and the tip broke off," I retort.

He chuckles. "I had to make sure it wouldn't shatter."

"Of course," I mutter, jabbing him in the ribs.

Vergus rubs his side before slinging his arm around my neck and pulling me close. He messes with my hair until my head hurts from his knuckles rubbing over it.

I manage to get him off and immediately put some distance between us, not giving him another chance to grab me.

He laughs while I try to smooth down my hair. I feel it sticking up in several places and do my best to tame it. Vergus just keeps smiling as he pulls out something wrapped in a towel from behind his back.

"I found this while I was cleaning up the closet last week," he says as he pulls the cloth off.

Revealing the dagger he just asked me about.

The roughly wrapped leather handle, the broken tip and small crack at the base of the blade because of the throw.

I thought he had thrown it away.

"You kept it?" I ask, taking it from him.

"I did," he answers. "You were proud of it, and I was so very proud of you that I couldn't just throw it away. It has value for both of us."

Dragging my finger over the blade, I feel a faint smile form on my face. I remember it pretty clearly. The building frustration after not being able to even make a simple dagger after months of practicing and trying.

And the immense relief when I finally made it work, and it didn't shatter in the oven or cooling barrel.

"Keep that somewhere you won't lose it," Vergus says, tapping the blade. "It would be a shame to lose something that really helped you get out of that shell."

I put the blade down and come closer to him again. He sees my approach, immediately knowing what I want to do.

He opens his arms to me, letting me embrace him. I wrap my arms around his middle and Vergus puts his chin on my head.

"When you first came here, I was worried. So very worried about how you would react to everything and everybody around you," he says, rubbing his hand over my back. Knowing I'm still recovering to say it nicely from my childhood. "You didn't talk to me, you didn't want to do anything except stay in your room, and occasionally you'd eat and drink. But somehow, being around the fire here, your magic wanted to come out again. And it helped you break those walls down and you have no idea how hard I was trying to hold back tears when you said those first words to me."

"I don't even remember what I said," I whisper, burying my face in his chest.

Vergus responds, "I want to make something." He pulls back and puts his hands on my cheeks. "And those were the words I had been waiting for. You had found something you wanted to do on your own and I could help you with it."

"Thank you for getting me out of there," I mutter, showing him how grateful I am for him.

"Don't think of apologizing. I wish I had actually found you sooner," he says, the regret shining in his eyes.

I put my hands on his lower arms and give the most genuine smile I can. "What matters is that you found me. If you hadn't, I might've been dead by now."

Vergus lets go and ruffles my hair once more. "We definitely don't want that."

We both chuckle and leave that conversation for what it is. No need to stay in the past when he gave me a brighter future than I could've imagined all those years ago.

Something is suddenly thrown at me, and I fumble to catch it.

I look up to find Vergus pointing at the door as he says, "Now that we've had our heartfelt moment, you need to go before Dawn starts her trial."

With a mocking salute, I say, "Yes, sir." And head towards the door.

Vergus sighs and comments, "I could have you work overtime tonight."

"You wouldn't," I retort before I walk out the door.

He never makes me work overtime. He knows I have sleep deprivation enough already.

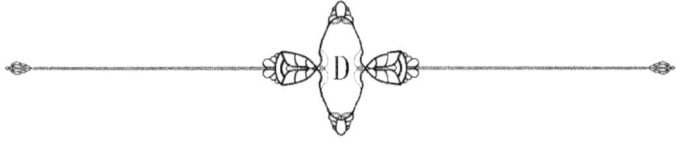

The day of the first trial is here, and to say that I am scared is an understatement.

I'm terrified. If I don't pass this trial, I won't be allowed to do the others. Well, if I don't pass, I've most likely died.

Jade finished my outfit, and it turned out to be as stunning as expected. It fits perfectly. I have enough storage for my weapons. At least for the ones that I'm allowed to have. My sword, two daggers, and four throwing knives.

I still don't know a single thing about this trial except for the shadow part. There have to be shadow creatures in this trial. They could hunt me, try to kill me. But it could also be the complete opposite. Maybe I have to be the huntress and kill them.

Speculating wouldn't get me anywhere, so all I could do was train as much as possible in various situations.

I emerge from my bathroom, fully suited up, and find a small note on my bed. No one has been in this room all morning. So I carefully walk over and pick it up.

~

Please watch your back, little one.

~

What?

Little one. Nobody calls me 'little one' anymore. My dad used to, but he couldn't have put this here.

A knock on the door startles me. "Dawn?"

I stuff the note away in my pocket, walk over to the door, and find Nate on the other side.

"What are you doing here?" I ask as I let him in.

Closing the door behind him, I lean against it. He stops in the middle of my room, scanning my bookshelves.

"I wanted to wish you luck," he says, still eyeing all the books. "And give you this."

He pulls out a sheathe from behind his back. One that matches my sword.

Simple, yet beautiful. No engravings or anything, just leather, beautifully shaped into a perfect bearer for the sword he made me.

"It's beautiful as always," I mutter as he hands it to me. "Thank you."

And that ended the small conversation we had. We just stand awkwardly for a minute before he clears his throat and asks, "And I wanted to ask how you are doing? Overall, with Leanne, the trials, everything."

The sincerity in his eyes and words just makes me want to break down right here, right now. But I need to keep it together.

I take a deep breath and clench my fists. "I'll be okay, eventually," I reassure him with a faint smile. "I just need to focus right now. Afterwards, I can cry and scream as much as I want or need to."

Nate crosses the distance between us and takes my face between his hands. "You are worth so much more than the tears you shed, Dawn," he says, with tears threatening to fall from his eyes too. "But don't think that crying is weak. Crying shows that you are strong enough to show people your emotions."

I place my hands on both sides of his face. "Thank you." And pull him slightly down to let our foreheads rest against each other.

We both shed a few tears as we stand there. Completely silent. Eyes closed. Breathing slow and quiet.

It's been a while since we did this.

It started when we were younger. Nate would have panic attacks every now and then, as did I. Mostly from nightmares that came flooding back during the day. And we figured out by just leaning on each other, matching our breathing and eventually our heartbeats too, we would calm down. No matter how bad it was, just leaning on each other, having that support, did the trick.

It was his support that got me through the mourning of my parents. He was there, Madion and Jade were there too, but Nate was the person who kept me going.

He is my light at the end of that darkness that surrounds me. And I don't think he even knows how much he did for me already.

I don't want this moment to end, but I have to go. Otherwise, I won't make it to the dome in time.

I pull him in for one final hug. He grips my shirt just as tightly as I grip his. "Thank you," I whisper in his ear, before parting with him to make my way to the dome where the first trial awaits me.

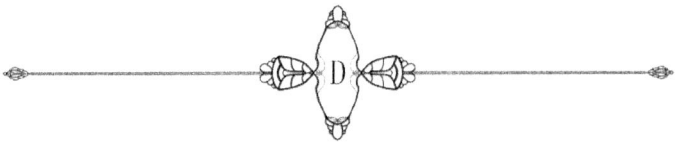

"Weapons ready?" Is the first question Madion and Jade simultaneously ask me when they spot me coming their way.

I pat myself down to show them I have the ones I'm allowed to have. "Yes, I'm ready," I answer them, "Nervous, but ready."

Then I notice Jade looking at me in a way that I'm not going to like what's going to come out of her mouth in a second.

"What did Nate want in your room?"

And there it is.

"He wanted to wish me luck," I say, and turn around to show the sheathed sword at my back. "And give me this." Madion reaches out to touch it, but I quickly turn back. "I have to go now. It's almost time."

They both fling themselves around my neck and hug me so tight I can barely breathe. A 'good luck' and a 'you got this' come from both of them before I peel them off me and start moving towards the entrance of the arena.

Let's see if we make it out alive.

Adrian and Jake meet me at the entrance. In full armor, sword at their side, Adrian has his blonde hair tied back and Jake might have brushed those black locks for once. They both give me a nod before taking their places beside me as I enter the arena.

My dad used to tell me about this all the time.

The great arena. Where the trials, but also horse races and tournaments, are held. It's shaped like a dome, with the seating areas circling around the whole arena. Hundreds of people can sit here and watch.

My dad always talked very highly of the trials. They are ancient and sacred. You can only stop one when you finish it or die.

But the challenges themselves are different every time. My dad had to show his strength in different parkour, magical and non-magical ones. Leanne had to hover over the ground at all times, otherwise, she'd burn to death.

Take a deep breath, take in your surroundings, and go for it. Use your instincts, your gut feeling, those are the things that keep you alive. That's the way my dad dealt with things. Your body tells you what you can and can't do, should or shouldn't do. Don't ignore it.

I won't let you down, dad. Not again.

The high priest that makes sure the trials go according to the rules is standing in the middle of the arena. Clad in a long black cloak with white stitching. In front of him is a table with a black bowl filled with a weird white liquid. I'm going to have to drink that, don't I?

As I come closer to the table, the priest raises his hand, gesturing to my guards to stop where they stand. I keep walking until I reach the table.

"Dawn Maria Rowena Sungust," he starts, hands tucked behind his back again. "Welcome to your first step towards your full potential."

I give him a nod, showing him I'm ready.

"Very well. You may remove your weapons and place them on this table."

I unsheathe my sword and place it on the table. The priest monitoring my every move. Next are my daggers, two beautifully engraved daggers from my dad, and my old and simple throwing knives. When the priest deems me clear of all my weapons, I take a step back. Feeling vulnerable without the weight.

"You shall have your weapons returned to you at the beginning of the maze," he states, gesturing to his right. A gigantic stone maze stretches out for what looks like forever. "You shall enter this maze with a riddle in mind. A riddle you shall have to solve before reaching the center of this maze. A riddle that is not that easy to guess, especially not with one being hunted." He stops, letting that sink in.

I'm going into that giant maze, trying to solve a riddle, while being hunted by something. Deep breaths. I can do this. I got this.

"You shall drink this brew before going in. It will enhance one of the elements you already possess power over, the other will remain at its current power. Understood?" the priest asks, hands remaining behind his back. Not letting me move further before my confirmation.

"Understood," I speak confidently. I look past the priest, to where Leanne is sitting on her throne. Crown atop her white hair, a red gown, and our dad's signet ring on her right hand.

She's smirking, as if she knows I will not make it. Let me prove her wrong, very wrong.

The priest gestures for me to take another step forward, making my legs almost touch the table. I look down at the white liquid. Liquid that could enhance my magic. I am not sure whether I completely trust this or not. Magic enhancing is something I've only seen with spells or jewelry. Never in liquid form.

"When you have emptied this bowl, you shall walk over to the entrance of the maze. There you may take possession of your weapons again. The riddle will come to you when you set foot in the maze."

I give him another nod, not daring to speak.

Place my hands on both sides of the bowl, I bring it to my lips and drink. It has a sweet flavor, but still feels very wrong. I can't place it, but this type of enhancing is not something I think I want to feel again. It feels forced, forcing my magic to go past its limit.

As I empty the bowl, I place it back on the table and pivot towards the maze. Nodding to Jake and Adrian.

My weapons are waiting for me near the entrance. As I put them all back in place, I look at the crowd. Trying to spot Jade, Madion and Nate. I sheath my sword as I spot them in the center of the right seating area. Frantically waving at me, mouthing 'good luck', I think. I give them an awkward wave back, before turning towards the maze.

Stone walls on both sides, with my first choice of going left or right in less than fifty meters from the entrance.

I almost jump as I find the priest a couple of meters to my left. I turn to him, waiting for any extra orders, but I get none.

He just points to the maze, as if saying to get in there.

I turn towards the entrance again. Steeling myself for what's to come, as I set one foot over the entrance line.

A sudden voice booms through my mind:

"You have me today, tomorrow you'll have more; As time passes, I'm not easy to store; I don't take up any space, but I am only in one place; I am what you saw, but not what you see; What am I?"

I clutch my head as I try to take in the riddle.

But I freeze when I hear a guttural growl from behind me. Looking over my shoulder to find three guards. Each of them has two leashed shadow hounds.

I look over to the priest, who merely says, "Let the first trial begin."

I bolt into the maze as the six shadow hounds are released mere seconds after me.

I'm being hunted by the creatures from your worst nightmares.

But they're not from my worst nightmares.

I can handle them.

They don't scare me.

CHAPTER 5

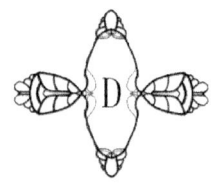

I take the first right.

Sprinting down the long hall, I look over my shoulder to find only three hounds on my tail. Where are the other three?

Ahead of me lies another intersection. Three options this time. I take the left hall.

I let my magic pool into palms, ready to pull up a wall to stop the hounds behind me.

The second I round the corner, I pull my magic up, creating a high wall behind me, cutting off the three shadow hounds. But I'm not rid of them yet and I still don't know where the other three are.

As for the riddle—*You have me today. Tomorrow you'll have me more.* Age? Hours? Time?

Why does this need to be combined?

Being hunted, solving a riddle, and trying to find your way in a maze.

I suddenly notice everything has gone quiet. No crowd cheering. No growls and no claws tapping on the floors of the maze. That's not good.

I keep running and running. Pulling up walls behind me every time I take a turn to make sure I won't be attacked from behind.

But then my last wall collapses behind me, revealing two hounds. Eyes locked on me, teeth showing, ready to strike. I make to unsheathe my sword, but then hear three more growls in front of me. I try to bring up the wall behind me, but something is blocking it. Or someone—I swear if Leanne is doing something.

The hounds in front of me have spread in half a circle, trying to drive me to the ones behind me.

I draw my sword, and one of them immediately backs away.

Interesting.

Nothing more than a warning growl comes from behind before a hound leaps at me. I slash my sword across his belly, and it does nothing. Yet when the hound hits me, it's solid. Like a real animal.

I fall to the ground, the hound on top of me, as I gather my magic.

A small burst of air shoots from my palm, lifting the hound off me, before pulling a spike made of earth out of the wall to impale it. The hound unfortunately solidifies at the wrong time. Killing itself instantly. The other hounds take a moment to let the death of their companion sink in, which turns into my window to run. I run through the gap, leaping over the dead hound, and pull up a wall behind me.

The hounds pass right through it. I keep running until I hit another intersection. I'm going right this time.

You have me today, tomorrow you'll have more. As time passes, I'm not easy to store. I don't take up any space, but I am only in one place. I am what you saw, but not what you see. What am I?

You'd think solving a riddle is easy unless you're being hunted. What could stop those hounds in solid and shadow form?

Air.

A wall forms before my eyes when I round another corner. I am not the one doing that. I do set up a wall of air behind me as I hear the hounds approaching, growling even more now that I killed their companion. And as they come around the corner, they bounce off my shield.

I smile as they try to break through. They're getting more agitated by the minute, scratching, and howling at the protection around me. I take a moment to look around, trying to figure out which way to go. I can't go my original way. But if I take the hall to my left, and then another left, I might get in the hall behind me again.

I scan the halls one more time when my eyes fall on a weird symbol at every corner. A small elemental figure, fire, water, air, and earth, they're on each corner. But only one has an extra ring, with a small arrow, around it.

Earth.

The one element that feels strangely stronger than normal, and the one I can use to modify this maze.

I need to follow those arrows, so my instincts to go left were right.

Now I only need to get past these hounds. I could try to run with the shield around me.

I shuffle a couple of steps to my left. The hounds follow.

I'll have to make a run for it.

Suddenly every hound perks up their ears and looks up. To the top of my shield, which is slowly crumbling down.

It can't be, I'm still fueling it with my magic.

I swear I'm going to kill Leanne if she is doing this.

I'll count to five. In five seconds, I'm making a run for it.

Five.

Four.

Three.

Two.

One.

I shove the remains of my shield towards the hounds, making them tumble into the hall straight ahead, and then I run into the left hall. Taking the next left, following another one of those earth-symbols at the corner.

I keep running and unnervingly hear nothing behind me.

Which means they're either coming up front or from the sides. I stop at the beginning of a long hall, four hopefully empty adjacent hallways.

An enormous stone and dirt wall at the end of the hall. Decorated in large swirls, all four elements, and my name. I assume that's the center.

I let thin walls of air cover each adjacent hall, like an alarm system.

And make a run for the door.

Suddenly, one hound slams into me from behind before I can even pass the first hallway.

My head collides with the floor as the hound bites down on my right arm. A scream escapes from my throat before I even fully register what's happening. Another hound grabs my calf, the pain radiates through my entire leg.

I bite down the scream and try to reach for the dagger at my thigh. I snatch the dagger from its scabbard and stab it into the neck of the hound at my arm. It hits home. Spraying black blood over its companions and myself.

I killed it, so as long as the hounds are in their solid form, they can be killed.

Shaking the dead hound off my arm, I try to sit up, just enough to reach for my sword. But the stretch causes the pain to spread across my entire arm, nearly making me lose my grip on the handle. The hound at my leg notices my sword too late, as I slash it across its neck, almost decapitating it. I unclasp the teeth from my leg and get back on my feet.

Nearly dropping to the floor again as I try to put my full weight on my leg.

I let my magic envelop and support my leg as I slowly walk towards the gigantic wall.

When I stop in front of it, I encase myself in an even stronger air dome this time. Two layers.

I'm at the center. The only thing left is getting through this wall.

"You have me today, tomorrow you'll have more. As time passes, I'm not easy to store. I don't take up any space, but I am only in one place. I am what you

saw, but not what you see. What am I?" The door suddenly 'says'.

I need to focus. It's not age, time, hours, days, or years.

Paws approach, and from every hall, a shadow hound emerges. But there are six of them again. I killed three—They would not release more, would they?

Of course they would. The trials aren't called lethal for no reason.

Apparently, one of my ancestors, my great grandpa to be precise, died during his second trial. He was supposed to make it to the center of a maze too, but he was hunted by shadow hounds and gendrils. A deadly combination when they're untrained and hungry. He made it to the center like I did, but did not have enough strength anymore to fight his hunters off. They ripped him to shreds, leaving behind five kids and his wife. My grandpa was crowned king almost the same day.

I won't die because of some shadow hounds.

My dad and I have talked about what happened to our family so many times. We read history books in the library, we talked over tea, or while walking through the gardens. Sometimes we'd even try our hand at riddles from ages ago, some we solved, some we didn't.

I wish I could still do those things, just relax, smell flowers, read books, or just laugh.

Smiles are very rare these days.

And the smiles I shared with my dad are all distant memories—

Memories.

I have them today, and tomorrow I'll have them more. I keep gaining memories as time goes on.

"Memories," I say to the wall.

It does nothing.

I push against it, knowing it won't do anything. A small crack forms when I push again. I push again and a tear forms beneath my left hand. I push again, but it does nothing. The cracks remain the same.

I have almost used all of my magic with pulling up all those walls and shields. And the brew the priest made me drink didn't help either. It was supposed to help me pass this trial.

Still, the brew felt wrong, like it was pushing against my very soul, pulling the magic out without my consent.

When I pass this trial, a layer of my soul will break, letting out the magic underneath it. What if that brew was pulling out the magic underneath that layer already? What if I need to push it that extra bit to shatter it? And how do I use that amount of power?

By breaking a stone wall.

I pull out every last scrap of magic that lingers around my soul, gathering it together. I also dare try to pull magic from underneath that first layer, forcing it to break when I release that magic.

I drown out all other sounds except for my heartbeat, keeping it steady. I hear faint growls around me, but pay them no attention.

I pull the extensive amount of magic beneath that first layer out as far as possible. Forming cracks in the first layer.

When it shatters, it's going to hurt.

I take a deep breath.

And let it all out.

My soul screams at the outburst, causing me to drop to the ground and scream with it.

The hounds are flung back and don't get up again.

I feel the remaining scraps of magic trying to heal my injuries, but this burst brought my healing almost back to zero. I need to rest and soon. So I stay on my knees for another moment until someone clears their throat in front of me. I look up to find the priest, standing in front of another table. This time it holds four bowls.

I slowly get to my feet, my calf barking in pain at the movement, but I bite through it. It can heal when I get out of here.

I walk and stumble over to the table, where the priest gives me a once over before saying, "Congratulations Dawn, you have almost passed your first trial. The only thing left to do is show you now have control over all four elements. Fire." He points to the first bowl, filled with burning wood. "Air." The second bowl, which is empty. "Water." The third bowl, filled with water. "And earth." The fourth bowl, filled with leaves and dirt. "Show me you can control all of them and you may walk out of here. If you cannot, we shall see what happens then," he states and places both of his hands behind his back.

I steady myself before I even dare try to gather up some magic. I get lightheaded for a second when I dare pull at a small piece of magic.

Please, I need this final bit of strength.

It slowly gives the last threads of magic left inside me. I reach out a hand and carefully let the fire twirl around my fingers. Next, I pull the air out of the second bowl to fuel the flames dancing around my fingertips. At the third bowl, I let the water slowly rain down on the flames, making them shudder and blink out in a matter of seconds. And for the final bowl, I let a small flower grow from the earth.

A blue flower, like the ones my dad always gave me when I was reading in the garden.

I drop my hand to my side and look at the priest, hoping to see any confirmation that I made it.

"Very well," he says, sounding as emotionless as always. "I am pleased to congratulate you, Dawn Maria Rowena Sungust. You have passed your first trial and gained control over the four elements in return." He raises his hand towards the wall to my left and makes it crumble down, all the way to the entrance of the maze without any effort. He gestures me to go, but as I make my way back to my friends, he whispers, "Watch your back, Your Highness, I would love to still see you at the second trial."

And with that he walks into the hall where the shadow hounds lay.

The newly formed road to the entrance of the maze feels like it goes on forever, no magic to heal me, no energy to keep me upright, but I will not stumble out of this maze.

I survived, so I'll show them I did. I pick up my pace, for as much as my leg allows me.

I'm met by Adrian and Jake as I reach the entrance. I look to the right and find Nate, Madion, and Jade waiting for me. They look concerned when they notice my slight limp, but I give them a reassuring look.

I walk over to where Leanne is now standing in the arena's sand. She gives me a smile, but it doesn't quite reach her eyes.

Then pulls me into a tight hug. I hug her back, but I feel something inside me almost boil up when I do.

My magic. It's refilling way faster than normal. I need to get out of here, who knows if I can control it fully.

"Congratulations, Dawn. I'm proud of you," she whispers in my ear.

"Thank you, but I would really like to return to my room, clean up and dress my wounds," I say in response. She pulls back as if she only now notices I'm injured.

"Of course. Take your guards with you to make sure you get there safely and have everything you need."

"Thank you." I squeeze her hand before turning to walk to my friends, looking very nervous.

As I look at all of them, I feel a small current of air wrap around my leg. Steadying it. I immediately know that's Madion's doing. I give her a knowing and grateful smile as I get closer to them.

"You made it!" Jade almost yells, as if she thought I wouldn't.

"I did."

"What's wrong?" Jade notices the all too familiar strain in my voice.

"I'm just tired and hurt, I'm going to try to get back to my room without falling down the stairs."

"We're out of sight, right?" Adrian suddenly asks, brown eyes scanning the corridors and arena.

"Coast is clear," Jake responds.

And before I know it, Adrian has hoisted me into his arms and starts walking towards the castle. Everybody else hurrying after him.

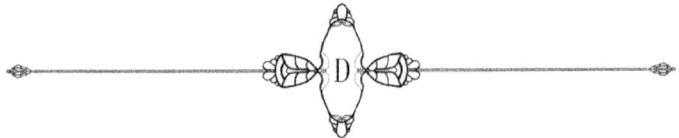

As we reach my room, Adrian puts me down. Giving me the choice of who I let in.

"I can handle myself from here," I say, smiling thankfully at him. He gives me a nod and a grin in return.

Adrian and Jake take their places by my door as I enter the room. I do not know where the other three are off to.

I close all my curtains, bathing my room in darkness. My clothes find a dark spot in the corner of my room before I almost run to the bathroom.

The shower is on within seconds, and the moment the drizzle of water touches my back, I slump to the ground.

But it doesn't give me the feeling of relief as it used to do. I calm down, but my magic doesn't lie down as it used to. I shouldn't be surprised considering the amount of power I just gained, but it'll take getting used to.

The shower was always my place of calm. It still works to a degree, I can feel that, but not completely. I'll have to cross that distance myself.

I pull my legs to my chest and place my arms around them. My forehead finds its place on my knees as I let the water stream down my back.

Bit by bit I feel my magic calming, as if it's laying down to rest too. Some pieces I have to push down by myself, forcing them to relax.

I hear a click of my door opening, but I don't pay it any attention as I see red hair in the corner of my eyes. Madion drops almost all of her clothes except her underwear on the ground, next to Jade's.

Jade sits down on my right and Madion on my left. Giving me the support that stops me from falling over in exhaustion. They both place their heads on my shoulders.

After a moment of silence, Jade dares to ask, "What happened in that maze?"

I don't give her an answer, as I'm still trying to make sense of it myself.

"Someone was working against me," I say bluntly. Jade and Madion share a look over my head.

Madion asks, a slight concern growing in her voice, "What do you mean?"

I look her in the eye and say, "I was pulling up walls after me to stop the hounds from coming from behind, but someone blocked me when I tried it a fourth time. Giving one hound the opportunity to attack me. And when I figured out I could keep them at a distance with air, I made a dome of it around me. It dissipated before my eyes, while I was still fueling it. You think that's a coincidence when someone powerful was very against me taking on these trials?" My magic flares up slightly as I say that last sentence. The memories of what she has done are not just my memories, my magic remembers the cold and dark nights in the dungeons, too.

Jade's faint smile drops immediately as she puts the pieces together but says nothing. Madion knows, Jade knows, and I know, that Leanne will go to far greater lengths to keep me from these trials.

But she is not the only one that can fight.

I'll show her just how much she has underestimated me.

CHAPTER 6

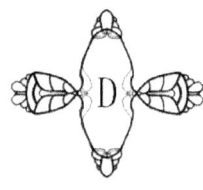

"Why are we here again?" I ask Madion as we reach a remote part of the training court, positioned at the edge of the woods.

Madion stops, turns around, crosses her arms over her chest and says, "Since you just gained even more magic, you need to train it. You need to learn how to control it. So I told Jade to hide somewhere in these woods." Pointing her finger at my chest, she adds, "You will have to get to the other end and touch the ring I hung from a tree without getting shot by her or attacked by me."

She's looking at me as if I am some kind of novice warrior, and I know how harsh she can be on them.

Every time new soldiers arrive, they get grilled by her and Jade. In every group, there is at least one person who tries to flirt with either of them. They usually let the person fight them, where his or her ass is sorely beaten.

They also always manage to get one person to run away crying.

She approaches me until she is only a few inches away from my face. "But beware Dawn, Jade is not using normal arrows." She leans closer and whispers in my ear, "See it as payback for last week."

And then she's gone, vanished into the woods.

I braid my hair into a tight braid. Then pull my sword out from behind my back, flexing the muscles in my lower arm.

The shadow hound did a lot of damage, but it healed quite quickly.

I scan the woods looking for any sign of movement, red hair, the tip of a sword, anything, but come up empty.

Of course I can't see them. They're trained to blend in. They're like wolves, and I'm some helpless bunny being hunted by them.

I make my way towards the tree line and see I have about a hundred meters to cross. The ring is on the other side of the woods. It almost looks golden in the sunlight.

A hundred meters with two deadly killers if they want to be.

Jade has her bow and some type of special arrows. Madion has daggers and a sword. I only have my sword.

The odds, when it comes to weapons, are against me, but I have more power than them. I could blast them out of these woods if I wanted to, I think.

I reach the first line of trees. There is a distinct path to the ring, one I will not take.

Too obvious.

So I slink into the bushes to my right.

After a couple of meters, I hear rustling in the bushes behind me. Yet nothing is there when I look over my shoulder. I move a bit to my left to stick my head out of the bushes and look how far I have to go. I crossed half of the distance already. Where are they? More rustling comes from my right again when I pull my head back into the bushes. I angle my sword to my right as I walk, knees bend, further.

I make it to the end of the forest line, with neither a sign of Jade nor of Madion. They're going to jump me, they have to.

An arrow zips past my head, missing me by inches. It came from my right, but I see nothing. I call up my magic, not wanting to be shot. I throw a thin wall of air to my right, hoping it will bump into someone, but it only hits a tree. She already moved to a new spot.

I'm going to make a run for it. I create a shield of air around, just like the one I used in the maze, to stop the arrows from hitting me.

Three.

Two.

One.

Why do I always need to count down before I do something?

I run for the ring, but don't make it.

An arrow hits my shield.

And goes straight through it.

It skims my arm and I go down. It feels like fire burns through my veins. My shield collapses and my magic shoots back into my soul, away from whatever was on the tip of that arrow.

On my knees, I cradle my arm and hear people coming up from behind.

"Thank you for not putting it straight through her arm," Madion says, annoyance resonating in her voice. "Now help me."

They get closer to me, and I feel someone grab my shoulders, turning me around onto my back. A shadow looms over me and Madion stands there, rope in her hands. I feel someone else tug at my legs, binding my ankles together.

I try to struggle, but the burning that courses through my arm is too much. I can barely move.

Jade comes up next to Madion. "Grab her wrists," Madion orders Jade. "Keep them tight together." As Jade pulls on my arm, I let out a small whimper, making her go easier on me.

Madion wraps the ropes around one wrist, then the other, pulling them together, before spinning the rope around my wrists a couple of times. Fastening it with a tight knot.

"You think this is a good idea?" Jade whispers to Madion, as they step away from me. I still lay on the ground, trying to breathe through the pain.

"Trust me, Jade," Madion answers. "She needs to be able to do this."

Madion reaches out her hand, palm down, and turns it up. The burning feeling in my arm starts to dissipate when Madion turns her hand further and further. Until the feeling is completely gone.

Just then, it fully hits me. They tied me up. I don't know why, but my magic notices the same moment I do. And it fights.

I sit upright fast as I try to wiggle out of the ropes. They're too tight.

"Madion, untie me, please," I plead to her.

But she just stands there. Monitoring me.

My magic starts pushing more and more, begging me to break the ropes, but I can't. It's like the ropes are enchanted, rendering them unbreakable. I trash, trying to get at least my feet free, but nothing works. I take deep breaths, calming myself down. It doesn't help.

Normally, deep breaths and focusing works, but with this extra weight battering down on me from the inside, I can't grasp the complete focus I need to calm down.

I think at one moment, tears start streaming down my face. I hear Jade whispering to Madion to help me.

And the moment Madion sees my magic is seeping out, she steps in.

She goes to take her previous spot on top of me. Grabbing my wrists, she carefully pushes me back to the ground. Then she places one knee on each side of my stomach and keeps my arms flush against my chest, letting them move with my too fast breathing.

"Dawn, listen to me," she says calmly. "Listen to me, okay?"

I manage a tight nod. My magic is slamming into my skin, wanting to come out.

"Try to match my breathing. Inhale." She inhales, as do I. "Exhale." She exhales, I do too. "Good. Keep breathing, calmly, nothing is going to happen."

I keep breathing steadily, in sync with the rising and falling of Madion's chest. Jade is quiet the entire time, letting Madion do her thing.

"Why?" I bring out after a deep inhale.

"Because as much as I dislike saying this, Dawn, Leanne is going to lock you up again. We all know it. And with your magic now even more destructive, I need you to be confident you can calm yourself down, no matter the situation." She lets out a broken laugh. "I can't bear seeing you completely losing it when she locks you up again, but I can't do anything about it. The only thing I can do is prepare you, give you the means to get through the night. I can't bear seeing you look like that empty shell whenever you come out in the morning. I just can't." She glances at Jade, who's looking solemnly at us. "Jade might be my mate and the love of my life, but you are our best friend. We both love you. And seeing you like this, seeing you suffer, we can only bear that so much." She loosens the ropes on my wrists as Jade moves to my ankles.

"I don't want you two to see me like that. Broken and slowly crumbling down." I sigh. "But when I see you, I can't help but feel like I can break down in front of you. I can let it all out."

Madion and Jade finish untying the ropes simultaneously. As she pulls her hands back, I take Madion's hands. "I want you both to know that I love you with all my heart. I will fight for you, I will always fight to come back to you." Tears have started coating Jade's dark cheeks, too. I release one of Madion's hands and beckon Jade to come sit beside me. "We always fight to stay together, no matter the odds. We are a team, and nothing will break us apart."

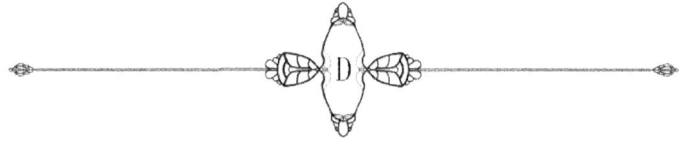

I remain in my room for the rest of the afternoon. Absently flipping through pages of a book that just can't grasp my attention.

This morning was emotional, to say the least. When I finished talking, Madion got off me and took her spot next to Jade, who was not doing very well. I stayed right where I was, not wanting to interrupt Madion while she was comforting her mate.

But it got me thinking. Jade isn't originally from Iluniel, she's from Yedel.

Could my mate be in a whole other kingdom? Could he be dead or right in front of me? Would he be more like Jade, sweet on the outside, but deadly when you get on her bad side, or more like Madion, a fierce warrior, but as sweet as you can get them on the inside?

I don't know and I don't think I'd care.

I will meet him when the moment is right. Until then, I'll just fantasize about what he would be like.

A faint knock on the door snaps me out of my daydreaming. I put my book back on the nightstand and make my way over to the door.

I once again find Nate on the other side.

"State your business here," I say. Not letting him enter just yet.

"My business involves checking in with my friend, looking at how she is doing," he says. "Permission to enter?"

I look him dead in the eyes for five second before smiling.

"Permission granted."

"Thank you, Your Highness."

"I can still revoke that permission, you know," I threaten him when closing the door.

"You can, but you won't," he retorts with a wink, but his eyes immediately go to my books again. He's always been invested in reading, just like me.

"Have you looked in the mirror lately since the trial?" he bluntly asks.

"No," I counter. "Why should I?"

"Did neither Jade nor Madion mention your hair?" he asks, eyes on me again. "It looks very nice, to be honest."

I make my way over to the bathroom and look in the mirror. I won't mention how tired I look, but he was right about my hair. It's not completely brown anymore, it's littered with white streaks. The first physical change I'll go through. And when—if I reach the final trial, it'll be fully white.

I do like it, the white streaks. It looks a bit messy now, but once there is more white than brown, it'll look much better.

I make my way back to my bedroom and plop down on the bed.

"You scared me during the trial," Nate says bluntly. "When I heard you scream, I wanted to run after you into that maze, to make sure you were alright. But then everything went quiet again. Until that final scream came, which just tore right through me. As if I could feel your pain." His voice turns to a whisper. "It scared me, Dawn. It terrified me that you might not walk out of that maze."

He keeps his gaze on the floor, his breathing fastening. He won't leave me hanging like that.

I walk over to him and put my forehead against his. Our almost ancient but still working move.

"I am okay, Nate. That last scream was the layer of my soul breaking. As you can imagine, that hurt, but it was needed for me to pass the trial."

"Does your magic feel any different?" he quietly asks.

"It feels stronger, more present. But it doesn't feel different. It's as if a part of me finally gasped for breath, giving it life," I answer just as quietly as he asked.

"Can you show me? The earth since I'm not able to control it. Can you show me how it looks?"

I pull away and take his hand, guiding him to the balcony.

The flowers are moving in the wind, a couple of pink and blue petals float past. I take a deep breath to steady myself.

Every time I see these flowers, at least one memory of my parents comes floating to the surface. I usually ignore them, but sometimes I want them, even need them.

"I don't think this garden will ever not have me in awe," he breathes, taking it all in. "It is as if it grows more beautiful every day."

"I try to work on it at least once a day, just the simple things. Healing a broken flower stem, giving a flower its color back, just to keep it alive."

"I can see the work you put into it, and I'd love to see you in action," he says, giving me a smile.

I put my right-hand palm upwards and place his hand upwards on it. I place our hands around a broken flower stem and let my magic pool out.

Swirling around the stem, sealing every broken fiber back together, forming one solid stem again.

Nate's mouth drops open as I remove our hands, but I'm not done yet. I let my magic twist around the stem, asking it to form another flower.

It happily obliges.

A small bud forms at the end of a newly grown, thin stem. It slowly opens, revealing a light pink flower.

"It is absolutely beautiful," he murmurs, before turning around and hugging me tightly.

"What's this hug for?" I ask.

He puts his head on my shoulder. "Showing myself you're here."

"I'm here," I whisper, burying my nose in the nape of his neck

I didn't know it affected him this much.

"I'm not leaving you, nor Jade, nor Madion. I'm here," I reassure him. "And I will be until the day I die. That day will not come soon, I promise you."

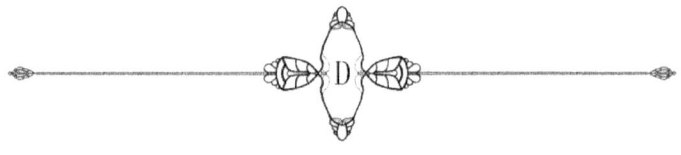

The next couple of days flew by and the castle was quiet. I barely saw Leanne or my friends. I just locked myself in my room. Trying to get through this day.

My birthday.

But also the anniversary of my parents' deaths.

I dread this day every year. Every year I lock myself in my room, Jade and Madion usually come in the evening to spend time with me, but I told them no this year.

It's just all becoming a bit too much.

The council has been pressing Leanne and I for a meeting, which will be held tomorrow. They had much to talk about if we have to believe their messenger. But Leanne and I have some things to say too, starting with those shackles. They have no right to order them and use them against us.

My bedroom door opens, and I already know who it is without looking over my shoulder. The only person in this castle that can just barge into any room.

My sister, better known as the queen.

I keep my eyes on the garden below my balcony as Leanne stops somewhere in my room. "Can I help you?" I ask her calmly. I'm not feeling like picking a fight right now.

"I wanted to ask if you wish to come with me to mom and dad," she responds, making my breathing still.

"What?" I blurt out as I turn around.

She's wearing a less elaborate dress than usual, her hair is even loosely falling over her shoulders. As if she didn't even have the strength to dress up like she usually does.

"I have been ignorant of this day for a couple of years now and I know you struggle on this day, too. I want to be there. This is supposed to be a happy day for you. But because of past events, it's not," she says as she steps closer. "Let's pay them a visit. I know we both haven't done that in a while." She holds out her hand to me and I take it.

Hoping to have my actual sister back, even if it's just for an hour. Leanne leads me to the royal cemetery just outside the castle.

I haven't been here in months. There are various graves here. Lords, ladies, even servants lay here. But the most prominent and floral grave lies in the middle of the cemetery.

My parents' grave.

I read their names.

Ricon Armen Sungust and Rowena Elizabeth Sungust
Beloved parents and friends
Forever watching over us

I drop to my knees on the first step. I should've returned here sooner. They always said that no matter what happened, they'd watch over me. And I do feel like they're watching over me.

Sometimes I find a blue flower on my bed, when nobody has been in my room since that morning, or I find a book open on a certain page where I hadn't left it.

All these little signs, telling me they're still here.

Leanne places her hand on my shoulder, giving it a light squeeze, but says nothing. Giving me space.

I keep saying that I wish they were still here. I do wish they were, but life goes on, and I know I am not alone in life.

I have people that can hold me together, even in the darkest places of this world and my own mind.

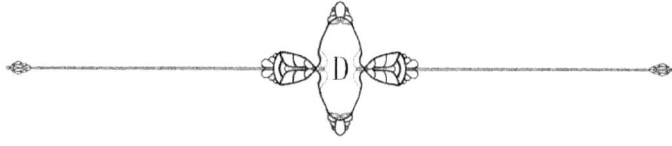

The next morning, Leanne is back to being coldhearted. No hello or good morning in greeting as I enter the council room, not even a glance in my direction. She's sitting at the head of a long table. I stand to her left with Jade, Madion, and Nate leaning against the wall behind me. I chose to wear my sword to this meeting, knowing the council always has a trick up its sleeve. The three behind me are armed to the teeth too, showing they're not just friends I invited to an important meeting. They will step in if anyone dares to threaten any of us.

The council is seated at the table. Seven lords are present, which means one is missing. We haven't heard anything from him yet.

Four councilmen are not looking happy, the others barely show any emotion at all.

Lord Akrin is one of the worst lords at this table. His already greying hair and dark brown eyes give him a tired but wise look. I can almost say for certain that he pushed the other council members to order Vergus to make the shackles.

"Your Majesty, we have asked for this meeting to discuss certain happenings. Railon to begin with,"

Akrin says, face stone cold. "We believe he is moving his armies. Towards us."

"And what makes you think this?" Leanne questions him.

"My informants." His spies. "They have picked up pieces of information regarding the current standing of Draven's armies."

Ah, Draven. King of Railon, my father's biggest enemy, and now ours.

"They are gathering, going from town to town to take young and strong men with them," Akrin states, wringing his hands together.

"Why would he be doing that now?" another lord asks. Lord Remin is his name.

"Because he believes we are outnumbered against his armies. He is sorely mistaken," Leanne says smoothly. "He might be gathering and expanding his armies, but he knows very well that my sister and I are a force to be reckoned with once she finishes her trials."

This is the first time she almost sounds happy I decided to do the trials.

"Which is why he is gathering them now, to take both of you out before you get too powerful." Remin counters.

"Is that why you had those shackles made?" Leanne says with a hint of rage, "To be able to control us if we are too powerful for your liking? You all might be lords, but I still have a say when they are used."

No one dares to contradict her.

Charon clears his throat. "We did not mean it as a way to control you, but we do not wish to see both of you at each other's necks. We need you both alive, and if it takes two sets of enhanced shackles to do so, then we are satisfied with that."

My anger rises now too. I know we both need to stay alive, but I am most certain that neither of us would ever go for the killing blow.

"Fine, you ordered those shackles. But my biggest problem is that you did it behind our backs. You ordered a way to restrain us without our consent or knowledge over it," I snap at him. "Do you like being restrained and locked up?" I can feel Jade, Nate and Madion tense behind me, "No, you don't. So you have no right to do so."

Leanne gives zero reaction to me, but the lords look away. Some look almost ashamed, except for Akrin. He just glares at me.

"And what do you wish us to do then, when the two of you are at each other's throats again?" Klan asks. A lesser lord from the West.

"You shall let us handle ourselves," Leanne says. "And if I ever find those shackles around my wrists again, let's say you don't want your wife to find your body when I am done."

A knock sounds on the door of the room as eight guards enter. Six stay at the door, the other two make their way over to me and Leanne.

"Yes?" Leanne asks.

"Lord Bren has fallen ill. He cannot attend the meeting. Next week he will be present again," the guard closest to me explains.

The other has taken a place on the other side of Leanne.

"Thank you for the news, we wish him all the best," I say, inclining my head slightly. But the guard gives no response at all anymore.

He just stares at me.

And I notice the dagger in his hand a second too late. He plunges it between my ribs and pulls me close, whispering in my ear, "For Railon."

CHAPTER 7

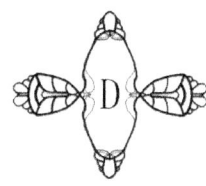

I immediately push him off me, causing both of us to stumble backwards. Someone catches me before I fall to the ground.

Then the room bursts into chaos.

The soldiers that entered are fighting the guards that were already here.

Our guards are leading Leanne out of the room while I'm surrounded by my friends, back against the wall, dagger still between my ribs.

"It's not made of Alk," I choke out. The blade hit one of my lungs. "Which makes it a warning."

And it has to be pulled out for me to heal.

Jade's hands hover over the knife, debating whether to just pull it out fast or slowly to avoid more injuries.

"Just pull it out," I mutter.

Concern is visible in her eyes, so Madion puts her hands around the knife instead. Nate grabs my hand, giving it a squeeze. Madion pulls it out in a second and I bite down on my tongue to keep from screaming.

Moments later, I'm hauled to my feet. Madion slings her arm around my waist, keeping me upright as I take in the chaos in the room.

They got Leanne out, but left me with my friends. The other guards are fighting the Railon soldiers. Even two lords have thrown themselves into the fray. Even though the Railon guards are outnumbered, they're winning.

Jade palms two fighting knives and joins one of the fighting lords at the door. Madion stays at my side, but Nate decides to join in, too. He helps two guards to my left.

Both guards go down, leaving Nate to face off against the Railon soldier. My head snaps to the door as someone screams in pain.

Jade.

One blade cut across her ribs, leaving a large bleeding gash, and one found its way into her calf, bringing her off balance and to the floor. The guard is about to make the fatal blow as Madion clashes with him. Rage shining in her eyes.

No one hurts someone's mate and gets away with it.

I stumble back to the wall as Nate lets out a grunt to my left, the guard has slashed its blade across his thigh, leaving a long and deep cut.

Enough, no one bursts in here and goes after my friends.

I take a deep breath, leaving some magic behind to heal my wound. The rest I gather in my palm.

Every human needs air to breathe, so what happens when you take it away?

I extend my palm, locking onto every single bit of air in each Railon guard. And I just pull it out. I pull the air from their lungs, and they all drop their swords and grab their throats, somehow hoping they can get air down.

One by one, they drop to the floor. Unconscious, but not dead. I won't cross that line.

As I take another deep breath, I notice I'm on my knees, with every single pair of eyes in the room on me.

I feel faint as I reach for the wound just above my heart. My shirt is soaked, but the gash is almost closed. I get back to my feet with a grunt, but almost stumble back to the ground because of lightheadedness. I brace myself against the wall, taking deep breaths, letting my head clear.

"Lock them up in the dungeons. I want to have a chat with them later," I order the remaining guards.

Walking over to Nate, I help him up. Then we move over to Madion and Jade. The latter is breathing shallowly and needs to lie down soon so she can heal properly.

When we're all back on our feet, we leave side by side, leaving the rest to clean up this mess.

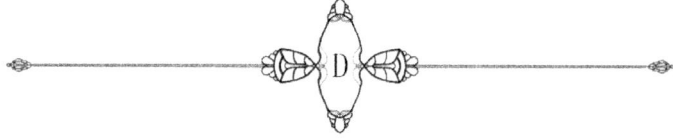

The next day I receive word that Madion wants to talk to me.

My entire chest is stiff. But my lungs feel okay, just an occasional hitch in my breathing. I put on the first shirt and pair of pants I can find. Then strap on my weapons and make my way towards the town.

I haven't seen Leanne since the attack yesterday, neither have Jake and Adrian, which is weird because they are supposed to report to her what happened to me.

She is nowhere to be found.

I walk through the small streets, stopping at a small bakery to buy an amazing-looking pastry. It's covered in strawberries and chocolate, just what I need. I bide the woman goodbye and resume my way.

The garden is cleaned up, which most likely means that Jade was asleep and Madion didn't know what to do with herself.

I knock on the front door, and it immediately swings open. Revealing an almost frantic Madion. Her hair isn't tied up in her usual braid. Bags under her eyes, indicating she was with Jade all night, awake.

"Did you even sleep last night?" I ask her, laying a hand on her arm and closing the door with the other.

"No—" she mumbles, looking sheepishly at me.

"She is okay, Madion. We all are." I grab her hand and take her with me to the bedroom.

Jade is sprawled on the mattress, hair in one large loose braid, probably done in haste by Madion.

As we enter the bedroom, she cracks one eye open and smiles at us, holding out a hand to Madion. She takes hold of it and Jade pulls her in, whispering in her ear that she's okay. Madion nestles herself close next to Jade in the bed, not letting go.

I clear my throat. "Madion, I got your message. What did you want to talk about?"

Still clinging to Jade, she asks, "Have you seen Leanne today?"

"No."

"Do you know where she went after the attack?"

"No."

"Do you know that she was seen outside the walls?"

"No."

"Then I think it's time you and her have a talk," she says, "without attacking each other."

I take a spot at the other side of the bed and let out a breath. Closing my eyes, I rest my head against the wall. "I know we need to. But the fact that she lashes out every time I say a word about our parents or anything involving them, makes it pretty difficult to properly communicate."

"Then you don't bring any of it up. Don't give her a reason to lash out," Jade snaps hoarsely. I don't think she slept a lot either last night, even though healing takes up a lot of energy. "Talk to her about the things that matter at that moment, you can leave talking about and processing their death for another time, when you are both ready to talk about it."

"I know, but our conversations always end up with talking about them," I say. "And either she pushes the conversation that way, or I do. But when she does it, it almost feels as if she does it on purpose. Just to be able to hurt me, to let that anger out."

"Then let her take that anger out, but not on you," Madion cuts in. "She has no right to get mad at you when none of this is your fault."

Her eyelids are drooping, the sleepless night finally taking its toll. Jade notices too and whispers her to sleep. Madion kisses her once before closing her eyes. She's out cold in seconds.

"Has she been awake all night?" I ask.

"Yes. No matter how many times I said that I was already halfway healed, she wouldn't go to sleep or even eat," she answers. "I know either of us being hurt brings back memories we'd rather put away. But no matter how hurt I am, she needs to take care of herself as well. Because I can't see her like this either."

Madion tightens her arms around Jade, almost as if muscle memory kicked in. Jade just pulls her in even tighter in response.

I know the whole story of how they met and what they went through, but without some of the minor details they'd rather forget about what they had to endure.

It took Madion a long while to recover, physically and mentally. She had nightmares, back problems from the lashings, and numerous other things. However, she got through it. They got through it together.

"She'll be okay. It might just all be too much for her right now," I reassure her, noticing the fatigue is catching up to Jade too. "You two rest, I'm going to check on Nate."

I slide off the bed and put my hand on Jade's. "I'll see you both tomorrow."

I take my leave when I notice they're both already sound asleep.

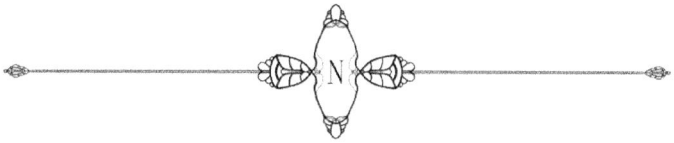

"Vergus?" I call out as I dip a sword into the cooling bin.

A silence follows, with no response from him.

Is he out?

After a moment, I pull the sword out and leave it on my bench. Taking off my apron, I walk away from my station, towards the back of the forge.

If Vergus is out, his ovens should be cold.

As I glance around the corner, I indeed find his ovens to be off, not even smoldering anymore.

When did he even go out?

I didn't hear him leave.

With a sigh, I make my way back to my station to continue on the sword. He'll come back from wherever he had to be when he can.

But before I reach my bench, the doors open, and slam shut. I look to my left to find Vergus coming in, looking rattled as he rushes to the back. I'm confused for only a second until I follow him.

Once I reach him, he has already lit his ovens and put his gloves and apron on. Without even acknowledging me, he grabs a bucket full of metal and throws it on his bench.

I carefully approach him and brace my hands on the wooden board. "What happened?"

His eyes snap up, and I swear they're filled with regret and anger as he mutters, "Nothing that concerns you, Nate. Please get back to those orders I gave you."

"I only have one order left," I counter, trying to keep the conversation going.

Vergus turns to his ovens and takes out a small bowl to melt the metal in. "Then you can find more on my desk."

I lean towards him and say, "Vergus, something happened wherever you just were. Talk to me."

"It is nothing that concerns you right now, Nate. Please leave it," he repeats.

"Since when do we keep things from each other?" I retort. "Don't start shutting me out now. I know how much it hurt you when I used to do it."

"Then now you know even more how it felt when you did it," he snaps suddenly.

I'm taken aback and lift my hands from the bench. He never talks like that.

Something set him off, and I want to know what.

"Where did you go?" I ask, trying to look into his eyes.

"I went for a walk." A lie.

He never goes for a walk when it's raining. It messes up his beard and hair, especially the few curls he has in it.

"Vergus, don't lie to me. You're always talking about your beard getting frizzy when you take a walk in the rain," I say. "And as far as I know, it's currently still pouring outside."

Vergus sighs and walks to the oven. He puts the bowl with metal in the flames before lifting his face to the ceiling, seeming to blink back tears.

"Please, get back to work," he mumbles.

"Vergus—"

"Get back to work," he grinds out, glancing over his shoulder at me.

"For heaven's sake, just tell me what happened."

"No," he snaps. "And now you're going to get back to that order or you can go home."

I stumble back because of the second time he now raises his voice at me. Vergus doesn't even look at me as he returns to his bench to gather his tools. I take a deep breath and turn around to do as he said.

"Very well. You can come talk to me when you're ready to act normal," I mutter, voicing my disappointment.

An awful feeling fills my chest as I walk away from him.

He never acts like this, no matter what happens.

Passing my finished orders, I make way to turn right towards my workstation.

"Nate?" Vergus suddenly says.

I stop in my tracks, waiting for him to continue.

"I'll tell you later, okay?" he mutters, his voice slightly shaking. "Just no—not now."

With a nod, I leave him be and return to my station.

Whatever he did in his absence affected him in a way I haven't seen before.

So I truly hope he'll open up to me soon.

CHAPTER 8

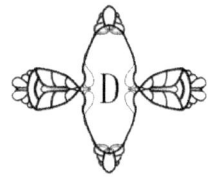 I make my way to the other side of town, getting rained on while passing even more shops, food, and clothes. I love how much this town works together. If you need the smallest thing, numerous people would be happy to help.

Even when I pass the streets, they just greet me as if I am not the princess. It feels more like home here than at the castle.

I even got invited to dinner by a small family that saw me coming back from the woods.

It was one of those nights where I felt normal. Just Dawn. Not Dawn Sungust, Princess of Iluniel.

In the distance, the forge appears, the dark building almost merges with the mountains. Camouflage is something they definitely thought about when building a workplace for the best blacksmith in the kingdom.

I'm met by the smell of fire and burned wood, and the sound of hammers clashing with steel.

Nate is standing at his bench, working on what looks like a dagger. Vergus is farther back. Sweat is dripping down Nate's head, soaking his white shirt. I send a small wisp of air over his forehead, making him look up. He smiles and I give him a broad smile back.

I call out to Vergus, but it's as if he doesn't want to look at me. He solely focuses on his work.

I shoot Nate a confused look, but he just shrugs. "He's been like this ever since your sister apparently summoned him this morning."

"This morning?" I ask. "And you don't know what they talked about either?"

"Beats me, but I certainly hope he starts talking to me again soon. I need help."

"Can I help?"

"I don't know," he mutters, laying down his tools. "Have you ever done this before?"

"Never too old to learn something new, right?" I trace my fingertips over a newly forged sword. The heat doesn't bother me as it used to.

He makes his way over to me, handing me an apron. "If you want to help that bad, you can help me make some arrowheads. Jade ordered them a couple days ago, and I'm afraid she'll have my head if I don't finish them soon. Especially after yesterday."

I put my hand on his shoulder. "She will definitely come after you if you don't finish them soon."

We burst out laughing but compose ourselves when Vergus yells at us to be quiet. At least he can still yell at us.

"Talking about yesterday, how is your leg?" I ask as I put on the dark brown apron. "I thought the cut was pretty deep."

"Almost fully healed," he responds, tracing his fingers over his thigh. "How about you?" We make our way over to a barrel full of metal, as he adds, "You were looking worse than I was."

"Good thing I heal quicker than you, then." I absently rub the spot where the blade went in. "I'm lucky it was a warning and not an assassination. If the blade had been made of Alk—I don't think I'd be walking right now."

Nate lets out a sigh. "Thank the heavens that you're lucky."

I don't respond to that, instead I stare at the molds for the arrowheads. Just simple pointy arrowheads, except for the inside.

These will be hollow arrowheads, not solid as usual.

"Did Jade order these before?" I ask curiously.

"She did. Last week, she ordered four of them. Now she wants ten more," he answers, noticing my stare. "You have seen them before, haven't you?"

"I think Jade might've used one to get through my shield while training. She had infused it with some type of burning substance," I explain. "When it skimmed me, it felt like my arm was about to fall off."

"Of course she did," he muses. "She had been bugging me about making these for weeks until I finally had the time to make a few."

"Well, let's make the rest then," I say, picking up a hammer, which is heavier than I thought. Before I drop it on the ground, Nate catches it with one hand. Then he takes my hand with his other and leads me to the other side of his workbench.

A vise on the right corner, multiple hammers, pincers, even a wrench, scattered across the bench. Numerous pieces of metal glistering with the reflection of the fire behind us.

Nate walks over to one of the ovens, picks up what looks like a bowl on a stick, and fills it with pieces of metal. Then places the bowl in the fire and detaches the stick.

"Now we wait for a bit until the metal is fully melted. Then we carefully fill these molds and let them harden," he says, taking a place next to me to lean against the bench.

"Do you think if we enhance the flames, it'll melt faster?" I question, my magic eager to show itself.

Nate seems to notice it, too. "We could try."

He takes my hand the same way I took his a couple days ago with the flower on my balcony. This time my hand is in his. A faint tingle passes between us as we intertwine our fingers. "Have you practiced with fire yet?" Nate asks, lowering his head to be at the same height as me.

I shake my head. "Not really."

He lets our palms face the oven. "Then let me be the first person to teach you."

His magic wraps around our hands, rousing mine. I let my magic flow to the flames, following and entwining with his. As my magic meets the fire, it slightly retreats. But the flames are no longer the enemy from when I didn't have control over them. It starts to feel warmer as the flames grow higher and higher, while Nate and I continue to fuel them with our magic.

The metal is melted in seconds. So I prepare the molds when Nate returns to the oven to grab the molten metal. He slowly pours it into the molds, telling me when to close one and when to open one. All ten molds are filled to the rim before I have to close them.

"Teamwork," he says as we high-five.

"Glad to help," I counter. "It is really amazing what you create here. I would've never thought of a hollowed-out arrowhead."

It almost looks as if Nate starts blushing, but it could be from the heat of the ovens. "Thanks." He then motions to the sword strapped across my back. "Do you want to fix your sword too? Because I thought I saw it was a bit bent and chipped."

I unsheathe my sword and indeed notice faint cracks. Swinging it around also feels unbalanced and as I hold it vertically in front of me, I can see a slight bend in the middle of the blade.

"It could use some repairs," I admit.

I hand Nate the sword and he puts it back in the fire, the flames completely engulfing the blade.

We work on my sword for the rest of the afternoon. Bending it back into its original state, filling up several chipped-out places, and reforging every single crack.

Until we end with a perfect sword, sweat-soaked clothing and smiles on our faces. I even dare to say that Vergus looks at us with admiration.

His apprentice teaching someone else his craft.

Nate hands me my sword back after he cools it down one last time.

"Thank you," I mutter. "As I said before, you're amazing at this."

"No problem. Are you going to test it?" he asks, fidgeting with a small piece of metal in his hands.

"Not today. I'm going to have an early night," I state. "But I asked Madion and Jade to meet me tomorrow morning at the training court. Want to join?"

"What are you going to train?"

"All kinds of things, sword skills, defense, magic, anything you want."

"Count me in then."

I embrace him, and he returns it luckily. "See you tomorrow. Don't overwork yourself on those arrowheads. They can wait. I don't think Madion is going to let Jade use her bow, anyway."

"I don't think so either." He chuckles. "I'll see you tomorrow."

I pull away, sheathing my sword before wrenching some sweat out of my shirt. "See you tomorrow."

I wave both him and Vergus goodbye before making my way back to the castle.

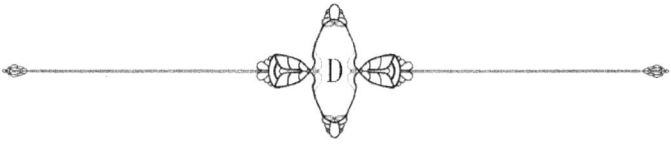

I arrive at the court bright and early. Clean clothing, hair in a tight braid, weapons all polished and ready to get dirty again. Madion is sitting on a pile of rocks, sharpening one of her daggers. Jade is, surprisingly enough, practicing with her bow.

I shoot Madion a questioning look. She just shrugs. "I couldn't convince her to leave it at home." And continues sharpening her dagger.

Even though she was injured a couple of days ago, it didn't affect Jade's aim. Arrow after arrow hits the center of the target.

"When are you going to teach me to shoot like that?" I ask, leaning against a target across from Jade.

She aims slightly my way. "Whenever you're free."

"You know, I figured out how you and Madion got me down," I muse, staring into the distance. "Hollowed out arrowheads. I never would've thought about that."

Jade just aims straight at me now. "How good of you to figure that out. Can you get out of my way now? I want to practice."

"Why not practice with me?" I challenge her, placing my hand in the middle of the target, fingers spread.

"It is not my fault if I chop off one of your fingers," she says, re-aiming her arrow. "Are you sure?"

I wiggle my fingers. "Why else would I put my hand in the way of your arrow? You say you never miss. Prove it."

She sighs. "Your funeral."

Pulling the bowstring tight, Jade seems to aim precisely in between my fingers.

She releases her breath and string simultaneously.

The arrow hits home, right between my index and middle finger.

"Not bad," I mutter as I make way to remove my hand from the target.

But a dagger embeds itself between my ring and middle finger, and another pins my sleeve to the target.

Jade and I look in the direction of the culprit. A wicked smiling redhead, now leaning against a pillar, playing with three more daggers in her hand.

"Want me to throw more knives at you?" Madion asks.

I rip out the one holding down my sleeve. "No, thank you very much."

Someone entirely different clears his throat behind Madion.

"Hey," Nate says quietly.

"Hey, what are you doing here?" Jade asks, counting the number of arrows left in her quiver.

"I invited him," I state. "I thought it would be fun to try some two against two combat. Nate and I against the two of you."

Madion seems to think on it, but Jade already counters, "That's not fair, together you two are stronger when it comes to magic than we are."

"How do you propose we team up, then?" Nate asks. He's taken a place next to Madion, his own sword dangling at his side.

"Dawn and I against Nate and Jade," Madion says, putting away her daggers.

"Why don't we make it a bit more interesting, then?" Nate adds, "Let's make it a small competition. Two different skills. Accuracy and strength."

"Go on," I encourage him.

"One person from each team will show their accuracy, by knife throwing and archery. The others will face off in the ring by using magic and other weapons," he explains, crossing his arms over his chest to wait for our response.

"Let's do this," Jade shouts excitingly. "I want to start with accuracy." Shooting a glance in Madion's direction. "Let's see how you are with a bow and arrow, honey."

Madion's eyebrows shoot up in a questioning look, but Jade ignores it and grabs Madion's hand, dragging her towards their designated spots.

"I have never seen you work with a bow," I say as I take my spot next to my teammate.

"You haven't even seen half of what I can do, Dawn," she retorts as she knocks an arrow. "And watching Jade do this for years teaches you what to do, and what not."

"Good luck then."

Madion breathes in deeply, focusing solely on the center of the target. Bowstring tight, pulled all the way back, arrow ready to fly.

She releases her arrow, and it hits its mark. Right in the center. As does Jade's arrow.

"Not bad, honey," Jade teases her mate.

"Keep calling me that, sweetheart," Madion says smoothly. "And you can feed yourself tonight, no dessert either."

Jade's mouth opens and closes several times, shocked by her threat. Madion winks at her before resuming her shooting. Jade is still pouting as she brings up her bow.

They each fire off four more arrows, all of them hit their marks.

All five knives they throw hit home, too.

Leaving me and Nate to fight out who wins.

We make our way over to the stone circle. Once you step outside of it, you're done.

Madion and Jade take a spot a couple of feet away, just to be safe from potentially flying weapons. You wouldn't want to be too close when that happens.

"You ready to get your ass kicked?" Nate asks, sword raised.

"I should ask you the same question." I raise my sword to meet his. Steel shines in the sun.

"Ready?" Jade asks us both.

"Ready," we say simultaneously.

We start circling each other, assessing where to strike. My magic is humming beneath my skin once again, pushing against it to get free, to take Nate down.

But this is my fight first. Magic can come into play later.

I notice Nate has a vulnerable spot. His left side. It's because he has his sword over to the right, almost pushing himself off balance. Which gives me a window to strike.

I faintly swipe right, but immediately go left to hit his exposed side. But he sees what I was about to do and blocks perfectly.

I might've underestimated Nate. He knows his way around a sword better than I thought.

Nate tries to go for my legs. I jump over his sword and try to land a blow to his legs, but his sword is already there.

I pump a bit of magic into my arms and sword, giving it that small boost of energy. I notice Nate doing the same. Madion and Jade notice too as I see them shuffling back, getting out of reach. I smile at them before bringing down my sword on Nate again.

I strike, he dodges. He strikes, I block. I strike, he blocks. I strike again. He does not block.

My sword skims his arm, leaving a streak of red coating his white shirt. Nate slightly stumbles back but pushes even more magic into his sword before bringing it down on me.

I don't have enough time to recharge mine, as Nate brings his sword down and shatters it. I stumble back, having the hilt in one hand, and nothing in the other.

Nate smiles wickedly at me, thinking he won. I smirk at him, not giving him the win just yet. So I throw the hilt aside and palm one of my daggers. I let my magic envelop it, add to it, make it a larger blade than it originally was.

Nate only stares at me. The sheer power it takes to hold this sword up is tremendous, which means I have to finish this quickly.

I bring my dagger down, striking Nate's sword. Neither break.

As I slash to his right and Nate's sword groans at the impact. I immediately hit from the right again and his sword slightly cracks. Steel is not always the best choice for a fight that involves magic.

I slam into Nate and bring him to the floor. My knees hit the floor on either side of his stomach. His sword is leveled at my throat, daring me to move an inch.

Challenge accepted.

I hit his sword from the right once again, and this time, it shatters. Leaving him with only a hilt, too.

I pull back my magic from my dagger and hold it against his throat. "Do you admit defeat?"

Silence. He just stares at me.

I lean in closer. "Do I need to repeat myself?" I whisper.

"Of course not, I heard you clear enough the first time," he says proudly, as I feel a sharp sting in my stomach.

I keep my dagger at Nate's throat and pull back to see him holding one of my daggers pointed at my stomach. He must've grabbed it when I leaned in.

"Nice try," I remark, effortlessly twisting the dagger from his grip. Pointing one dagger at his throat now and the other at his stomach. "Shall I repeat myself again?"

He raises his hands. "Congratulations."

I pull the daggers away and lay next to him.

"You know, I didn't think you could fight that well," I say.

"I didn't know you were that powerful," he responds.

Two shadows loom over us, one of them is smiling, the other not so much.

"Nate, you were winning. Why did you not win? Now I need to cook for myself tonight." Jade pouts.

I look at Madion, who is standing at my feet. "You made a bet with her. How did you know I was going to win?"

"Because I trust you can handle yourself, Dawn. And besides, I didn't care if I won or lost that bet. I had nothing to lose. Jade, on the other hand," Madion says with a sideways glance.

"I barely know how to cook," Jade says. "Will you please make food for me tonight too?" Putting up her puppy eyes.

"We'll see. Maybe I'll cook for you, maybe I won't. It would be good for you to learn it yourself though," Madion shrugs as she sits down at my feet.

Jade sits down beside her and puts her head on Madion's shoulder. "If you want to teach me, I'll happily learn how to cook."

"I have been wanting to teach you for years now. You always say no. Yet when I won't cook for you, you suddenly want to learn."

"Yes," Jade mumbles very innocently.

"You're lucky I love you," Madion whispers, a faint smile tugging at her lips.

"And I love you," Jade says as she kisses Madion on the cheek.

Madion pulls her in for a proper kiss. I glance to the side to find Nate's cheeks heating up, so I quickly grab his hand and pull us up. With a grateful nod, he leads us back to the town, leaving Madion and Jade to do their desired business.

CHAPTER 9

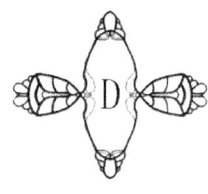

"She has been dead for approximately eight hours," Jade says while assessing the body. "Cause of death—I haven't got a single clue. It's as if the life was sucked out of her."

Jade roughly hauled me out of bed this morning to go to a nearby village. She threw my clothes at me, luckily not my weapons, and then rushed me out of the room. To Adrian and Jake, who were waiting for us at the gates with our horses.

My horse, Lio, a beautiful black stallion with black manes, was waiting excitedly for me. I hadn't been out with him for a while, which meant he missed me, and I missed him.

The journey to the village was short, no problems there. But once we reached the town, we ran into problems. Some villagers were not happy with us being there, because we apparently wanted to cover it up and never speak of it again.

"Sir, I can assure you that I want to find out what happened here as much as you," I said to her father, who was walking a fine line between rage and grief when we arrived. "Please, let me help. I want to bring whoever did this to justice."

They luckily hadn't moved the body yet. It was a beautiful girl, short blonde hair, around twenty years old, my age, named Anna. And she was just ripped out of her life as if she was meaningless.

"What do you mean 'the life was sucked out of her'?" I ask Jade, as I kneel beside her.

"Look at her skin." She gestures to the girl's arms. "She's almost grey." Then she gently opens one of the girl's eyes and shows all the tiny blood vessels have been torn open. There is no white left around her irises. "That doesn't just happen. She was attacked by something, either a monster or very powerful, dark being."

"Why would they go after her?" I question, "She was a kind and loving girl from what I've heard."

"I don't think her death was meant for this village." Adrian sighs as he plucks a piece of paper out of the girl's pockets. He hands it to me. "I think it was meant for you."

"What?" I blurt out, my hand trembling as I grab the paper.

~

Railon is watching you, Dawn.
Day and Night. Night and Day.
No one escapes once we get in control.

~

I incinerate the paper right there and then in my hand. Small flakes of burnt paper float away in the air.

"We need to get back to the castle now. I'll ask if we may take her with us," I say.

I make my way over to the small crowd gathered behind us. They part before me until I come face to face with Anna's father. "I am very sorry for your loss." I incline my head to him.

"Thank you, Your Highness." He nods. "What will you do now?"

"I want to ask for your permission to take her with us, to examine her further in the castle."

A couple of disapproving words murmur through the crowd, but the man in front of me silences them. "Why do you want to take my daughter with you?" he asks, sadness clouding his eyes.

"I hope we might find the cause of death with our supplies there. Within two days, I will bring her back," I say to him, the sadness resounding in my words too. "So you can properly bury her as you wish."

This girl is dead because of me. Because they wanted to send me a message. If I find who did this, they're going to suffer. I don't care what I have to do. But this girl is getting the justice she deserves.

"Very well, but please bring her back safely," he responds, fear now coating his voice.

I take both his hands in mine. A few shocked gasps resound through the crowd. "I will take care of her. You have my word."

The man squeezes my hands before I let go.

I walk back over, instructing Jake and Adrian to gently lay the girl on my horse. I promised I'd take care of her, so I'll be the one to take her to the castle.

We bid everyone goodbye before making our way back to the castle.

Once we return, Adrian lifts the girl off the horse and carries her in his arms to the lower levels. Jake leads the horses to the stables, but Lio fights him as he sees me walking to the castle.

I run back over to him and take his face in my hands, gently stroking his hair.

"I'll come back soon. We'll go to Yuno, to the large grass fields, to the apple orchards, where you can eat as many apples as you want. Deal?" I try to bribe him, looking into those deep black eyes. He nickers in approval. This time when I walk away, he lets Jake pull him towards the stables.

When I enter the room, Anna's body is already on a stone table, partially covered with a white sheet. Madion is there to assist Jade.

"You have everything you need?" I ask.

"Yes, Adrian is getting the last of the supplies I need."

I put my hands behind my back. "Do you think you can figure out what happened?"

"We'll have to wait and see for that, I'm afraid. I have seen a lot of dead bodies, but never one like hers."

I nod to her as I take in Anna's face, and I remind myself of my promise. I will do her justice. She did not die to just deliver a message. That can't be the reason her life was ended.

"Do the best you can." I take a sharp breath. "I'm going to report this to Leanne."

Madion looks at me, assessing whether or not to come with me. "You got this. If she gets angry, just leave. Don't fight over this."

"I wasn't planning on fighting with her today. Definitely not over the death of this girl."

I close the door behind me, preparing myself once again to talk to my own sister.

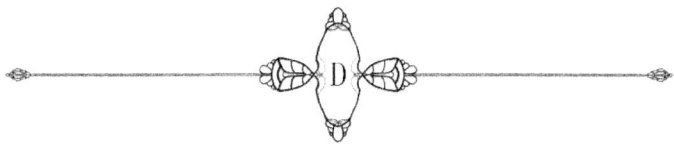

I decided to put on some clean clothes instead of the muddied ones I had on. One thing less for Leanne to complain about when I enter the throne room.

She is sitting on the elaborately decorated throne. One our father had made a couple of years before his death.

A stone chair, covered in vines, leaves and flowers carved out of wood and attached to the throne. Besides that, because of my dad's powerful magic, he added while making the throne, it still grows real vines, leaves, and flowers. You don't always see them, but they are there.

I don't bow as I reach the steps in front of the throne. I don't have to.

Guards are on either side of the throne, one hand on their sword, the other behind their backs. Their hands have been on that sword the moment I stepped in.

"Dawn, where were you off to this morning?" Leanne asks, the black fabric of her dress shifting as she slightly leans forward.

"I was informed that a girl was murdered in a nearby village," I say. "I set out with my guards to see what had happened."

"And what did you find out?"

"That she was indeed murdered, but not with a blade or anything in that category. She was killed with magic."

Leanne's face stays neutral, as if it doesn't bother her one bit that someone was murdered. I almost dare to say a small smile tugged at her lips.

"And what are you going to do with this information?" she asks, propping her chin on her fist.

"We brought the body back here, and Jade is examining it at the moment. That's all we can do at the moment," I respond.

Mentioning that note right now is not the right move to make. She'll just start blaming everything on me. "I'll report back once Jade finds something."

"Good," she says, her attention already on some papers beside her. "I think those soldiers from Railon would love a visit from you."

"I'd love to pay them a visit," I mutter through clenched teeth. I hate it when she thinks she can just order me around as if I'm not her sister. "I'll pay them a visit right now."

I pivot around towards the door, but Leanne calls after me, "But be careful, Dawn. If they have the nerve to stab you, I don't think they'll be easy to interrogate."

"I'll keep it in mind," I shout back.

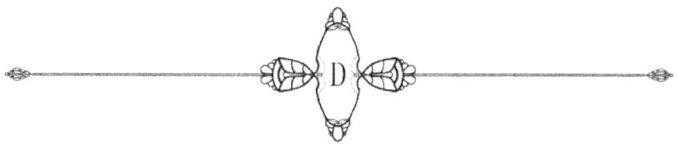

The dungeons are damp, cold, and dark. When you have nothing to keep you warm, the nights are tough. The iron around your wrists and ankles only cools you down even more. The shadows dancing in the corners of your cell, ready to jump on you if you dare to close your eyes. But when you've been down here long enough, you get to appreciate the shadows.

I lean against the wall for a moment, telling myself I am not going into one of those cells. Not today.

A guard stationed at the entrance of the dungeons greets me and leads me to the two cells the soldiers are in.

As I approach the cells slowly, something already feels wrong. Both cells are too quiet. All four of the soldiers are laying on the ground. No movement. No breathing either.

"When was the last time someone checked in on them?" I ask the guard.

"I think last night, your Highness," he responds, fear sounding in his voice.

"No one has checked in on them yet?" I ask again.

"No, we were supposed to check on them within the hour," he answers.

"Open the cell," I order him.

"But they'll attack you."

"I don't think they will. They're dead," I state.

The color now fully draining from his face. He quickly opens the door.

Two soldiers lay side by side, faces turned to the right, lips colored purple. They must have smuggled in poison, or someone gave it to them.

"Has anyone been with them besides you and I?" I ask as I squat down to take a better look at the dead men.

"Her Majesty spoke to them briefly yesterday, Your Highness."

Seriously, she sends me here to talk to them when she already did it herself. Does she want me to have a panic attack?

"Thank you for the information. Make sure they're dead and then please bury them at the edge of the town," I order him.

"Of course, Your Highness." He goes on one knee. "I will take any punishment you see fit for the situation."

I gesture for him to rise. "No one is getting punished because of this. You did your job, and you couldn't have known they had a way to kill themselves."

"Thank you, Your Highness. I'll get rid of the bodies immediately."

I nod once to him before almost running out. The walls were closing in on me.

I hope I don't bump into Leanne on my way out of the castle, because those guards will need their swords if I do.

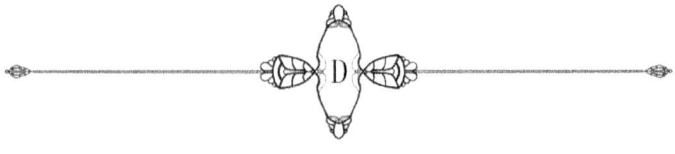

"She is just always getting under my skin. Sending me to the dungeons only to find the soldiers dead, not caring one bit about the murder," I rant to Yuno, who has her head in my lap, looking up at me with her bright yellow eyes. "I don't know what to do anymore sometimes. We can't even have a normal conversation."

Ever since our parents died, she's been distant. But locking me up didn't start until two years ago. I was out with Madion to check on Yuno after she got hurt while hunting. I hadn't told Leanne about it because I thought it would be okay.

We came back after dark. I dropped Madion off at her house and went to my room, where I found Leanne on my bed, looking angry. She started yelling at me that I was irresponsible, and I yelled back at her.

I didn't notice the guards until it was too late. They had knocked me to the ground before I could do anything. I was struggling so hard that one of them threw me over his shoulder and carried me to the dungeons. A servant tried to interfere, but was pushed aside.

Then I was shackled to the wall in the last cell at the end of the dungeons. The darkest cell of them all. Leanne didn't speak a word to me as they restrained me and then she just left after making sure I wasn't going anywhere.

That was the night my nightmares started again, too. They came back hard, and I remember myself screaming for half of the night.

Adrian and Jake are always the ones that get me out in the morning. They would take me to the grass fields, to Yuno, to the woods, to let me come back to myself while I'd stare into the distance for hours. But lately, they have to take me straight to my room or to Madion and Jade. Because just taking a deep breath and thinking is not helping anymore. The only thing that helps is the running water that streams down my back. The water that feels like my dad rubbing his hand up and down my back, calming me down.

"What do I do?" I whisper.

"You get up and fight us," a voice behind me shouts.

I look over my shoulder to find Jake and Adrian out of armor, swords in their hands.

"Why?" I question them.

"Because you're angry and you can't go back when you're angry. If you go back while you're still angry, you're going to clash with Leanne, and we don't want to be forced to use those shackles again," Jake says. "Never again."

"Leanne already forbade them from being used."

They both give me a look. I give them a look back.

"We all know that won't make them magically disappear," Adrian says, crossing his arms over his chest.

I pick up my sword, causing Yuno to jump up and step beside me. I get to my feet and bring up my sword, gesturing for them to come closer.

"You want to fight that bad?" I provoke them. "Come at me then."

"Do you want to use magic or not?" Adrian asks.

"That wouldn't be fair to the two of you, would it?"

"We can manage. Let's all use magic," Jake says. Winking as he adds, "Full power."

He's taunting me. I just give a scheming smile back.

Let's blow them off their feet.

I let my magic pool into my left hand, the right holding my sword. Jake and Adrian both conjure up the amount of magic they can handle, which is significantly less than mine.

I let my magic grow and grow. "Are you both sure about this?"

They let their magic flare up in response. "Come and get us," Jake yells.

I run towards them. Jake stays in my path, but Adrian diverts to my right. I clash swords with Jake and notice Adrian coming in from the side. I form a wall of air to meet Adrian. He slams into it, but I suddenly bring it down to make him trip. Jake brings his sword to my legs, trying to throw me off balance. I step back, but Adrian suddenly comes from behind and wraps his arms around me.

"Get off me," I snap at him.

"Make me. You are the strong princess with powers over all the elements," he whispers in my ear, clearly enjoying this. "Show me just how strong you are."

"Oh, I'll show you." I push my magic out to rip Adrian away from me. He skids back and comes to a halt a few feet away.

"That was nothing. Everybody says you are so powerful," Jake says. His sword is still raised at me. "Show us."

"Indeed, I haven't seen the smallest bit of that power lurking beneath the surface," Adrian says, brushing some dirt from his sleeves. "Where is that big, powerful blast you used to shatter that wall? Where is that power you'll need to defeat the second trial?"

"Stop that," I sneer. My magic is flaring up even more. I need to control it. My anger can't let me lose that control.

"Stop what?" Adrian asks, "Talking to you? Pushing you to your limits?"

My magic is pushing against my skin, wanting to come out. *I'll let you out,* I whisper to it. *We just have to do it at full strength.* Wipe those smirks off their faces.

I drop my sword. Adrian and Jake both tense up. Good.

My magic pools into my right hand, matching the strength in my left hand. I can blow them both away at half my strength. Let's not waste the rest.

Stretching my arms to the side, I open my hands and close my eyes, breathing in the scent of the flowers and the nature.

"You brought this upon yourselves," I mumble, not sure if they hear me as my eyes snap open and I bring my hands down. Blasting my magic out.

I hear two screams of terror as the two men are ripped off their feet and flung back, landing further away.

I let out a deep breath, quieting the rest of my magic that didn't come out to play. I open my eyes to find both Adrian and Jake on their backs in the grass, wheezing.

"You brought this upon yourselves," I repeat.

They both answer me with a grunt.

I sit on the grass, Yuno comes to join me again. I let my fingers slide through her fur, a welcome feeling beneath my fingertips.

After a while, Jake and Adrian get up with an even louder grunt and sit beside me. We talk, we laugh, we're just us.

No titles, no princess with her guards. Just friends.

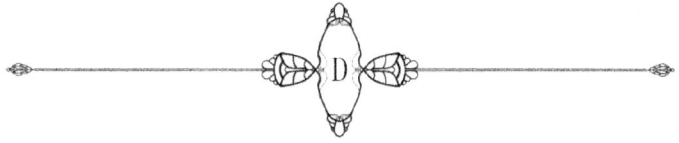

By the time I return to the castle, it's already dark outside. I need to hurry before Leanne finds me outside of my room. It's a small distance between the front door and my room, so I should be able to make it.

But before I can even round the final corner to my bedroom, I feel I'm not alone.

Peeking around the corner, I find Leanne, accompanied by four guards at my door. I could try my balcony, but that would take too much time. I'm going to have to talk my way out of this one.

I round the corner and the guards immediately tense up, guilt showing on their faces. Leanne merely stands there, looking too calm for what's about to happen.

"Leanne. What can I do for you?" I say, as I fake a yawn. "I'm pretty tired, so I'd like to go to bed."

"I was informed you were out in the woods again, with that creature and your guards. Did I give you permission for that?" she asks calmly.

I swallow my pending fear as two of the guards seem to get closer to me, "No, but I thought with my guards there, it would be okay." I take a step back, ready to make a run for it.

"As long as your guards were there, it's okay. But why did you not get back hours ago?" Leanne says. "Before it got dark."

I take another step back as I see her make a small gesture for the guards to close in on me. "Because I want to have some freedom for once in my life," I snap at her. "Instead of having to find you every single time, I want to go outside the castle. Where did you run off to when they stabbed me at the meeting? You didn't let me know where you were. So why should I come to you every single time I want to go out? Maybe I just want some peace for once!"

At this Leanne snaps too, motioning to the guards.

They close in on me, but I'm already bolting down the hallway.

I am not spending the night in the dungeons. I can't handle that right now.

As I round the corner, I slam into three other guards, ready to apprehend me. I fight against their grip, but the four other guards are already upon me. I try to fight them, but seven against one is too much.

"Please don't fight this. We don't want to hurt you," one guard quietly says to me as my arms are wrenched back and iron is clasped around my wrists.

My magic instantly retreats at the touch. These are the enhanced shackles. As Jake and Adrian already said, she doesn't keep her promises when it comes to me.

One guard pats me down, looking for all of my weapons. When he finds them all, he puts them safely in my room. As he emerges again, he doesn't dare look in my direction. They all don't look at me, guilt on each of their faces.

Every guard that has taken me to the dungeons has apologized the day after. They know what it does to me, how I come out of there.

I plead with her as I'm hauled away, still struggling in their grip. "Leanne, please. Let me go."

"You would not listen, Dawn," she merely says, walking in front of us towards the dungeons. "You know these are the consequences."

I yell and struggle the entire way down, but no guard or servant dares to intrude. They have learned these years that when I am led down here, there is nothing they can do to stop it.

Sometimes I escaped, but with these shackles, there is no way I am getting out.

I am dragged down the stairs, feet scraping over the stone. We take the first right. The only cell that is always available is straight ahead.

And as soon as I come closer and see the inside, I start kicking the guards, yelling at them to let me go. But they do not. They keep dragging me forward.

The cell is small, but it has enough space for a metal plate on the ground, with two pairs of shackles.

And a collar.

She can't put that on me.

My magic tries to fight against the enhanced shackles on my wrists as I start to panic even more. But it can't do anything.

I'm dragged into the cell and pushed onto the metal plate.

Tears have started rolling down my cheeks by the time the shackles are around my ankles. My hands are put in front of me, shackled to the metal plate, too. The guards walk out and leave the collar on the ground. Thank the heavens.

Leanne walks into the cell and stops out of my reach. She grabs the collar, absently playing with it in her hands, as she says, "How many times do I have to do this before you listen to me?"

"Before I listen?" I yell at her. "I listen to you every second of the day. You just don't want to see that. You only see the things I do wrong."

Leanne quietly walks to my back, still fidgeting with the collar in her hands, opening and closing it. "I see not only the mistakes you make, but the mistakes are what I notice. Those are the things I want you to stop doing." She puts a hand on my shoulder, "Mistakes get you killed, Dawn."

"Mistakes let you learn. You act as if you've never made a mistake in your life, but I know a lot of times you made a mistake," I sneer at her. Still hearing the closing and opening of the collar behind me. "You are only pushing me away by judging me every single time."

"Like I said, mistakes can be lethal," she reprimands.

"Then let a mistake kill me. I might learn something from it. Instead of you locking me up every single time, I don't follow your rules," I say, tears still dripping down my cheeks.

"Forgive me for not wanting to lose the only family I have left," she says, opening the collar.

My response is something I've been thinking for a long while now. I take a deep breath and close my eyes. "You already lost me."

Leanne jerks my head back by pulling my hair and snaps the collar around my neck.

She walks out of the cell and slams the door shut, leaving me in the dark with only a flickering candle down the hall.

When I don't hear any footsteps anymore, I scream.

Letting it all out, tears streaming down my face.

I plead, I scream, I cry, until there is nothing left.

A familiar voice suddenly speaks from another cell. "Dawn, breathe."

But I can't breathe.

"Dawn, you'll get through the night." Another familiar voice tries to calm me down. "Just breathe, we're here."

"Please," I whisper as I slump to the floor. "Get them off."

I close my eyes as I lay on my side, still breathing way too fast. Madion's techniques aren't working.

The collar feels as if it is constricting me. The air cannot reach my lungs.

"Dawn, you're going to pass out if you don't breathe." Adrian, his familiar voice snaps into focus. "Inhale. Exhale."

Through my sobbing, I get a couple of breaths down, but it's not enough. My vision starts to darken.

My shackled wrists drop to the floor, metal on stone resounding through the hall.

"Dawn!" Jake yells.

She locked me up. Again.

I just lay there, breathing shallowly, tears streaming down my face.

The darkness being my only friend tonight.

CHAPTER 10

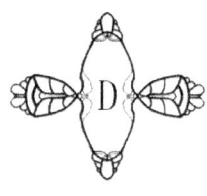

I'm awoken by the sound of keys jamming into a lock, yet my eyes remain closed. Afraid of it being another nightmare.

A cell door opens. "Get her out of here, please," the guard of this morning pleads.

"We'll get her out," someone responds.

The door to my cell opens and two people step in. One takes a place at my feet, the other kneels before me.

The collar has been slicing into my neck all night. I felt blood drizzling down to my chest multiple times when I moved.

A hand slowly moves towards my neck. It wraps around the collar and mine shoots out to grab their wrist. The owner of the hand grabs my shackled wrist in return.

"Hey, it's me," someone says gently.

I open my eyes to find Adrian and let out a sob as I see the keys in his lap. "Let's get you out of here," he whispers.

He slides the collar around to find the keyhole. As soon as it snaps open, I feel relief flowing through my body. My hands tremble as Adrian moves to my wrists. My left wrist is freed, my right wrist is freed, and as soon as the chains fall to the floor, I wrap my arms around Adrian's chest. He holds me tight as he hands the keys to Jake so he can free my ankles.

I keep holding on as the shackles slide free.

I'm free. I can get out of here. My magic slowly starts to come to the surface again, no longer repressed.

"Get me out of here, please," I beg him.

"I got you," Adrian whispers back.

He unwraps my arms from his chest and gets me to my feet. I stumble a bit, but Jake catches my elbow and keeps me upright. They both wrap an arm around my waist, but don't carry me.

If I can get through the night, I can walk out of here.

The stone floor is cold beneath my bare feet, but I keep walking. I will not fall. I hear faint words of encouragement coming from several cells. Even the prisoners are more reasonable than my sister.

I do need more support to get up the stairs. Jake grabs both my hands and goes backwards up the stairs. Adrian is behind me to make sure I don't fall back, since my legs are numb from the cold night. I channel a bit of magic into my legs, warming them, giving them more strength on the way up.

But my magic wants more, demands more.

It wants out.

I need to get out of here. I make it up the stairs quite fast, but the halls of the castle are a different story.

They feel longer and smaller than they normally do. My vision blurs again and my magic pushes more and more to come out.

"We need to get her to Madion and Jade right now. She's burning up," Jake says as he holds the back of his hand against my cheek.

"I'm not letting her walk one more step," Adrian states, lifting me into his arms. "You make sure no one gets in our way."

Adrian picks up his pace as I desperately grab onto him. My skin feels like it's burning yet freezing at the same time. The distinct elements fighting inside my body.

I hadn't been in the dungeons since the first layer of my soul broke and a lot of magic was released with it. I think my magic being suppressed is going to be even more traumatic for me and my soul from now on.

Jake swings open the front door of the castle, scaring the guards on duty. They try to step in, but one look at me makes them keep their mouths shut. I give them a faint smile before Adrian is walking down the stairs.

The streets are bustling, people going from store to store, buying food for tonight.

"Adrian, I can walk," I say, faintly. "I can make it to their house."

"No, you're not doing well. And you're no longer inside the castle, so I can carry you wherever you need to go," he retorts.

"You were already carrying me while we were still inside the castle," I say with a hint of a smile.

"Glad you still got some humor," he says, a smile forming on his face, too.

I hear Jake pounding on Madion and Jade's door as Adrian comes to a stop.

Now he puts me back on my feet, keeping an arm around my waist.

The door swings open, and the two females take me in, the strain showing in my eyes. They rush forward to get me inside. Straight ahead, through their bedroom, into the bathroom. I'm seated on their toilet. Madion kneels in front of me and takes off my clothes, while Jade is regulating the right water temperature and pressure. I wince slightly at Madion's chilly hands, and she silently apologizes.

When I'm fully undressed, Madion checks the water temperature one more time before guiding me to the floor of the shower. Jade makes the water flow over me in different places, cooling me down as much as possible, giving my magic the rest it needs after fighting the entire night.

"Keep breathing, Dawn, just breathe through it," Madion says as she takes my hands. "We're here."

I feel the warmth slowly pull back, back to the deep corners of my soul. Madion is cooling me down with her magic internally, and Jade is cooling me down externally.

I could never ask for better friends. They are by my side, every minute, every day, whenever I need them. Friends like them are what gets me out of bed in the morning. Just the thought of laughing with them, being in their presence, gives me the strength to get through the day, or nights like these.

When most of the heat has receded, I sag backwards against the wall. With the water going in streams down my chest and face, washing all the dirt and tears away and I just take a deep breath. A deep breath to pull myself out of that dark place I went last night.

A dark place where my nightmares are like photographs flashing past my eyes.

"Dawn?" Jade carefully asks.

"I'm okay," I mumble, not quite ready to face everybody else yet. "Thank you," I add.

"We're going to talk to Adrian and Jake for a moment. Clothes are on the bed, towels are on the sink," Madion says, letting go of my hands. "We're just on the other side of the wall if you need us."

I nod.

They walk out of the room, leaving it quiet and empty, except for the continuous sound of water falling down.

A sound that will always bring me calm.

Because no matter how big the storm is, you can always dance in the rain.

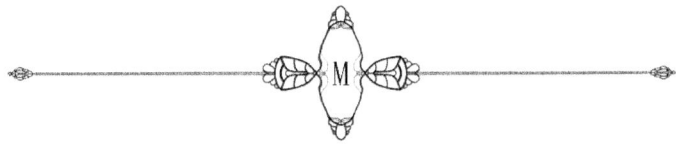

"What happened after she was dragged down there?" I ask.

Jade and I were still on the lower levels when Dawn's shouts echoed through the halls. We rushed out of the room to see her in shackles, once again being dragged to the dungeons.

"Leanne locked her up again. She used the enhanced shackles this time. Shackling her wrists, ankles, and—" Jake trails off, as if it is too painful to say.

"What did she do to her?" Jade demands beside me. "She has not been this close to breaking for a long while."

"A collar," Adrian mutters. "Leanne put a collar on her."

I have to take a deep breath to stop myself from killing Leanne right now. She has put Dawn through so much. After their parents died, she basically abandoned her. She tried to punish Dawn for every mistake she made, but most of all, she left the only family she had left to rot in a dungeon. Leanne was always this kind girl, ready to do anything for her sister. Dawn's eyes always lit up when Leanne entered the room and called her 'little droplet.' Now I haven't heard those two words in five years.

Jake takes a deep breath. "They had a conversation before Leanne left her down there. That fear in her voice, that wasn't the worst, the pain and determination in her voice when she said that—that she'd rather die. That's what made Leanne snap and use that collar."

"I can't take this right now," Jade says. She grabs her coat and rushes out the front door.

"Leave her," I order the two men. "She's having a very hard time with this, too."

I know what Dawn is going through, what's going on inside her head. I was tortured and beaten too, but with Dawn, everything went a step further.

I was imprisoned by people Jade trusted.

Dawn is being locked up by her own blood.

My torment was ended the moment Jade snapped and I'm afraid one day Dawn will snap, too.

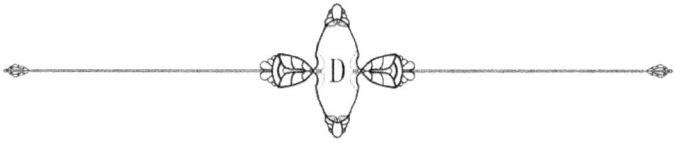

I heave myself off the floor and stumble into the bedroom. My legs still feel slightly numb, but I can stand on them. Madion laid out one of her warmer pair of pants and a green shirt. I tie my hair into a sloppy bun, white and brown strands sticking out everywhere.

Peeking through the gap at the door, I find Madion at the dining table fidgeting with a piece of fabric. I silently open the door and walk over to her. She has a distant look in her eyes, remembering something, yet I'm not sure whether it is a good or bad memory. So I gently hug her from behind, wrapping my arms around her and resting my chin on her shoulder. She slightly tenses before recognizing me. She puts her hands over mine and lets out a deep sigh.

"How are you?" I ask her.

"I should ask you that," she counters.

"I'll be okay. It was just harder this time with the different shackles," I explain to her. "I know this brings back memories every time, ones that you'd rather forget. I know that and I am sorry you two have to take care of me almost every time it happens."

Madion turns her head to look up at me. "You have no reason to be sorry. And we gladly take you out of that dark place you go during those nights." She fully turns now, "We are here Dawn, we will be here. Now, always and forever."

"I know and I will always be here, too." I give her hands a squeeze. "Like we always say, nothing will break us unless we allow it to."

Madion pulls me into a hug, arms around me, face buried in my neck. "We won't break. Nothing would be strong enough to do so."

And if we go down, we get up, no matter the pain.

"Nothing," I whisper. "Things got too much for Jade, didn't they?"

Madion pulls back. "Yeah, I think she went to take one last look at Anna's body."

"Did you find anything?"

"No, there are no obvious signs as to what or who killed her. Only the things you and Jade already noticed. I don't think there's much left to do except for getting her home."

"I'm taking her home then," I say, as I stride for the front door.

"We could take her home if you want to rest," Madion offers.

"I made a promise Madion, I will not let a night full of nightmares keep me from fulfilling it."

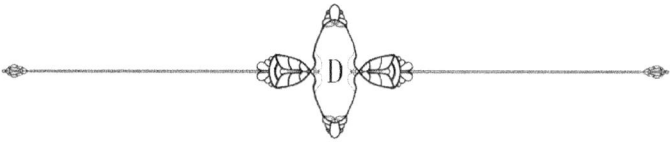

The ride to the village is quiet. I decided to go alone, no one around, just me. When I went to pick up Anna's body, I passed several servants. One by one they said kind words, and that they were very sorry this happened again.

Leanne apparently wasn't present at the castle. She went out early in the morning and hadn't come back yet.

Why is she always gone suddenly?

She never informs me or anyone else of her departures.

I can see smoke rising from the chimneys of the village. Everybody is waking up and starting their day. No worries on their minds, just getting to their duties of the day, making food, washing their clothes.

How I would love to just stay here for a day.

I am greeted by a few villagers as I arrive. I dismount Lio and strap him to a nearby pole.

"Where can I find her father?" I ask a nearby woman.

She points to the edge of the village, to a cloaked man sitting on a rock. "Thank you. Could you get a few men to carefully get Anna off the horse?"

She nods and takes off towards what I think is a small tavern. I approach the cloaked man carefully, not wanting him to lash out at an unknown threat.

"Sir?" I say carefully.

He slowly turns around to face me. "So the princess returns."

"I promised you I would bring back your daughter myself," I state. "Unharmed."

He looks over my shoulder to see four men watchfully lower his daughter from Lio and place her on a blanket. A single tear streams down his cheek as he looks at me again. "Thank you for bringing her back and for risking your own safety."

"Risking my own safety?" I blurt out.

The father approaches me. "We all know what happens to you inside that castle, but don't think for one minute we approve any of it." He reaches for my hand. "Please know that everyone here will stand with you if a time ever comes where we have to pick sides. We will stand by our rightful queen."

Now my eyes are blurring with tears. Not just from the determination in his words, just the fact that everybody knows what happens in that castle. I thought nobody knew or even cared.

"Thank you," I say as I grab his hand. "It means a lot to me, to hear that people care about me."

"People care more about you than you think, Your Highness."

"No titles please, just call me Dawn."

He inclines his head. "Of course, Dawn."

"Did you prepare anything for her funeral yet?" I ask him.

"I made a flowerbed to put her on and slide her into the river, but I have nothing to light it on fire with. Would you want to do it?"

"If you would trust me with that, I'll gladly give her that last honor."

Anna is lifted onto the flower bed minutes later and the whole village gathers around the shore of the river. Her father and I standing at the front, at Anna's feet.

"Go, my little girl," Anna's father mutters, his voice thick with tears. "Go to your mother. She'll welcome you with open arms and keep you safe. I will join you both when my time has come."

He waves two men forward. They place their hands at the sides of the flowerbed and push Anna onto the river. Flowers fall off, leaving a trail from the shore to her. Anna's blonde hair looks almost as if it is glowing in the sun, her white dress flowing over her body.

"Dawn?" The father gestures to his daughter. "You may."

I give him an empathetic nod, knowing how it feels to lose someone that means the world to you. A parent should never have to say goodbye to their child. Never.

I extend my right hand, my magic carefully coming out, still riled from last night. I demand every fiber of the flower stems to vibrate, creating heat. Soon the flower bed catches fire. I guide the flames to envelop Anna's body. The red flames stark against her pale skin and dress.

A tear is streaming down my face, at the gesture this man allowed me to do, and the amount of grief I still haven't fully processed myself.

The moment my parents died, I cried. I cried so much, but that was it. I don't think I ever fully came to terms with the fact that they died, that they left me. That grief is still deep inside me, waiting to either come out and tear me apart, or to be accepted and be processed.

Soon, almost nothing is left of Anna. The flower bed is slowly sinking to the bottom of the river. Thus, becoming her final resting place. I don't think she would mind all the water. Her father told me she was always playing along the river, practicing in shaping the water to her will.

It is only suitable that she may find her peace in these very waters that brought her so much joy.

I bid the village goodbye as I make my way back to Lio. He slightly lowers himself for me to climb onto his back.

With one last wave and a smile to the father, I urge Lio to ride back to the castle.

Where I will hopefully have a peaceful and quiet night.

CHAPTER 11

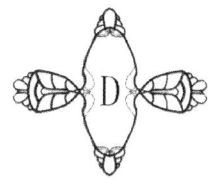

I hand Lio over to one of the stable servants and ask them to give him an extra apple as gratitude. Lio nudges me with his head once before walking into the stables towards his apples.

The hallways are still quiet. They always are after a night like we just had. No one dares to talk, not to Leanne, and some don't even dare to talk to me. Afraid they'll break me on the spot.

Then I notice my bedroom door is ajar, meaning someone was, or still is, inside. I palm a dagger and lift it in front of my face. Then I push the door open with a gust of wind and peer into my room. No one seems to be present. But I won't take any chances.

My balcony door is closed, my bathroom door is open, as I left it yesterday afternoon. My weapons are neatly placed on the chest at the feet of my bed. The only thing out of place is the all too familiar envelope on my bed.

I pick it up and cut it open with my dagger. Revealing the message:

~

Dawn Maria Rowena Sungust,
We hereby summon you for your second trial.
In two days, when the sun rises, be at the sacred dome.
Memories will be brought to light, but will they be the ones you seek?

~

I chug it on my nightstand and walk into the bathroom, not in the mood to fully take in the content of the letter. I wash my face, brush, and braid my hair, put on my light blue pajamas, and plop onto my bed. Picking up the bookmarked book I left on my nightstand.

Reading myself to sleep seems to be the only way to take a nap.

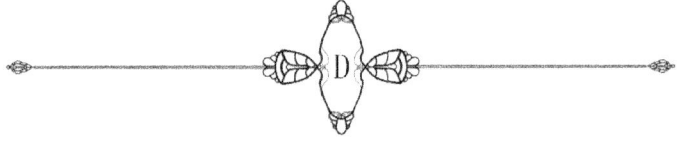

I wake to a commotion in the hallway several hours later. Servants preparing breakfast, guards changing shifts, councilmen asking for things. The usual.

I roll myself over to face the window. The sun peaking through the gap between my curtains, bathing my bed in light. I throw the purple sheets off as I notice something moving behind the curtains. It almost looks like another note, like the one I received before my first trial. It read: '*Please watch your back, little one.*'

Now what does this one say?

I pull open the curtains and catch the note before it hits the floor.

~

I love you so much, little one.

~

'Little one'

Only Leanne would call me that, or my dad, when I was younger. What kind of trick is someone pulling on me?

I place it in my drawer, next to the other piece I already received.

They might come at weird times, but they almost feel familiar or rather safe.

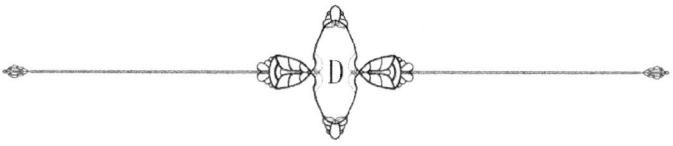

"What was that last sentence again?" Nate asks, leaning against the wall. Jade is sprawled on her stomach across my bed, and Madion actually pulled out the chair from my desk and took a seat.

"Memories will be brought to light, but will they be the ones you seek?" I recite, leaning against the wall opposite him, next to the open balcony doors. "I am guessing it'll be a full-on memory overload. Just old memories coming back at full speed."

"What if it's not just old memories?" Jade asks, propping her chin on her fists. "Think about it. '*The ones you seek*'. What is one memory you can never finish?"

"My repeating nightmare and headache." I sigh as I drag both my hands down my face.

"Exactly. What if you finally get answers?" she asks.

I hadn't even thought about that.

"But what if that memory was so traumatizing for Dawn that it will never come back?" Madion debates. "There has to be a reason she doesn't remember."

"We can never know for certain until I do it. So speculating won't help." I retort, "Did you manage to salvage the suit you made for the first trial?"

Jade jumps up from the bed and walks to the suitcase she left at the door when she arrived. "I most certainly did. Were you really doubting my sewing skills that much?"

"I would never," I say with a smile, teasing her. Madion lets out a chuckle, and Nate smiles as well.

Jade drags the suitcase to my feet and clicks it open. "See? Not a hole or damaged part present."

"I do hope there are four holes in the shirt, otherwise I might have a problem putting it on," I say, dead serious.

She takes a moment to process what I just said, while Nate and Madion are already laughing.

As soon as Jade gets the joke, she smacks me upside the head. "Bad joke, Dawn, terrible joke."

I give her a little nudge with my elbow before lifting the shirt in front of my face. The blue fabric is completely unstained, no blood anywhere. The bite holes on the forearm are neatly stitched closed, and the ripped hem is fixed too. "Thank you, Jade. You do wonders."

I look the clothes over once more before neatly tucking them back into the case. Then Nate pushes himself off the wall and leans on the bed.

"Just a random question that popped into my mind just now," he starts. "What would this trial mean for you? Magically and physically. The first one gave you all four elements and white streaked hair. What could this one cause?"

"Well, I still feel three layers covering the rest of my soul. We know one of those will definitely break. But besides that, I do not know," I state.

Madion braces her forearms on her thighs. "I think your hair will get even whiter. When you compare it to Leanne and your father, theirs only got whiter and whiter. As for the ring around your pupils, I think that'll come in the third or fourth trial."

I had completely forgotten about those defining rings around someone's pupils. My dad, mom, and Leanne all have a silver ring. The queen of Yedel, Agrema, has a bronze ring. And Draven, king of Railon, has a golden ring.

"I completely forgot about the fact that even my eyes will change," I admit.

"You would've noticed, eventually." Nate juts his thumb at the mirror in my bathroom.

I stick out my tongue to him, and he sticks his out in response.

"Children," Jade says, "be silent for a moment. We have something else to add to your outfit, Dawn."

She lifts an expertly engraved and decorated dagger before my eyes. Long blue swirls cover the hilt and heft, flowing out into small cobalt stones.

"Oh my." I gape. "Where did you find this?"

"Nate helped me and Madion make it as a late birthday present." She smiles and presses the dagger into my hands. "You didn't feel like celebrating this year and we respect that, but that doesn't mean you're not getting any presents."

I smile at all of them. "Thank you so much."

Then I urge Madion and Nate to get over here, as I already pull Jade into a hug. They both join in, and we embrace each other.

Four friends, four flowers, four flames, whatever you want to call us. We need each other to move, to move forward.

These people have pulled me from depths I didn't think I'd ever come out of on my own. They are three amazing people, people I'd give my life for so they could live to see another day.

CHAPTER 12

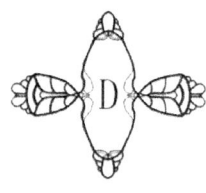

My new dagger is secured at my waist as I tie my boots. The gems shining in the sunlight coming from my windows. My clothes look as good as new and still fit perfectly. Maybe even better than before.

I have to admit that this trial is going to be harder than the first one. The first one was skill, tactic, and will. This one will most likely depend on me handling old and maybe recent memories.

I know I am not good with those. The nightmares and panic attacks tell that pretty clearly.

But I can face my past, as can I face my future. I will not fail because I have trauma I'd rather put away.

The hallway outside my room is quiet. I hear the occasional whispered conversations between Adrian and Jake, but that's it. I think everybody is still avoiding me. Only Remina and Calis have come by with my clothes and meals.

I strap my sword across my back and stride for the door. Adrian and Jake immediately perk up as the door opens.

"Ready for this?" Jake asks hesitantly.

"I have to be," I say and walk past them. They immediately jump up and follow me.

The road to the arena is filled with guards and townsfolk. People are pushing others away to get a front-row seat to the trial. Good to know I'm that enjoyable to watch.

Luckily, I can take a quiet side entrance, guarded by four soldiers. They nod in greeting before they open the big wooden gate.

I'm met by stone walls on either side of me once again. Several stones are cracked, but still standing strong and keeping the walls up. As well as other stones holding the cracked ones up, the ones that'll never crumble beneath the others as long as necessary.

Broken, on the inside and outside, but still keeping others up to stop everything from falling down. As well as others holding them up, that'll never crumble from underneath them as long as they need each other.

Madion, Jade, and Nate are already waiting around the corner. All dressed in black, all of their weapons with them as usual. Jade has her two signature French braids, and braided Madion's hair into her usual red crown. My hair was braided tightly too this morning. As for Nate, I think he just brushed his hair.

"Nice of you to all look presentable." I greet them. "I like the color coordination."

All three of them give me a look. "You know you always start joking when you're nervous," Nate says, his arms crossed over his chest.

"Let me be," I counter as I wave him off. "I'm shitting my pants over here."

Madion approaches me and fishes something out of her pocket. One of her bracelets. A silver ring intertwined with a red and white thread, a couple of black beads between the threads.

She places the bracelet in my hand and wraps my fingers around it.

"I got this bracelet from Jade right before we had to fight in the pit. She promised me we'd get through it, that we'd go to you and build our home here," she says with her hands tight around mine. "Wear this and get through your own fight. Don't let the memories decide the outcome of this trial. You decide it."

I place my other hand over hers. "I know what this bracelet means to you. And to Jade." Who is standing beside Nate, looking away from us as she seems to get emotional. "So thank you for trusting me with it. I will make it through this, I promise."

"Good," Madion says as she wraps an arm around my shoulders and leads me to the other two.

"By the way, Dawn. We always look good." Jade jokes, earning a laugh from me.

At least Jade jokes with me. Madion is just looking at the both of us while Nate is scanning the halls, as if he saw something.

"You go in, you listen to what you have to do, and you do it." He turns to me with a smile. "Nothing more, nothing less. You got this."

"I know I got this. I just can't help but feel scared of what might come back to me."

"And you are allowed to feel scared. Nothing is wrong with fear, as long as it's not the only feeling you have," Madion says, as she points at my chest. "There is courage in there, too. Use it."

I want to counter her, but someone clears their throat behind me. I turn around to find Adrian and Jake ready to enter the arena, just waiting for me.

I slide the bracelet around my wrist and take my place between them. One final deep breath before I set my sights on the arena.

But that breath doesn't come back out as I see what's in front of me. I freeze at the sight of the same priest, the same table, the same weird bowl. However, they're accompanied by a metal plate and chains this time.

Jake and Adrian notice them the same time I do, and both place a hand on my lower back. "Easy," Jake mumbles. "She can't do anything to you here."

I let out the deep breath I was holding and nod.

The walk to the table seems endless. I hear faint cheers all around me, feel the sand beneath my feet move, but I am solely focused on those chains. The ones that are most likely going around my wrists again.

Yet I keep on walking, not faltering a single step.

I see Leanne smiling broadly from the corner of my eyes. She probably thinks she can get me to back out with this. Wrong thinking, sister. I won't give you the satisfaction.

"Welcome once again, Dawn Maria Rowena Sungust," the priest starts, both his hands behind his back, as usual. "Your second trial will start shortly. You will drink the content of this bowl and it will set you on a journey. A journey through memories, old ones, new ones, altered ones. Ones that have not yet come to pass and ones that did not happen because of previous choices. Your task is to embrace them. Let the good, the bad, the old and the new memories in. If you try to fight one of them, it won't be pleasant."

I nod in understanding.

"Very well. You have already noticed everything in front of you. The memories can be vicious," he reminds me. "So, for your own safety, we will have to restrain you. Do you understand?"

I glance in Leanne's direction, who is still smirking. "I understand."

The priest gestures to the empty part of the table. "Good. You may once again undo yourself from your weapons and place them on the table."

I unclasp the buckle from my sword and gently lay it on the table, still mesmerized by the sheer power it holds while being so plain and simple. My dagger goes next, the cobalt stones and blue lines stark against the silver sheathe. I'm without weapons after a few more unbuckled belts and sheathes.

"You may kneel on the plate." He gestures to Adrian and Jake. "And the chains will be fastened around your wrists."

My knees hit the cold metal, a shiver runs up my spine at the contact. I hold my arms at my side, giving my guards the space to put the shackles on.

Jake takes my right hand, and I instinctively recoil. "Nothing is going to happen."

I hold out my arm and he puts the shackle around my wrist. Adrian does the same on the other side. They both give my hands a light squeeze before standing at a distance behind me.

I then raise my head as the priest approaches me with the white bowl in his hands.

"Let the second trial begin," he announces as he brings the bowl to my lips.

The second I empty it, a headache blooms on my forehead, meaning this is going to hurt even more than I thought.

My vision darkens as I am pulled into my memories.

My dad is sitting at his desk, Leanne on one knee, and me on the other, while he is reading a report.

I think I was around 8 years old here, barely able to make a small gust of wind or create a flower. But dad was practicing with us every day.

"Did you ever go to Yedel, dad?" I suddenly ask.

"I did," he answers. "They have the most beautiful beaches and seas. And exquisite flowers."

"Will we ever go there?" Leanne asks in the kind voice I remember her with.

My dad looks at both of us and says, "If you want to, I could try to ask their king and queen if we could visit."

A smile blooms on my face. "Then I can see all the flowers and I can find shells on the beach."

"You most definitely could, and you could bring the most beautiful shells and flowers home if you ask the king nicely," he says as he pulls me closer.

"I love you, dad," I mutter.

Dad then pulls Leanne closer. "I love you both very much, too. I promise I will always be here."

I feel tears rolling down my face as I whisper, "No, dad—"

But I'm already pushed into the next memory.

This is not something that has happened, and I immediately try to pull back.

I see Jade, Madion and Nate, dead on the dark floor of the dungeons. A faint flickering light of a torch washes over the room. Bathing the horrific scene in front of me in an orange glow.

Jade's throat is cut, her bow hanging limply in her hand. Madion is impaled by her own sword. Eyes open and empty, yet still looking loving and longing at Jade. And Nate—Chains are draped over his arms. His chest is black and burned. The chains are glowing hot as they eat away at his arms.

Beaten by the element he trusted most.

I scream.

I scream at the sight of my friends.

Nate lets out a small whimper and cracks open his eyes. "Dawn," he breathes. "Why?"

I bring my hands to my face and notice the horror on them. They're coated in blood. It's dripping from my fingers onto the floor, dripping on the red-coated dagger at my feet.

I killed them—

No, I didn't.

It couldn't be me.

I wouldn't.

Nate's chest rises one last time before the light leaves his eyes. His pale blue eyes staring at me, looking right through me.

My friends are all dead, at my hands.
That can't happen.
It wouldn't happen.

I'm dragged back in time to where the memory starts.

I walk into the dungeons, where my friends are waiting, all armed to the teeth. I smile at them before bringing my sword down on Madion. Jade tries to aim her arrow at me. Nate is merely waiting for the right moment to bring his sword down on me.

The split-second Jade shoots her arrow, Madion doesn't pay attention to her lower body and I—I twist her arm and drive her own blade through her stomach. Jade screams in horror and runs to me. Madion slumps to the floor as I grab Jade at the throat. Lifting her in the air. Before she can reach for any other weapon, I drive my sword through her chest. And as she comes down, I slash my dagger across her throat.

I could never do that on my own free will. I would never do that.

Please—Please make it stop.

Nate lets out a battle cry as he charges me. Our swords clash, but I am absently leading the chains all around us closer and closer, ready to wrap them around him. And I—I bring my sword down with ten times the strength I should possess and shatter Nate's sword. He falls to the ground where the chains are ready for him. I stretch out my hand and begin—

His screams forever haunting my nightmares.

I'm sobbing, tears rolling down my face as I'm thrown into the next memory.

My mom is digging small holes to give plants a new home in our garden. A variety of blues, yellows, pinks, and oranges are spread around her. Leanne and I are chasing after each other. As I run past my mom, I accidentally step on a flower. I lift my foot and peel the flat purple flower off. My mom holds open her hands, urging me to put the flower in. I gently put it in her hands before Leanne takes my hand and tells me to sit down.

My mom grabs one of my hands and places it over the flower, then puts her hand over mine and lets her magic flow out. I feel the leaves come alive beneath my fingers. Bending and shaping itself into a beautiful flower again.

As she lifts our hands, we reveal a lively purple flower in my mom's palm.

"Nothing is broken forever," my mom muses before placing the flower between the others in the garden.

I trail after Leanne as she approaches a bush at the far end of the garden. Broken twigs and leaves stick out of it.

"Do you want to heal it?" she asks me, holding out her hand to me.

I step up and grab it, letting our magic meet. Leanne grabs a broken twig, barely hanging on to the rest of the bush. And let our magic fuel its growth.

We reconnect every single twig and leaf, reshaping it to its former glory. But it takes a toll when you use this much magic at once.

We slump against a tree, still holding hands. Keeping that deep connection we made.

"Dawn?" she asks.

"Yes?" I respond.

"You know I will always be here for you, right?" she says as she tugs me closer. "I won't leave you alone, no matter what."

I wrap my free arm around her. "I know. And I will never leave you either. We're connected," I say, lifting our hands. "We can only be disconnected by ourselves."

"And we won't let that happen," Leanne promises.

She closes her eyes and drifts to sleep. I close mine soon after.

The next memory is one I remember as if it was yesterday. The day Jade and Madion landed, all bloodied and bruised, on my doorstep.

"Madion!" I shout as I see her approaching, with Jade stumbling beside her.

I reach them right before Madion drops to her knees. Jade is there in an instant, but slightly backs away when I kneel in front of Madion. I look Madion over and find several large bruises and cuts covering her arms, legs, and back.

"What happened?" I ask to no one in particular, still assessing Madion's injuries.

"Dawn, meet Jade. My mate," Madion declares.

My eyes shoot up to Jade, who just gapes at Madion. That she just exposed that bond between them.

I hold out my hand to Jade, letting her decide whether or not to trust me. Jade has fewer injuries and blood on her, but is still not in the best state.

After a moment of hesitation, her hand grabs mine and I pull her up with me.

"We need to get both of you home. Come on." I sling one of Madion's arms around my shoulder, and Jade does the same.

It's a struggle to get them both all the way back to Madion's house. But we make it.

Madion lets out a grunt as I drop her on the bed. Jade lingers on the doorstep.

"Are you going to help me undress your mate? Or shall I do it on my own?" I say to her, trying to provoke her to work with me.

Jade lets out a low grumble. She stalks over to sit at Madion's side on the bed. They both undress, one without and one with help.

And that's when the full extent of their injuries shows. Madion has cuts from several lashes down her back. Jade has cuts on her stomach and legs. I put them one by one under the shower and dress their wounds.

Madion's back requires stitches. And since she has never been a hero when it comes to needles, I put together a sedative to let her sleep through it. Jade is watching my every move as I work on closing every cut on Madion's back.

"May I ask how all of this happened?" I ask Jade, who is struggling to keep her eyes open.

"It's a long story," she mumbles.

"As you can see." I gesture to the sleeping woman in front of me. "I have time."

"I was around bad people, who only got worse when Madion and soldiers arrived."

"You're from Yedel?" I ask as I finish another stitch.

"Yes, and you're a princess from Iluniel."

"I am."

"How come a general and a princess to be friends?" she questions, suppressing a yawn.

"Mutual interests, hate on the same people, needing people to trust and support you, do I need to continue?"

"No, I'm glad she had someone to fall back on. I hope I won't ruin that by being here."

"You don't," I retort, trying to show gratitude in my eyes. "You're more than welcome here."

"Thank you." Is the last whisper I hear from Jade before she slumps back onto her pillow and gets her well needed rest.

This memory brings a little smile to my face.

But I am ripped away from it in a second and thrown into a nightmare once again.

I'm restrained. My arms are spread wide, clasped in long chains that are bolted to the walls.

I take in my surroundings. I'm in a cell once again, but I'm not alone. My friends are chained to the wall in front of me.

Jade is unconscious, blood running from her nose. Madion is awake but barely conscious. Blood coats her temple. She has to be close to a concussion. And Nate, his arms are burnt. They heated the chains before tying him up. But he is awake, the pain shining in his eyes.

I let out a grunt as the pain on my chest worsens. I look down and find my shirt almost completely burned away, my chest blackened and bruised. My breathing goes faster and faster because of everything around me.

"Dawn," Nate urges me. "Calm down. I don't want you to pass out again."

I manage to get my breathing slower. "I'm okay, just in pain." Looking him over, I mumble, "As are you."

"We'll be okay." He exhales as he hangs his head back against the wall. "Do you remember anything?"

"I remember Leanne and a lot of guards."

"Those were not soldiers of Iluniel."

"What?"

"They're from—"

He's cut off as I'm pulled into my mind again, aiming for the next memory.

A memory I will always call a nightmare.

I'm already yelling down the hallways of the castle. Searching for my parents. Not knowing the horror, I'm about to witness.

I pass their open door and stop. Peering inside to find my parents on their knees. The hooded killer in front of them, the Alk knife ready to end it all.

"Why?" my dad asks, reaching for my mom's hand.

They answer, "I don't have a choice."

A slight tremble in an emotionless voice.

"Please, think about her, please. Think about your little droplet," my mom mutters with tears streaming down her face as she grabs my dad's hand.

"No," I whisper. I feel people closing in on me as the memory continues.

I push the door open further, but lose my footing and stumble into the room. The killer pulls up their mask quickly before grabbing my mom's shoulder. They kick my dad in the stomach, making him double over.

"I love you, m—Goodbye." The Alk dagger is driven into my mom's heart and my dad screams in agony.

Losing your mate is the most painful feeling anyone could ever imagine. It is like having your own soul ripped in two. Your other half stripped away from you and never coming back.

Mom slumps to the floor, looking me in the eye one last time. Saying goodbye, before releasing her last breath in this world.

Dad tries to get to his feet, but the dagger has already found its second mark. My dad lashes out with the last scraps of his power and punches the killer across the face with a burning hand. He then collapses to the floor and has the light leave his eyes, too.

"I'm sorry, d—" The killer stops themselves as they remember I'm still there. Gawking at the scene before me. My parents were dead at the hands of someone they knew.

The killer puts away their blade and stalks over to me. I back away but hit a wall. I stare into the stark blue eyes, lined with a silver ring around the pupil. White hair is peeking from under the hood.

"Why?" I whisper as tears are streaming down my cheeks. I look over the shoulder of the killer and notice my dad's outstretched hand.

He didn't just want to wound the killer. He was reaching out for mom, too. His hand now covering hers. It still looks as if he is gripping it with all he had left. He couldn't let her go, not even in death.

The mask of the killer is slowly sliding down, being half burned away by my dad.

I pull it down and stop breathing entirely.

The burn on her face is not healing. It stretches across half her neck, up towards her cheekbone.

I look into my sister's eyes, cold and distant, as she starts choking the air out of me.

My vision fails me as I slump against the wall.

She killed them.

Leanne killed our parents.

CHAPTER 13

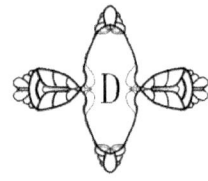

I can't look at this.

I can't.

I push the memories away. The polar opposite of what I'm supposed to do.

She can't be the one that killed them. She was the person who got me out of there. She took me outside and calmed me down.

A sharp pain suddenly courses through my body, and I double over in agony.

I need to go on. I can't stop here.

But what if she killed them and hid it from me all these years? It would explain so much from the past years.

But the burn on the side of her face wasn't there when she got me out and it couldn't have healed that fast.

Another bolt of pain goes through my body. It gathers around my heart and spine.

I try to let my magic soothe it, but it stays back. Afraid of what it might do to me.

I'm thrown into the next memory, while my mind still lingers in the previous one. And this one might be even worse.

Mom and dad are in chains, being led to their execution. An execution that never happened.

I'm next to the throne. As I notice who is on it, I stumble backwards.

Leanne has the crown on her head and a scepter in her hand. Smiling at the sight in front of us.

The blade that the executioner is holding is forged out of pure Alk. Even the tiniest bit of that at the right spot could kill us. This will cease their entire existence.

"Leanne!" I shout, barely audible above the cheering crowd. "What did you do?"

"I freed these lands," she merely answers. Still staring at our parents in chains.

"You did no such thing," I sneer at her. "They are our parents. They did nothing wrong."

"I will not argue about this with you. Either stay quiet or leave," she snaps right back.

I keep my mouth shut as mom and dad are pushed onto the blocks. They try to reach for each other, but the chains are too short. They're inches away from each other, yet so far.

"At least give them the decency to go together," I plead as I grip the armrest of the throne.

Leanne grabs my arm. "They can go together, if you can make it to them in time."

I stare at her for one more moment before taking off. If I can make it to them in time, I might even save them from this.

I push people out of my way. The ones that see who I am immediately disperse.

I let a small strand of magic go ahead, to notify my parents I'm coming. As it reaches my dad, his eyes scan the crowd.

His eyes fall on me, those silver eyes softening. He signals my mom, who looks in my direction.

I notice the shadow above them, Alk reflecting in the sun, ready to make the final blow.

I feel tears welling up. No—I can't lose them again. Not again.

They both mouth 'we love you' as the swords drop and a gut-wrenching scream shatters from my throat.

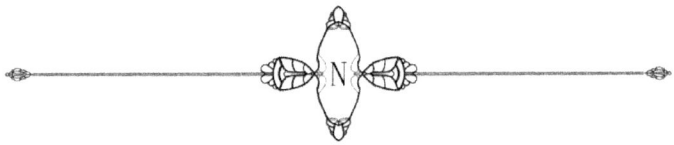

"She's fighting," I whisper. Madion and Jade are looking distressed beside me. Debating whether to just run in there and get her out.

"There's nothing we can do," Madion murmurs.

The scream Dawn just let out—it made everyone in here go silent. The pain that came with that scream is nothing anyone should ever experience.

Yet she can't stop now. She has come this far already.

"We have to calm her down," I state.

"How?" Madion responds. "We're not allowed to get closer."

I gather a small current of magic in my hand. "We don't have to get closer."

"He will notice that," Jade counters as she comes up to my other side. "The priest is keeping a close eye on us."

"Then I show him I only want to calm her down before she burns the entire building to the ground," I say as I point at the small flames gathering in a circle around Dawn. "She is not going to last much longer."

A moment of silence, the only sound coming from Dawn. A faint whimper and tears streaming down her face.

I can't even imagine what she is seeing right now.

"Okay." Madion sighs. "But you need to alert the priest first of what you're doing, otherwise we won't even be allowed near the third trial."

"Leave it to me," I say, a small tendril gathering in my palm.

If I guide this just right, it will cause the priest to look this way. But if I miss the priest, we can kiss watching the other trials goodbye.

I let the tendril flow out of my hand and float it towards the priest. It passes Dawn, with Adrian and Jake still at her side.

She will never lose them. They will always protect her. That's one thing that'll never change.

The tendril passes Leanne, who is looking almost satisfied with herself, seeing her sister struggle like this.

At last, I attach the tendril to the robes of the priest and tug at it. It takes a few times before he looks our way. I let the tendril dissipate and signal to him that

Dawn needs help to calm down. Otherwise, she'll blow this whole arena up.

I point at Dawn, as I let my magic create a miniature dome in my other hand. Showing the priest what I'm going to do.

He cocks his head slightly to the right and takes a momentary look at Dawn, assessing the situation. Until giving me his approval as a slight nod, right as he hears Dawn call out again.

As she calls out my name.

I shake it off and gather my magic to throw a larger dome over her, an invisible one. Nobody can know anybody helped her.

The dome slowly takes form around her, building itself from the ground up. Until it closes at the top. I let it slowly close in on her, making it feel like a weighted blanket.

Like somebody is holding her.

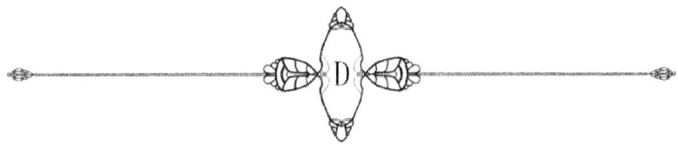

More and more memories are overlapping. Past, present, and future merging together.

It's becoming too much.

"Get away," I whisper as I feel something or someone close in on me. It presses down, as if it wants to push me down.

What's happening?

No one can use their magic on or around me. Unless it's Leanne, thinking she can finally get rid of me when I'm at my most vulnerable.

But no, it feels familiar. It's magic from someone I know.

And It's not trying to hurt me, it's comforting me. Almost like a hand on my shoulder, that it'll stay with me for as long as I need them to.

Nate.

This is Nate's magic.

I let out another sob as his magic weighs down on me.

I can do this.

Memories do not make your future. You make it. You can only let the memories guide you. Guide you to what you want to achieve.

The next memory might be something I want to forget, but every time I think of it, it earns a smile.

"Madion?" I shout down the halls of the castle. "Jade? Where are you?"

Where did they run off to?

They told me to meet them right here, between the front doors and the throne room

I pick up faint sounds coming from—from a storage closet. You have got to be kidding me.

I put my hand on the doorknob, bracing myself for what's happening inside.

Madion and Jade both bump their heads against the shelves as I pull open the door.

"Really?" I mutter, bracing my hands on my hips.

Jade has Madion's dark red lipstick all over her neck and mouth. Madion's hair is a complete mess. They both look sheepishly at me, breathing heavily.

Jade lets out a sigh and starts fixing Madion's hair. "You took way too long."

"Don't blame me. You said ten, which means I'll be here at ten, not nine, not eleven. Ten," I declare.

"Let's just go," Madion says as she bats Jade's hand away and exits the closet.

Jade and I trail after her, out of the castle, into the fresh air.

I feel a small smile tug at my lips as the memory dissipates and twists into another one.

One I will cherish forever.

"Dawn, meet Nate Marblebender," Vergus says as he pushes me and Nate to shake hands. *"Nate, meet Dawn Sungust."*

Nate extends his hand, which is slightly trembling.

Vergus has already told me that Nate was hesitant to touch people. He hasn't had the best childhood, parents killed when he was eight, left on the streets because of his magic, beaten for sleeping too close to someone's garden.

I carefully take his hand. "Nice to meet you."

"Nice to meet you, too," he softly says back.

We both let go and awkwardly stand there. Suddenly, Nate's breathing speeds up. As if this handshake was too much contact already.

"Nate?" Vergus says as he notices what's happening.

He tries to reach out, but I put my arm in front of him. "Let me help."

Vergus looks confused for a moment, but nods as it clicks that I know exactly how to handle these panic attacks.

"Nate, breathe," I say as I slowly approach him. "I don't want you to pass out."

"I—I—I can't," he chokes out.

Before I can warn him, he's with his back against the wall. He lets himself drop to the floor and buries his face in his hands. I drop to my knees in front of him, leaving some space between us.

"Nate, look at me," I say as I let my hand hover over his knee. Not yet touching him.

He lifts his head a bit, just enough to notice the hand hovering over his knee and my eyes on him.

"I—I ha—have this—a lot," he stammers out between labored breaths.

"So have I." I let my hand rest on his knee. "I know what it's like to feel constricted. To not be able to breathe when you want to so badly."

I carefully put my other hand on the side of his face. He recoils slightly at first, but allows it. My hand that was on his knee moves his hand towards my back, letting him feel my breathing. Then my hand goes to the other side of his face.

I slowly tug his head towards mine, making the move to let our foreheads touch.

Nate's breathing is not getting much better. He has gotten pale, and I can feel his hand trembling on my back.

"Breathe with me," I say as I put my forehead against his.

He faintly nods as he tries to breathe in at the same time as I do.

The breaths come easier by the second, and as he calms down, his hand finds my shoulder. "Thank you," he whispers.

"I don't know what you've been through, but I promise I'll be here," I reassure him, letting go of his face. "If you ever need a friend, I'll be here."

He stares at me for a moment before he mutters, "Likewise."

And that's how our friendship started.

Two souls supporting each other, making sure we don't bend so far that we break.

Memories are there to guide you. Either by pain or happiness. By grief or joy.

And I do have good memories. Not everything that has happened to me is bad. I gained people along the way too. Madion, Jade and Nate. Vergus, Adrian and Jake.

No matter what, we stay together. We don't let each other down.

I feel the same sharp pain flow through my chest, just like I felt at the first trial.

My soul cracks, more power leaking out.

I have to hold on for a bit longer. Just that final bit to finish this.

Keep those memories coming. They're a part of me. Things I've always carried with me, things I will always carry with me. They won't stop me anymore when they come back to the surface.

More and more cracks are forming. They're spider webbing across the outer layer of my soul.

And as the last memory fully disappears, my soul breaks.

CHAPTER 14

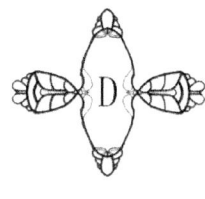

Whilst the light of my soul breaking dies down, I slowly open my eyes. Letting them get accustomed to the daylight once more. Everyone has taken a step back, probably from the sudden power burst that came out of me.

"I am once again pleased to congratulate Dawn Maria Rowena Sungust for completing your second trial," the priest muses. Then he lifts his eyes to the men behind me. "You may free her."

I'm breathing heavily as my guards approach me. Adrian grabs my hand. "You gained some decorations," he mutters.

I lift my hand to see the silver lines spiral over my fingers into my palm and around my wrist. Both hands are identical, swirls and small leaves covering them.

"Let's get you out of these," Jake says while nudging Adrian to unshackle my other hand.

The chains fall to the floor, and I let my fingertips trace the lines on my hand. A shiver goes down my spine as I touch them, as if they're connected somewhere deep inside.

"Come on," Adrian mumbles as he throws my arm around his neck and hoists me to my feet. "Away from these prying eyes."

"Thank you," I say through gritted teeth. Walking is not very pleasant as my legs feel numb yet on fire at the same time.

But we make it back to the stone halls underneath the seating area. We round the corner and at the sight of my friends, alive and well, I make a run for it.

They fling their arms around me and pull me close. Jade in front of me, Madion, on my right, puts her arm around my waist and squeezes once. Nate does the same on my left, pulling me closer.

"You're okay," Jade says. "You made it."

"I'm not okay," I counter.

My breathing goes faster and faster as tears threaten to fall again.

I break away from our hug and take a few steps back. "I'm not okay," I gasp as I bury my face in my hands.

Nate sets one step in my direction. "Dawn, what happened?"

"I killed you all," I whisper, not believing it myself.

"What?" Madion asks.

"I killed you all," I repeat as my back hits the wall. "I killed you."

Jade stands beside Madion. "What do you mean, you killed us?"

I pull my face from my hands. "I killed you!" I shout at her. "I slit your throat," I say as I point at Jade. "And impaled you with your own sword." I gesture to Madion.

I look at Nate, tears blurring my vision. His eyes aren't clear either. "And I burned you to death."

I slump to the floor as the walls start closing in on me. As I am just completely swallowed by everything around me.

"Dawn, look at me," Nate says as he kneels in front of me. "Look at me."

I don't. I can't look at him after what I saw.

But Nate then wraps his hands around mine and pulls them away from my face. "Look at me."

I take in his teary eyes, breaking into tears myself, too.

"We're here. We're all here," he says as he lets go of my hands and places them on the sides of my face. "You have done nothing to us. And you never will. We know that."

I take his face in my hands too and pull him close, placing our foreheads against each other. No matter how many times we have done this, for some reason, it hasn't lost its magic. We both calm down, as if some deep laying connection sparks up as we touch.

Nate wants to pull away, but I wrap my arms around his neck. "Please stay."

"I'm not going anywhere," he whispers as his arms come around me.

"I remembered the first time we met and did this." I mumble. "I remembered how you didn't want to touch anyone or anyone to touch you. Yet you let me. Why?"

"Because you felt safe. You felt like home after all those years."

"I'm glad I can be that person for you," I breathe.

Now I pull away and look into his gentle eyes. "I'm glad we can get each other out of those dark parts of our lives."

Nate gets to his feet and holds out a hand. "We'll never let the other fall."

Madion and Jade stand behind him, looking proud. I grab Nate's hand and let him pull me to my feet.

"Do you want to talk about what you saw?" Madion carefully asks.

"Not here," I mumble, wiping away my tears. Then Jake hands me back my weapons and I say, "Let's pay Yuno a visit."

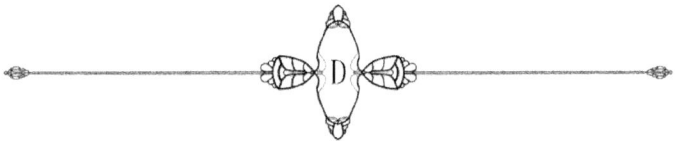

With Yuno asleep in my lap, I finally calm down completely. The fresh air clears my thoughts. Nate, Madion and Jade are seated in front of me, eagerly waiting for me to talk about what I saw.

"Where do you want me to start?" I ask no one in particular.

"Why don't you start at the beginning?" Madion offers. "What was the first memory?"

I trace idle circles in Yuno's fur as I answer, "My dad, Leanne, and I were in his office. He had just received the peace treaty from Yedel. And we were talking about visiting it one day."

"So, nothing special happened there?"

"No."

"Did you see any other memories of your mom or dad?" Jade asks.

"Yes," I answer, trying not to relive the forged memory.

It did not happen. They met their fate in another way.

Jade leans closer, putting on a faint smile. "Do you want to share what happened?"

"Leanne had them executed," I say, dragging both my hands down my face. "I tried to reach them, but I was too slow. They were killed right before my eyes, again."

"Wait, Leanne?" Nate blurts out, sounding confused.

"Yes, Leanne was seated as the queen on her throne. Crown on her head, scepter in her hand. Smiling at the sight of our parents in chains."

"As if she wasn't awful enough already," Jade mumbles, earning her a jab in the side from Madion.

"But I did see some nice memories, too," I say with a faint smile. "I remembered the day I met Nate. Which was pretty eventful."

"To say the least," Nate murmurs as he looks into the distance.

"And I relived my meeting with Jade," I say. "You both looked like shit by the way."

"You're kidding, right? We looked fabulous with all the blood caked to our hands, streaming down our arms, legs, backs," Jade says, very sarcastically.

Madion sighs. "Not one of your finest moments."

Jade leans her head on Madion's shoulder and grabs her hand. "It's over and done. It's not happening again."

Madion smiles down at her mate, leaving us all in silence for a moment.

"Moving on. Remember when we were supposed to meet up at ten at the front doors of the castle?" I muse.

Jade and Madion stay quiet, trying to remember what I'm talking about.

After a full minute, Jade slaps her hand against her forehead, and Madion lets out another sigh.

"Did you really have to remember that?" Madion asks, probably remembering the exact circumstances she was in.

"Believe me, I'd rather have forgotten that, too," I confess to her. "But I have to live with it for weeks now before I forget it again."

We stay silent for a moment. Nate, Madion and Jade, all contemplating whether to ask me about my confession just now.

"Did you really see yourself kill us?" Nate asks at last.

I let my hand lay on Yuno's fur as I answer, "Yes, and it can either be something that never happened because of previous choices or something that will happen. And I really don't want it to be something that will happen."

"It won't," Jade says confidently, locking eyes with me.

"But if it does," I plead, "then I don't care what you have to do. If I ever try to hurt any of you. Take me out."

They don't answer, just nod.

"I saw something else," I breathe. "I finally finished my nightmare."

"Did you see who killed them?" Madion says.

I look at her, showing the confusion and exhaustion in my eyes. "Yes, and now I'm even more confused than I was before."

"Why?" Jade asks. All three of them inching closer to me.

"Because the person who killed them was not someone I expected or even thought of. I don't even know if it is true or yet another made up memory."

"Who did you see?"

"Leanne," I say. "Leanne killed our parents and hid it from everyone."

CHAPTER 15

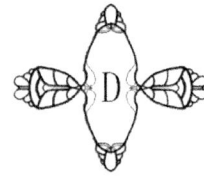

"What?" Jade blurts out. "You can't be serious."

"I don't know anymore," I admit. "It was identical to my nightmares, and i—it felt real. As if it was actually what happened that night."

"But you don't have proof," Nate grunts in annoyance.

"Precisely," I mumble in a similar tone.

"And you're not even sure she did it, right?" Madion asks.

"No, I'm not," I counter. "But something tells me there is more to this than just Leanne stabbing them. Either I need to talk to her or go exploring myself."

"You really want to risk talking about this with her?" Madion asks, a hint of disapproval in her words. "One wrong word and you're not sleeping in your own bed tonight. You know how that went the last time. I don't know if we can even calm you down enough next time before you blow up the town."

"I know that, Madion. No need to remind me."

She raises her hands in defense. "Just stating facts."

I mumble, "Very annoying facts."

"What are you planning to do now?" Nate cuts in, steering us away from that conversation.

Yuno stirs in my lap. "It seems like my best option is to go look for evidence myself, but where to begin is another thing I'll have to think about."

"Is there a way to get into her office?" Jade cuts in. "I would hide things in an office too if I had one."

"You already have an office. Also known as our living room," Madion says. "You really need to clean up all of your stuff. I almost broke my neck this morning."

Jade looks surprised. "I literally cleaned up four days ago."

"Four days, Jade. Four."

"I'll clean it up when we get home," Jade mumbles.

Madion gives her a shoulder pat. "Good, otherwise I would've thrown it all out of the window."

"Hey! No need to get violent with my fabrics."

"I will get violent with them if you don't clean them up."

I look at Nate, pleading for him to break them up. He winks and clears his throat. "Ladies, let's leave the disputes at home. Our former king and queen might be murdered by their daughter. I think that's more important than the mess in your living room."

They both give him an apologetic look and keep quiet.

"Any suggestions on what to do?" I ask, knowing all too well they don't have a clue either.

"I still think somehow getting into her office might give us at least some insight into what she's doing," Madion says.

"Then I need to get in there without her knowing about it," I say quietly.

"How?" Jade counters. "That room is guarded almost every hour, every day."

"I'll figure it out," I mutter, as I gently push Yuno off of me. "I have to."

And start walking back to my room, really in need of a good night's sleep.

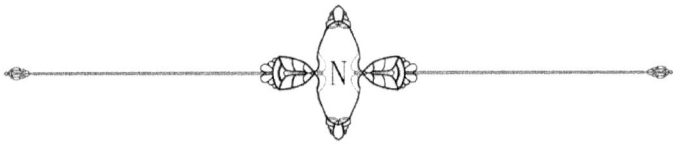

Dawn walks to her room, with Jade, Madion and I trailing behind her.

"Someone needs to talk to her," I mutter. "She is not going to sleep tonight if she goes to bed like this."

"I think in this case, you are the best choice," Madion states, looking me over.

I give her a questioning look in response.

"Don't look at me like that. We all know you two calm each other down better than Jade and I ever could," she declares. "So just talk to her, get her to sleep. Because she will collapse soon if she doesn't."

"You're right, I'll talk to her," I say as I wave them goodbye and head inside Dawn's room.

She is on her balcony when I close the door behind me, overlooking the garden. The moonlight reflecting on the white parts of her hair.

"Hey," I innocently say.

"Hey."

"What's going on in that head of yours?"

"Too much."

"Talking with someone tends to help, or so I heard," I say, silently urging her to come inside.

She picks up on the signal and moves away from the railing to go lay on her bed.

"It's just all becoming too much," she whispers as I take a seat at the edge of the bed. "I knew what I was getting into with these trials. But everything around it, Leanne, Anna's murder, the constant nightmares and fear that I'll end up in chains again." Her eyes focus on mine. "It's just overwhelming."

"Make some room," I order her.

She moves to the middle of the bed, and I lay down next to her. "You'll be okay," I mutter as I pull her close to me. "I know you. You might think all of this is too much, but you work the best under pressure." I move my fingers up and down her arm. "When you have to make your plan on the spot, that's what makes you shine. And that is exactly what you have to do now. You passed the first trial with ease, the second trial can almost be considered a low blow, but you still got through it."

"With help," she mumbles.

"No one said you couldn't have someone to support you," I counter her.

She has no response for that.

"And I know your parents are immensely proud of you," I say with a smile as I tug her closer. "I know they are still looking down upon you every second and smiling at how strong you have become."

"Do you remember anything about your parents?" she asks me in return.

"Not much. I know my dad had the same hair and eyes as me, but that's about it. Yet I find it weird that, even though I was eight at the time they died, I can't remember everything about them." And I add with a weak voice, "I even feel like they are not the only ones I lost that day."

Dawn looks up at me. "What do you mean?"

Rubbing my free hand down my face, I explain, "I feel like they weren't the only family of mine that left for that camp and didn't return. I have this vague memory—of me having a brother."

"But you can't remember anything about him?"

"No," I grumble as I look down at her. "The only thing I know is that he had the same hair as me. That's all I can get from the memory."

"Hold on to that memory, then. Maybe you'll get you answers one day," she says, faintly gripping my shirt.

We stay in silence. Comforting each other, I'm rubbing her back as she plays with the hem of my shirt.

"I lost someone in that camp, too," Dawn suddenly murmurs.

"Who?"

"Amel."

"And who is that?"

"A boy I ran into in the town one day. We started talking and before I knew it, we were friends," she says. "One day, he had to go with his parents to the same camp your parents went, and well, we all know what happened there a couple days later."

I just nod. We have both heard the story of what went down at that camp too many times.

They had gathered at the center of the camp for some sort of meeting, but the moment soldiers ambushed them from all sides, things went downhill. Most of the men were killed on the spot, but the women and children—Some were used in horrible ways, some were taken away and killed later, some women even had to kill their husbands before having to kill themselves.

It was a massacre. And my parents were among the casualties.

"I know your parents are proud of you too, Nate. My mom and dad told me about them, and they were so proud of you. You were the most valuable thing they had."

"Thank you," I breathe as I wipe away a stray tear running down my cheek.

"And I am proud of you, too," she says as she intertwines her fingers with mine. "I know you have nightmares like I do. I know you sometimes still don't like to touch people, so I am truly proud of how far you've come."

I squeeze her hand and rake my fingers through her hair. "We're proud of each other, and we'll always be here, no matter what."

"Promise?" she whispers as her eyelids droop.

I gently stroke her head, trying to let her fall asleep as peacefully as possible. "Promise."

As Dawn falls asleep, my thoughts go to the trial. To the amount of pain and grief that radiated off her.

It was the first time I actually saw someone in their trial. In the first trial, she wasn't visible, but during the second, she was out in the open for everyone. I have to admit I was scared, not just for her, but for the reaction of the audience. I thought they might laugh or mock her, but the moment she started whispering, everyone went quiet. Because everybody knows that King Ricon's death hurt Dawn deeply.

It left cracks in the depths of her soul.

Cracks so deep they might never heal.

The first time a layer of her soul broke was terrifying. Yet when you actually see the cracks spider web across her soul, you truly fear for her life.

But then, you see the light receding, her soul releasing the magic that was hidden behind that layer. You see the magic one layer can hold. The immediate power that radiated off her.

I am almost afraid of what might be the full extent of her magic once she breaks that last layer.

But I know one thing, she will use it for good. Not to hurt others.

She'll make her parents even more proud than they already are.

CHAPTER 16

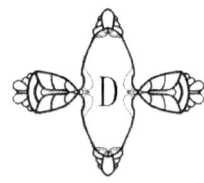

I wake to the pillow slipping from underneath my head and falling off my bed. Besides that, I am tightly tucked in, blankets pulled up to my chin. Who?

Nate.

I lift my head to survey the room and my eyes fall on a snoring Nate, slumped in a chair in the corner of the room. He's the one that tucked me in last night. He could've slept on the other side of the bed instead of that uncomfortable chair, though.

It was in that corner, turned around, for a reason. Apparently, he didn't grasp it.

I pick the pillow up from the ground and sit up straight. Drawing my arm back, I aim the pillow at Nate's head.

And throw it.

Hitting him right in the face, scaring him awake. He glares at me as I double over in laughter.

Rubbing his eyes, he mumbles, "Good morning to you, too."

"You could've slept here." I pat the bed beside me. "I wouldn't have minded. Definitely not if I knew you'd sleep in that awful chair."

"I didn't sleep that bad," he says as he rises from the chair. Immediately regretting his words as he tries to straighten his back, which does not go without a pained grunt.

I give him a look, but he waves it off. Right as someone knocks on the door.

"Who is it?" I call out as Nate walks over to me and sits at the end of the bed.

"It's Adrian. Leanne left you an invitation."

"What kind of invitation?"

"Well, let me in and I'll show you."

I sigh. "The door is always open."

The door opens, and Adrian stops short as he sees Nate at the edge of my bed. He clears his throat and moves over to me.

"She wanted to barge in here at first." He glances at Nate, who is awkwardly inspecting some spots on my ceiling. "Glad I could stop her."

I open the envelope and read the contents.

~

Her Majesty Leanne Sungust hereby invites you to the ball.
In honor of her sister Dawn Sungust, who just passed her second trial.
It would be wonderful if you could join us tomorrow evening.

~

I let my magic pool into my palm and burn the invite on the spot.

"It would be amazing if someone would tell me they were planning something for me before they let other people know," I grumble.

"You're a princess. People want to see you in fancy dresses instead of pants and dirt," Adrian says as he picks up a few pieces of burned paper.

"I hate being a princess sometimes," I mutter as I heave myself out of bed. "Can I come with you to the forge, Nate? I haven't seen Vergus in a while and I feel like he's still avoiding me."

Nate nods. "Of course. I'll wait outside so you can change. I wouldn't recommend a fancy ball gown, though." He adds a wink before turning around. My hand shoots to a pillow, and it's already flying through the room before my brain processes what I'm doing.

It hits Nate right at the back of his head. He swirls around, looks at the pillow now on the floor, then at me.

And then the pillow is flying back at me. I duck in time and make a run for the bathroom.

"I'll be out in a few minutes," I shout from the safe side of the bathroom door.

"And I'll be waiting," Nate states. "With more pillows ready to be thrown."

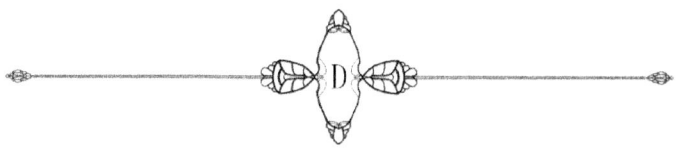

I wash my face quickly and put on a pair of pants and a shirt. Besides that, I'm carrying my sword and six of my daggers.

As I open the door of the bathroom, Nate's words go through my mind a second too late because I am hit with two pillows. One to the head and one to my legs.

"Nate!" I yell as I throw the pillows back. "I'm going to kill you."

The only thing I hear is laughter rumbling through the hall as I chase after him. Dodging guards and servants all the way to the front door, where I shoot out a burst of air and make him trip. All the way to the bottom of the stairs. But he keeps laughing, even as I loom over him.

"Sorry," he heaves, his voice filled with amusement.

I hold my hand out to him. "Let's just go before I do something I'll regret."

"And what would that be?" he asks as he grabs my hand.

I haul him to his feet and look him straight in the eyes. "You don't want to know."

Before Nate can respond, I start walking. I wouldn't have done anything to him. Although suffocating him in his sleep with a pillow sounds very attractive. I'll keep that in mind for the next time.

Nate catches up to me as I'm almost halfway to the forge. "You walk fast."

"Or you just walk slow," I say with a smirk on my face.

He lightly punches my arm before slinging his around my shoulder.

And like that, we walk the remaining distance to the forge talking, laughing, teasing.

The front doors of the forge are closed as usual, so we both grab one and heave them open. They weigh like ten times as much, maybe more, as I do. But with some effort, you can get them open.

The forge is quiet—very quiet. No raging flames are to be heard, no hammer hitting steel. Nothing.

"Vergus!" Nate calls out, cupping his hands around his mouth to let his voice travel farther through the building. "I'm back."

No answer. We take off to the other end of the factory, to Vergus' usual spot and find him. Staring at a set of shackles hanging limp in his hands. He once again refuses to make eye contact with anyone. He's just blankly staring at the humming iron shackles.

Those are the same shackles the council used on Leanne and I. And a while later Leanne used them on me again.

Something like pain or even guilt is etched into his face. That his hands could make such things.

"Vergus?" Nate asks.

"How?" Vergus whispers as his hands wrap tightly around the chains.

I take a step towards him. "Vergus? Talk to us. What's wrong?"

His hands are shaking from the force he's using to grip the chains. "How could I?"

"What do you mean?" I say carefully, not wanting to push him too hard.

He finally looks up at me, tears in his eyes, a slight tremble in his voice. "How could I make these?"

I take a hold of the chains, hating the power they contain and gently tug Vergus to release them. He squeezes them harshly one last time before letting go. I let them drop to the floor, the sound of the iron hitting the stone floor reverberating through the whole forge.

Then I look Vergus in the eyes as he says, "I let them hurt you—I let her hurt you when I promised Ricon I'd protect you."

I stumble back at his words. My dad went to Vergus, asking him to protect me.

As if he knew something was going to happen.

I shake off the thought and redirect my gaze to Vergus.

"You didn't let anyone hurt me," I whisper.

His voice breaks. "She threatened to hurt everybody around you if I didn't do it."

"If you didn't do what?"

Tears start rolling down his face. "Make three sets of these. She wanted me to make three sets for you."

I step so far back I bump into Nate, who catches me before I drop to the ground. "Three sets," I mumble to myself.

"We've only seen one so far," Nate counters.

Vergus buries his face in his hands and mutters, "I know."

"So, the other two are still missing," Nate says, still keeping me upright.

"Vergus," I whisper as I step out of Nate's hold.

I close the distance and stop in front of him. He slowly removes his hands from his face and looks at me with so much guilt in his eyes.

I pull him into a hug, putting my arms tightly around him. He freezes for a moment, but quickly wraps his arms around my shoulders.

"I'm sorry," Vergus says, his voice thick from the tears.

"It's okay. You couldn't have said no, even if you wanted to. I'm almost glad I know they're out there, waiting for me. At least now I know what to expect if something bad ever happens again."

"How are you so calm under this?" Vergus asks as he pulls away and grabs my shoulders.

"Because I have let fear drive me into dark corners I never want to go to again." I take a deep breath. "I prepare myself every day to spend the night in the dungeons. Just because I don't know if Leanne found my behavior acceptable that day. I let those thoughts of being down there drive me into panic attacks way too many times. And I won't let that happen again. I know the shadows in the corners of that dungeon cell are waiting for me to crumble, but I won't give anybody that satisfaction."

They both stare at me, trying to comprehend what I just laid bare.

That I indeed sneak back to my room every night, afraid of Leanne standing around the corner, ready to put me in chains again.

"The only person here to blame is Leanne. Thinking she can get away with all of this," I say to both of them. "But we're going to let it rest for now and get back at her on our own terms and in our own way."

They both nod. Vergus wipes his tears away as Nate embraces him. We might not be family by blood, but Vergus treats all four of us as if we're his children. And I am very glad for that, but it makes seeing him like this even worse.

I have seen Vergus cry three times since I met him.

When my parents died, after the first time Leanne locked me up, and right now.

He's always the tough guy, towering over everybody, keeping his emotions in check. But everybody needs to let them out from time to time. Even the brightest men and women.

Nate breaks the hug and mutters a few words of encouragement and understanding to Vergus before announcing he wants me to help him fix his sword.

Since he apparently broke it. Wonder how that happened when he was slashing it across rocks and iron poles.

The rest of the afternoon is quiet. Vergus resumes his work. Nate and I work on rebuilding his sword. And that was that. All the emotions are out in the open and we can just be around each other with no one feeling guilty.

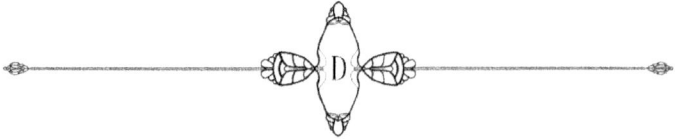

My night on the other hand is restless. I can't seem to fall asleep, no matter how much I relax or close my eyes. I toss and turn for over two hours, but get nowhere near being asleep. So I decide to pay the sweet couple another nightly visit.

I take off my pajamas and put on the outfit I wore today again. However, I'm not going to drag my sword all the way over there, so let's hope I don't run into any assassin. I leave my sword in its place, propped against the side of my bed.

Then I quietly open my balcony doors and close them behind me. I peer across the garden to see if there are any guards close by. Luckily not, which means I'm free to climb down and run into town.

I unlock their front door by pushing a wisp of air through the lock, through the mechanism on the inside. Letting my eyes adjust to the pitch-dark house before I resume my way towards the bedroom.

But unfortunately, I don't make it to the bedroom soundless. I trip over one of the fabric rolls Madion told Jade to clean up and fall face first on the floor.

A moment later, I hear noise on the other side of the bedroom door and less than five seconds later, Madion and Jade swing open the door, sword and daggers raised.

Until they spy me grunting on the floor. They both let out an amused chuckle as they help me up.

"What made you try to creep up on us?" Madion muses, "Are you trying to finally get rid of us?"

"I couldn't sleep," I admit.

"And you always decide to don't let us sleep either," Jade mutters, a taunting smile on her face.

I sigh. "I just really needed to get out of the castle."

Madion grabs my wrist and pulls me to the bedroom. "Come on then, you can spend the night here."

I hear Jade kick the roll of fabric aside before joining us in the bedroom. Probably not wanting to break her neck in the morning, either.

Madion pushes me onto the bed and plops down beside me. "Okay, talk. What's keeping you up?"

"Is everything a valid answer?"

"No."

"Fine. It's just that we couldn't figure out who killed Anna. Leanne might've killed our parents, and then the surprise ball she's throwing tomorrow," I ramble. "I assume you got invites, too."

Jade lays down on my other side and says, "Yeah, we did. We were expecting her to do something, but not some elaborate ball."

"I hadn't even thought of her planning something, so you can imagine my shock this morning," I grunt, pulling a pillow against my chest. "I am not looking forward to an evening full of dancing and laughing while the tension between Leanne and me is sky high."

"We'll be there right beside you, but you'll have to face her," Madion states. "She'll be trying to find you in the crowd, ask you to dance, ask you to sit beside her. She's going to push your buttons tomorrow night as much as she can."

I grunt once again and pull the pillow tighter to my chest.

Jade coaxes me to lie down completely and pulls the blanket over me. "Well, from what I hear, you need a good night's sleep. You're safely going to be tucked in between Madion and I and sleep. We'll wake you in the morning when it's time to get ready." She looks in the direction of the living room, as if seeing something through the door. "I might've put together four outfits for tomorrow. One for each of us, including Nate."

"Thank you, Jade. I really don't know what I'd do without the two of you," I mumble as I look at them.

"You'd fall flat on your ass or face, and no one would be there to pick you up?" Jade smiles at me.

I lightly punch her bicep. "Not funny. Didn't Madion tell you to clean those up?"

From Jade's facial expression, I make out she has yet to listen to Madion's words.

Shocker.

"She'll clean it up tomorrow, very quietly, so she doesn't wake you," Madion whispers from my left.

They both crawl under the blanket too and mutter silent good nights before falling asleep.

And as expected, it doesn't take me a long time to fall asleep either.

I have to be rested for that ball tomorrow.

CHAPTER 17

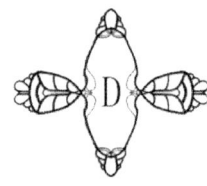

"Holy shit," I mutter as Jade enters my bedroom with the dress she made me. "How did you manage to make that?"

"A lot of long nights and bleeding fingers." She gives me a look. "So if you dare spill anything on this dress, you better hope Adrian and Jake are close by, because I don't know yet what I'll do, but it'll definitely hurt."

I stifle a laugh and gesture for her to put the dress on the bed.

"Do you need help to put it on?" Jade asks as she lays it down.

I run my hand down the fabric, the dark blue fabric. "No, Remina and Calis are coming any moment to hoist me into it and block off my airways with a corset."

Jade lays a hand on my shoulder. "The hard life of a princess."

"I might be a princess, but I still want my lungs to supply the necessary oxygen for the rest of my body." I slap her hand away. "Why don't you put Madion in a corset, see how she responds to that."

"She'll lock me out of the house if I even come near her with one," she says with a sigh.

I poke her shoulder. "Then don't say I'm complaining."

A knock sounds on the door before Jade can answer. "Your Highness?"

"Come in."

Remina and Calis are wearing their usual white, simple dresses with dark green aprons.

"How are you doing, Your Highness?" Remina asks me.

"I'm nervous. How are things at home, Calis?"

She thinks about her answer for a bit, or she's debating whether to talk so casually with me. "My mother is doing better. Thank you for asking." She slowly inclines her head, her blonde braid falling over her shoulder.

"Good." I turn to Jade again. "You, go dress yourself."

"Yes, Your Highness." She bows.

"Get out," I say flatly.

She throws me a wink before leaving the room.

"Shall we get you ready?" Remina asks once the door clicks shut.

"Yes, let's," I say and walk to the bathroom to scrub myself clean before they complain I stink.

They let me do it myself for about five minutes before interrupting and finishing the job themselves.

Then they lead me out of the bathroom and coax me into a chair in front of the mirror. Remina brushes, braids, and styles my hair to make me look as regal as possible tonight. She parts my hair horizontally and makes two braids out of the top part, which she ties together. Then she uses her control over fire to curl the bottom half of my hair, letting each curl fall over my shoulder or my back.

Last, she places my crown in front of me on a small table, letting me decide when I'm putting it on.

Next step is putting my dress on.

Calis wraps the corset around my chest. I take one final deep breath and she pulls it tight. Like I said, this is going to be a fun night.

The next thing is putting on the actual dress. I slide my arms into the long, lace sleeves, going all the way until they cover the top of my hands. The bodice is the same azure as my sleeves, covered with white beads in intricate patterns. My skirt falls over my feet, a bit too long, covered in the same bead patterns as the bodice.

Jade once again outdid herself. Though I am curious what Nate, Madion and her are wearing if my dress is already this spectacular.

When Calis and Remina deem me ready, they step aside to let me properly look at myself in the mirror.

The dress is stunning on its own, my hair is beautiful. But it's not me to dance in dresses. I fight in the mud and ride my horse through the woods. So nothing has ever intrigued me during these balls. It's watching other people have fun, dancing with older men who want to shoot their shot and guards constantly breathing down your neck to make sure you don't get killed.

But I can do this, it's only for one night.

I raise my hand to hold my necklace. The golden half moon, containing a cage with two crystals between its tips. My mom gave it to me for my seventeenth birthday.

"I love you, mom," I whisper. "I love you, dad."

I notice Remina and Calis bow at my words. We stay a moment in silence before they add the finishing touches. A dark red color is applied to my lips, my lashes are darkened.

"Thank you both," I say to them as they finish their work. "I'll see you at the ball."

They bow again before leaving me to my thoughts.

I let my hand trace the crown in front of me, made of various silver curls bending inwards to a large, light blue opal. A gem carved from the mountains surrounding Iluniel.

The queen's crown contains a crimson red ruby, the king's crown has a white sapphire and Leanne's crown used to have jade gemstone, but it went missing the night our parents died.

Knocking on my door snaps my attention away from the crown. A moment later Adrian enters. A more elegant blouse, still together with his sword, is his clothing choice for tonight.

"You look exactly like your mom," he says as he approaches me. "She would've been proud of the woman that is standing here today."

At those words, my restraint snaps. "I miss her—" Tears start rolling down my cheeks. "I miss them both."

Adrian kneels in front of me as I sink to my knees and bury my face in my hands.

I used to be able to get through these balls with ease. Dad would always sneak over to me after a couple of hours and take me outside to catch our breaths. We'd experiment with our magic. Sometimes we even ran off to the woods. Ever since he's gone, I have refused every single ball Leanne held.

I just couldn't do it, not without him.

"Dawn," Adrian says as he pries my fingers off my face. "Look at me."

I look into his dark brown eyes, filled with sorrow and pity.

"I know you miss them. I miss them every day, too. But I also know that they have been by your side every single day. Do you really think that a dagger ripped them away from you completely?" he takes a deep breath. "I am certain they fought their hardest to have a place beside you. To help you through the day. To help you up when you fall. But most importantly, to still love you unconditionally. Even if they're not physically here, they keep loving you with all their hearts."

He lets go of my hands and reaches behind him, grabbing my crown. "Now. Why don't you show how proud you are to be one of the late king Ricon's daughters?"

Adrian carefully places the crown on my head, twining a few strands of hair around it to make it stay in place. Then he grabs my hands and pulls me to my feet.

He stands behind me, hands on my shoulders. "I am glad that I get to be your guard, Dawn. I wouldn't trade it for anything in the world."

I turn around to face him. "You're not just my guard, neither is Jake," I say, earning me a questioning look. "I consider you my family after all these years of having my back. You couldn't be anything less after ten years of being by my side."

Now it is his turn to cry as he wraps his arms around me. "I love you too, sis."

We stand in our embrace for another moment before Jake knocks on the door. He notifies me I'm expected at the entrance of the ballroom in ten minutes.

They let me freshen up quickly before leading me to a night, which is hopefully full of dancing, laughing, and talking.

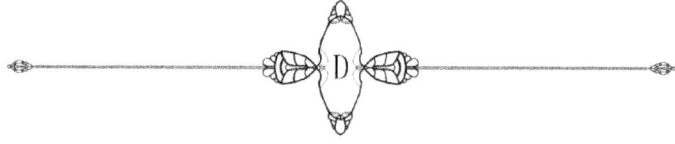

I stand in front of the enormous doors, which are about to be pulled wide open to reveal me.

Adrian and Jake stand behind me as usual. They'll follow me inside for a few meters and then take their assigned places at one of the large windows.

A faint voice starts inside. "Ladies and gentlemen, may I present to you, Her Highness Dawn Sungust."

The large doors are pulled open, and I make my way inside. The crowd parts before me as I walk all the way to where Leanne is sitting on her throne.

I incline my head as soon as I reach her. "Sister."

Leanne inclines her head. "Dawn, you look beautiful this evening."

"Thank you. You look rather good yourself, too," I say.

She gestures for me to sit beside her as she speaks to the people present. "Resume the dancing and music."

Everybody quickly bustles together again as the music starts. Each and everyone have a smile on their face. I even saw two people already sneaking off.

Wonder what that will lead to.

After a few minutes, I notice three shapes shuffling through the crowd towards me. As they emerge, I almost gasp at their clothes. Jade has definitely been pulling all-nighters to finish all of this.

She is wearing a dark green dress, sleeves going till her elbows, with lace covering her skirt and bodice. Several more earrings peek out from beneath her thick braid.

Madion is wearing a dress that matches her hair. It's a vibrant red, sleeves covering a part of her hands just like mine, with white pearls decorating her waist and neckline. Her hair falling over her shoulders in curls.

Nate is wearing a dark purple, almost black, suit, with a black shirt underneath. Several bracelets decorating his wrists as usual.

Nate holds out his hand to me. "May I have this dance, Your Highness?"

Leanne is already embroiled in another conversation with lord Akrin, so I take his hand. "You may." And hurry after them.

We huddle together at the window guarded by Jake and Adrian. "Why are we in this dark corner?" I ask.

"Because you looked pretty uncomfortable next to Leanne, and we thought why not get you away with some dancing? She wasn't even paying attention, so no harm done," Jade answers.

"Okay," I say with a sigh. "I might—"

I'm cut off by a couple of lords approaching me. Lord Bren, Klan, Emris and Nigal.

They all bow, and Lord Klan speaks, "Good evening, Your Highness."

I slightly bow my head. "Good evening, lord Klan, lord Bren, lord Emris and lord Nigal. To what do I owe this pleasure?"

"We would all like to congratulate you on your victories," Lord Emris declares. "We are thrilled to see your father's courage back in you, Your Highness."

"Thank you."

"We shall leave you to it," Lord Nigal says as the lords bow again. "Have a good evening, Your Highness."

"You all as well," I say before turning back to the window to look at my previous conversation partners.

"The switch you flip to talk to others is still odd and confusing sometimes," Jade mutters, straightening out her skirt.

I look at her. "Well, I can't just joke or not be serious when they're around, can I?"

"Not really." She fidgets with her sleeve.

I put my hand on her shoulder. "I just have to change the way I speak and act when it involves this kingdom."

"I know." She puts her hand over her eyes.

I remove her hand and say, "It's okay. Why don't we join the dancing couples?"

"Good idea," Nate says as he holds out his hand to me. "Shall we?"

I lay my hand on his. "We most certainly shall."

Nate leads me to the center of the room, Jade and Madion taking a spot beside us.

I place my hand on his shoulder as he lays his hand on my lower back, while our other hands grab hold of each other.

And away we go, slowly dancing to the music playing in the background.

"How did you sleep last night?" Nate suddenly asks. "The girls said you came to them again in the middle of the night."

"I just couldn't fall asleep after what happened with Vergus and my nerves for tonight. And most of the time, going to them tends to help me fall asleep and actually feel somewhat rested when I wake up," I respond.

He eyes me for a moment. "And are you feeling rested?"

I look at him. He definitely noticed the underlying exhaustion. "No, I'm still tired. But no matter how much I sleep, that exhaustion stays."

Nate pulls me a tad closer. "Is that because of the constant nightmares, or something else?"

"Everything. Every damn thing that has happened since that awful night has made me into this. An emotional, exhausted person, with way too much weight on her shoulders for it to be healthy."

"Then why don't we, the four of us, go on a trip once you finish these trials? Just to throw everything off those shoulders," Nate proposes.

I notice Madion carefully placing her head on Jade's shoulder, just to make it a tad more intimate without making it too much for the room.

"I think that would be an amazing idea if Leanne allowed me to go," I whisper.

Nate places a light kiss on my forehead. "We'll figure that out later. Now we're just going to dance and relax."

"I'd like that," I say.

After that, we fall silent and slowly dance around the room. Just dancing, nothing more, nothing less. It's more relaxing than you might think.

Until your sister taps on your shoulder.

"May I borrow my dear sister for a moment?" Leanne asks, her hands on my shoulders.

Nate shoots me a look. "Dawn?"

I let go of his hand and shoulder. "I'll be okay."

Nate bows. "Your Majesty." Before leaving me to it.

Leanne grabs my hand and puts us in the same position I was just in. In the corner of my eye, I see Nate pulling Jade and Madion aside.

Leanne guides me away from their hushed conversation and starts one on her own. "It's nice to finally have a moment to speak with you. You seem rather occupied these days."

"You could always pay me another one of those nightly visits, with numerous guards. Those conversations are always fun," I say as my eyes focus on hers. "Or would you rather have a normal and free conversation?"

"I would like to just talk as sisters. Instead of wild animals tearing at each other."

"Then don't lock me up like I'm a wild animal," I say, my magic faintly rising to the surface. "It would help me have a normal conversation, like the one we're having right now."

"Dawn, I have told you so many times why I do what I do."

My anger and magic rise even further. "Yet you have not given me one reason, one good reason, why you'd lock your own sister up and suffocate her magic," I snap.

She takes a deep breath, probably trying to come up with another excuse. "You know why I do it and I will not discuss it with you at this moment."

"Fine, if you don't want to talk about that, why did you ask me to dance?" I say with a light sneer.

"I wanted to ask you how you were doing after the second trial?"

That question leaves me speechless. She hasn't asked me a question like that in five years.

"I've been better," I admit, while I feel a faint, very faint thing prodding my soul. "But I have people that help me through it."

I try to trace the tendril, but it recedes as soon as I try to hook onto it. However, the magic was familiar. If I could get a better look, I would know who it belongs to.

Leanne suddenly pulls me closer, placing her face next to mine. "What about the memories you saw?"

I try to look at her, but she holds me tight. "What about them?"

The magic started prodding at my soul again, looking for what lies there. The power that lies there.

I hook onto it as the magic recedes again. And I am led straight back to my dear sister.

Yet it doesn't fit, something is wrong with it. Leanne's magic doesn't feel like that. Hers is soft and light, not harsh and dark.

I try to pull away again as the tendrils now start to dig into the outer layer of my soul. "What the hell are you doing?"

I let my magic flow out like a barrier, keeping hers at bay.

"I'm merely asking you a question," she says sweetly. "Did you see mom and dad?"

"Yes, I did," I mutter through clenched teeth. "What about them?"

"You didn't have to experience that dreadful night once again, did you?" she says, almost sounding sorry for me. "I know about the nightmares that keep you awake at night."

My magic is flowing further and further away from my soul, still keeping Leanne at bay. "I'm glad you can sleep peacefully, sister. Now if you'd excuse me, I'd like to get something to drink," I say to her, trying to escape from her grip.

"Now wait a moment. I was not finished," she whispers, slamming her magic harder into mine. "Did you finally see who killed them?"

With that question, I lose another bit of the restraint I still have left.

"I saw who killed them," I mumble.

A smile faintly tugs at Leanne's lips as she finally pulls away to look at me.

"And I know you know who killed them," I grind out.

The pressure she's putting on my soul is getting more and more by the second.

"If I knew that, wouldn't I already have them executed?" she questions me.

She pushes her magic harder and harder into my soul, darkness enveloping it, until the outer layer almost cracks. I'm fighting the heavier magic she's pressing on my soul as best as I can with what I have.

I let out a faint whine of pain as I try to push her off me. My magic still trying to push hers away.

"Get off me," I snarl at her.

"Not until you tell me who killed them," she snaps back.

"You know damn well who killed them," I say, louder than intended.

A few people turn our way. Nobody dares to speak of that day with me present. No one.

But faint whispers spread across the crowd as more people notice me struggling in Leanne's grip.

Leanne leans closer one more time, her magic slightly retreating. "Who killed Ricon and Rowena?"

And as the last words leave her mouth, her magic slams full force into me.

I stumble away from her and clutching my chest, eyes wrenched shut as I fight her off. My magic builds up in response, leaking out of the small cracks Leanne caused.

And when her magic lessens, I slam right back into her. She stumbles back a few steps and smiles at me.

She's provoking me.

"You killed them," I snap at her. "You killed them so you could have all of this. That crown on your head. The apparent authority to lock me up if I don't listen. The guts to subdue my magic, because you apparently need to teach me a lesson if I don't get home in time."

She stays silent as everybody in the room stands still, completely still. Not knowing what to do when Leanne and I have a falling out. Even though we have them a lot, we have them behind closed doors, not in the company of others.

But tonight is different. Let them know what she does, let them know what she has done.

"You even tried to get me killed in the first trial. You stopped me from keeping those hounds at bay," I sneer.

"How do you know that was me? There were hundreds of people watching you," she merely says.

"Because it was the same magic that you just hurled at my soul," I retort.

Surprised gasps make their way through the room. The thin line of restraint I still have almost at its breaking point.

"Why? Why would you do it?"

"I did nothing. You can throw any accusations at me, but you don't have proof," she counters.

"I don't have proof?" I scoff. "Let's ask any servant or guard in this castle, or even nearby villages. Because they all know what happens if I'm not back before dark. I'm dragged in chains to the only cell that is always unoccupied. I'm chained to the floor or wall, whatever you feel like at that moment. And then the grand finale, a collar."

Leanne eyes me, her magic still pushing against mine.

An internal battle. One I don't intend to lose.

"That might be so, but you have no proof that I killed them. Everybody here knows I loved them with everything I had," she says, before she snaps that fine line I call restraint. "What makes it you didn't kill them?"

My magic rams hers like a battering ram, sending both of us to our knees. While Leanne gets back up, I do not.

My magic is riled up and will not go back to where it came from. I am losing control as my magic makes some kind of protective dome around me.

Magic sometimes gets its own will. Right now, it wants to protect the person it's housed in.

But it hurts me as my magic leaks out of my body. It is coming from behind the cracked layer of my soul, pushing the cracks open wider.

My soul is not ready for that. It has barely had time to heal from the last shattering.

If I don't stop this now, I could die right here, right now.

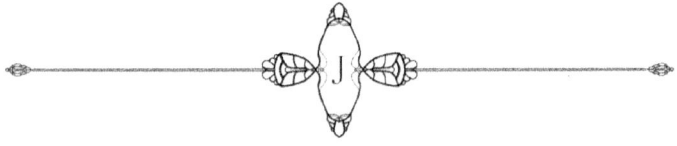

Madion and I watch as Dawn collapses to her knees and starts pulling up some kind of protection.

Everyone in this room can see the major leak her soul has.

"She could die if she doesn't stop that leak," I whisper to Madion and Nate. The latter slowly stepping closer to Dawn.

Several guards are rushing in to surround her, but when she flinches at their arrival, Nate orders them to stand back. The rage and determination in his eyes doesn't make them think twice about disobeying him.

"I know that, Jade. But there is nothing we can do until that barrier around her is broken," Madion whispers back.

Nate raises his hand as he comes closer to the dome. A thin layer of his magic covers his palm. He is going to try to calm her down with it.

"Just watch, Jade. Watch closely," Madion mutters in my ear before placing her attention on Nate and Dawn again.

Nate places his hand very carefully on the dome. His magic slithers in small wisps over the whole dome, calming it.

"Dawn?" he mumbles. "Let me in."

Everybody in the room is just staring, staring at Nate, not giving a single shit about what could happen if Dawn breaks completely.

Nate puts more pressure, his magic spreading across the whole dome.

A small tear forms right where he is standing and as soon as it is big enough, Nate slips in. He falls to his knees in front of Dawn. The tear immediately closing behind him. As if it was only meant to give Nate an entry.

As if it would only let him in. Only trust him to not cause even more pain.

"Dawn, look at me, please look at me," he whispers, concern and sadness in his voice.

Nate's hand hovers over Dawn's hands, which are lying in her lap.

"We need to help him," I say.

"No, we don't," Madion counters, gesturing to the scene unfolding in front of us.

A faint glow starts to emerge from Dawn's hands and a similar one coming from Nate's hands as they close in on hers.

"Looks familiar, doesn't it?" Madion muses, looking at me over her shoulder.

A distant memory from Madion and me floats to the surface. A memory we will forever treasure.

"Wait—" I blurt out as it clicks. "They're—"

"Yes, they are. I've had my suspicions for a while now. Didn't think they'd be confirmed this soon," Madion says as she grabs my hand. "Just watch. Maybe it'll bring back memories."

"Oh, it already did," I say and lay my head on her shoulder, just like she did during our dance, and firmly hold her hand.

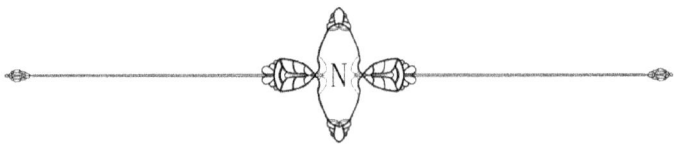

I place my hands on top of Dawn's and a shock goes through me. Through both of us, apparently, because Dawn's bright blue eyes snap up and focus on me.

"There you are," I say as one of my hands goes to cup her cheek. "Just let it slowly come back in. Slowly."

I let my magic press more onto the dome from the outside, guiding it back to her soul. But we're held back by something else happening between us.

I notice both my palms are faintly glowing, as are Dawn's.

And only two occasions can make that happen. One of which is certainly not happening right now.

Which leaves me with one other option.

One I would not mind one bit.

I lift my hand to the space between us, coaxing her to place her hand against mine.

Slowly, she lifts hers. The closer our hands get, the brighter they illuminate. Right as her fingertips hit mine, I feel something ripping loose from my soul. An almost imperceptible piece of my soul twists around our hands. Her soul doing the same.

Both pieces lock onto each other and split again. Making two identical, faint yellow swirls of our souls.

And as each swirl floats back to Dawn and me, I whisper, "You're my mate."

CHAPTER 18

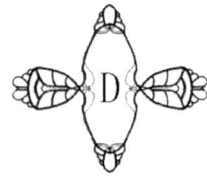

He is my mate.

Nate is my mate.

How did we never figure it out?

Our magic has touched so many times.

"How did we never notice?" I whisper as I look into his eyes. Those vibrant blue eyes, lined with tears.

"I don't know," he whispers back as he puts his hand on the back of my neck and puts our foreheads against each other. "Shall we get you out of here?"

"I can't, I can't get it back in."

"Yes, you can," he says, and I feel his magic pressing harder against mine. "Let it flow back in. Breathe with me."

And as I slowly match my breathing with his, I feel my magic slipping back through the cracks in my soul. Safely tucked behind their protective barrier until they're truly ready to come out.

"It's working," I breathe.

"I know," he answers. "I can feel it."

Suddenly, a faint tingle forms in my head. *Almost. I've got you, Dawn. I'm not letting go.*

Nate, I mumble back over that bridge.

I feel him stiffen, as he must feel the same thing.

We can talk mind to mind, he says, grabbing my face with both hands. He places a soft kiss on my forehead.

It seems like we can, I answer.

"Let's get you out of here," he whispers as he places his hands on mine.

I feel the final whip retreat, but the calmness doesn't come back.

All eyes in the room are directed at me. My magic is still buzzing, on the verge of exploding.

I hear people approaching. "Get her out of here, now," Madion says to Nate as she and Jade step in front of the crowd that is closing in.

"Come on." Nate grabs both my hands and pulls me up. I almost trip over my feet, but Nate wraps his arm around my waist just in time. Jade and Madion turn and follow us out of the room as I see Jake and Adrian block the doors after us.

The stairs up to my room are tough. My legs feel like mush, ready to collapse, and my vision goes from blurred to normal every few seconds.

"We're almost there, a few more steps," Nate mumbles as he tightens his grip on me.

Jade runs past us to open the door to my bedroom. Madion enters first and goes straight for my curtains, closing them when I enter. Jade locks the door behind us, blocking out everybody else that might've followed.

Nate lightly touches my forehead. "She's burning up."

Madion nods towards the bathroom. "Shower. Now."

She leaps over the bed, Jade right behind her.

They've had to do this so many times in the past years, that I really feel bad about how much I depend on them. I should be able to keep my magic in check on my own.

But I snap out of my thoughts as I'm led into the bathroom. Nate guides me to the floor and starts to untie my dress and corset. Madion kneels in front of me and untangles my crown and hair. Several curls fall over my face before she can lift the crown from my head. She places it on the sink, then takes out my earrings and helps Nate undo me from my dress.

Once I'm fully undressed, Nate and Madion help me into the shower.

The water hits my back in force, massaging the tight muscles. Nate takes off his jacket before he squats in front of me. He then takes both my hands in his and starts rubbing idle circles on the back of my hands. I lower my head to let it rest on my knees, the pounding headache still present and getting more intense by the second.

Jade and Madion have a whispered conversation and then decide to leave the room. Not wanting to come between us.

They know exactly how all of this feels. The weird but nice feeling of being connected with another soul.

A piece of your soul intertwined with a piece of someone else's.

A lifeline, one that you will have till the end. No matter what that end is, they will be there.

And I have found mine when I needed him most. When I was at my end, he was there when I opened my eyes. I might've always hoped Nate was my mate. Because I had never come across someone I formed a bond with so fast.

Now my soul is slowly filling in the smallest cracks, stopping the leak before it can actually kill me. I let the magic I can use guide the water all over me, my head, my back, my feet, down to my wrists.

And when my headache has finally receded enough to let me lift my head, I look at Nate. His eyes focused on the silver lines decorating my hands. He traces them, from the tips of my fingers to my wrist.

"Nate?" I say, my voice hoarse. His eyes shoot up, a questioning look passing his face. "Can you help me up?"

"Are you sure?"

"Yes, I'd rather lie in bed than sit on this stone," I say as I cut off the water.

He lets go of my hands and moves to a cabinet filled with towels and washcloths. He grabs the largest towel I have and wraps it around me.

Nate's hand finds a place around my waist again as he helps me up. My legs are still unstable, but I manage to walk the short distance to my bed. I plop down on it, towel wrapped tightly around me, my wet and tangled hair dripping water down my back.

"Anything specific you want to put on?" Nate asks, standing in front of the chest filled with clothes.

"No, some pants and a shirt are okay."

He nods and starts rummaging through my clothes. Coming up with my most comfortable pajamas a moment later.

"Do you need help putting it on?" he asks, holding up the pants and shirt.

I push myself up from the bed, but immediately stumble into him. Nate drops the clothes and catches me in his arms.

"I'll take that as a yes. Come on, let's get these clothes on, then you can lie down for the rest of the night," he says as he picks me up and carries me to the bed.

He tucks in my towel, so it stays around my body, then motions me to raise my arms and slides my shirt on. He pulls the towel down next, my shirt now covering my chest, and lets it cover my legs. I put on my underwear as he lifts me off the bed. My pants are a bit more work, but we get it done.

The towel disappears into the bathroom as Nate goes after it to freshen up himself.

He's my mate. And even though I feel like I'll collapse at any second, I couldn't be happier. I know everyone dreams of meeting their mate one day. I dreamed of meeting him one day and I am glad to know that he has already been by my side for years.

So for now, I close my eyes and lay down as my head has started pounding again. What Leanne did literally broke something inside me, and my body needs to heal before I can get going again.

I hear the water in the bathroom stop running a moment before Nate emerges. He got rid of his shirt, showing off muscles he has gained by hitting a hammer on iron all day.

I want to turn over to make room for him, but my body just says no.

Nate's gaze lands on my face and hair, noticing the giant knots of hair. He gently turns me over onto my belly. I place my hands underneath my head as he climbs on the bed next to me.

He sits on his knees beside me and starts untangling my hair. "Do you feel better after that shower?"

"It helps most of the time, not always," I say. Glancing at him from the corner of my eyes, I add, "And when they don't work, I have you, I hope."

Nate smiles. "You're not getting rid of me that easily. Well, you're not getting rid of me at all anymore."

"What a shame," I mumble, a faint smile spreading across my face.

Several more strands fall over my shoulders, Nate's fingers expertly untangling them. For someone working at a forge, he has surprisingly gentle hands. And with a glance to my left, I can see the concentration on his face, just taking his time to expertly unravel my hair.

And just him being this calm, this focused, makes me wonder. "How do you do it?"

"Do what?"

"Keep your magic in check. You're powerful. Everybody knows that, but how do you control it? How does your magic not lash out?"

He exhales sharply as he untangles the last strands of hair, then he lays down beside me, looking straight into my eyes. "How do you think I do it?"

"I don't know. That's my problem." I sigh.

"Because I have an outlet," he explains. "I use it daily. I tire it at the forge. You need to find something you can do every day to take off that edge. I know training, with or without us, can help expand a lot of energy. It might even help you fall asleep at night.

"But I think the other problem for you is the fact that your magic is not whole yet, in a way. I've had the same amount of magic since I was born. I can train to become more powerful, but the amount will most likely not change. Yours is becoming bigger and bigger in a short amount of time. Besides that, you don't really have anyone who can help you control all the elements. The three of us can help, but we don't cover all four."

"Jake could help with earth," I mutter.

"Then you ask him if he can help you. Asking for help is allowed. No one says you have to do everything on your own," he says, taking hold of my hand. "You're not alone, not in any of this." He places a kiss on the back of my hand. "Never."

I shuffle closer to him, placing my head against his bare chest, his calm heartbeat calming me down. "How did we never notice or figure it out sooner?"

"I don't know," he says. His arm comes around my waist, his hand laying on my lower back. "We had our weird moments, but nothing that pointed to this."

"There was one time, when we were walking in the woods and a feral gendril attacked us," I say, trying to recover that old memory. "We fought it off, but both of us got injured. Remember when I was leaning against the tree, and you tried to feel how bad my injuries were?" I look at his free hand. "Your hands started vaguely glowing."

Nate stays quiet for a moment, probably trying to remember the day from three years ago. "I think I remember. You had a large cut running across your ribs. You didn't heal that fast yet. I almost had to carry you back."

"Not my fault it went for my heart." I swat his arm.

We both laugh at that but fall silent soon after. Not knowing what could be said at this moment.

"Are you happy that it's me?" Nate suddenly asks. "Am I enough for you?"

"Enough?" I blurt out. "Nate, you're everything I could've ever wished for."

I lift my head to look him straight in the eyes. "Nate, don't you ever think you're not good enough for anyone. I have always dreamed of who my mate, my soulmate, would be. And if they had said it would be you, I wouldn't have believed it. I wouldn't have believed I'd be blessed with the most loving and kind person I had ever met."

I shift so I can put my hand on his cheek, his bright eyes focused on mine. "Never think you're not good enough for someone. They're the ones that don't deserve you."

He kisses the palm of my hand. "I think I might've loved you for a while now." His other arm comes around my waist, pulling me closer to him.

And the silence that follows has enough answers for him.

I feel the same way, because I have always felt something for him. I just never dared to admit it until now. "I think I love you too."

Silence falls over us again. Silence I don't want.

"I don't think I ever really asked about your bracelets," I say, fidgeting with a golden bead hanging from one. "Why do you always wear them?"

He looks at them himself for a moment, lost in thought, lost in what he's going to answer. Then he grabs one charm, one in particular. A small silver coin, no bigger than my nail, engraved with three elements. Fire, water, and air. The elements he can control. "To remind me that I'm not the monster people think I am, that I do not deserve to be locked up."

I lift myself with my elbow, leveling my face with his. "What?"

"There are scars underneath those bracelets, scars that remind me every day of how people used to see me."

I let my hand slide over the thick leather band, reminding me of the shackles that are around my wrists too often for comfort. "Can—can I see?" I hesitantly ask.

I had never actually thought about why, why someone would feel comfortable wearing leather bands and other bracelets around their wrists.

But this is not just for comfort, it's protection.

He turns his wrist, showing the locking mechanism. He unfastens the small hook, letting all the loose bracelets drop on the bed. The leather band follows soon after.

Revealing a thick, rugged scar looping around his wrist.

I have the same scars, in the same place, but not as striking as his. Without those bracelets, people would stare at his wrists all day.

"Who did this to you?" I whisper, my fingers hovering over his wrist.

"A man that wanted revenge on me for hurting his wife," he says with a shaky voice. "When my parents left for that camp, they left me in the care of a woman named Esmeralda. Whenever I missed my mom, she'd stay with me the whole night, singing songs to me, holding my hand, anything I needed.

"No one knew then how far my power reached, how deep that well went, until the day news about my parents came. They were supposed to return that week. When I heard Esmeralda talk to the soldier, I could feel the magic surge through my whole body, and I did not know how to control it yet. So, when the soldier left, I unknowingly let it all out. Cups flew off the table, glass shattered, and Esmeralda was pressed against the wall by the enormous current of air that was circling through the room. I was slowly crushing her with it."

He takes a deep breath, as if bracing himself for what he has to say next. "I almost killed her that day. But her husband came home soon after and knocked me out before I could do more harm. I woke in their basement, in chains, my vision blurred. Because, as I'd later learn, he was drugging me. Day in, day out, to keep my magic as deep in my soul as possible. I was only allowed to come up to the living room to bathe. Sleeping and eating happened in the basement."

He looks at me with what I'd call gratitude and love. "But every time I could bathe, I'd look outside to the children running there with their parents. And I saw you. Sometimes with your mom, sometimes with your dad. And it got me through the day. Seeing you run there brought me joy." His voice breaks. "Joy that one day I'd hopefully be running right beside you."

I fling my arms around his neck, almost causing him to tumble backwards off the bed, but he catches us. His hand rubs soothing circles onto my back. "Hey, I'm okay now."

"I know," I mutter, a tear hitting his bare back. "But no one should go through that. No one, no matter who or what they are."

His arm now fully wraps around my back and gives my side a squeeze. "And I completely agree with you on that, but it got me to where I am today."

"How did you get out?" I bury my face in the nape of his neck.

"Vergus got me out," he states. "Esmeralda's husband asked him to come by. I don't remember the reason, but he ended up in the basement, where fourteen-year-old me was huddled in a corner. He unchained me and we were almost at the front door when Esmeralda walked in. She looked at both of us, at the state I was in, and said 'take care of him, take better care of him than I could', before walking further into the house to stop her husband from following us."

He pulls me away to look at my face, at the tears no doubt running down my cheeks. "I got out, I survived. Just like you survive all those nights."

His thumbs brush over my cheeks, rubbing away the tears. I grab his hands and ask, "Do you know where Esmeralda is now?"

"I think she moved to a town close by, but I haven't seen her since that day. I don't know if she'd even want to see me again," he answers, the mere thought of those six years already haunting him again in his head.

I nestle myself against him again. "I think she'd love to see how much you've grown. If she never wanted to see you again, I think she would've stopped Vergus from taking you away that day."

"You might be right. I'd just rather not talk about it too much." He sighs.

My hand lands on his exposed wrist, replacing the comfort of that bracelet. "Then we'll talk about it whenever you want, if you want to."

His answer is an appreciative kiss on the top of my head.

I'm not going to push him to talk more. No one pushes me to talk about what happens in this very castle. I know how he felt, and I hope that might make it easier for me to fully understand his fears and panic attacks.

Nate's hand drifts to my necklace, moving the blue crystals inside. "This was your mom's necklace, right?"

"It was, why?"

"Ever wondered what the two crystals stand for?"

"No, what do you know about them?" I ask, my curiosity rising.

He lays the moon in his hand. "I read about this necklace in an ancient book. These two crystals represent the person who wears it, the light blue crystal, and their sole partner, their mate, the darker crystal. Mates, trapped together under a moon, stands for their will to survive, to get the other out, no matter what it would take from them." He plants a small kiss on my forehead. "I would do anything to get you back if you were ever taken. Anything."

"Then I hope Leanne doesn't have any plans to do something soon. I don't want you to burn down the castle," I say, entwining my fingers with his. "And if she did, don't make yourself a target for her. I won't break that easily anymore down there. But if I knew she went after you, I think I would."

Nate looks at me with something I'd call sadness in his eyes. "Dawn—"

I interrupt him. "I can handle Leanne. Just leave her to me."

He rests his forehead against mine. "You're my lifeline, Dawn. You're all I'll ever need to survive something."

I stare at him, into those loving eyes, and think of how lucky I am. How lucky I am to have this man as my lifeline, as my safe place. I will show him how grateful I am, how happy he has already made me these past years.

I slightly lift my head and place a faint kiss on his lips. "You're the only person who has ever made me feel this alive. Don't you dare leave me."

"I won't," he promises.

And as my eyelids droop, he whispers one last thing with a kiss on the scars on my wrist. "We're both broken, but together we can put those pieces back together."

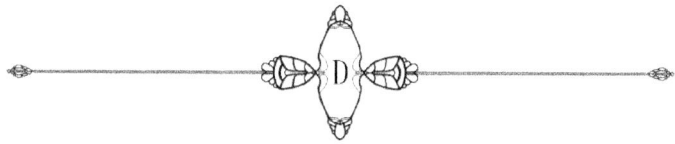

It's been over an hour since Dawn fell asleep, but sleep doesn't seem to grasp me. No matter how long I close my eyes, they'll eventually flutter back open.

It could be the adrenaline or happiness that my body is still full of.

Or the memories I revisited when I told her about that dark part of my life. The only person who knew what happened those years is Vergus. He has always given me free range in what I wanted to do with it. If I wanted to turn them in with the king, if I wanted to take matters into my own hands. But I always said no. Revenge wouldn't make me feel better, it would start eating on me from the inside.

They might've caused me immense misery, but I would not inflict it on them.

I wouldn't have been able to look at Dawn's peaceful face if I had killed them. I couldn't have looked at her innocent face without wanting to scream what I'd done.

So I let them be. I know Esmeralda is still alive. Her husband apparently died from some strange accident a couple of years ago.

She is also finally free of him, whether or not she loved him. He was a man that was never supposed to have a woman. Not in the way he treated her or me.

But it made me think those years what love really was, was it something that everybody carries with them? Or was it something that blossomed or grew when certain people met?

My mom used to say, *"Love is not made. It is always there. You just have to dig a little deeper to find it."*

And I dug deeper. I found the person I could love with my whole heart.

So I'll be damned if I let anything happen to her.

CHAPTER 19

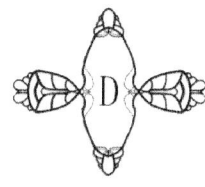

I awake, feeling rested. A thing I haven't felt in a long while. A thing I have longed for years.

An arm is draped over my stomach. Nate's arm, to be precise. I turn my head to find him sound asleep. Slow and steady breathing. His dark brown hair a mess from turning all night.

He woke me up a few times with his tossing and turning, but eventually settled down and fell asleep. A few faint whimpers cut through the silence of the night, telling me he had several nightmares.

I let my hand slide through his messy hair, moving aside the strands of hair covering his face. He looks peaceful now. Just sleeping without a worry on his mind.

I notice he left his bracelets off, his scars stark against the dark blanket. He was either too tired to put them back on or he felt safe enough to leave them off.

No matter the reason, I'm glad he even allowed me to see what had happened to him.

But as everything from last night sinks in, I untangle myself from Nate's arm and slide out of bed. I walk to his side of the bed and pull the blankets up to his shoulders.

Let him wake up when his body and mind are ready.

I tiptoe into the bathroom and when I look in the mirror, I finally see what last night did with me. Dark bags under my eyes, my hair looking like a bird's nest.

I brush and braid my hair and try to soften the bags under my eyes as well as possible.

I don't want to look completely sleep deprived.

Then I quietly change into my training leathers, slip on my belt, put on my shoes, and make my way out the door. Where I find Adrian leaning against the wall, twirling a throwing dagger in his hand.

He tenses as he hears the door open, but sags against the wall when he sees me. "Morning."

I softly close the door, and when I don't hear Nate wake up, breathe out. "Morning."

"May I ask where you're going?" He points the dagger at me.

"Just getting some fresh air. Can you make sure no one bothers him?" I say as I nod to the door.

"Of course, we wouldn't want to have a grumpy mate." He smirks.

I snatch the knife from his hand. "And you don't want me being grumpy either."

Throwing the knife across the hall, I embed it in between two bricks. "So, pretty please, let him sleep."

Adrian looks from me to the knife and back, mumbling, "Aye, aye, princess."

I sigh before walking towards the kitchen.

The halls are quiet, very few servants darting past me, but the kitchen is bustling with people. Cooks preparing large meals, servants bringing it to everyone in the castle. But my meal is sitting at the end of the counter, waiting for me, as it does every morning.

"Good morning, Leia," I call out to the head cook.

A spatula appears in the air. Her usual greeting.

"What's on the menu for tonight?" I ask, shoving a piece of egg into my mouth at the same time.

"Steak, potatoes, and vegetable soup, is that sufficient for Her Highness?" she responds with a wink.

"I'd rather have a full four course meal." I smirk.

"Definitely not happening," Leia retorts.

I finish my meal in five minutes, cleaning my mouth with a napkin, when I bring my plate to the dishwashers. "Thank you."

I get a thankful nod in response. Leia is flipping a pancake when I step in front of her at the other side of her workstation. "Have you seen Leanne this morning?" I ask.

Her pan stops abruptly, and a silence falls over the kitchen. I never ask for her. Never.

"Why do you ask?" she counters.

"Because I don't want to run into her today," I say as I put my hands on the edge of the counter.

Leia continues her pancakes before they turn black. The whole kitchen starts to move again in her wake. "Understandable. I think I saw her ride off this morning," she says. "And I think after last night congratulations are in order."

A blush creeps over my cheeks. "Thank you."

"Be happy with him, Dawn. Don't let anybody deny you that happiness, not even Her Majesty."

"I will. But if she dares touch him, she'll be dead on the floor within a second," I sneer, my magic heating the wooden counter beneath my hands. "She can do whatever the hell she wants with me, but she'll regret it if she goes after the others."

Leia suddenly points her spatula at my face, then at my hands. "Calm yourself down before you burn my kitchen to the ground."

I lift my hands from the counter, black burns in the shape of my hands cover the surface. "Sorry."

"Don't be. I can't even imagine what it must feel like to have so much power buzzing beneath your skin. Having to contain it every day," she says, a sweet look on her face. "But you'll get the hang of it. If I know one thing, it's that your father believed in you. The happiness that shone in his eyes whenever you were practicing, he knew you'd do great things when you got older."

"Thank you, Leia."

"Any time, sweetie," she whispers while flipping the pancake in the air. "Now go. Do whatever you need to do these days."

I snatch the pancake right from the air. "Will do." And run to the door. "Bye everyone."

A goodbye in unison sounds behind me as I round the corner, munching on my stolen pancake. Leia makes really good ones.

And as I roam the halls, not having any direction I want to go, my mind wonders what it might've been like if my parents were still with us today.

How the kingdom would've looked, how the spirit of our people would've been. I know everything got darker the moment the news came out. The whole town got quieter, maybe even more dangerous. Thieves started roaming the streets after dark, attacking anyone they came across. Patrols were multiplied for the night, trying to keep everyone safe.

It was as if my parents were the only tether keeping this kingdom together.

But I will not let this kingdom fall to ruin because someone decided they didn't want their king and queen around anymore. I will find who killed them and they'll pay. Pay dearly for what they took away from me.

When my thoughts float away from me, I finally look at where I am.

An oak door, the edges deeply cut from years of opening and closing it.

My dad's old office. Now Leanne's.

And Leanne is not present at this castle at the moment.

Time to hopefully get some answers.

The door mercifully opens without a sound. I quickly slip inside before locking it behind me.

It looks exactly the same as five years ago. That's how long I haven't been here. The giant bookcases still cover two out of four walls, all stacked to the rim with books. Various papers scattered across the gigantic desk, the sun coming from the window highlighting each one.

One paper in particular catches my attention, one holding the seal of Railon. Why would Leanne be in contact with Draven?

I walk to the desk, plop down on my dad's old chair, and read the letter.

And in all shock, drop it. I pick up the next one, also with Railon's seal and a similar message.

Leanne has been talking to Draven all this time. She's been lying even more than I thought she was. She's been talking about our armies, our trainees, annual events, everything. Draven knows everything.

That's how those soldiers got into that meeting a couple of weeks ago, why Leanne remained so calm, why she was gone in the blink of an eye when they attacked.

She was never in danger. Everybody else was. And she just casually moved on after I was stabbed.

This is at least one reason she has been so cold. But not enough.

I leave the papers and move on to the desk drawers. Pulling them all open one by one, three on my right, all filled with empty sheets, quills and ink.

The top two on the left are empty, the bottom one sends me reeling back in the chair.

I only catch a glimpse of the contents and I am scared to truly see what this drawer holds. I swallow that fear and creep closer. My hand grabs the handle and pulls the drawer open fully.

Showing a glass case with a bloodied dagger inside. I don't even need to feel it to know that this is an Alk blade. An Alk blade with my mom and dad's blood still on it.

Leanne never even bothered to clean it. She still holds onto it as if it is a trophy.

I reach out with a trembling hand and open the glass case. I grab the hilt and lift the blade to hold it in the sunlight. This very blade caused my dad so much pain before his death. Not just the fact that it was Alk, but that Leanne went for our mom first.

As if she wanted to hurt dad even more than she already would.

His scream is the one scream that haunts me the most. Not my own, not anybody else's, his. His loss. The suffering you could hear in his voice. No one deserves that.

I let my eyes trail the blade up and down, but there is nothing more than blood and Alk. Nothing more than the only thing that can kill the entire royal family if you have enough of it.

Not that there is much left of that family.

I carefully place the blade back and close the drawer. I take a deep breath before standing up, walking to the door, and leaving this room behind me.

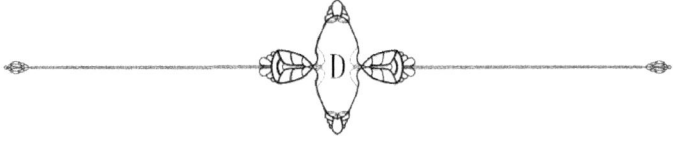

"I think I found out who killed you," I say, my knees on the cold stairs before my parents' grave. "I just don't know why. We had everything. She had everything she could wish for."

I drag my feet up the stairs and lay my hand flat against the giant tombstone. "But I'll get to the bottom of it. Just so you can rest peacefully."

My fingers trace my mom and dad's names, the stone freezing cold beneath my fingertips.

I should come here more often, just to maybe find peace. Find peace with the reality that they're gone, but that I can keep going. That I can make them proud.

Their grave was partially made by me. The large arch stretching over the entire staircase was the first thing I created after they placed the tombstone. I sat here all day, letting my magic, magic connected to theirs, cover over them one more time.

A couple weeks later, I made stone flowers that would always lay at the tombstone. I made roses, lilies, even daffodils. Until a whole bouquet of never dying flowers laid before me. Right now, it's just missing one last flower. A forget-me-not.

I reach for a small rock to my right. I wrap both my hands around it and let my magic form it into a beautiful flower. Leaf by leaf, it changes, a stem forming.

And as I open my hands, a perfectly shaped forget-me-not lays there. Five stone blue leaves.

I place it with the others, and promise myself I won't forget them, never. But I need to move on.

"I'll come back tomorrow, I promise," I whisper before walking down the stairs, back to the castle.

But a faint voice in the cemetery stops me in my tracks. I follow it and stop when I see Nate slumped against a for me unknown tombstone.

He's talking to it. And as I quietly approach, I see whose grave it is.

His parents'.

I didn't know they were buried here. But I'm glad they are. They deserve to lie here and not in a grave outside the walls.

I lean against a nearby tree and listen to his words.

"I found her, mom," he says. "And I couldn't be happier with who it is. I think I've always wished it was her. From the moment she walked into the forge, from the moment she got me to calm down, I had hoped it would be her." He puts his face in his hands. "She makes me happy, mom. I feel like I can breathe and not be afraid to be alone."

Together till the end, I whisper into his mind. I see him tense and open his eyes as he removes his hands from his face to find me leaning against the tree. *Or no end at all.*

"Together," he whispers as he gets up and says his goodbyes to his mom and dad.

He approaches me and wraps his arms around my waist. Only now I can see his puffy red eyes.

I let my hand drift to his cheek. "You've been crying," I say, my thumb stroking his cheek.

"I'm okay. Don't worry about me." His eyebrows knit together. "Where did you run off to this morning? I woke to a cold bed."

"I didn't want to wake you, so I went to get some breakfast." I glance down. "And then ended up in Leanne's office. Alone."

Nate's grip on my waist tightens. "What? Did she see you?"

"As far as I know, she did not. But I'm being careful today," I say as I put my arms around his neck. "I found some other things, too. I wanted to go to Jade and Madion with you to share everything."

He plants a kiss on my forehead, causing a smile to form on my lips. "Let's go then. I'm curious about what you found."

I put my head against his shoulder. "A lot, so it'll take a while to get through everything."

"No time to waste, then."

He grabs my hand and starts pulling us away from the cemetery. His gaze lingering on his parents' grave and mine on my parents'.

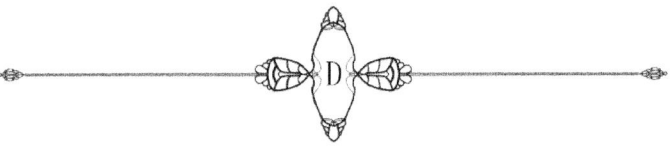

After a few knocks, the door finally opens. Revealing Jade seated on the couch, sewing something, and Madion in front of us, looking exhausted.

"Yes?" she says with a lazy smile. "What can we do for our newly mated couple?"

"We need to talk," I bluntly say.

Jade lays down her needle and moves herself to the table. "Go on."

Madion gestures for us to enter and then closes the door behind us. I take a seat next to Nate, and Madion sits across from me, taking the seat beside Jade.

I plant my elbows on the table, rest my head in my hands, and let out a deep sigh. "I got into Leanne's office this morning."

"What?" Madion blurts out.

"I was wandering through the castle and ended up at the door. I knew she wasn't anywhere close, so I went in. And I found some disturbing things," I answer.

"What did you find, Dawn?" Jade asks more insistently.

"Letters. A lot of letters, going between her and Draven."

A collective gasp sounds through the room. We expected a lot from Leanne, but not this.

"Did you read the letters?" Nate asks.

"Some of them. They were mostly about the size of our armies, how many trainees we get every month. Even dates for banquets and balls were shared."

"I can understand the army information, but why would he want to talk about balls and banquets?" Jade says, deep in thought as she looks down at the table. "Why are those important?"

Madion sighs. "Because at balls and banquets, people are least prepared to fight if an attack happens."

"So, should we prepare for an attack? He knows everything now," Nate questions.

I let my hand drift to his. "We can, but we can't do much yet. We know he can come, but not when."

He intertwines his fingers with mine. "We'll prepare the basics. Just extra weapons when we go somewhere."

"That's a good idea. There's nothing else we can do," Madion says.

I take a very deep breath. "I found something else, too."

All three of them eye me, like they can see the pain and grief in my eyes.

"I found the dagger," I say, my voice surprisingly even.

It takes a moment before they understand what dagger I'm talking about. Nate's hand immediately tightens around mine. Jade and Madion just stare at me.

"How do you know it's the one?" Jade asks carefully.

I let my other hand wrap around Nate's hand already holding mine, "Because the blood was still on there." I let my head rest on Nate's shoulder.

"Oh heavens," Jade and Madion simultaneously mumble.

Breathe. I don't want you to have a panic attack, Nate whispers between us when I hadn't even noticed my breathing had become shallow. I take deep breaths, my heart rate slows, and I calm back down.

"Did you take it with you?" Nate asks.

"No, I didn't want her to notice I had been there."

"Do you want to go back for it?"

"One day. But not now."

Good, just one step at the time with this, Nate says.

This can come in handy in certain situations, you know, I say back.

What kind of situations?

During fights, when I can't find you, or just to piss off Madion and Jade. I look up to find both of them glaring at me. *I think we already did that last thing.*

"It's rude to talk like that without involving us," Madion comments.

"You two have most likely been doing this for years behind our backs. So don't get grumpy now that we can do it, too," I retort.

Madion stares at me for another moment, before grunting, "Fine."

And that's the end of our conversation. We try to have fun for the rest of the afternoon.

And what tonight will bring, I have yet to find out.

CHAPTER 20

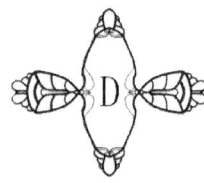

After dinner, Nate drops me off at my room. I decide to relax there and read a book. But when I open it, I'm met by another surprise.

Another sliver.

With trembling fingers, I fold it open and read:

~

I loved them as much as you did, little one.

~

Are they talking about mom and dad?

Once again, they used '*little one*'. Only dad and Leanne called me that.

I don't understand who is sending these. No one can slip into my room unseen, and no one would know I would pick up this book. So how do they get it in my room, and plant these notes in places I tend to look in the first ten minutes after I enter?

It's confusing to me. Are there good intentions here, or is this just a big joke to throw me off my game?

A knock sounds on my door, and a moment later Jake and Adrian enter, a sorrowful look on their faces.

"What's wrong?" I ask.

Jake clears his throat. "Leanne wants to see you."

A thousand thoughts rush through my mind. Did she find out I was in her office?

If she did, there is only one thing I can imagine she'll do to me.

"Lead the way." I motion to the door.

A minute later we arrive in front of the same door I was this morning. This time with a reason to be here.

One knock on the door makes it fly open, allowing me to enter. "I want to talk to Dawn alone. Everyone else can wait in the hallway," Leanne orders.

I nod to Adrian and Jake and walk into the office.

Leanne is sitting in her big chair behind the desk, pointing at the chair on the other side. I sit down and look her straight in the eyes.

"Let me start off by saying congratulations."

"Thank you." I incline my head.

"Onto other matters," she says, "Draven is moving in even closer. His army is growing more by the day behind those mountains."

Can't imagine why, when you've been trading secrets with him. That's what I say to myself, but I actually answer with, "And I can help with that, how?"

"You can help me figure out a plan to keep him at bay. If we work together, we can keep him away as long as possible."

"Okay, how can I help?"

Leanne leans forward and props her chin on her fist. "We can start by talking normally. Without either of us starting a fight."

"I can do that," I say, just to satisfy her.

"Good."

"Was that all?" I ask.

"I think so."

I stand up. "Good, then I'll head back to my room." And make my way to the door.

I reach out for the door handle, but bonds of air wrap around both my wrists, tugging me back.

"Let me stop you right there, dear sister." Leanne chuckles from behind her desk.

I try to move, but I'm stuck. "What are you doing?"

"I got some news about your whereabouts this morning," she muses.

"I was in bed this morning," I sneer at her.

"Not all morning," she snaps. "Don't think I am not informed when you do something. Especially when you decide to enter my office."

She gets up from her chair and stands in front of me. "You must already be running all scenarios of how tonight is going to go in your head." She snaps her fingers. "Guards."

The door opens behind me, and I feel strong hands wrap around my arms and wrists. I struggle in their grip, but a third guard joins them. The sound of the iron already triggering my nightmares. I suck in a sharp breath as the shackle snaps around my right wrist. Soon after, it finds its way around my left wrist.

"You know what the consequences are when you step out of line," Leanne whispers to me.

She releases the air bonds around my wrists now that they're secured with iron instead.

"Mom and dad would be so disappointed in you if they were to see this," I snap at her.

Leanne places her finger underneath my chin, urging me to look straight into her eyes. "It's good then that they're not around anymore to be disappointed, right?"

I want to lash out at that sentence. I want to beat her for it. But I'm dragged into the hallway before I can make another move.

Hearing a struggle behind me, I turn my head just enough to see Adrian and Jake being held down by six other guards.

"Let her go!" Adrian yells at them.

He gets one arm free, but it's immediately wrenched behind his back again.

"Adrian, don't," I say to him.

He looks up at me and once again pain shines in his eyes. "We're getting you out first thing in the morning.".

"I know you will," I say with a sad smile.

The guards haul me down the halls, not even giving me time to get my feet underneath me. I try to struggle, but it's to no avail.

I can't win from the six guards surrounding me while I'm in these shackles. I just can't.

The dungeon floors are cold as usual. Several prisoners filling up the cells on both my sides. The cell at the end of the hallway is unoccupied, as usual. It has become my private cell. Only I get to stay there.

I'm dropped onto the metal plate. My ankles are put close together, shackled, and then wrapped in chains. Giving me no way to even run out of here.

My wrists are freed, only to be restrained a second later with the thicker, more magically enforced shackles. Vergus' most regrettable creation.

I notice the collar in front of me too, but I don't let my attention linger on it. Let them forget it, please let them forget it.

My prayers are unfortunately dismissed when the youngest and kindest looking guard picks it up as he squats in front of me. "I'm sorry," he mumbles as he swipes my hair aside and snaps the collar around my neck.

My magic completely vanishes. Retreating so deep into my soul, I can barely feel it. My breath seizes and all the men step back. Not knowing what could happen.

They leave one by one, the kindest one lingering for another moment before slamming the cell door shut behind him.

Now I slump to the floor, at the awful feeling that spreads through my body when my soul and magic are subdued. It feels unnatural. My body is made to hold large amounts of magic, not to be completely stripped of it.

When I lay my head on the floor, I think about tomorrow morning. Adrian said Jake and him will come first thing in the morning.

Then my thoughts wander to somebody else.

Nate.

What will he do when he can't find me?

Please, be careful Nate. I can't have you get hurt for wanting to protect me.

My breathing speeds up again, and it does not slow down. I can't have a panic attack down here again. I want to make it through the night. Not pass out from the sheer panic that is making my body numb.

As my vision darkens around the edges, I try to reach out to him. But without my magic and with the fear coursing through my veins, I can't.

Then my vision almost completely blackens out and I try to reach him one last time.

But as my mind slips away into unconsciousness, I fail.

I'm met by darkness and my night is filled with nightmares.

CHAPTER 21

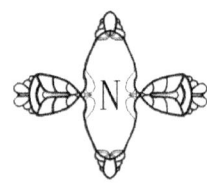
"Where is she?" I shout through Jade and Madion's living room.

Dawn was not in her room this morning. And every guard and servant I asked ignored me or ran away.

Madion pushes her finger into my sternum. "Calm down right now."

"I will calm down when you tell me where she is," I sneer at her.

"Leanne called her to her office last night," Jade says, trying to diffuse the tension.

And then it crashes down on me about what happened. She found out that Dawn was in her office yesterday.

"No," I whisper. Not again.

I hadn't seen her the last time she came out, but I could still see the haunted look in her eyes days after she spent a night down there.

I know I have had that look in my eyes too, when Vergus got me out of that basement. I was mute for over a month before he finally got me to talk.

"No," I say, livid.

I turn around and reach for the door. But a hand wraps around my wrist. I glance over my shoulder and find Madion looking me straight in the eyes.

"You will not get her out acting like this. You'll make her panic if you stomp into that dungeon," she states.

And she's right. I can't rush in there like this. With a sharp inhale, I try to get rid of the lingering anger. "I'll be gentle with her."

"You better," Madion says as she releases my wrist. "Now go get her out. She needs you."

After a quick nod, I open the door and start walking to the castle. Leanne better be somewhere on the other side of that castle, because if I bump into her, she's dead.

I reach the stairs to the dungeons in minutes and I'm down them in less than five seconds. A guard immediately perks up and stands in my way.

"Who are you? You are not allowed to come here," he says, but my hand is already around his throat.

"Keys, now," I order him.

"Why do you need the keys?" the guard chokes out.

I hear more people coming from the stairs. My hand is filled with my magic and pointed at them before I can even think of what I'm doing.

Adrian and Jake come rushing down the stairs, but stop in their tracks when they see me.

"Nate, let him go. The keys are right over there." Jake points to my right. To the keys, dangling from a ring embedded in the wall.

I squeeze tighter. "No, they locked her up again and did nothing to stop Leanne."

"Nate, they have no right to go against her orders. We're powerless when Leanne wants her down here," Adrian says, his voice unsteady from frustration and maybe even sadness.

I drop my hand to my side, but the other remains around the guard's neck.

I know they can't do anything, but I want them to do something. I want them to stand at Dawn's side and not listen to Leanne.

Something rustles behind me, but I pay it no attention.

"Nate," a weak voice mutters. "Please, don't hurt him. He did nothing wrong."

I let go of the guard and turn around to find Dawn laying on her side, restrained with chains and shackles. I grab the keys and run to her cell door. My hands are shaking as I jam the key into the lock and swing the door open.

Dropping to my knees in front of her, my hands immediately find her face. "Hey."

Her hands try to reach for mine, but they're tied too close to the ground. I fumble with the keys when a hand lands on mine.

"Let us help," Adrian offers.

He takes over the keys and frees Dawn's wrists, and then takes off the collar.

That goddamn collar.

He hands the keys to Jake, who's taking care of the chains and shackles on her legs.

Dawn's arms fling around my neck. My hand digs into her hair, the other presses her tightly against me. "You're okay. I'm here now. I'm sorry I wasn't."

"Shh, you couldn't have known," she says as the last shackle falls to the ground. At the same time, her grip on me tightens. Her magic is returning like a flood and she's trying to hold it all in.

"We need to get her out of here," I state to the men now staring at us.

They both get up and wait for me to exit the cell with Dawn. I help her off the floor, her arms not leaving my neck, before lifting her in my arms. She's trembling when we reach the top of the stairs and make way to the front doors. I'm not letting her stay in this castle for one more minute.

Adrian and Jake move past me to open the giant front doors. Guards on either side point swords at us, but one look from me makes them look the other way.

"Where are we going?" Dawn mumbles.

"To my house," I respond.

"I don't think I've been there before," she whispers.

I place a kiss on her hair. "You'll love it."

Jake and Adrian are still trailing after us as the crowd in the streets parts for us. Several gasps ring in my ears, but most people stay quiet. They're used to this, used to this sight the mornings after.

I see my house in the distance. Just a small cottage with a living room, kitchen, bathroom, and one bedroom.

Enough for just me. And now for Dawn. too. She is not going back to that castle if she doesn't want to.

Adrian opens the door, and I immediately take a turn right into the bathroom. I don't have a shower, so the bath will hopefully be enough.

I set her down on the rim of the tub as Adrian and Jake follow us in.

"I got her," I say to them, my hands never leaving Dawn's.

"We'll let the girls know that you're both here," Jake says.

I give them a nod before they turn away. A moment later, I hear the front door slam shut.

Only then do I let go of Dawn's hands and let the tub fill with water. I help her undress down to her underwear. Swinging her legs over the rim, I let her slide right into the tub. She sighs in relief as she submerges in the water. She pulls up her knees, wraps her arms around them and lays her head on them. Taking slow and steady breaths, I can see her magic slowly creeping back.

"Please, sit behind me," she pleads to me.

I take off my shirt, pants, and shoes before I let myself sink into the water. My legs on either side of Dawn, my arms leaning on the edge of the tub. Waiting until she wants to make a move.

And she does. She lies on her side against my chest. One of her hands gripping my bracelet, the other laying flat on my chest. Her eyes closed, listening to my heartbeat and breathing.

I fold my free arm around her shoulders.

And we just lay there, floating in the water, savoring the calm and quiet. We don't have to say anything to speak a thousand words.

But after a while, I have a question. "Why is it water that helps you?"

Dawn lets out a breath, clenching my bracelet even tighter. "I figured it out after she locked me up for two days and I was about to explode."

"And you found out by just jumping in the water?" I say, trying to lighten the mood.

It earns me a chuckle. "No, I had done it in a way before in my room. But this time, I had to run to Madion and Jade's house because my room was closed off for no apparent reason. They put me under their shower and the pain, the tension, just everything that hurt, went away," she explains. "So ever since then, I either go to my own room, or I go to them if I can make it. And after a while, I figured out why the water helped. It felt like my mom or dad was rubbing soothing circles on my back, just like they used to do when I was younger."

"Well, from now on you can come here too if you need to. The door is always open," I promise her.

"Thank you."

"Don't thank me, Dawn. You're my mate and my best friend. I'll always be here."

She lets go of my bracelets and closes her eyes while I gently stroke her hair. Letting my magic spread across the water when I feel it heating up from an upcoming outburst. Her magic quickly calms when it feels mine and entangles with it.

I feel her relax even more, to a point where she almost falls asleep. "Why don't we move to the bed? Sleeping in a tub tends to get uncomfortable."

A small smile forms on her lips. "Okay."

She sits up and sways slightly but steadies herself with the rim. I pull my legs back and stand up. The water disappears through the now open hole at the bottom of the tub. I reach for the two towels I laid out earlier and wrap one around Dawn's chest. Then I step out, wrap one around my waist and help her out.

We cross the living room to the bedroom. I hand her a shirt, underwear, and some pants. Then I grab some pants for myself and wait in the living room.

Moments later, she emerges. The clothes are too big for her, but they're good enough for now.

"Come on, let's get you to bed," I say as I approach her. She nods and turns back to the bedroom.

She plops down and lays back on the pillows. I throw the blanket over her and lie next to her. She turns on her side and gazes at me.

"What?" I say when I look at her.

"Nothing. I just didn't expect you to come."

"Why not?"

"You didn't even know where I was."

I put on an innocent smile. "I might've yelled at Madion for a bit."

She slaps me on the bicep. "You could've just kindly asked her, you know."

I rub my arm. She slaps pretty hard. "I panicked when I couldn't find you."

"The next time you can't find me, you either reach out with your soul." She pokes me in the chest. "And if I don't respond to that, you can yell at Madion, okay?" she says.

"Fine."

Together till the end, she whispers between us.

We'll stay together, no matter what.

Or no end at all, I respond.

She shuffles closer. I let my arm be a pillow for her head and wrap the other around her.

"Rest. I'll wake you when it's time to eat something," I whisper in her ear.

But she's already out. Sleep claims me soon after, too.

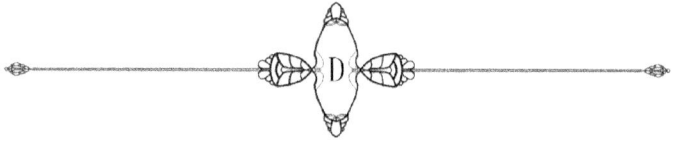

I wake to the door of the bedroom being swung open. One figure sprints inside and lands on Nate and me, the other just casually strolls in.

Jade lands on my legs, and I let out a grunt of pain. "Careful with the legs, please."

She climbs off them. "Why?"

"They're sore from being wrapped in chains all night," I say, untangling myself from Nate's arms.

"Oh."

"Don't worry, you couldn't know," I reassure her.

Madion sits cross-legged at the end of the bed. "Was he still angry when he got you out?" she asks, her eyes fixed on Nate.

"He started choking a guard to give him the keys, while they were literally hanging from the wall to his right. But Adrian and Jake came to help him," I say, glancing at Nate, who is blushing from embarrassment.

And Madion gives him a look. "You and I. Training court, right now."

She steps off the bed, walks into the living room, and comes back moments later with Nate's sword and three daggers. She throws all three daggers at Nate, circling them around his head in the wall. His sword she neatly lays on the end of the bed. "If you want to lose some anger, you can come to me. So, as I said, training court, now."

And with that, she leaves. I look at Nate. His face is as pale as can be, as he mumbles, "She's going to kill me."

I look at Jade on my other side, and we burst out laughing. Nate sits up and pulls the daggers from the wall. I push Jade off the bed and get out myself.

"I brought you some clothes, too," she says, pulling a stack from her bag and handing it to me.

I stash them under my arm. "Thank you."

Nate stands in front of his dresser, digging through his clothes. I give him a kiss on the cheek before retreating to the bathroom to change.

I change out Nate's comfortable clothing for my tight training outfit. Then I clip my sword to my belt, sheath my daggers, and tie my hair up. Let's see if my magic wants to come out and play.

Jade is lounging on the couch by the time I emerge from the room. Nate is in the kitchen making himself tea.

"Are you ready to go?" Jade asks as she perks up from the couch.

Nate turns around, still sipping from his cup. He looks at me with raised eyebrows as I hold in my laugh. "What?"

"You look cute when you're drinking tea like that." I smirk.

He almost chokes and quickly puts away the tea. "Let's go."

I laugh even harder and grab his hand before he exits the house. Jade trails behind us, but after we pass one street, I grab her hand too.

Together we stroll through the town, all the way to the other side of the castle, to the training court.

Madion is already waiting, tapping a dagger against her thigh impatiently. "Took you all long enough."

"You know how slow these two dress themselves," Nate says, but falls silent when Madion glares at him.

She stands up. "I know you are not the fastest either, dear Nate." She gestures to her right. "The circle. You know how it works."

I give him a pat on the shoulder. "Good luck."

"Thank you for the vote of confidence," he grumbles.

Then he unsheathes his sword and stalks to the circle.

Madion has her sword already pointed at him, while Jade and I take a seat near the side.

"The next time you get angry at me, Nate, think twice. You can come to me with anything, you know that, but not to yell at me for something I don't have control over," she says, motioning him to take a defensive stance. "I know this is all new to both of you, but try to not let it come out like this. I know you two will be more protective of each other. Jade and I are the same, but we don't let it affect others."

Nate lets out a sigh. "I know, and I'm sorry for yelling at you. I just panicked when I couldn't find Dawn and took it out on you."

"Apologies accepted," she says, "but I'm still going to beat your ass for it."

"Great," Nate mutters under his breath.

Nate and Madion circle each other as Jade whispers in my ear, "Want to bet that Madion takes him out in two minutes?"

I look at the concentration on Nate's face, that unwavering focus on Madion and her sword.

"I say Nate takes her out in less than two."

"Deal," Jade says, right before Madion and Nate clash.

Steel sparks and breathing quickens. Jade's eyes are fixed on Madion's movements, trying to see if she'll win or lose this bet. I know I'm not losing, because I know what Nate can do when he gets this deep into his focus. Almost as if he triggers some kind of survival instinct.

He'll win.

She blocks an attack from above but doesn't have enough time to block Nate's dagger coming from below. She tries to jump over it, but it nicks her ankle, and she goes down.

Jade gasps at the sight of Madion, almost undefeated, going down. She lands flat on her back, gasping for air as Nate points his sword at her chest.

"Do I win?" he asks.

Madion props herself on her elbows. "Definitely not."

Her sword is up before I even register it.

She slams into Nate, who stumbles back. His dagger clatters on the stones, but a new one is almost immediately in his hand.

Madion brings her sword down, again and again. Nate stands strong against her, his sword groaning under the strain though.

Madion reels her sword back for the final blow, but Nate is ahead of her. He swings his to her ribs. Madion deflects on time by a mere second. But the move brings her off balance, giving Nate the opportunity to knock her down again.

He brings up his arm and knocks her in the face with his elbow, causing a nosebleed. Madion grabs for her nose, most likely broken. It'll heal within the hour, but it has only pissed her off more.

Madion tries to do her signature move, but Nate has seen it so many times that when Madion wants to turn, he slams the pommel of his sword into her back and brings her down. She lands on her stomach, Nate on top of her, pinning her arms behind her back.

"Do I win now?" he asks, knowing he outsmarted Madion this time. And only this time.

Madion struggles beneath him. "If you let go." She looks in my direction, "Otherwise you'll be fighting someone else too."

But she's not looking at me, she's looking at Jade. Who is looking mad, either at the fact that Nate has her mate pinned beneath him, or that I won our bet.

Nate lets go of Madion and gets off her.

Madion immediately jumps up and stands in front of Nate. They're about the same height so she can stare him right in the eyes.

Then, in the blink of an eye, she whacks him upside the head. Nate looks at her in disbelief, clutching his head. Madion's face slowly shows a smile. "Good work."

He smiles sheepishly. "Thank you."

Madion cradles her nose. "But try not to break my nose the next time."

"Sorry."

She waves him off and sits beside Jade, who immediately inspects Madion's nose. Nate walks to my side and wraps an arm around my waist. I immediately melt into him.

"You did great," I say to him, sliding my arm around his waist in return.

"Thank you."

"Nate," Jade starts, "why don't you come help us train the next batch of soldiers we're getting next week? I think you could teach them a thing or two."

Nate is quiet for a moment. I rub his back when I feel his heartbeat quicken.

"You don't have to decide right now," Madion wheezes. Her nose is clogged with blood. "You can come whenever you feel ready for it."

Nate inhales deeply and exhales. "I'd love to come next week." His hand finds mine behind my back and gives it a squeeze.

"Dawn." Jade points her attention to me as she grabs her weapons. "You up for it, or are the legs still too sore?"

I let go of Nate, grab my daggers, and walk to the circle. "I will never be too sore to beat you."

I indicate her to get over here. She gives Madion a quick kiss and takes a fighting stance in front of me.

"Magic or no magic?" she asks.

"Mine might've been suffocated all night, but that doesn't mean you suddenly got stronger than me," I retort, feeling my magic responding to my comment.

"Just you wait. I have some new tricks I want to try," she responds.

"Bring it on," I taunt her.

The second the words leave my mouth, Jade drops her sword, her dagger remains in her other hand. What is she planning?

I glance at Madion, but her face is blank. Either not knowing what Jade has planned or she does not want to betray her plans.

"Jade?" I mumble, adjusting the grip on my sword.

She's going to lash out suddenly. Jade closes her eyes and takes a deep breath. I feel the ground underneath us shaking as she does so.

Jade kneels to pick up her sword, and when she lifts it an inch from the ground, I strike. But this time my blow doesn't land.

My hands are lodged behind me, not moving an inch. I look to my right to find my sword and hand covered and wrapped up in earth. I glance to my left and find the same scene. She used my own trick against me, but she can't even control earth. Only water and air.

"You used my own tricks against me? How?" I question her, trying not to notify her of my magic creeping through all the cracks she left in the bindings.

She squats down, the tip of her sword digging into the ground. "I might not use the earth, but if I channel water and air precisely right, I could mimic the same thing you did."

"Clever," I say with a grin. "But not clever enough."

I push all the air I gathered between the cracks and let it expand in seconds. The earth explodes outward. My sword knocks her aside, opening an opportunity for me to bind her down completely. Her hands next to her head, her feet together, and her waist pinned to the ground. She plasters the same look on her face she had when I first did this. Complete and total rage.

I casually saunter over, looking at Nate's proud face and the growing smirk on Madion's. I kneel at Jade's side. She turns her head to me and snaps, "Screw you."

I pat her on the head. "Love you too."

"I really thought I finally had you." She sighs.

She wriggles her hands and feet, but me being able to control the earth makes it a lot more difficult for her to break free. I don't leave the cracks she had to leave because of her combination of water and air influencing the earth.

"You'll get me, eventually," I say and release my hold on her.

She props herself on her elbows. "Promise me one thing. If we ever go to war, both of you will be on our side." She looks at Nate and then back at me.

"Why wouldn't we be?" Nate asks her curiously, his head cocked slightly to the side.

"I don't know, it just popped into my head," she says as she sits up. "And the only time I will fight my friends is during training."

She holds out her hand to me. "We either fight together or I won't fight at all."

I smile down at her and grab her hand. "Only together."

The rest of the afternoon we talk and show off tricks we fabricated.

I try to teach them mine, but they can't get it just right to hold me down, not even all three at once. Nate comes close, though, but I could throw him off with some effort.

We'll get there.

And if we ever go to war, I'll be right there fighting beside them.

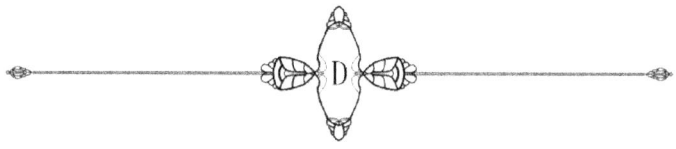

It's already dark when I reach my room. No Leanne in the hallways, luckily, but I am met with another surprise.

A dark blue envelope on my bed.

The third trial.

I drop my weapons on the floor and walk to the bed. The letter is out of the envelope in seconds.

~

Dawn Maria Rowena Sungust,
We hereby summon you for your third trial.
We expect you at the mountain vault in three days.
Death comes for us all. Some just have to go sooner than others.

~

What—What does that last sentence mean?

I sit on the bed and open my nightstand drawer to throw the letter on top of the others, but then my eyes fall on the three smaller pieces of paper. The weird slivers I keep finding in the most random places and times. But I can't seem to figure out who sent them and why.

Little one is something only my dad or Leanne called me. But it couldn't be my dad, no matter how much I wish it was. And I doubt Leanne would send me these notes instead of just screaming it at me.

It is someone that loved my parents just as much as I did. The only person I keep thinking of stays the same.

Leanne.

Yet it makes little sense, and the more I think about it, the more confused I get.

I slam the drawer shut and storm into the bathroom. I untie my hair, let it fall over my shoulders and throw water in my face. Bracing my hands on the sink, I look in the mirror at my tired face. Sometimes I wish everything would just be over. The trials would be done, no threat of a war, no more nights in the dungeons. Just me, my friends, and peace.

I put my pajamas on and crawl under the covers. But it feels empty, the whole bed feels empty without him. Since the bond snapped in place, I haven't even slept without him beside me, and only now I see how much I actually need him there.

I clench the covers in my hand and close my eyes. Giving sleep the chance to take me, but it won't. Tossing for what feels like the entire night until I hear a loud thump outside.

On my balcony, to be precise.

A moment later, a knock sounds on the glass doors.

I jump from the bed, reaching for my dagger with one hand, the other pooling with magic. I creep closer to the doors. It's now completely quiet on the other side.

I let the curtains open slightly with a gust of wind, and when I see the eyes and hair of the perpetrator behind them, I tug the doors open. "I thought someone was coming to finish me off."

Nate leans casually against the door frame. "I would never kill off my beautiful mate."

I give him a flat stare. "What are you doing here?"

"I couldn't sleep," he mumbles as he rubs the back of his neck. "I'm sorry if I woke you."

I extend my hand to him. "Come on."

He grabs it. So I pull him inside and close the doors behind us. He takes off his shirt before creeping under the blankets with me. I immediately lay against him as close as possible.

"I couldn't sleep either," I whisper, pulling his arm around me.

He tightens his arm around me and kisses me on my head. "Now we can both sleep."

I smile. I smile at the man I have with me. The man that was already there before I even knew we were connected like this.

A man I've loved since the moment he showed me. It was not pathetic to show my fears.

A man I've loved since the moment he showed me what it truly means to be loved.

CHAPTER 22

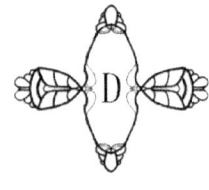

"We're going to the mountains," I say, holding the letter in front of Nate's sleepy eyes.

He rubs his hand down his face. "What?" Then he grabs the letter and reads it over. "Why would we need to go to the mountains?"

"Do you think I know? I only know that I have to pack warm clothes and a lot of weapons. Departure is tomorrow, by the way," I add, running my fingers through his wild hair.

He relaxes under my touch. "Then why don't we lay down for a bit longer?" Nate then runs his hand through my hair, too. "And tell all of this to the other half of our group in the afternoon."

He turns me over and presses my back against his chest, his arms completely enveloping me. "Because I am not ready to share you with the others yet."

I try to wriggle free as he buries his face in the nape of my neck. "That tickles."

He moves a hand under my armpit, tickling me even more. I laugh and try to push him off, but he's too strong. "Nate, stop it!"

"Never. I want to hear your laugh," he whispers. "It makes me happy."

I squirm in his grasp and laugh as he continues, under my feet, my armpits, my neck. I try to slap him off, but he just holds tight.

He stops tickling me when I finally manage to turn to him. "You make me happy," he mutters.

Putting my hands on his chest, I look up at him. "Glad to be of service."

Then a thought comes into my mind, and I ask him, "Do you maybe want to stay here every night? I know we both sleep better that way. At least I haven't slept this well for a while."

"I'd love to."

"I do think I'm going to have to ask permission," I say. "But I'll ask for it, and if she says no, I'll just come and live with you."

Nate kisses the tip of my nose. "I don't care where we live, as long as we are together."

"Good. You're not getting rid of me anymore." I smile as I nib at his nose.

He wraps me in a tight hug and pulls the blankets back over us.

We stay in our warm cocoon for a long while. Occasionally exchanging a few words, but other than that, we just lay here. We even fall asleep again at some point.

A while later, I wake to Nate snoring loudly. I want to push my pillow in his face, like I promised myself I'd do after he threw those pillows at me, but I don't. He'll panic if I do.

I shake his shoulder, but he wakes to the door of the room being swung open instead.

Nate and I sit up as the other half of our group enters. Jade and Madion look at us for a moment before sighing.

"Of course he's here," Madion grunts, voicing something like annoyance.

"What's wrong?" I ask.

Madion waves me off. "Nothing. We heard of the location of the trial and wanted to pick up Nate and come to you. But of course he is already here. Since when is he here, anyway?"

"Last night," Nate bluntly says.

"Last night—" Jade narrows her eyes as she looks us over. "You two didn't do the dirty, did you?"

I lift my hand, a pillow in my hand. "I dare you to say that again."

Nate snatches the pillow from my hand and throws it at Jade's head. She jumps out of the way but crashes right into the uncomfortable chair I still didn't turn back around.

"Why do you still have this one?" she questions, picking some flint off the armrest.

I look at Nate, who gives me a questioning look. "Because Nate here likes to sleep in it."

He looks at me even more confused until it dawns on him. He gives me a lazy smile before he tickles me again. "If I remember correctly, you threw the same pillow at my head that morning."

After a minute or so, he stops. I'm breathing heavily when I look at Jade and Madion, both with a big smile on their face. "What?"

"It's good to see both of you this happy," Madion says, the genuine smile on her face not faltering.

I smile at Nate. He grins down at me and touches his forehead to mine. *I'm really happy,* he whispers between us.

Me too.

The room is quiet for a moment before Jade, as usual, interrupts. "Okay, enough with the mushy love. We have bags to pack."

I shove myself to the edge of the bed. The floor is cold when my toes hit it. Nate steps out of bed and throws the curtains open. Flooding the room with sunlight.

"I'm going to fill my bags, and then head into the woods," I say. "I want to ask if Yuno will join us."

"Doesn't Leanne still hate Yuno?" Madion asks, now leaning on the armrest of the chair Jade is seated in.

"Yuno is not allowed within the walls, but since we're moving away from them, I see no reason I shouldn't let her tag along."

"Fair point." She agrees.

I know Leanne might still loathe Yuno, but this is one of my ways to bend her rules. She never said Yuno couldn't travel with us. She only said she could not roam inside the walls.

"Shall we meet at the front gates later?" Jade says.

"Definitely," I answer.

Nate kisses my forehead before following Jade and Madion out the door.

I throw open the balcony doors to let the wind flow through my room. I make my bed, rearrange all the pillows. Including the pillow that landed in the corner of my room when it flew at Jade's head. When that's all done. I move to my clothing.

Mountains tend to be cold, right? I haven't been there in years. I remember the vault as a big hole in the ground. Tournaments or fights would be held there. Sometimes the toughest criminals would have to fight against animals. And now I have to go there, with the last sentence of the letter in the back of my head.

Death comes for us all. Some just have to go sooner than others.

The only thing I know is that no one is dying. No one else.

I pack warm clothes, underwear and a coat. Anything I'd need. I put the bag at my door and place most of my weapons beside it. Those weapons are going to be fastened to either me or Lio.

You never know who would dare to attack a group with two royals at the head of it.

Now let's see what Yuno is up to. I haven't seen her in so long.

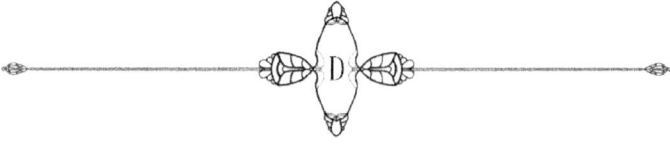

"Yuno!" I call out across the plane. She's always around here somewhere.

I don't get a response though, and my worry rises. She always comes when I call out to her.

I walk towards the thick forest in front of us. "Yuno, this is not funny. Where are you?" I shout.

I bat leaves and branches away, opening a path. Rustling sounds all around me, yet still no sign of her.

Her home should be around here somewhere. It's a small cave near the waterfall. Which I spot in the distance, with nothing seemingly out of place. The waterfall is quiet as usual, an occasional fish jumping out of the water.

My approach to the cave is careful and slow. I have no idea if she's even here. I squat in front of the entrance. "Yuno?" I say, my words resounding through the whole cave.

I jump back at the snarl that answers me. She'd never do that. I squint my eyes to look further into the cave and I'm not met by Yuno's beautiful yellow eyes.

I'm met by bright red eyes.

On near silent paws, the gendril exits the cave, slowly closing in on me. I walk backwards, my eyes never leaving theirs, but I stumble over a branch and fall flat on my ass.

The gendril strikes. He jumps on top of me, his teeth snapping inches from my face.

Nothing I say will change this situation. The gendril opens his mouth, breathing heavily on me. This is where I either get hurt very badly, or where I draw my final breath.

The gendril is a second away from ripping out my throat when a familiar growl sounds from behind me.

Yuno.

She barks at the one on top of me and he immediately backs off.

Her shadow falls over me a moment later, and Yuno licks my face.

"I missed you too." I chuckle. "But I already showered, Yuno."

She stops and walks over to who I think is her partner. Yuno growls shortly at him, making him bow his head in submission. She has him covered, good.

I dust myself off and get back on my feet. "I was going to ask if you wanted to join me on a trip to the mountains for my third trial."

Yuno eyes me for a moment, then looks at her companion, then back at me.

She walks over and sits in front of me. We stare at each other, and I do not know what she wants until she lets her nose touch mine.

Our sign of agreement.

"I'm glad you're joining me. What about your friend?" I ask, looking past her to the red-eyed male eyeing us.

She shakes her head. He's staying here.

"Okay. Meet me tomorrow at the edge of the woods. I don't want you coming too close to the walls of the town."

She again lets our noses touch.

"I'll see you tomorrow," I breathe.

I scratch her head, and she lays it against my chest. Eventually, the male carefully approaches me. He sniffs everything on me. And when he eyes the relaxed state Yuno is in, he lays down next to me. I slowly lower my other hand to him, letting him sniff it before I scratch his head, too.

We sit there, listening to the rush of the waterfall, listening to the birds, and relax.

These upcoming days are going to be stressful enough.

CHAPTER 23

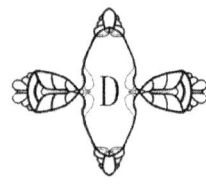

I'm riding Lio, with Nate next to me on his horse, and Madion and Jade right behind us. Leanne is a couple of rows ahead of us, surrounded by several guards. Our company is not the largest you could come across, but definitely not harmless.

"You know, Nate. You snore," I say to him.

Nate gives me a disappointed look. "You don't even want to know what you sound like while you sleep, and that is saying something when we've only slept in the same room like four times."

I wink at him, but immediately sigh after. "Why are these rides always so boring?"

"Because the only thing you can do is sit and talk to whoever is beside, in front or behind you," he answers with a sigh of his own.

He reaches for my hand, and I grab his.

Are you sure this isn't just nerves talking? he asks.

I squeeze his hand. *I'm okay. Those nerves will come sooner or later, though.*

You've got this. You aced the first two trials, you can finish the final two as well.

"Are we always this mushy and in love, too?" I hear Jade whisper to Madion behind me.

"I think we might be even worse than this at times," she whispers back.

"Damn right you two are," I say, glancing over my shoulder. "Remember the broom closet? Because I still remember that all too well."

Jade sneers at me, "Dawn, I swear I'll push you off that horse. I don't care about all those guards around us."

"I think you should care if you don't want a sword at your throat," I say provokingly.

She grumbles, "I'll get you one day."

"Sure you will," I taunt her as I refocus on the road ahead.

We've been riding for almost two days now and the trial starts tomorrow morning. Two days that my nerves have been skyrocketing. I might say that I have them under control, but everyone can see that I do not have them under control.

However, holding Nate's hand, or even just talking to him, calms me down. Which is almost everything we've been able to do these past days.

Also, making sure Lio doesn't stress himself out over a leaf that is hanging out of line has been a challenge. I really should take him out more. He's getting scared way too easily and I don't want him to hurt himself or me.

Yuno has been walking either beside me or very close by, moving through the trees. And the occasional look from Leanne forces her to move to the surrounding woods every couple of hours.

The rest of the morning is quiet. Yuno joins my side as we finally approach our campsite. Several tents have already been set up by the scouts we sent ahead yesterday evening. Mine is close to the forest's edge. Madion and Jade are a couple of tents over, and Nate is sleeping with me.

That makes me realize I still have to talk to Leanne about a certain situation.

I dismount Lio and hand him over to a caretaker. Then I follow Leanne's path and match my steps with hers as I walk next to her.

"Sister," I say, to get her attention.

She keeps her eyes straight ahead. "Dawn. How are the nerves?"

"Manageable, for now," I answer, she momentarily looks at me.

"Good," she says before she looks at me. "Now, I don't think you're here for idle chit-chat."

"No, I am not," I admit. "I'm here to ask for permission."

She comes to a full stop. "Asking for permission. You? Just like you asked for permission to bring your beast along." She throws an angry look in Yuno's direction. Who is laying next to Madion and shows her teeth in response.

"I ask for permission for things happening inside the walls, not outside of them."

"Okay. What do you want?"

I take a deep breath, preparing myself for a no. "I wanted to ask if Nate is allowed to live at the castle from now on."

She crosses her arms over her chest and looks at me. Then leans in even closer, but I don't back down.

"Okay." Is her answer.

I'm taken aback at first. Saying okay just like that doesn't happen often. I would almost call it unique.

"Wait, that easy?" I blurt out.

She places a hand on my shoulder, a cold, almost unbearable feeling, and says, "He's your mate, Dawn. What happens between mates is not something I'm going to come between."

"Thank you," I say, letting the gratitude show in my eyes.

"Don't thank me, just go to him. Be happy while you still can."

"I will."

She lets her hand drop to her side, and I walk away. But something just doesn't feel right. Something feels off, yet I can't put my finger on it.

"Dawn," Leanne calls out after me.

I turn around. "Yes?"

"A word of advice. I would stay close to the camp while we're here. Especially at night." She gestures to the woods on our right. "Dark things tend to roam these woods."

I swallow. "Thank you for the advice."

She nods and resumes her way to her tent. I walk over to Nate and let him wrap his arms around me.

"Hey, what's wrong?" he breathes against my hair.

"She said yes."

"That's great." He pulls me away from his chest and gives me a prodding look. "Something is still wrong. Talk to me."

"She was too forthcoming. She said yes too easily. It felt wrong."

He grabs my hand and kisses my knuckles. "Lets not think too much of it right now, no stressing."

"Okay. Let's see the interior of our hideout." I grin at him.

He pulls me along towards the tent. "Is that what we're calling it now?'

I bat the opening flaps aside and I'm amazed by the space on the inside. "I'm still calling it a hideout."

I jump on the bed and let myself sink into the pillows. But get up immediately when I feel my dagger stab into my side. I pull it out of the sheathe and toss it on the table at the end of the bed.

"Dawn?" Nate says from the entrance of the tent, not having moved an inch since I dropped onto the bed.

"Yes?" I mumble, my head now buried in a pillow.

"I wasn't finished with you when Jade and Madion interrupted us a couple of days ago," he says, walking to my side of the bed.

I pull the pillow away from my face and stare at him. "What do you mean?"

He throws his jacket off and drops his sword on the floor. "I wasn't done cuddling yet."

As he throws himself on the bed, I yell at him not to fall on me. He has his arms around me before I even see them coming. "Come here," he whispers.

He pulls the blanket around us, making a cocoon of warmth again, and trails a series of kisses down my neck, my forehead, and even my nose.

"I like this," I whisper, stroking my finger over his arm.

"Me too." He pulls me tighter. "Why don't we just lay here all afternoon to just take your mind off tomorrow?"

I observe him, the twinkle in his eyes when he says something genuine, or the small smile that is always on his face. "I'd appreciate that."

"What do you want to talk about?"

"We didn't finish our conversation about you snoring," I say to him.

He gives me another disappointed look. "Really?"

"What?" I try to sound as innocent as possible. "I would be lying if I said you didn't."

"You little—" he mutters as he launches a full tickle attack on me.

I squirm, toss and turn, but there's no escaping.

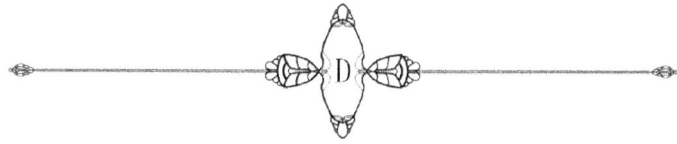

This time I'm the one that wakes to a cold bed. Nate's side of the bed is messy, as if left in a hurry. I jump out of bed myself and move over to the small water basin. I wash my face, brush my hair and braid it tightly.

By the stand of the sun, I make out that the trial is starting in less than an hour.

I put on my clothes, then my jacket, the fabric tight around my arms. I lace up the boots I've been walking on for the past two years now. And lastly, all of my weapons. My sword pressed solid against my spine, two daggers strapped to each thigh, one dagger up each sleeve.

Let's see if I can find anybody this morning.

I exit the tent and I'm greeted by Adrian and Jake, as usual.

"Morning," Jake says from his stool.

"Morning. Have either of you seen Nate leave?" I ask them.

They look at each other before Adrian says, "No, why? He's not with you?"

"No, he's not. And I'm worried because it looks like he left in a hurry."

They're both on their feet in an instance. "We'll look for him. I'm sure he's around here somewhere."

"Thank you. I'll go look for Jade and Madion before I head over to the vault."

Adrian drops his hand on my shoulder and squeezes lightly. "You got this. Everything will be just fine."

I pat his hand. "I hope so."

We break apart, each going another way. I walk to Jade and Madion's tent.

As I open the entrance, I stop in my tracks. Their bed looks the same as mine. On both sides, the blankets are thrown aside, multiple pillows are on the floor. All their weapons are still waiting for them.

Something is wrong here.

Something is very wrong.

I don't even step a foot into the tent before turning around. Maybe they're already at the vault.

Maybe nothing is wrong, maybe I'm just overthinking this.

But when your friends are all suddenly gone one morning, you'd be scared, too.

Almost as if she senses my distress, Yuno comes to walk next to me. Occasionally rubbing her head against my leg. I reach down to pet her right before I'm about to enter the vault.

I have about half a dozen staircases to walk down before I reach the bottom, and Yuno strolls all the way down with me.

I could really use a hug from Nate right now or an encouraging speech from Madion or just a joke from Jade.

At moments like these, I truly understand how much my friends help me, stop me from breaking completely.

When I reach the bottom, I say goodbye to Yuno. She gives me a few encouraging licks and huddles close to me, trying to give me a hug.

I send her back up, but she stays where she is. She'll wait until I'm done.

So I give her a grateful smile before taking a deep breath. Bracing myself for what this trial has planned for me. I push open the massive stone doors.

And stop in horror as I find the people I'm looking for on the other side.

Jade, Madion and Nate, bound and gagged, on their knees, on one side of the plane. A growling wolf on the other.

And the priest standing calmly in the middle. He turns his head to me and says, "Welcome to your third trial, Your Highness."

CHAPTER 24

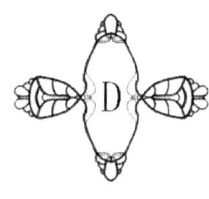

I feel the anxiety already boiling up inside me. What are they planning here?

Dawn, breathe. We're okay, Nate's careful voice sounds through my head, as he feels the panic coursing through me. *A bit uncomfortable, as you can imagine, but we're okay. So take a deep breath for me, calm yourself down.*

I take deep breaths, trying to match them to his. The panic faintly lessens, but it's still there and it'll stay there until I can hold him again.

Good, now just take step after step, until you reach the table.

Okay.

One step, one breath, one step, one breath.

All the way to the table. I put my back to my friends, keeping the wolf right in front of me.

I'm already proud of you, Dawn. You—

A searing pain goes through my head. At the same time, I hear Nate groan in pain behind me.

"No communication in any way during this trial, understood?" the priest states, still a fully neutral look on his face. "Otherwise, your mate will meet the consequences."

I glance back at Nate, sweat now coating his forehead. Madion and Jade look at him with concern. He takes a deep breath before meeting my eyes and then nods.

I can do this on my own.

So I look back at the priest and say, "Understood."

"Very well. Dawn Maria Rowena Sungust, welcome to your third trial," the priest starts. "You have already taken notice of your surroundings. You have your companions, the ones that are always by your side. But you also have your enemies, represented by the white wolf behind me."

He places his hands on the rim of the bowl on the table. The same liquid I've had to drink at the previous trails. The liquid that makes a layer of my soul shatter if I'm worthy of it.

"There are no specific actions you need to complete during this trial. The only task you have to fulfill is protecting your friends from your enemies, no matter what."

I nod, my fingers pensively fidgeting with the dagger at my thigh.

"Remember that sentence that has been running through your mind for days now, 'death comes for us all, some just have to go sooner than others'."

The priest moves his hands underneath the bowl and lifts it to me. I take hold of it and empty it. That odd, crushing feeling around my soul forms again.

The priest snaps his fingers, and the table vanishes.

His magic still works in mysterious ways, which I have yet to fathom.

He takes a step towards me. "Think of this one thing. How important are the lives of your friends?"

My eyebrows knit together as the priest dissipates in front of my eyes.

That will never not be creepy.

I draw my sword and place myself in between the wolf and my friends.

It's not getting through me. It won't reach them.

The wolf scrapes its claws through the sand. The sound reverberating through the entire clove. Its piercing blue eyes focused on me as it shows off its long canines.

I do the same thing with my sword. I let the tip hit the floor and drag it behind me as I approach the wolf.

It pounces and I'm ready.

I slash my sword across its belly, but the wolf still crashes into me.

We both fall to the ground. The wolf is up faster than me and tries to make a run for it, but my arm is just long enough to grab its back leg and yank it out from underneath its body. The head snaps back to bite my hand, but I'm already reaching for a dagger.

I scramble back to my feet, putting myself between the wolf and the three behind me again.

With my sword in one hand and a dagger in the other, I try to close in on the wolf. But every time I put one foot forward, it puts one back.

It's playing with me, and I don't like it.

I let myself take one daring glance to the side, checking for any surprising guests, and make the mistake I shouldn't have made.

The wolf goes for my legs. I try to jump out of the way, but his jaw snaps around my ankle and yanks me off my feet.

I collapse on the floor, knocking the wind out of me. The wolf takes no time to let me recover and jumps on top of me. Its body is almost as big as me. My sword has fallen just out of my reach, and I can't reach for the daggers at my thighs.

Warmth pools into my hands as I let flames grow there. Once the wolf leans closer, I slam them onto both sides of its head.

It doesn't even flinch.

Magic does not work.

Before it can attack me again, I slide one of the daggers I have out of my sleeve.

And when the wolf is close enough to my face, I plunge it into the wolf's neck.

It whimpers as it falls to the ground beside me.

Magic does nothing but solid objects, like my blades do harm.

Sucking in a shallow breath, I push the wolf off. I pull my dagger out, but almost let it drop to the floor when I find it completely clean. Not a speck of blood.

Then I look to my left and find that the wolf is gone.

I jump to my feet, expecting an attack from any side, but nothing comes.

What is happening here?

I glance over my shoulder at Nate. His face set in disbelief, too.

A startling growl sounds in front of me. And when I turn my head towards it, I find the wolf, completely fine, a couple feet away from me, in the exact same position as before.

I snatch my sword off the ground and point it at the wolf. I get another snarl in response.

This time I take off running, trying to get the first attack and maybe the upper hand with it.

But the wolf sees exactly what I'm doing and jumps over me. I nick its legs. However, it keeps running, right towards Jade. I sprint and try to tackle the wolf to the ground. My knees scraping over the hard ground, rocks slicing them open. But I ignore the pain, grit my teeth, and try to get a hold of its legs.

I come an inch short, and it barrels on towards Jade, who is watching in horror.

No one's getting hurt, not on my watch.

I gather a substantial amount of magic and throw it around them. A wall of air now blocking the way of the wolf.

It slows down and stops a few meters from the wall. In the meantime, I get back up and step closer, but the wolf creeps closer too, ready to attack.

Then my wall starts to lower, slowly crumbling down, and no matter what I do, it goes on. I see Jade trying to crawl closer to Madion, but she's held in place by the hand of a guard.

The wolf smiles, actually smiles at the sight of her fear.

And the second the wall hits the floor, the wolf jumps, and so do I. My dagger poised to drive itself into the skull of the wolf.

It does.

My dagger finds its mark and goes up to the hilt into the head of the wolf. I turn my gaze up to see Jade very relieved. I let my hand touch her knee before pulling the dagger out.

And like the first time, there is no blood.

Nothing.

Everything is clean.

The wolf vanishes in front of our eyes. I look everyone over, making sure they're fine.

Another growl sounds behind me.

I stop dead in my tracks.

I'm protecting my friends, aren't I?

When I turn around, I find the same wolf I just killed back in its original place and state. Not a scratch or drop of blood on its fur.

This is going to be a long morning.

I sheathe my sword and grab another dagger. Getting close to the wolf is the only way to bring it down.

I wait for the wolf to run, to do something, but it does nothing. No movement at all.

Until I step back.

Then it dives to my feet. I jump over it and land right on its back, snapping the spine clean in half.

But the wolf does not stop. I stumble off of it as it gets back up and starts running. Towards Nate.

That is definitely not happening. My grip tightens on the blades in my hands as I take off.

I need to slow it down so I can catch up.

I let several clumps of earth emerge from the ground, slowing the wolf down in its hunt. One even reaches so high that it hits the wolf in the face, yet it still doesn't slow down. Even the broken spine, one I can see moving in parts under its fur, does nothing.

When I dare take my eyes off the wolf to look at Nate, I see him looking directly at me, not at the incoming threat. He doesn't even glance at it. His focus is completely on me, and I dare say I see a faint smile on his lips.

He fully trusts me to do this. I push my legs to speed up, to catch up with the wolf. Air pushing at my heels as I desperately try to reach him.

But I can't make it.

And when Nate sees it too, he just closes his eyes. Waiting for that fatal blow to come.

Yet it doesn't.

The wolf dissipates when it barely touches Nate.

I didn't protect him. I couldn't protect him.

Does this mean I failed? The trials stop and I die?

My answer is yet another growl behind me.

And when I turn around, I find two wolves instead of one.

So I did not fail, but if the wolf disappears even when I don't make it. What's the purpose of this whole trial?

I can't think of it while fighting these two opponents. Because they seem to have set their eyes on me, and me only. With two of them, I take my sword in one hand again. Just to be able to keep at least one at a distance.

I raise my sword and dagger into a defensive stand, and wolves howl in response.

They part, one going to my left, the other to my right. It's almost as if I'm fighting Jade and Madion with this setting. But they don't try to kill me. At least not always.

The wolf on my right takes off in a sprint when the one on my left takes off for a jump.

I roll back and spring back on my feet, hearing the wolves crash into each other. I look at Nate and he looks like he's smirking again. As much as he can with that gag still in his mouth.

I stay with my back to the wolves another second until I hear one make a move. I spin around and drive my dagger right into its eye. My sword is almost right behind it, going for the neck.

The wolf goes down, choking on its own blood. The time I take to see if the wolf disappears almost costs me my neck.

The second wolf jumps on me from behind, its jaw going for my throat.

I won't die here. I need to protect them. I can't leave them behind, not like this.

I tighten my grip around my sword, ready to swing it. But the wolf is yet again gone before my sword even comes close.

And I just lay there, staring at the sky. Breathing ragged and heavy.

When I said I didn't want to die, when I begged it not to kill me, it disappeared. Just like with Nate and just like with Jade. Nobody wants to die. Nobody.

The last line of the letter suddenly resounds through my head. *Death comes for us all, some just have to go sooner than others.*

But who is death coming for?

A moment later, the whisper of the priest goes through my mind. *How important are the lives of your friends?*

And I think over and over about that question.

My feet get me back up and I see only one wolf stand in front of me. Not as far away as the previous ones. Just a few steps away. Its teeth exposed, ready to kill me.

Then the answer to that one question hits me.

How important are the lives of your friends?

I let my arms go slack at my sides, my sword now dangling from my fingers.

How important are they?

My sword tumbles from my grip.

How important are the lives of your friends?

I look straight into the bright orange eyes of the wolf and whisper, "More important than my own."

I hear a muffled scream from behind me as the wolf leaps straight for my throat.

But it doesn't hit me.

Instead, a burning pain slams through my chest. I drop to my knees, my hand going to where my soul lays beneath my skin.

It cracks, and cracks, and shatters.

Light explodes from me.

And the third layer of my soul vanishes, replaced by a large amount of new magic now flowing freely.

I brace my hands on the hard ground as my vision blurs. The light emanating from me fades and is replaced by applause sounding through the ravine.

When I force myself to lift my head, I find the priest in front of me. He holds out his hand. I grab it and let him haul me to my feet.

"Congratulations on completing your third trial. You fought tremendously, but as you now know. Fighting will not always get you what you desire," he says.

I nod, not knowing what to respond.

He gestures to the scene behind me. "You may free them and leave. I will see you at your final trial."

I nod again. Then grab my sword, sheathe it and palm a dagger instead.

The guards still have their hands on each of my friends' shoulders. And even when I approach, they do not back down.

"Let go," I order the one holding Jade, who completely neglects the order.

My hand shoots out, grabbing him by his collar. "I suggest you all let go right now." I glance down the line of men. "Because I am not in the mood for this."

He hesitates for a moment before letting go. His fellow guards do the same.

I squat down and cut through Jade's ropes. She immediately moves to get the gag out of her mouth.

She gives me a grateful smile before I move to Madion. She removes her gag and grins. "I'm proud of you."

I give her a smile in response.

Then I move to Nate, who is looking confused at my eyes. I ignore him and cut through the ropes binding his now red wrists.

They took his bracelets off.

I pull his gag out as he keeps staring into my eyes. "What?"

His hand drifts to my cheek. "Your eyes, they—they have a golden ring."

My eyebrows knit together at his statement. When he notices my confusion, he just pulls me in for a hug.

I let my arms wrap around his neck, savoring his touch. I was so scared this morning.

"Why don't we get out of here?" he whispers.

I pull back and grab his hands. "Where are your bracelets?"

"Stuffed in the pocket of the man behind me, I think."

I only have to glare at the man and his hand shoots into his pocket. I hold out my hand to him and he drops the bracelets. Nate shows his wrists to me. I cover both scars with his bracelets, several beads catching the light of the sun.

"Now we can go," I say to him, both of us with a smile on our face.

"Let's go," he whispers and grabs my hand.

The four of us walk side by side to the entrance.

Three trials down. One more to go.

CHAPTER 25

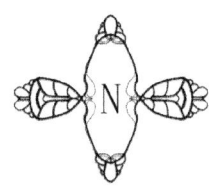

Dawn hasn't let go of my hand since the moment she could hold it again. She was scared. I was scared. We were all scared.

Back in our tent, we all sit down, everybody discarding off their weapons somewhere in a corner before sitting down on the bed. Dawn snuggles close to me, still holding my hand.

"How did I not notice you were all taken?" she asks after a moment of silence.

I look at Madion and Jade. Who will tell her what went down?

The choice lands on me as Jade and Madion both keep silent.

"The priest and two men came in the middle of the night. I barely had time to open my eyes before they had my hands and feet tied together. And when I wanted to talk, I couldn't. The priest silenced me in a way I still don't understand. And to make it even worse for me, as you already saw, the men thought I could escape if I had my bracelets on." I take a deep breath, because their reaction was not pleasant. "I think the priest paralyzed me or something, because I couldn't fight back as one man took off my bracelets and stuffed them in his pocket. Then they saw the scars and without a warning started touching them, hoping to figure out what happened. I think I even heard the words awful and good riddance drop a few times, as they seemed to figure out who I was. I tried to get them off, but I was helpless, just like when these scars were created."

Dawn's hand tightens around mine as she puts her head on my shoulder. I put mine on hers in return and let the bad things from last night flow away. They were awful men and had no right to do what they did.

Once I've gathered my thoughts again, I continue the events from what I call our abduction. "The priest finally stepped in and ordered them to take me away. They grabbed my feet and shoulders and carried me out of the tent. All the way across camp to one of the underground dungeons of the vault." I gesture to Jade and Madion. "Where I was thrown down next to them."

"Right before your trial started, six men came into the cell, gagged us and told us to keep our mouths shut until we were told otherwise, and herded us to the plane," Madion finishes.

Dawn whispers, "And then I came."

"Yes." Madion sighs.

Silence falls over us again.

"What did you say to that wolf in the end?" Jade suddenly asks, bracing her forearms on her thighs.

"The priest whispered something before he vanished. He asked how important are the lives of your friends? When the wolf kept attacking, yet not hurting you or me, the answer to that question slowly dawned on me," she mutters.

Jade leans forward. "And what did you answer?"

"More important than my own," she says, as if it's the most normal thing in the world.

We're all taken aback by the casualness of her voice. As if she'd jump in front of a sword if it meant to save any of us.

"Dawn—" Madion says, pain in her voice.

"I mean it, Madion," Dawn cuts her off, determined by what she's saying. "If giving up my life means that you get to live, I wouldn't hesitate. I just wouldn't."

"And you know I would do the same thing, Dawn," Madion counters.

"We'd all lay down our life if it meant that someone else could live," Jade says, looking us all over.

We all know the sacrifices we'd make to help one another, giving up our life could be one of those sacrifices in the worst scenarios. But I truly, truly hope that never has to happen. Because even though we might lay our life down if needed, we would also do everything in our power to all make it out alive.

No one is left behind if that option is there.

I look down at my mate. My beautiful and brave mate. Someone who gives her all for everything.

Yes, she might have her shortcomings, but those things make her perfect.

I plant a kiss on her head when she shuffles even closer. Then I notice her eyelids drooping, followed by a small yawn.

Her body needs sleep. She expanded magic, but also gained a massive amount. Her soul needs to adjust to that.

"We'll leave you two to it," Madion says as she follows my line of sight. "We all need our rest after this trial."

"We'll see you both tomorrow," I say.

Even though the afternoon is just here, I know we're all going to sleep, long and deep.

They wave us both goodbye before letting the flaps close off the entrance.

I slide down the pillows and pull the blankets over Dawn and I. My fingers tangle with hers, her thumb brushing over the leather around my wrists.

She's sound asleep by the time we're fully settled in.

And seeing her be so careful with what I carry around my wrists and the first thing she noticed when she cut me loose being my missing bracelets, made me fall in love with her even more.

But what those men did last night hurt, it hurt more than I had wanted it to. I thought I was used to being called a monster and could just let it slide. However, the fact that after all these years, they still don't understand my side of the story. I was an eight-year-old child that barely had control over his magic and just heard that his parents had been brutally murdered.

Yet I grew, ever since I got out of that basement. I've been training every single day to keep my magic under control. To never let something like that happen again. And my wrists are a factor for me that keeps me going. I was locked up for being dangerous, but not anymore.

I have control over everything, and if Dawn needs help with whatever is loitering beneath her skin, I will help her. Every step of the way.

Maybe, when we get back, I could make her a set of bracelets. To cover the small bands on her wrists. Bands she formed over the past years of spending nights in the dungeons.

I know she can be ashamed of them. I've seen people look at them and then at her. They only look away when they see who she is, not at the first sight of the scars. Only when they notice they're staring at the princess, they look away. Which is so, so wrong.

Scars are memories for people. They are visible on the surface, but you never know the full story. Someone with a scar down their back could've been tortured, but it could also have been a stupid accident. You never know until you ask, instead of staring and trying to figure out what happened.

So maybe bracelets like mine could help her feel more comfortable. I'll gladly make her anything to feel more comfortable, just like she did with me. She made me feel more secure over the years and I want to help her feel safe, too.

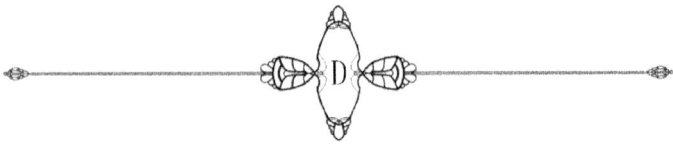

I wake in the middle of the night to a loud noise coming from outside the tent. Nate is already upright next to me. We lock eyes and agree that something is wrong.

We both reach for the weapons on our nightstands. Something or someone is about to enter this tent.

Grunts come from outside before we hear bodies hitting the ground. Unconscious, hopefully.

But it's not Jake, nor Adrian, who enters. Three men enter, two of them armed, and the third one armed with what looks like a syringe.

A syringe filled with a metallic liquid.

Nate and I jump from the bed, several pillows hitting the floor in our wake. Nate gives me one resolved nod before taking on the man in front of him. I focus on the one in front of me.

The third one is just waiting, patiently waiting.

Nate clashes with the man, but he doesn't budge. The man in front of me swings his sword in my direction. I knock it aside, but it brings me off balance.

In the corner of my eye, I see Nate being pushed back, colliding with his nightstand. He trips and lands on his back. I conjure a ball of water to send it down the man's throat, but he already has Nate in a headlock before I can do anything.

"Don't do anything stupid now," he muses to me, satisfaction gleaming in his eyes.

I look down at Nate to see him clawing for breath. I let the water go into the lungs of the man in front of me instead. He chokes on it and drops to the floor.

One down, two to go.

That's when I notice the third man is gone. He's nowhere in the tent.

My hand is outstretched to the man holding my mate's life in his hands. "Let go of him," I sneer at him.

His only answer is his arms tightening around Nate's neck. Nate's eyes droop because of the lack of oxygen. I let my magic slowly fill his lungs with air again, but it makes no difference. Nate looks up at me one more time, like he feels the next thing coming. The man holding him squeezes once too hard and knocks him out.

He drops to the floor like a rag doll. Leaving me with one unconscious bastard at my feet, one who just knocked out my mate and one unaccounted for.

I focus completely on the man in front of me, not thinking about the man at my feet.

My fatal mistake tonight.

I didn't render him fully unconscious because he has enough strength to yank my feet out from underneath me. I topple over him and land hard on my back, knocking the wind out of me.

Suddenly, the man unaccounted for emerges from the shadows, the syringe still in his hand.

I try to get up, but he's already on top of me. Straddling my legs with the needle of the syringe pressed against my neck.

"She didn't say how pretty you'd be," he says, putting a bit more pressure on my neck.

I look at him, slightly confused. "Who are you talking about?"

"No one for you to worry about anymore. The only thing you should be worrying about is us and what we have."

Dread coils in my chest. "And what might that be?" I dare ask.

He glances at the syringe. "Alk."

He smiles at the fear now coursing through me. The syringe pierces my skin and I want to scream, but the man covers my mouth with his hand, "Diluted Alk, for now."

He jams the needle fully into my neck and my whole body seizes up at the one thing it can't handle now entering my bloodstream.

I manage to look at Nate's peaceful face one more time, maybe the last time, before I lose feeling in my arms, legs, chest.

Before I'm swallowed by darkness and taken to a place I most likely won't leave again.

CHAPTER 26

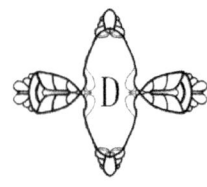

The pounding headache that is spread across my head, combined with the searing pain coursing through my whole body, is not the way I want to wake up. Shackled to a chair, no less.

I try to sit as still as possible, not yet notifying the people that took me I'm awake.

Three men attacked Nate and I.

One of them knocked Nate out, barely giving him the chance to fight back. Another pumped me full of Alk. They wouldn't do that if they ever thought of letting me get out of here alive.

I'm going to die. Plain and simple. If no one finds Nate or me, I'll be dead by morning.

I hiss when I feel several drops land on my neck, sliding down my back.

A hand suddenly clamps around my chin, jerking it upwards. "Hello there, beautiful," a man says with a sickly-sweet voice. "Why don't you open those pretty eyes for me?"

I tug at my wrists once, trying to get any movement in them, but nothing. And when I reach out for my magic, I feel it retreated all the way to the depths of my soul. Which gives me a good indication of which shackles are around my wrists.

When the man tugs on my chin again, making my head pound even more, I dare to open my eyes. They take a moment to adjust before I'm met by dark brown, almost black eyes, and long blonde hair falling over his shoulders.

"Ah, the eyes of royalty," he says, staring at my eyes. "Pity you'll never open them again when we're done with you."

My pain now gets tangled with the fear of what they have planned.

Then another drop falls on my back, biting into it.

The man lets go of me. "Ah, that. Our employer was so kind to give us the one thing that could hurt you." He grins. "Permanently hurt you."

He gestures to something hanging over me. A sack, with several holes in the bottom, leaking a silvery substance.

Alk. The same diluted Alk they injected me with.

The drop from just now slides all the way down my spine, burning everything in its wake.

I look to my right, finding another man, a twin to the one in front of me, and a table. A table filled with tools, Alk and no Alk. Even two of my own daggers laying on it.

"As you might've already guessed by now, this will not be pretty," the first man says as he walks to the table. "We could do whatever we wanted with you, as long as it led to your death at the end." He turns to me, his hands braced behind him on the table. "And with the payment we were offered, we happily obliged."

He grabs my daggers, sharpening them with a block he had in his pocket. "And it didn't matter how you met your end either, we just had to make sure the body wouldn't be discovered."

He moves on to the second dagger. And I try, try so hard to get any movement in the chains holding me.

If they never find me, if these men just bury me somewhere. What would become of this kingdom? Would Leanne destroy it even more than she already has?

And what about Nate? Will he know I died? Or will he search for me until he drops dead himself?

I'm startled as the sharpening block is dropped on the table, and the man now has one dagger sheathed at his side, the other ready in his hand. I press my back flat against the chair, my hands gripping the armrests, knuckles turning white.

He chuckles at my distress as he squats in front of me. The dagger tipped against my sternum. "You already know this is going to hurt, so I'll spare you the talk."

He pushes harder, drawing blood, and I trash even more. "Mul?"

The man at the table perks up. "Yes, Kreinn."

"Hold her arm for me, will you?"

He rounds the table, squats down next to me and grips my arm, pressing it firmly against the wood of the armrest. My heart is pounding in my throat as I try to keep my fists clenched.

Kreinn lays the dagger in my lap. He needs both his hands to pry my fingers off the armrest. He turns my hand around, the palm now facing upwards. "You move too much."

And before I can even register it, his hand shoots to the dagger and plunges it through my hand.

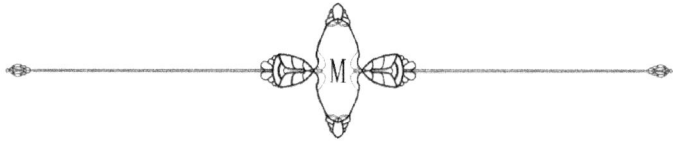

Jade and I decide to go check on our two lovebirds. It's the middle of the night, we know, but maybe they woke from their nap too.

When we're about two tents away, we both stop. A hand is peaking out from behind the tent.

Something is wrong, very wrong.

I look at Jade once, seeing she followed my line of sight, and then we take off running.

We're struck with terror when we find Jake and Adrian unconscious on the ground, hands on their weapons. They were going to fight off whoever barreled towards them, but they didn't have enough time before it hit them.

I leave Jade with them and silently move aside the covering at the entrance. The tent is completely trashed, pillows on the floor, the blankets thrown aside in a hurry, and Nate's nightstand is toppled over, with him motionless next to it.

I rush towards him and drop to my knees, my hand on his neck to feel for a pulse. "Jade!" I shout.

A moment later, she comes running inside and sees the mess. I turn Nate over onto his back and see the bruising on his neck. He was strangled and Dawn is nowhere to be seen.

Jake and Adrian stumble inside after Jade, sorrowful looks on their faces. They couldn't protect the one person they were supposed to defend with their lives.

"Nate?" I mutter, shaking both his shoulders. "Nate, wake up."

He lets out a grunt, but doesn't rise to consciousness yet. "Help me put him on the bed," I say to the men behind me.

They grab Nate under the armpits and at the feet and hoist him from the floor. I sit at the edge of the bed and take his hand, trying to wake him up. And slowly but surely, he comes around.

His free hand drifts to his neck and then to the empty spot beside him. That's when the panic hits him. He shoots up, trying to get off the bed, his breathing shallow and quick.

"Nate, breathe," I order him, cupping his cheeks with my hands to make him look at me. "Breathe."

He buries his face in his hands. "I—I—ca—can't."

But he tries, he desperately tries to get the air down, he just can't. I pull him into a tight hug, making him feel my breathing and heartbeat. Keeping him from passing out again.

He still doesn't calm down.

This is why they're mates. They're the only ones that can calm each other down. That bond between them goes way deeper than just mates.

"Breathe. Just try to match my breathing," I whisper in his ear.

His arms are tight around me, his fingers digging into my back. Then I feel drops falling on my shoulder, and something inside me breaks with it. I've never seen Nate cry like this.

"They took her," he breathes. "They just took her, and I couldn't do anything about it."

I rub soothing circles on his back. "Tell me what happened." He tenses slightly. "At your own pace."

"They came out of nowhere." A deep breath. "Three men. One disappeared." A very deep breath. "Right before one knocked me out." A long pause, his breathing slowing to a normal pace. "One of them had a syringe."

"And you have an idea what was inside of it?" Jade asks behind us.

Nate swallows and pulls away from me. His breathing less shallow, but the haunted look in his eyes remains. "They went for Dawn, not me. I was just someone to take out, like Jake and Adrian. And if they came here for Dawn, I can think of only one metallic substance that could incapacitate her."

Alk.

"No one is supposed to have that," Adrian mumbles.

Nate looks at him. "Have people ever played by the rules when it comes to her family?"

Adrian stays quiet at that. Nate gets up from the bed, straps on his belt, and starts gathering all his weapons.

"Nate?" I quietly say.

But he ignores me. He stalks out of the tent. We all run after him.

"Nate!" I yell at him. "What are you doing?"

He stops, looks over his shoulder and says, "Hunting down the bastards that dared take her from me."

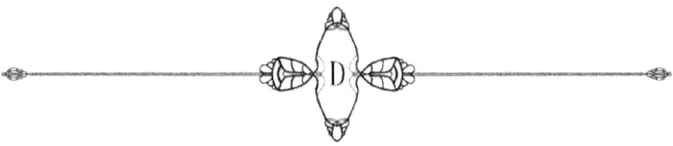

My vision is blurred when I come to again. I've been switching between conscious and unconscious for what feels like hours. And every time I wake, I'm met by Kreinn's haunting grin.

"There she is again," he muses. "The three of us have been thinking while you were out. What to do now, since we're not planning on letting you die just yet. So we came up with a little game."

His fingers grip my chin, forcing me to look at him. I again try to pull back, but whimper as I accidentally pull at my hands. Which are still pinned to the wood by my daggers. Any other weapons haven't found their way into my body, but it's only a matter of time.

"I'm going to get creative, and if you make a sound, I'll keep going. But if you keep still and silent, I might give you a five-minute break."

"Damn you." I spit at him.

He wipes a hand down his face and punches me in the face with the other. My head snaps to the side, blood drips from my nose onto my shirt.

Mul is just smirking, safely standing behind the table. The other, very tall male, Grem, is still standing behind me, monitoring my movements, but also controlling the sack hanging over me.

Whenever I fight too much, he'll hit it, causing a flood of the Alk to course down my back.

I'm snapped from my thoughts as Mul moves from behind his table with several needles, thick needles, in his hands.

Kreinn takes one and puts it on my fingertip, right where one of the swirls starts. "I've never seen anyone with such beautifully decorated arms." He puts pressure on the needle, making it pierce my skin. "They're perfect to trace, too."

He drags the needle all the way to my wrist. I bite down, not making a sound. Because he does not know how deep those lines run, he can not know those lines are connected to my soul. He'll only push further if he does.

So I suck it up as he drags it further and deeper to my elbow. "You know, I have another task, too."

He stabs the needle into the end of a swirl, and I manage to just keep my pain hidden. "What do you know about our dear northern neighbors? Any plans about them you found out?"

I say nothing, I just stare at him. Kreinn eyes me for a moment, before motioning Grem to come closer. I brace myself for the flood, but it doesn't come. Instead, the pain explodes at my shoulder blades as Grem stabs two small blades into them. And because they came so quick and unexpected, I make a noise.

I dare look up and find Kreinn playing with an Alk blade in his hands. "You made a noise. You know what I said about making noise."

I suck in a deep breath, steadying myself, preparing for the pain. All three men chuckle at the dread coursing through me. Kreinn grabs my already shattered kneecap. He took a bat to them earlier, and squeezes. Then, again, without any notice, stabs the blade into my thigh.

A scream shatters from my throat.

I couldn't hold it in anymore.

And because of that scream, a second blade finds its way into my other leg.

The Alk burns through my muscles, searing off any blood that wants to escape. Heavily breathing, I close my eyes. I need to think of other things. Not the pain, just anything else.

"You can breathe all you want. It won't take any of this away," Mul says, looking at me like a predator looks at its prey.

"And you can stand there all you want," I counter, "but it won't make you the person who killed someone from the royal family."

I try to flex the muscles in my hands, but they're either stiff from the adrenaline or the tendons that are cut. Which won't heal until the knives are pulled out.

Mul makes way to stand in front of me, but Kreinn steps in his way. "Don't let her get to your head."

"She won't, I just wish to give her an answer." He smirks.

After eyeing him for another moment, Kreinn steps out of the way and looks at me with satisfaction.

Mul has a short sword in his hand as he stomps my way. His hand grabs my hair and pulls me flush against the chair, causing the knives in my shoulders to bury themselves deeper, the daggers in my hands to shift slightly and my vision to blur again.

"Let this be a lesson," he whispers as he drives the sword into my stomach.

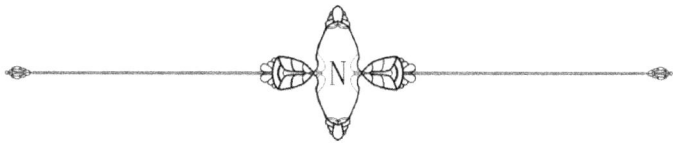

I just stalked into the woods like I knew where to find her, but I don't. I have no idea where to start. They could have taken her anywhere in the time I was out.

Madion has been following me for a while now, Jade and the rest most likely not far behind her.

"Nate, stop. You have no idea what way to go," she reminds me.

I whirl around. "Do you think I don't know that? I'm trying to find something, a scrap of that bond between us, blood, anything. But there is nothing, not a trace is left of her."

"Then stop and think," she says. "Don't let the emotions drive you to just wander around. It'll only cost you more time."

She's right.

Hold on, Dawn. I'm coming for you. I send down that bond.

No response follows.

"Okay, you're right." I admit and drag my hands down my face. "Where do we start?"

She leans against a tree, lets her head fall back against it, and closes her eyes. "Do we know of any buildings or cabins nearby?"

It's been too long for me to even remember half of these woods, let alone any residences. "No."

"Okay," she mumbles, right as Jade, Adrian and Jake emerge from the bushes. Madion opens her eyes and leans her head in their direction. "Do any of you know about any residences in these woods?"

They all think about it for a moment, before Jake responds, "I remember several cabins spread across this part of the woods. I don't know the exact locations, but I think there are five of them."

"Good," Madion states.

"Do you think they're stupid enough to take her to one of those?" I ask.

Madion opens one eye and looks at me. "They're already stupid enough to take her in the first place, let alone take her from her own tent where anyone could've heard or seen them."

I sit down on the trunk of a fallen tree behind me. "What do we do then? Check every cabin until we find her?"

"No, we wait for a moment." Madion pushes off the tree.

"What do you mean, we wait?" I say, agitated.

We can't just wait around. Who knows what they're doing to her right now.

Madion ignores me, and we wait. And we wait for two minutes until she raises three fingers. "Three." One finger goes down. "Two." Another one. "One." She makes a fist as something shoots out of the bushes.

Then she squats down to take something from Yuno's mouth. "While you immediately walked away without a plan, I sent Yuno out to look for anything that could lead us to Dawn. And if she did, she was to bring it to me."

She holds up Dawn's necklace. "And it seems she found something valuable."

Everybody has gone quiet, even the forest barely makes a noise. Madion steps in front of me and holds up the necklace. "Use that bond. Your souls are connected." She grips my chin to make me look at her. "Find her."

She presses the moon into my hand, and I stare at it, noticing a few specks of blood.

I'm coming Dawn. And whoever took you will wish they were never born.

I wrap the necklace around my wrist and clench the moon in my hand. My magic immediately responds to what I hold. I let it spread out as far as I can reach until I bump into a similar mark. I pull back and fling it all in that direction.

I need a precise location.

And as if she feels me too, she tugs on it.

"Found her," I say with a grin. My sword in my hand as I look at the still waiting friends before me. "Let's go."

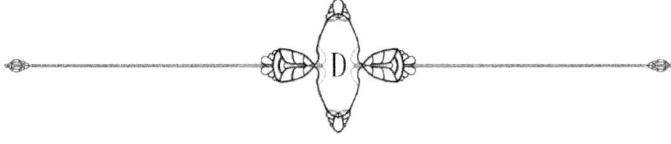

I did not know I could be in this much pain and yet be this numb at the same time. The Alk in my legs is slowly poisoning me and I don't know how long I can hold on anymore.

My knees are shattered, my fingers are non-responsive, the blades in my thighs are burning away everything they touch, and let's not forget the long blade Mul left in my stomach.

Everything hurts, breathing, talking, even the smallest movement sends an immense pain through my whole body.

And now they're just casually talking about what to do to me next.

Eventually Mul steps forward. Stretching his fingers, mocking me for not being able to do that. He stops in front of me, and I slowly raise my head, trying to keep the headache at bay.

"Now, you still haven't answered our questions." He drums his fingers over the hilt of the blade that is still stuck in my stomach, sending tremors of pain through me. "So, I'll ask again." He fully grips it. "What do you know about Railon's armies?"

I lean forward as far as I can. "Nothing."

The sword is twisted inside me, and I feel blood running from the corner of my mouth. That is not good. I feel my fingers twitch as I want to ball my fists.

"I can either keep turning, making you eventually pass out again, or you can just tell me what I want to know," Mul says, his face now inches from mine.

I focus on his eyes, not the pain radiating from my stomach. "Railon has armies, but Iluniel has bigger ones."

He twists the blade around twice, two full times, shredding everything around it. I let out a guttural scream at the immense agony spreading through me.

"She will not say anything," Grem says, his deep voice sounding bored, as I slightly slump back in the chair.

Mul steps back, another satisfied grin on his face.

The sound of a dagger sliding free sounds behind me. From the corner of my eye, I see the shadow of his arm moving upward to the bag hanging over me. He's going to dump it all on me.

I feel a few drips on my back, and a spurt follows. Sucking in a deep breath, I try to stop myself from screaming as it floods over my back.

I don't understand how they have so much Alk. Everything was supposed to be destroyed ages ago.

"The pain can stop once you tell us exactly what you know," he whispers from behind me.

"How many times do I have to say this?" I snap at them, the anger in my voice quickly replaced with exhaustion. "I don't know anything."

Suddenly the bag drops beside me. Grem snatches it up and covers his hands with the contents.

His hand then wraps around my throat, throbbing pain wrapping around it with him. "Speak. You know things you're not supposed to know."

I just glare at him. My face has to be looking like a mess with the blood running from my nose, my mouth, and my temple. The tears coating my cheeks spread the blood even further.

Kreinn puts his hand on Grem's shoulder. "She knows nothing, which means her time here is up."

Grem lets go of me and I inhale deeply. But my breath seizes when I see what appears from behind Kreinn's back.

He walks to the small fireplace to my left and sticks the long Alk poker into it. "I've been thinking long and hard about how this night was going to end. Well, how your life was going to end." The Alk is almost glowing now. "And what is a better way than dying just like your lovely parents?"

My eyes snap up to look at his face. "Did you kill them?" I mumble, trying to hide the fear that is now taking over.

Kreinn turns to me, armed with a glowing Alk poker. "Oh no, that honor was given to someone else. You remember perfectly how they died, don't you?"

Flashes of that night shoot through my head. I wrench my eyes shut in response to the memories.

"Why don't you walk me through it?"

"No."

"No?" Kreinn squats down in front of me. "Did she just say no to me?"

"Just end it already," I sneer at him.

He points the poker at the spot where my heart beats beneath my skin. "Oh, I'll be taking my time. It's not every day you get to kill a princess and get paid."

I try to lean back but I push the daggers in my shoulders only further in.

Grem steps closer to my back. "Shall I pull them out?"

Kreinn gives him a nod, and only a second later, the blades are out. Pain is replaced by a paralyzed feeling, meaning that my body will slowly start healing there. Not that it matters.

I'm pushed back against the chair by Kreinn's hand on my shoulder, the poker still hovering over my heart. "I'm just going to slowly, very slowly, let this pierce your skin. And then your beating heart. Until we never see those pretty eyes again."

I take a deep breath and close my eyes.

If I'm going, I'm doing it on my terms. I let myself sink deep into myself, right where my magic coils around my soul. My magic will never come out again. It will be snuffed out alongside me.

I let it wrap around my soul, protecting me for as long as possible.

I wish I could just hear his voice one last time or just look at him. That's all I ask.

The poker is pressed against my chest, but I only feel a distant pain.

Nate... I love you. I wish I would've said it earlier.

And right at that moment, I feel a wave of his magic flood over me.

He's trying to find me.

But before I can grasp it, it pulls back. He didn't notice me.

I dare my magic to flow out as far is it can, leaving my soul exposed.

I need to get to him.

His magic shoots out more precisely this time, straight at me, and my magic lashes out with it. It tangles together and faintly tugs on it. *I'm here.* I show him. *I'm here.*

And in response, a tug comes from his side.

A sob escapes from my throat.

I need to hold on a little longer. I can't just give up and I can't leave him behind like this.

With my magic no longer wrapped around my soul, I feel the Alk piercing my skin. The sob is instantly turned into a scream of pain.

Nate and I have so much more to do. I want to finish that final trial. I want to figure out what happened to my parents. But most of all, I want to live happily with Nate. Just wake up next to him every morning. Kiss him under the stars. Walk through the gardens. Maybe even start a family when we're ready.

I want so much, yet I have so little time.

I exhale deeply as Kreinn pushes further. The poker pierces my skin and I cry out.

Then the front door of the cabin bursts open. The poker clatters to the floor and all three men whirl around to the door. Through sagging eyelids, I see Nate standing in the doorway, Jade and Madion right behind him.

With a world-ending rage, my mate says, "You made a very big mistake."

CHAPTER 27

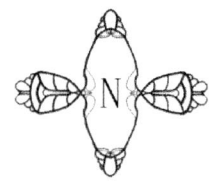

At the sight of my mate stabbed, broken and covered in blood, I lose it.

At the heart-wrenching sob she lets out when she sees me, I explode.

I go for the man in front of Dawn, the man that was just holding an Alk poker over her heart. He's going to perish first.

He snatches a dagger from the table and meets it with mine. He might tower over me, but the rage coursing through me makes up for my disadvantage.

In the corner of my eye, I see Jade and Madion moving to the man behind Dawn, and on the other side, Jake and Adrian are going for the one at the table.

I crash into the man from the left, not wanting to fall on top of a now unconscious Dawn. We need to get her out of here, fast.

On our way to the ground, I dig my knees into his chest, causing him to gasp for air as we hit the floor.

At the same time, I see Madion driving her sword through the second man. He crumples to the floor and doesn't get up again.

Everyone falls silent. The only thing audible is Dawn's heavy yet shallow breathing.

I start punching, just punching the man's face to a bloody pulp. He almost killed her and felt good about it. How dare he think he can do that to anyone?

When the man is near passing out, I snatch the hot poker off the floor. If he thinks he could kill her with this, I'll show him just how much it hurts.

I lift the poker to make the fatal blow, but a hand wraps around my wrist. "Stop. Just knock him out. I have plans for him," Madion says. "Same goes for that one." She motions for Jake, who has the third man in the same headlock I was in a couple of hours ago.

His eyes meet mine and recognition flickers there before Jake squeezes his airways close. He falls to the ground with a thud. I flick the end of the poker against the temple of the man underneath me, knocking him out cold as well.

I throw the poker in the fire and get up.

Everybody is silent, staring at the scene before them.

Dawn, shackled to a chair, several blades still inside her. Blood dripping from her nose, mouth and temple. Tears dried on her cheeks.

I drop to my knees in front of her, Madion and Jade coming to stand on either side of me. My hands drift to Dawn's wet cheeks, slightly lifting her head. "Dawn?" I whisper. "Please, open your eyes."

No response.

I carefully lift her head higher, leveling it with mine. "Please, Dawn, don't leave me," I whisper, tears forming in my eyes.

Another moment passes until she takes a slightly deeper breath. Her eyes flutter open, but that usual brightness is dimmed. Only pain and exhaustion are there.

"Nate?" she whispers.

"Hello, love," I say, my voice cracking. "Why don't we go home?"

She manages a pained nod.

I let go of her face, looking at what we'll have to pull out of her. My hand hovers over the blade in her stomach, but I can't push myself to grab it.

"Let me," Madion offers.

I move aside as she steps in front of Dawn. She presses her forehead against Dawn's, her left hand finds a spot at the back of Dawn's neck and her other hand wraps around the hilt.

"This is going to hurt," she mumbles.

Dawn merely whispers back, "I know."

And without any countdown, Madion pulls the blade out.

Dawn cries out in pain, but Madion holds her tight. She throws the sword aside and presses a clean cloth to the wound. "Shh, you're going to be okay."

I see her trying to clench her fists as tears start streaming down her face, but she can't. The daggers have cut off every tendon in her hands.

"Jade, pull the ones from her legs," Madion orders us. "Nate, be ready. Those daggers are made of Alk."

Meaning they're going to bleed heavily, heal slowly and leave scars.

Jade takes a deep breath to ready herself. "Okay."

Madion keeps Dawn in the same position to keep her steady. Jade grabs one dagger and instantly pulls it out. I press the cloth to the wound as Jade moves on to the next one. Jade takes over as I give Dawn a once-over.

Then we all notice what remains to be removed and I feel Dawn's panic rising, her breathing quickening with it. Causing her stomach to bleed more heavily, too. Madion moves out of my way and steps behind the chair to let me take over, but keeps the cloth pressed against the gaping wound.

My hands gently grab Dawn's face, making her look at me. "Almost there. Just these two left." I see her fingers twitching from the corner of my eyes.

I grab them and slowly massage her fingers down to her palm, trying to calm her down. "Do you want me to count down?" I ask her.

She shakes her head. I just have to pull them out when I can.

My fingers reach her palm, right in front of the dagger. My right hand stays on her cheek, making her look at me. "Just look at me." I smile faintly at her and see that sparkle in her eyes slowly rise to the surface.

Then I pull the dagger. She momentarily closes her eyes to take a sharp breath.

Her fingers tremble as she tries to make a fist. So I lay my hand on her palm. "Let it rest."

She listens and lets her hand go limp again.

I do the same thing with her other hand. I massage her fingers all the way to her palm, making them relax before I pull the second dagger.

It luckily comes out smoothly.

Jade already has the shackles open, causing Dawn to topple forward. I catch her as her arms go around my neck. She tries to grab onto my shirt, but her hands won't let her. She buries her face in the nape of my neck instead, letting out every emotion she's been holding, and I do nothing else but hold her tight.

"Do we have anything to properly wrap her hands and thighs in?" I ask, everyone now staring.

Adrian opens the bag he has been carrying with him and reaches out several rolls of bandages to Madion.

I lift Dawn off the chair and put her sideways in my lap, so she can rest her head on my shoulder. Madion kneels down and gently grabs one of Dawn's bleeding hands. She wraps them expertly, stopping the bleeding as much as possible. And by the way Dawn lifts her hand to my neck, I can see it's starting to heal.

Her second hand is done before I even blink and Madion goes straight to Dawn's heavily bleeding legs. "This is going to require stitches," she mumbles to no one in particular.

Then Madion glances over her shoulder. "Jake, Adrian. Grab the two that are still alive. Tie one to the chair and the other to the fireplace."

They look stunned for a moment at her order but quickly start moving.

Both Dawn's thighs are wrapped up, but blood is already blooming across the bandages.

"You're going to have to stand up for a moment," she says to Dawn, who just buries her head further in my neck. She's exhausted.

Madion points her attention to me. "Just hold her up. I only need to have access to her stomach."

Jade comes on the other side of Dawn and wraps an arm around her waist. I do the same. Together we carefully lift Dawn until her feet are beneath her again. Her full weight is leaning on us, because walking is not going to happen soon.

Madion lifts Dawn's shirt and presses the cloth against the wound, which she then fastens around Dawn's stomach with several rolls of bandages, fastening them with a knot at the end.

"You're going to have to carry her back," she says.

I nod in response and carefully slide my arm under Dawn's knees and lift her in my arms. Madion steps in front of us and cautiously reaches a hand to Dawn's arms around my neck. She takes Dawn's hand and puts another cloth against Dawn's stomach as blood blooms there too. "Try to keep as much pressure on it as possible, okay?" she tells Dawn.

She nods in return, and Madion gives her a light kiss on her temple. "You'll be okay."

At that, Dawn cracks a small smile.

I turn to leave, but I'm stopped by a hand on my shoulder. "You two go with him," Madion says to Adrian and Jade.

"What about you?" Adrian asks.

I hear a grunt of the man I knocked out behind me as she answers him, "Oh, I wouldn't worry about us."

She chuckles, something dangerous gleaming in her eyes. "Those two are the ones that should be worried, or rather terrified."

Jake and Adrian decide not to ask more questions and step out of the cabin.

I lean back slightly and mumble to Madion, "Hurt those bastards for what they did to her."

Madion only glances over her shoulder at me, the look in her eyes now cold and out for blood. "Oh, Nate. When I'm done, they're going to wish they never laid a hand on her. They'll be begging for me to end it."

I swallow deeply at those words, but one look at Jade tells me I'm definitely not the one that should be worried. She has the same look pointed right at the men who are now getting aware of what's happening.

With her gaze still on the men, Jade says, "Get her back to the camp. We'll handle things here."

And that's my cue to leave this hellhole.

The door slams shut behind me. I hear the door lock and then only silence.

One of them throws a shield of air around the cabin, keeping unwanted guests out and noises in.

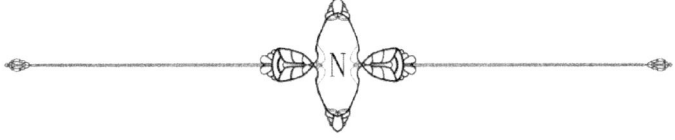

I gently lay Dawn on our bed. Her breathing has gotten more relaxed and no longer shallow.

Then I send Adrian off to grab stitching supplies, and Jake for water and towels. When they're off, I turn to Dawn, who is now sleeping soundly on the blankets. I tear open her ruined shirt and take off her pants. And when she lays there, the full extent of what they did to her hits me.

Her knees are black and blue, her face and neck coated with blood and all the stab wounds. The ones to the stomach, legs and hands we already knew about, but in this light, I see what else they did.

Small, very small dots cover the swirls on her arms. They traced those lines. There are bruises between the streaks of blood on her neck as well, just as purple and blue as her knees.

When I hear people approaching, I cover her chest and legs with a blanket. Adrian enters a moment later with the things I asked for.

The bowl with warm water is put on my left and the stitching supplies on the nightstand.

I grab the needle and thread, but only then I notice how badly I'm shaking.

And I can't get the needle threaded. I try and try, but fail. Warm hands wrap around mine as Adrian kneels beside me. "Go lay next to her. I'll do this."

"Thank you," I mumble as I get up, and I take off my bloody shirt.

Then I climb onto the bed on the other side and pull Dawn closer to me.

Adrian pulls aside the blanket and wants to start with her stomach. "Is she conscious?" he asks as he gets the needle threaded in one try.

"I don't think so," I say, tucking her hair behind her ear.

He leans forward to push the bandage down and show the gravity of the wound. The bleeding has almost stopped, but this still won't be able to heal properly without stitches keeping the wound closed.

Adrian dips a towel in the water and starts wiping away the blood as careful as he can. He hands me a second towel to clean her face and neck.

Slowly but surely, the wound gets clean, and Adrian can start stitching, but the moment the needle pierces Dawn's skin, she writhes in my arms.

"Damn, I was hoping she'd be out cold," Adrian grumbles.

I scan the tent, looking for anything that might help. "Wait, Madion told me about some vials she brought. They numb the skin."

She always brings them in case she is the one that needs stitches. Her fear of needles is the whole reason for that.

Adrian pushes the cloth back on the wound, telling me to put pressure again. Then gets up and walks to Jake. They exchange a few words before Jake hurries off.

Only moments later, he returns, a leather bag in his hands. Adrian empties it until the vials, filled with a dark purple substance, roll out onto the bed. "This should be it."

He spreads some of it around the wound. We wait for a few minutes, and when we see Dawn settle down, Adrian tries again. This time she doesn't respond once.

"Okay, now we need to turn her over. That blade went right through her."

We carefully lay her on her freshly stitched stomach and fall silent at her back. It's burned, completely burned, with two more stab wounds we hadn't even noticed until now.

"Oh heavens," I mutter.

That's what was in that sack on the floor. They've let the Alk drip down her back the entire time.

Adrian lets his hand graze over her spine. "It's not as bad as it looks. I think this will heal for the biggest part."

And in minutes, he has all three wounds closed and covered up.

Then our concern drops to her hands. Adrian slowly unwraps one, not wanting to do more damage.

We both let out a sigh of relief when we find the hole partially closed already. Her hands will be fine.

The legs are a different story. Several muscles are seared away, straight through the middle. With time, they'll heal, and I really hope they'll do so before the final trial. Whenever that may be.

Adrian smears the purple ointment on both legs and starts again.

First, stitching the muscles back together as well as possible, then closing the skin and wrapping it in bandages, too.

He packs the needles and threads back up and stands. "Just let her sleep. We'll see how she's doing in the morning."

"Thank you, again," I say, tossing the blankets over Dawn and I.

He turns right as he reaches the tent flaps. "You two have nothing to thank us for. I'd almost say you should scold us for letting those men walk in with no resistance."

I hear Jake inhale sharply from outside, and I see the guilt flooding Adrian's eyes. So I reassure them, "You have nothing to be sorry for. It happened, it's done, there is nothing else we can do besides help her get back up."

He thinks on the words for a moment. "You're right." He sighs, pushing aside the flap. "Sleep tight. We'll be here if you need us."

I let myself fall back against the pillows and lay on my side to look at Dawn's face.

I just stare at her, taking in every single detail.

I was scared that if I lost her today, I might not remember every small thing about her.

How she has a tiny freckle just in front of her left ear, or the—

"You know," she suddenly rasps, "staring is considered inappropriate."

A faint smile tugs on her lips as her hand touches mine, and I cautiously interlock my fingers with hers. "Hello to you, too."

"I thought I'd never see you again," she whispers, her smile instantly disappearing.

Together till the end, or no end at all, I whisper between us. "I wouldn't believe this was the end."

She tightens her hold on me, not showing if it causes her any pain. "Stay with me, forever."

Her other hand lies on her stomach, absently rubbing the bandages. I wrap an arm around her waist and pull her closer until she's flush against me. "I'm not going anywhere."

Dawn nestles herself closer against me, mumbling, "Good."

And with that, she falls back asleep, and I follow her soon after.

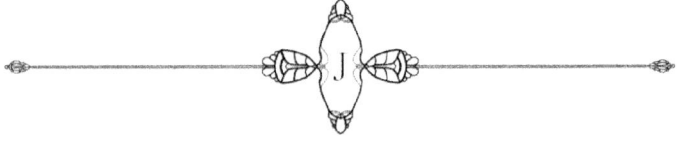

Madion is casually leaning against the doorpost, twirling a dagger between her fingers. I squatted in front of the chair that holds one of the men whose days are numbered.

They both started waking up right before Nate left with Dawn, but they have yet to wake fully. And we want them to be awake for what's going to happen.

I know Madion will do anything. She has to get information out of them, and I won't stop her. I've seen this persona of her before when she was the one being tortured. The usual brightness in her eyes dims, leaving a cold void.

She always apologizes afterwards for what she had to do, but I don't care. I know it's still the woman I love underneath it all. Glancing back at her, I whisper to her with a faint smile, *I love you.*

And I swear a smile flashes across her face when she responds, *I love you too.* Before it's completely gone again.

My thoughts drift away from me as we hear both men grunt.

Let's get to work.

"Good evening," I say.

Their eyes shoot open and panic when they see the predicament they're in.

"Already regretting your previous decisions?" Madion muses from behind me.

"We'll give you anything," the man in front of the fire blurts out.

Madion pushes herself off the doorpost, simultaneously as I rise to my feet. "The time for giving is over. You made a mistake and we're here to show you the consequences," she says.

"What do you want?" the man in front of me grumbles.

I place my sword under his chin, making him look at us. "Answers." Blood dribbles down his neck as I put pressure. "Otherwise you'll find out just how creative torture can be."

"We know nothing," he mutters.

One look between Madion and me, and we know what we're going to do.

We stalk to the fireplace. Madion lets the fire grow bigger and hotter, not even lifting a finger. And I grab the collar of the man in front of it and push him backwards, stopping him right before the fire touches him.

"Talk," I snap close to his face.

His face pales as it finally becomes clear to him, he is not getting out of here. "We know nothing," he shouts.

"Tell that to the person you just tortured," Madion sneers at him. "Because I am fairly certain she kept saying the same thing. Yet you kept going."

I push him closer to the fire, his shirt almost catching it. "Why? Do you enjoy it when people are in pain? Do you enjoy your own pain just as much?"

His shirt is now inches away from catching fire and burning him alive with it. "I'm not repeating myself. You know what to do," I say, my face inches from his.

"We were cornered in an alley last week," the man in the chair answers.

"Keep talking," Madion says, creating a small fire in the palm of her hand. "What did they look like?"

"I didn't see much. I kn—know it was a wo—woman," he stammers out. "She wore a long cloak that concealed her face."

Madion walks over to the man. "What did she say then?"

"If we got to the princess, she'd pay us in gold."

"What was the exact assignment?" She brings the fire to his face.

"We were to take her away with no casualties, then we could do whatever we wanted as long as we got information on what she knew about Railon and Iluniel, especially the strategies and armies."

Madion narrows her eyes at him. "Is that so? And you decided to torture her for the information, right?"

At that, he stays silent.

"I thought so." She lets the flame touch the tip of his nose and he recoils. "Now it's my turn to have my fun with you."

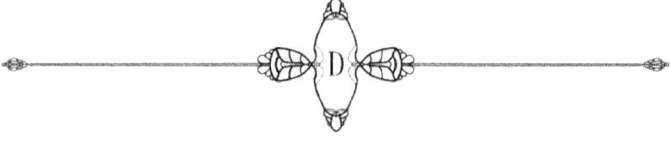

"How shall we carve him up now?" Kreinn laughs, his blade hovering over Nate's chest. "We did the

legs and arms. What about the chest?" He drags the blade down Nate's chest.

I struggle in my bonds. They took him. When I was giving up, they went for Nate.

He was tied to a table, his bracelets tossed in the fire, and the first thing they did was put the same daggers through his hands as they did with me.

I started screaming when he started. I felt his pain exploding between us and my heart felt like it was being ripped out of my chest.

Now I'm gagged and crying, crying at the broken man in front of me.

I know nothing, but they don't believe it. Soon Nate's heart will give out, just like mine. Because I am not staying in this wretched world without him by my side.

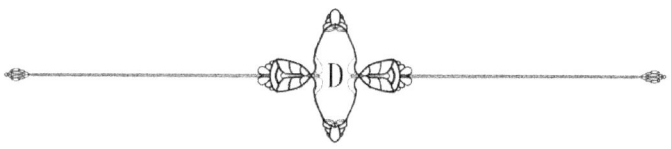

"Dawn!" Hands on my shoulders are shaking me, trying to pull me from the nightmare as they shout, "Dawn!"

I'm screaming, screaming at what I just saw.

The hands find my face. "Dawn, breathe."

I listen.

"Again."

I breathe in deeply.

Slowly, I open my eyes and I'm met by Nate's concerned eyes hovering over me. Those beautiful baby blue eyes.

He looks deep into mine, trying to figure out what happened. "Hey. You're okay. No one's going to hurt you anymore."

I wrap my bandaged hands around his waist, my muscles throbbing with every movement. "They were hurting you."

He puts his chin on my head. "I'm right here."

I dig my fingers deeper into his back, not wanting to let go. "I was so scared."

He slightly tenses. "I know. I think I felt it. The panic."

"And then I felt you—I felt you and I held on," I whisper.

Nate lays next to me again and gently pulls me against him. "You don't know how relieved I was to feel you. But that relief vanished completely when I saw you." I lift my head from his chest as he confesses, "I thought I was too late."

My head drops against him again, and my hand rubs soothing circles on his back. I might've been the one in pain, but he was most likely having a panic attack.

A sharp pain shoots through my hand. I hiss and pull it to the moonlight. It's still covered in blood. My fingers start trembling again at the amount of blood coating to them and the wound beneath the bandages.

Nate's warm and calloused hands wrap around mine. "Why don't we get you cleaned up?"

I barely manage to nod. Nate reaches over me and grabs a warm and wet towel. Then very gently, he rubs all the blood off my hand. Beneath my fingernails, my wrists, exposing the now even more recognizable scars.

He removes the bandage from my hand to clean the last bits of blood, and I'm comforted to see the wound almost closed and healing.

My other hand is clean soon after. We decide to leave the bandages off to let the wounds breathe and heal during the night. Nate tucks them safely between me and his chest, wrapped around each other.

He throws the blankets over us again and sighs. "I'm so grateful to still be able to hold you in my arms." His arm snakes around my waist and he kisses my nose. "Now sleep. I'll be right here."

"Okay," I whisper. Exhaustion is taking over fast.

Healing uses a lot of energy, and since my magic is still shy and has yet to come out again, I'm going to be exhausted for a while.

The last thing I feel is his lips on the top of my head before sleep drags me under.

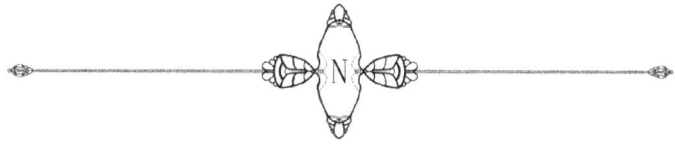

I know she noticed it, too. Her wrists. The scars are now almost as bad as mine. And there are going to be even more scars to remind her of tonight.

It might have been only four hours, but what damage they managed to do in those hours is horrendous.

And if we had only gotten there a few moments later, I'd have lost her. And I would have exploded.

Because I love her.

And since I met her, I can't imagine a life without her.

Seeing and feeling her safe in my arms, sleeping peacefully, calms me and my magic.

Yet, I don't feel her magic now. It's like it has retreated so deeply into her soul that it won't or can't come out.

She's going to need time. Her nightmares are already worse than before, not to mention the panic attacks I know are coming when she looks at herself in the mirror and sees all the scars.

Whoever ordered and paid those men to hurt her, and eventually kill her, will be found eventually. And when they are, I'm going to hurt them in ways they can't even imagine.

Too much has been taken from me over the years, my parents, my childhood, my freedom, but I'm not letting anything, or anyone take her away.

When my thoughts finally die down enough for me to fall asleep, someone pokes their head inside the tent. I look up to find Madion there, urging me to come with her. I throw on a shirt and a coat, not even bothering to put my shoes on, and follow her outside.

Jade is sitting on a log and Madion takes her place next to her.

"How is she doing?" Jade asks, fidgeting with a twig.

I drag my hand through my hair. "As well as can be expected. In the past two hours, she has woken up twice from a nightmare, but she's calm enough now that I hope she'll sleep until morning."

"Good. Because she can't hear yet what we found out," Madion says. "And before you ask, yes, the men are dead. We took care of it."

"Even better," I mumble.

Jade chimes in with an approving nod and grabs Madion's hand.

This is going to be bad.

I sit down on a log and brace my forearms on my thighs. "Just lay it on me."

"They said it was a woman. She cornered them in an alley in a nearby town and offered them gold," Madion says, anger rising in her voice. "She would pay them in gold if they took Dawn. They could do whatever they wanted with her as long as her body was never found again, and if she told them what she knew about Railon."

"Did they know who Dawn was?" I ask.

"Yes. They knew exactly who she was, but still risked it," Jade says as she wrings her hands together.

"Tell me they had a description of the woman in the alley."

They exchange a worried look.

This is not going to be good.

"Eventually, they gave in and told everything they knew. Which wasn't much, but they gave some pointers on how the woman looked," Jade says, glancing at Madion.

She is not even looking at anything, just blankly staring at the ground, thinking of something. After a moment, she continues Jade's story. "She placed a dome around them, so no one heard of the transaction." Madion inhales sharply before her next words. "And she had white hair with blonde streaks peeking out from under her hood."

Now she does meet my eyes.

"Don't tell me you think—" I say, hoping it's not true.

Madion gives me a resolved but sad look. "That is exactly what I think."

CHAPTER 28

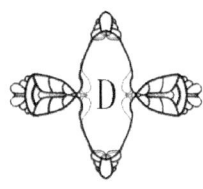

Every muscle in my body hurts when I feel the sun washing over me and a breeze coursing through the entrance of the tent.

At least I made it to the morning.

It's going to take a while for everything to heal, though.

I can bend my knees again, my hands are almost fully healed, my shoulders are a bit stiff, but nothing to worry about.

Then we reach my legs and stomach. My stomach will take a while because of how severe and major the wound is. My legs will heal with time too, but they'll scar on the inside and outside, which means I have to keep a close eye on the recovery. Otherwise, I could end up with a huge weakness compared to others.

So the best thing to do is just slowly walk on them, rebuild the strength that was seared away.

I try to turn over, accompanied by a loud grunt. "Godd—"

Strong hands grab my hips. "Easy." And help me turn over.

I look straight into Nate's eyes, his brown hair a complete mess, his eyelids only half-opened. "I'm sorry I woke you," I mumble.

"It's okay," he says, his hands drifting to my back.

He trails his fingers down my spine. "How are you feeling? Because from the noise you just made, everything is sore."

I stretch my fingers. "Some parts feel better." I rub my thigh. "Some don't."

"Good," he breathes.

My stomach tightens and lets out a grumble. "But I think I could use something to fill my stomach."

Nate gives my forehead a kiss before he lets go of me and gets out of the bed. "Then one plate of food is coming right up."

"Thank you," I say before laying back down.

He steps out to go get some food. When a moment passes, someone else steps in.

Adrian.

"Hey," he says, rubbing the back of his neck awkwardly.

I prop myself up on my elbows. "Don't just stand there, come here."

He hurries over and pulls me into a tight but gentle hug. "You have no idea how happy I am to see you in one piece, or how far you want to call it one piece."

"I'm okay," I reassure him. "Don't worry about me."

His grip tightens. "I should worry about you. We failed you last night. You got hurt badly because of us."

I let my hand go up and down his back, trying to soothe him. "Don't think like that. No one could've known that this would happen." I pull back. "I don't want you to beat yourself up over something you had no control over. It happened, it's done. Nothing to do about it now. Okay?"

Now Adrian manages a smile. "I think Nate might've said the exact same thing last night."

"Then you have to believe me, and him, that none of this was your fault," I counter.

"Okay," he finally says. The guilt in his eyes slowly recedes as I give him another smile.

More light pools into the tent as Nate enters with a plate and pitcher of water. He puts both on the nightstand, then moves to lay a board on my lap so I can properly eat without the plate toppling over.

Adrian bids us farewell and retreats to his spot outside. And while I eat my food, Nate gets to sharpening his weapons, since he doesn't really have anything else to do.

However, the sound of the block sliding down the steel already brings back memories of last night. I cringe at the sound, but I try to block it out.

Nate picks up on it and halts his movement. "What's wrong?" He looks down at what he's doing, then at me, then at my hands. "Oh."

"It's okay, that sound is just painful right now," I say. "Since it was the only sound right before—" I lift my hands to emphasize.

He stays quiet for a moment and then makes way to put his dagger and block down. "I'll stop."

"No," I blurt out, and he stops dead in his tracks. "Don't let me stop you, please."

Nate looks at me, not believing my words. But he mutters, unsure, "Okay." Before picking his dagger back up and continuing his work.

I swallow more of the food, my eyes focused solely on my plate, the sound of the dagger in my ears. More and more food I shove down my throat, but it's hard to get it down. I know nothing is going to happen, yet the noise is nauseating.

A dagger falling on the ground suddenly rings through the tent. I look up to find Nate with his hands set behind him on the table. "You can barely get your food down. I'm not doing this right now, no matter how much you tell me to do it."

I meet his eyes. "I don't want you to have to stop something you want to do because of me."

"Dawn." His gaze softens. "I won't even enjoy doing it if it makes you this uncomfortable, especially if it reminds you of last night."

I bury my face in my hands. "Why do you have to be this sweet and understanding?"

He outright laughs at it. "Because you are sweet and understanding when it comes to my problems, or rather traumas."

"We're both walking traumas, aren't we?" I joke.

The tent flaps fly open. "We all are, in a way," Madion says.

I put aside my plate as Jade comes in behind her. Her face lights up when she sees me. She runs over and almost tackles me with a hug.

"Easy," I gasp as she slams into my ribs, knocking the wind out of me.

Madion saunters in behind her. "Maybe a bit less enthusiastic, Jade. We don't want to break her in half."

She pulls away from me. "Sorry."

I pull her right back in. "Don't worry about it. I appreciate the enthusiasm of seeing me alive."

Jade laughs at my words and puts her chin on my shoulder. "I'm glad you're okay."

I keep silent, only showing my gratitude by embracing her tightly.

"My turn," Madion then says with a hand on Jade's shoulder.

Jade lets go with a grumble, but makes way for Madion, who is more gentle with her hug.

"Are they—?" I whisper.

Her grip grows stronger. "Yes. We took care of them. They're gone."

"Thank you," I whisper as I bury my face in her shoulder.

"Shh," she soothes as tears well up in my eyes.

Madion has always been like a big sister to me, more than Leanne has been these past few years. No matter the circumstances, she kept us all calm and collected, kept me calm. And whenever I needed someone, she was there.

"Why don't we take a stroll? Just to get all those muscles working again." She lets go and brushes the hair out of my face.

I nod and hoist myself to my feet with her support. I nearly topple over, but Madion catches me by the elbows just in time. Nate comes to my side and slides an arm around me. "Just one step at the time."

I mumble my agreement and try to make my legs move, which is not as easy as it may sound. It takes two minutes to even get to the entrance of the tent.

But eventually, after a lot of small steps, sweat and pain, I walk all the way to a clearing in the woods. Nate guides me to a log formation at the edge and props me on one.

I stretch my legs in front of me and rub soothing circles over the bandages around my thighs with the heel of my hand. This is going to be a tough recovery.

"Thank you," I whisper as Nate sits next to me.

His only response is a kiss to my temple and an arm around my waist.

My breathing slows down after a minute or two and nobody has said a word yet. All waiting for me to speak.

I take a final deep breath and slowly let it out.

"Maybe on the way back, you could use your magic to support your legs?" Jade throws in when I look everyone over.

I faintly smile. "Well, there I have a problem."

"Why?" Madion asks as she leans forward, sitting cross-legged, with her elbows propped on her knees.

I bury my face in my hands. "Because when he had that poker over my heart." My fingers start trembling again. "My magic coiled around my soul, and it has yet to uncoil." One hand drifts to my heart, to the small scar there. "But I don't know how."

After a moment of silence, Nate sighs. "I do."

He pulls the remaining hand off my face and intertwines it with his. "I had to do it too after Vergus got me out."

He sharply inhales at the memories that must be flooding his head. "It's a delicate process, but with the three of us helping you, you should succeed."

"Okay," I say, hesitant. "What do I need to do?"

"You'll need to stand first." Nate tightens his hold on my waist and pulls me up. "Then we're moving to the middle of this clearing."

He carries me there, since my legs give out after three steps. Then he lowers me to my knees, my thighs protesting harshly.

"Okay, now the three of us will sit in a circle around her." Nate kneels in front of me, Madion to my right and Jade to my left.

"Even though not everyone can control it, our power comes from deep within the earth," Nate starts. "So through the earth and us." He makes a circling motion with his hand. "We can uncoil each element separately from your soul."

"Jade will take water, I'll take air, and Madion will take fire. As for the earth, you'll have to do that one on your own."

"Okay, so what do I have to do, exactly?" I ask.

Nate grabs my hands. He spreads my fingers and presses my palms to the ground. "Try to feel that connection. Slowly breathe in and slowly breathe out."

I follow his instructions and keep a calm and steady breathing, while I challenge my magic to reach out to where it originally came from.

And very slowly, very carefully, I feel that faint thread between my magic and the earth beneath me.

"Good," Nate says. "Jade, let your magic flow through the earth to Dawn, feel for that strand of water wrapped around her soul. Once Dawn finds it too, guide her in uncoiling it."

Jade hums in agreement.

Moments later, I feel a faint magic pass through me like an arrow, right to my soul. I follow it to where it grasps one of the four strands wrapped around my soul. I grab onto it, too. Jade's magic gives me a light nudge, and I smile at the gesture. I nudge her back and we carefully pull on the strand, loosening it.

Eventually, it comes loose enough for Jade to let go and for me to finish the job.

I feel my magic filling me again, but it's not complete yet.

"One down," I whisper, and I feel Madion come in with her magic, which already feels heavier, more dangerous, than Jade's did.

She finds the fire strand in mere seconds and guides me to it. We follow the same steps as I did with Jade.

And my magic rises again.

"Halfway there," I say as Nate comes in.

His magic feels warm and safe as he steadily and gently moves through me to my soul. I let him guide me to the right strand of the two remaining, and we both grab on.

It feels as if he's holding me firmly, like his arms are around me, as we pull on the strand. And again, after carefully tugging and twisting, it comes loose.

That magic comes flooding into me and I let it roam free. I let it make sure I'm okay. Otherwise, it won't retreat to my soul when I ask it to.

"You'll have to do the last strand on your own," Nate mutters to me.

I nod and pull strength from the earth to guide me.

It leads me to the last thread wrapped around my soul. I grab on with the strength of the earth behind me. I tug on it, and tug, but it won't come loose.

I pull more from the ground below me. I will it to help me. Together, we carefully pull and pull until the end slowly gives way.

I give it one final tug, and it snaps loose. Releasing every last bit of magic I possess.

It explodes out of me, shooting in every direction. Knocking over Madion and Jade, but not Nate. I still feel him in front of me. He felt it coming, because he let his magic linger behind in case something went wrong or if I needed any help.

The moment he felt the final thread come loose, he retreated and braced himself.

I spy Madion and Jade a couple meters away, unfortunately they didn't feel it coming and were swung towards the trees.

Jade props herself on her elbows and looks at me. "I forgot how much of a punch you pack."

Everybody laughs at her comment. Madion gets herself into a sitting position, and Jade decides to just stay down.

So I turn my attention to Nate, who is still staring at me. "What is it?"

"Do you feel better?" he asks.

"A lot better," I respond.

"Good." He smiles.

Jade clears her throat. "How are you still in the same place, or the same position for that matter, Nate?"

He stares at her. "I felt it coming."

She sits up and stares back. "How?"

"First, mating bond. Second, I lingered behind to see if everything went right."

"Don't you feel it when I'm charging up for an attack?" Madion cuts in, looking at Jade.

Jade directs her attention to her mate. "I do indeed."

"And I can feel you using your magic for almost everything. Closing the door, picking up a needle you dropped. Everything."

"Why put extra effort into something when I can also train my magic with precise, directed movements?" Jade winks at Madion.

"Don't be a smart ass." Madion smirks as she leans against a tree.

"You love it," Jade says as she crawls closer to Madion. Once she reaches her, Jade nestles herself against Madion's chest.

I sit flat on my ass and look at Nate. "I'm going to need help to get up."

"Come here." He chuckles as he slides his arm under my knees and one behind my back. Then he pulls me in his lap, and I nestle close against his chest. As if I could never do it again.

He wraps his arms around me and places one of his sweet kisses on my hair.

And that's all we do the rest of the day.

Just enjoying each other's company, like we wouldn't be able to ever again.

CHAPTER 29

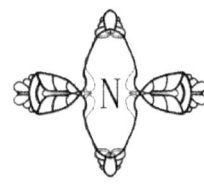

Dawn has been asleep for two days now. A peaceful sleep. No nightmares.

And nothing will wake her up, except for her soul.

I haven't left her room.

Occasionally breathing in some fresh air on the balcony, but most of the time I'm either in the uncomfortable chair reading one of the many books she owns or next to her in bed.

The journey back was difficult. Dawn was in so much pain after a couple hours on Lio that the guards had to clear out one of the weapon carts to let her lay there for the rest of the journey. Halfway through, she passed out, and she has yet to wake up.

I'm not worried about her not waking up again. I can feel her soul, I can check on it, just like she can with mine.

I can see that hers is hard at work to heal every injury she gained during the torture and during the trial. Her soul never had the chance to adjust to the new wave of magic she released after the trial. And the healing puts a lot of strain on her soul with it.

And because of that, this sleep is almost like some sort of unconscious state in which one of the most powerful women in this world can recover. A state in which Dawn can recover.

Because she might not believe it herself, but she's powerful. Maybe even more powerful than her father. I have seen his powers at work when I was little. And I think after this third trial, she might already match him.

After finishing my book, I'm now laying next to her, making sure nothing is amiss with her magic or soul, while waiting for her to wake up.

I brush a strand of hair away from her face and let my hand drift over her cheek. I still don't know what I ever did to deserve her as my mate, as my soulmate.

"You know," she suddenly whispers, "staring is still considered inappropriate."

I let my hand stay on her cheek. "Hello to you too, for the second time."

She puts her hand on mine as she slowly opens her eyes. "It's nice waking up like this."

"I'm glad you finally woke up."

"How long was I out?"

"Two days."

"And what have you been up to these two days?" she says, her eyes now fully focused and clear. No traces of her long sleep left behind.

I turn to lie on my back, my hand behind my head. "I've been here, reading and watching over you."

"You've been in this room for two days?"

"You've been here too," I counter.

Dawn gives me a flat stare before whacking me upside the head. "Really?"

"What else was I supposed to do?" I ask, as innocent as possible.

She hoists herself into somewhat of a sitting position. "I don't know. You could've at least gone outside for a walk."

My hand drifts to her thigh, slowly massaging the muscles. Dawn lets out a hum of relief as her hand clenches the blanket. "I've been outside on the balcony," I retort.

Her hand shoots to mine. She whacks me upside the head again, with my own hand this time. "You're way too sarcastic for your own good."

I intertwine my fingers with hers and lean in closer. "You love it."

She leans closer too, our noses now touching. "Maybe."

"And what do I have to do to make you say yes?" I mumble.

She doesn't answer, she just stares. And I gaze back into those rich blue eyes. Her pupils encircled with gold.

It's still odd that they're gold, but I wouldn't know any explanation for it.

One of the several mysteries yet to be uncovered.

But at this moment, all my thoughts seem to just float away. I'm here, she's here. This moment couldn't get any more perfect, except for one thing.

I move closer, our lips only inches away. I want to kiss her so badly. Her hand drifts to my neck, my hand goes to her cheek.

Suddenly the door opens, Adrian and Jake enter and Dawn and I part.

"Oh," Jake mumbles when he sees our flustered faces.

"Now would be a bad time to say that Leanne wanted to talk to Dawn as soon as she was awake," Adrian says, trying hard not to look too interested in what was going on moments prior to them barging in.

Dawn buries her face in her hands. "Tell her I'll be there in a moment. Let me just freshen up."

She slides out of the bed, steadying herself with the nightstand and slowly makes her way to the bathroom. When she almost slips at the door, I catch her and help her with the rest.

But the entire walk to the throne room is something she wants to do herself. So when we're at the threshold of her room, I let go.

And pray Leanne has some sympathy left for her sister.

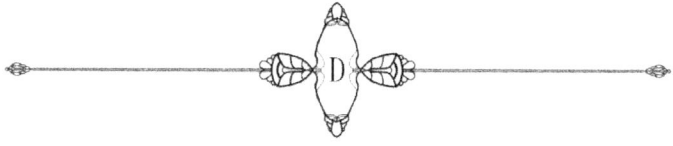

To say things with Leanne went bad is, once again, an understatement. By the time I reached the throne room, my legs and stomach were burning. I was holding back tears by the time I reached the bottom steps of the throne. Then she had the guts to ask me how I was doing with a big smile on her face, while seeing in how much pain I was. She didn't care.

After I said I'd be fine, she immediately moved to a conversation about Railon.

She didn't care what happened. She didn't care that I almost died.

Why would she?

She never does and with the thought of her killing our parents in the back of my mind, I'm not sure she ever did.

Another thing I need to figure out soon.

So much is coming at me, and I just don't know what to do anymore.

Those slivers I receive between the trials with their mystery sender. Leanne's reasons to hate me. The person who paid Kreinn and his cronies to torture and kill me. The person who killed Anna.

Things just don't add up.

The night of my seventeenth birthday, also known as the night my parents died, was peaceful. Nothing was out of the ordinary, so why did Leanne suddenly decide to kill them?

I know her letters to Draven could be an explanation, but according to the dates, they started the day after the assassination.

And with that comes the fact that she was rushing in with the guards while I was having a panic attack. She got me out. She was so kind, and still so much like my sister, prior to everything that happened.

But the day of the funeral, she completely turned. That was the first day she had me locked up.

Why did she turn like that? What caused everything that has happened?

So many questions, yet so few answers.

And it's eating me up on the inside.

Not knowing what my parents ever did to deserve a fate like this. Not knowing who the mysterious person is that sends me those messages, those slivers. I know they certainly knew my parents. They know Leanne and my dad's nickname for me. They know everything, yet I know nothing.

It can't be Leanne. She wouldn't go that far to torment me. I think she finds locking me up entertainment enough.

Neither my dad nor my mom could be it.

And that leaves me no one else that could be the mystery person.

I don't have any guesses as to who killed Anna or who tried to have me killed.

So I'm left with just thinking about each possible scenario.

"Why does everything need to be so complicated?" I grumble as I let my head drop on my pulled-up knees. Thankfully, my thighs granted me that movement.

Somebody sits down beside me. "Because life likes to screw us over."

Madion's emerald eyes look me over. "How did it go?"

"Bad. She didn't even care for a moment how I felt."

"That's Leanne, unfortunately." She sighs, mimicking my pose.

"It hasn't always been," I mutter sadly.

Madion gives me a sad smile. "I know."

I lay my head down on her shoulder. Together we just sit there, overlooking the plane I always go to when I feel like breaking down.

But I don't break because of the people around me. People I call friends, people I call family.

Madion breaks the silence between us. "You know, it's been a long time since I was scared."

I lift my head and notice the tears gathering in her eyes. I never want to see her cry, never.

"When I saw you slumped in that chair." She goes on, "I was terrified we were too late and scared that I broke my promise."

"What promise?" I ask.

"The promise I made myself the day your parents died." She takes a deep breath. "When I heard what had happened and saw you breaking down in that hallway. I never wanted to see you like that again, because you were in so much pain and I couldn't handle seeing it."

She lifts her head to look at me. "I promised myself I'd protect you, protect you from anything as long as I was still breathing. So when I saw Nate unconscious on the floor, with you nowhere in sight. I might've looked calm, but I was terrified of what was happening or what had already happened to you."

I wrap my arms around her, and she tightly hugs me back. "I love you, Madion." My hands clench her shirt. "Please, don't cry."

She buries her face in the nape of my neck, not wanting to let go. "I love you too."

"Then please stop those tears before they fall. I don't want to see you cry over me."

Madion lets go of me and almost furiously wipes her tears away. "Since we're already talking about that awful subject, Jade and I got information from the men."

I decide to not even ask about how they got it.

"And?" I ask, slightly curious what they found out.

"They gave us a description of the woman. Yes, a woman," she immediately adds, the disbelief must've been written across my face. "She had very distinct features. At least the one they could see."

"Which is?"

My curiosity is now replaced by fear at the look on Madion's face. "She had blonde hair with white streaks," she says, her hand already reaching for mine.

"No—No—No," I stammer out, my hands trembling as I lift them to my mouth.

Leanne tried to have me killed.

She tried to have the last obstacle in her way taken out.

CHAPTER 30

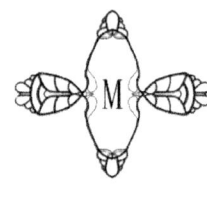

"Dawn!" I shout at her, my hands keeping her eyes directed at me.

She immediately seized up in panic as I told her. Her breathing hitched, and her hands are violently shaking as she buries her face in them.

Leanne wants her dead. Not just hurt or tormented. She wants her dead.

"Dawn! Look at me," I order her, trying to snap her focus to me.

"She—she tried to kill me," she mumbles softly to herself.

"Yes, but she failed. She tried, and she failed," I whisper, pulling her hands off her head. "You are stronger than her, Dawn. You survived everything she threw at you. Don't forget that."

She takes a few deep breaths, trying to calm that thumping heart down. "I didn't survive, at least not on my own. You all had to save me. You had to save me because I couldn't fight myself." She wipes away her tears with trembling fingers. "How could I ever save any of you when I can't even save myself?"

"Dawn—"

"You were crying because of me, Madion," she cuts me off.

I press her firmly against me, calming her. Her arms come around my waist in return.

Why does she always have to be so hard on herself? She doesn't have to take the whole world on by herself. That's why we're all here, not to save her, but to support her.

We'll hold her hand, be a shoulder to cry on, be a voice of reason. She just has to let us.

"Listen to me Dawn. I don't ever want to hear you say something like that again, you hear me? We are friends, we are equals. And I don't want anything in return for us saving you."

I place a kiss on her head, my only way of love I can show now.

Her arms slacken slightly, but don't let go. "Just let it all out," I whisper.

And she does.

Months, maybe even years of pain and suffering and grief, come out. She bottled it all up deep inside her, to never let it see the light of day again.

But every bottle has a limit, and she reached hers after all these years.

We need to take care of Leanne soon, because I don't think Dawn will last much longer living like this.

And after what feels like an hour, she lets go. Dried tears stuck to her cheeks, but no new ones forming.

She let it all out. She's empty.

"Thank you." She looks down at her hands, at the silver threads curling around her fingertips.

"You have nothing to thank me for." I take a hold of her hands. "Why don't you head back to your room and get some rest? I know your legs and stomach must be burning by now."

She merely nods before getting to her feet. She squeezes my hands one final time before sauntering back to the castle.

How I wish I could take this load off her shoulders.

How much I'd give to just take it from her.

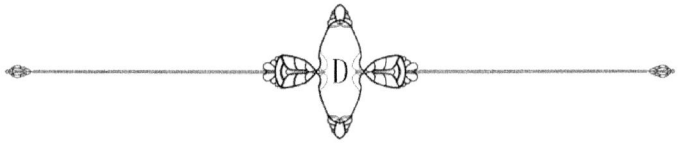

It's almost midnight when I feel strong arms wrap around me. Nate buries his face in the nape of my neck and lets out a deep breath. I tighten my grip on his arms and close my eyes again.

After a few minutes, his breathing slows down, yet the sleep doesn't let his grip on me falter.

I think he feels my pain, my distress, and knows that nothing can help me right now except for him being here.

I drag my fingers down his arm until I reach his wrist. His bare wrist.

Since we came back here, he's been taking his bracelets off before coming to bed.

And I love him for it. It might mean nothing to other people, but knowing he trusts me around his gravest scars gives me more courage with mine.

My eyes slowly close as his presence calms me, lulls me to sleep.

But hours later I wake again, this time not because of a nightmare, though.

A folded brown paper lies on my nightstand. Its presence feeling the same as those slivers.

I carefully lift Nate's arm off me and climb out of bed. Then toss on my silk bathrobe, still hate that thing, and walk to the balcony with the letter in my hand.

I silently open and close the doors, not wanting to wake Nate. Then I sit down against the outer wall overlooking the garden. Even at night, it seems like the flowers are glowing.

The letter is brief yet again, but at least longer than one sentence.

~

Dawn,
I can't say much, but all my previous messages are true.
I loved them with everything I had, just like you.
And my first warning still stands. Watch out, not everything is as it seems.
Find out what exactly happened that night, and everything will become clear.
I love you, little droplet.
Don't forget that.

~

The letter flutters down into my lap, my hands drop to my knees.

Why can't they just say who they are?

Telling me to figure out what exactly happened that night when I only remember and relive it in my nightmares.

They have become more vivid, and I've seen more of the complete picture, but it's not enough. I need to find out what happened the moment I passed out. That's the only way for me to get the whole picture.

The only thing I can do now is hope I get to see more of that night, or to get another sliver that might point me in the right direction.

Back inside, I throw the letter in the drawer of my nightstand with the other slivers. I have four things in total from the stranger now, yet no clue who they might be.

Almost as if feeling I'm sitting on the edge of the bed, Nate's arm wraps around me, his hand flat on the now closed wound on my stomach.

"What's wrong?" he mumbles, his voice heavy with sleep.

I lay down again and pull his arms around me. He puts his chin back at the nape of my neck and sighs. "You've been on edge all day. Talk to me."

"Just everything is becoming too much again. I thought I almost had everything figured out," I whisper.

Nate turns me around, so I face him instead of the windows. "Everything will be okay. You're not alone." He tugs me close to his chest. "Never again."

"I'm glad you're here," I say, my hand tracing around his wrist. He doesn't recoil at the touch.

"Me too," he breathes.

I pull my hand back, leaving goosebumps in my wake. Nate smiles at my gesture and puts his wrist against mine, then intertwines our fingers. He puts them against his chest and closes his eyes. "Sleep," he mutters.

"Okay." I squeeze his hand and fall asleep with him.

CHAPTER 31

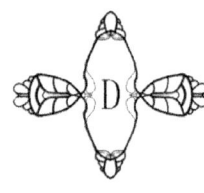

After a morning shower, I stumble onto the toilet. Fresh bandages waiting next to me on the edge of the sink.

If my legs are going to burn like this the whole day, I'll have to wrap those bandages around extra tight to get at least a bit of comfort and stability.

Almost everything has already healed. My hands are good, my back only has a few minor scars, my stomach is also turning out better than expected. I'm only left with a short but thick scar, which hasn't been inconvenient so far.

My legs are going to be the most difficult, with the Alk daggers having basically burned away parts of the muscles.

Adrian did a good job stitching it all together, there was nothing wrong on his part.

The mistake lies with my ancestors that decided to anger a pissed off person even more, causing us to have this one weakness.

Thanks again, great-great-great-great-grandfather. Much appreciated.

My legs feel and look better than I had expected though, but they'll need a few more weeks before I have full motion and strength again.

There come the bandages and extra tight shorts underneath my actual pants in. Just for that strength and stability.

When I deem them snug enough, I move to the bedroom, still occasionally seeking support from furniture. But my knees actually buckle when I see a familiar blue envelope on my bed.

The fourth and final trial.

But receiving the letter now means it'll be in a few days and my legs are still a mess.

I'll figure something out, I usually do at least.

Let's see what this trial is first.

I lean against the wall and thumb open the envelope.

~

Dawn Maria Rowena Sungust,
We hereby summon you for your fourth and final trial.
We expect you at the sacred dome in two days.

~

I stare at the summons a moment longer. Shouldn't there be an ending line that gives me a clue?

Or am I supposed to go in all blind for the final and most important trial?

I wouldn't be surprised if that was the case.

I'll have to get through it. I can't give up now, not when I'm this close to finishing it all.

My eyes fall on a folded piece of paper on Nate's pillow, which reads:

Meet me at the forge.
Bring your sword.
xxx

Nate was gone pretty quickly after he woke up this morning.

He's up to something.

Now, I'm going to Madion and Jade first to see what they're doing today and what their thoughts on this trial are.

I strap my sword to my back, brush my hair one last time, and head for the door.

"Morning," sounds on either side of me when I close it.

"I still don't understand why you're both here all the time. Do you ever sleep?" I say to the most stubborn guards in the world.

"We take shifts sleeping," Adrian answers, leaning against the wall with his eyes still closed. "Whenever you sleep, I sleep. Whenever you're awake, Jake sleeps. If he's able to, though. We switch it around every few weeks."

I roll my eyes at him. "Fine. I'm heading to Madion and Jade, and then I'm meeting Nate at the forge."

Adrian pats me on the head, and I shoot him a glare. "Have fun. We'll be following somewhere behind without disturbing."

"You better." I slap his hand away.

Their laughter scatters through the hallway as I make my way to Madion and Jade's house.

One day, I'm going to pull the biggest prank on them and they're never going to see it coming.

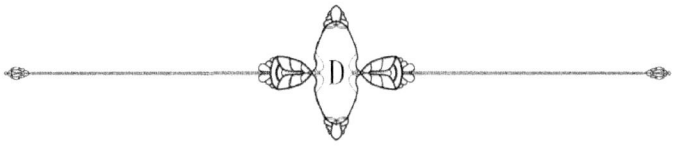

I find both women in the front yard. Jade is working on another dress, I've lost count how many she has made, and Madion is sharpening their weapons.

"Think you can do one more?" I point my sword at Madion.

Her eyes go to my hands. "I thought your hands had healed."

I sit down on the grass. "They have." I lay my hands, palms up, on my knees. "I don't know if I can do it. Physically I should be okay, but—"

She lays the arrow in her lap. "It's the feeling and sound of it in your hands."

My fists clench. "Yes."

Madion gets off her chair and sits down next to me. "We'll do it together. You hold everything first, then I'll put my hands over yours and make the movement."

The sound of the metal scraping against metal rings through my head and Kreinn's grin follows. I wring my eyes shut, trying to shut out the memories.

Warm hands wrap my fingers around the hilt of my sword and the block, then they cover my hands and start making the sharpening motion.

I take a few deep breaths before slowly opening my eyes. My hands are still shaking, but with Madion making the movements instead of me, I keep going.

"See." She pulls back. "You don't need any help. You can do it on your own."

My muscles keep going, the memory of doing this for days and nights on end somehow relaxing me. "I think I can."

My blade smooths, but as I reach the tip, the sound returns.

It returns with a vengeance.

Harsher and louder and I drop everything.

"I can't." I look at Madion, then at Jade, who dropped everything she was working on, too.

Jade gives Madion a nod and sits in front of me. "Then," she says as she takes my hands in hers, "like we always do, we take small steps until we get where we want to be."

The resolute look in her eyes immediately makes me smile and say, "Okay."

We smile at each other. And moments later burst out laughing because of the awkward silence.

"Okay, okay, now tell us what you came here for," Jade says.

I reveal the blue envelope and Nate's note from my pocket.

"Ah," Madion mumbles as she snatches the envelope from my hand. Her eyes dart across the page and keep rereading the final sentence, or rather the missing sentence.

She taps the empty space. "You thought the same thing, didn't you?"

I nod. "I did."

Jade takes the letter as Madion grabs Nate's note.

"I knew he was up to something," Madion mutters under her breath.

"Do you know what he has planned?" I ask, taking the note back from her and stuffing it in my pocket.

Placing her hand on her forehead, she says, "I don't know what he has planned, but he's been very absent since we got back."

"I noticed. Apparently, he was in my room the whole time I was unconscious and yesterday he only came back after midnight."

"I don't think it's something bad. He's just very invested in it."

I drag my hands down my face. "I know. I'm just very curious."

"We all are, so when you find out, let us know." Madion squeezes my shoulder.

"Will do."

Then Jade clears her throat. "About this final trial, though. You have no idea what it could be, right? Because if it's going to be running, you're kind of screwed."

I give her a flat stare. "No kidding."

She bites her lip. "Sorry, that was harsh."

"You were just pointing out the obvious." I put my hand on hers.

"But the question still remains. Is there any way you can prepare yourself for this one if you don't even have the slightest clue as to what will happen?" Madion reminds me.

"No, I don't," I state and start fidgeting with the strap of my jacket. "So the only thing I can do is keep training these upcoming days, rebuild the muscles in my legs, and train even more. That's the only preparation I can think of."

"I think that's the best course of action right now. You still have two days, so you should be able to get at least some improvement," Jade answers.

I give both of them a small smile. "I'm going to do my best, but I'll need training buddies."

They have daggers pointed at me in seconds. "You know you're not doing it alone," Jade muses.

I have my daggers pointing right back at them in mere seconds. "And you both know I'm winning on the magic part."

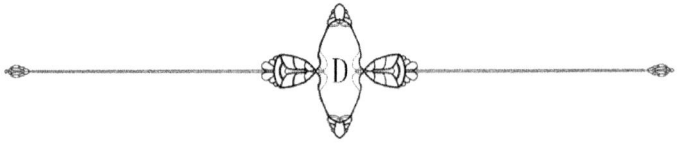

I barely get the front doors open but manage to stumble inside. The doors close with a loud bang, reverberating through the entire building.

At least Nate now knows I'm here.

The heat gets more intense the further I walk into the forge. Ovens are on either side of me, and there are even more behind the ones I can see. Yet no sign of Nate or Vergus.

"Nate?" I call out. "Vergus?"

A moment of silence follows, and I just make my way through all the scattered-out metal pieces, tools, and benches.

Until someone from the back of the forge comes running my way. "Dawn!"

Vergus wraps me in a firm hug, and I put my arms around him in return. "You have no idea how relieved

I am to see you in one piece. After Nate filled me in on what had happened, I didn't really want to think about all the horrors."

I clench the back of his shirt in my hands as I bury my face in his chest. "I'm okay now. They got me out and I'm almost fully healed."

He peels me off him and takes my face in his hands. "I was afraid I'd never see you and those beautiful eyes again."

"I'm not that easy to get rid of, you know that," I reassure him.

Vergus lets his hands drop to his side and gives me a once over. "And you're really looking more like your father by the day."

I start tracing the lines on my arms, not knowing what to say to that. Vergus eyes me and lets me fidget for a moment, before taking my hands. "He'd be proud of his little one, just like your mother."

He drops my hands before I can respond. "Now, I think your dear mate is waiting for you at his station. You better go see what he's up to."

Vergus winks at me before walking back to his work, whistling a melody from some old song that sounds vaguely familiar.

I weave through multiple benches, pieces of metal and steel, nails spread across the floor. "Nate?"

No answer.

Then let's try it the other way. *Nate, where are you?*

No answer again.

I take another step forward when hands suddenly cover my eyes. *Right behind you.*

I put my hands over his and chuckle. "Well, well. What does my handsome mate have planned that I cannot see yet?"

"Just listen to my directions and you'll find out," he whispers, his breath tickling my neck.

Nate keeps his hands in place and slowly starts walking forward. Eventually we go left, then soon after right. Until we come to a stop.

He removes one hand, only to cover my eyes fully with the other. "No peeking."

"Fine." I sigh.

I try to reach behind me to wrap my arm around his waist, but he pins it behind my back instead. "No, wait."

My arm drops to my side as he unsheathes my sword. "What are you doing?"

Tapping it on the floor, he says, "Getting rid of it in the fire."

"What?" My hands shoot to the one covering my face, but Nate moves quicker.

I hear him throw the sword on a nearby bench, then his arm comes around me, pinning my arms down. "Do you trust me?" he asks as he puts his chin on my shoulder and lets his finger trace a line on my arm.

"I do," I mumble, "but I'd love to know what you're up to."

"I'm going to remove my hand, but you have to promise me you won't open your eyes," he mutters, sounding defeated.

I'm ruining the surprise.

"I promise."

Both his arms disappear from my body. I feel him walking around me, hear him pick up the sword and stop in front of me. He grabs my hand and says, "Follow me."

Then he pulls me forward, only a couple meters. The heat is immense, but I feel Nate's magic pool around me, guiding the heat away from me.

"You can look now," he says.

I slowly open my eyes and find Nate in front of me, right as he tosses my sword in the blazing fire. "Why would you do that?" I blurt out.

He grabs my right hand. "Let me show you." And turns me around.

A bench, covered with a large black sheet, and something underneath it. Nate steps next to me, still holding my hand. He feels under the sheet with his hand before guiding my right hand, palm up, underneath it. "Just hold it there."

What are you up to?

Patience. Never heard of it, did you?

You are once again too sarcastic for your own good. I smile up at him.

And once again, you love it.

I do.

He just stares at me for another moment, and I stare right back. Until I notice the cloth slowly lifting in the air, revealing a sword.

A beautifully engraved blade, with a leather wrapped hilt. Nate presses the side of my hand against it, and that's when I see it.

The lines on my hand. He mirrored them and engraved them on the hilt. They match perfectly, every single curl brought onto the hilt.

"Nate," I whisper.

He moves behind me and wraps his arms around my waist before putting his chin on my shoulder again.

"How?" I mutter, not believing what he made.

He places a kiss on my shoulder. "I might've spent a long time looking at your hands when you were asleep. I know those lines help channel your magic. So I thought, why not make a sword that can help, too?"

I'm just speechless. The lines match perfectly, and as I wrap my hand around the hilt, I can feel my magic connecting with it. The sword faintly glows as the engraved lines fill with my magic, like blood through veins.

"It's beautiful," I whisper.

"You really like it?" he asks, still so unsure of himself.

I place the sword carefully back on the table and turn around. "It's beautiful. Thank you so much."

He places a kiss on my nose. "I have one more thing to show you."

My hands go to his shoulders, lightly pushing him away. "You know you don't have to give me anything, right? You're already more than I deserve."

"But I want to give you this." He smiles at me. "I promise it's the last thing, for a while at least."

I give him a smile in return. "Fine, show me what you've got."

We take a few steps away from the table. There he takes a silk black sack out of his pocket. I hear something like metal clinking inside of it.

Nate drops the contents in his hand and throws the sack aside. A smaller version of his bracelets lays in his hand. "I noticed you looking a lot more at your wrists since we came back, and the bracelets help for me. I thought they might work for you, too."

I stand speechless again, tears slowly forming in my eyes. He takes one of my hands and fastens the bracelet around my wrist. Then he does the same with my other.

They're the same as his. A leather band, encircled by thin metal chains with beads and charms dangling from it. And even though the leather might be tight, they give the comfort he said they give to him.

"I hope they'll help. I took some beads and charms from mine and added them to yours, but I also made some new ones." He takes a small red bead, next to a green, a dark blue and a light blue bead. "One bead for each element." He moves to the next charm. "This one has your mom's name and this one your dad's. I didn't know if you wanted me to add Leanne, so I left her out for now. But I could still add it if you want."

And he rambles on about every single charm.

"Nate," I say, snapping him from his rambling.

He looks up. "Yes?"

Tears well up even more in my eyes. "Stop talking."

"What?" His face drops.

And I slam my lips onto his, my tears streaming down my cheeks in earnest. His hand immediately goes to the back of my neck as mine go to his cheeks. "This is the most amazing thing someone ever gave to me," I breathe. "Thank you."

As we both deepen the kiss, I feel something inside me break free. Some final thread of doubt I had that it was all too good to be true. That Nate wasn't my mate.

But he is and I'm his. And I love him so much it hurts.

He—he's the person I love most in this entire world and I'm not going to wait any longer telling him.

I break the kiss and pull his forehead against mine. Then I whisper, "I love you. I love you with everything I am."

CHAPTER 32

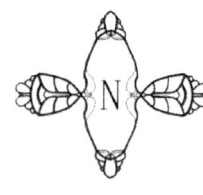
"I love you," she whispers.

My breath catches in my throat as she says it.

She really said it.

I take her face between my hands, stare into those bright, teary eyes, and say, "I love you even more."

Dawn smiles at that, and I bring my lips to hers again. Something seemed to snap in both of us when she pulled me in.

But I broke when she said she loves me.

How long have I wanted someone to say those words to me?

I think the last time someone said it to me might have been the day my mom and dad left.

And this time it fills me with warmth again, makes my heart beat faster, and it lets all my insecurities melt away.

I press her forehead to mine to let us both take a moment to breathe.

"Your bracelet has one last special thing," I whisper.

She raises her right hand, and I turn it over, showing the charm. Half of a moon. Then I turn mine around, showing the small counterpart of hers. "Now we both carry a piece of the other everywhere we go."

"Thank you."

I wrap my arms around her middle and Dawn throws her arms around my neck, then her legs wrap around my waist.

Her tears fall on my shirt, making me step back and lower us to the floor. She sits in my lap, and we hold each other.

"I don't have anything for you," she mumbles, trying to wipe away her tears.

I plant a kiss on her head. "You don't have to. You once said to me that me being with you is enough for you. The same goes for me. Just sitting here is more than enough."

"I really love you, Nate. I don't know why it took me this long to say it."

"Dawn, listen to me." I lift her chin with my fingers to make her meet my eyes. "I have wanted to say I love you so many times, but I waited. I waited because I did not know if you were ready. You said it when you thought it was the right time, and for me it couldn't have been more perfect."

Her voice breaks as she says, "Never leave me."

I rub soothing circles on her back, and she lays her head on my shoulder. "Never."

And that's the end of the conversation. Dawn closes her eyes and just deflates in my embrace, occasionally clenching my shirt or letting a tear stream down her cheek.

I know this was hard. It could be because no one else had said it to her for years either, or everything she's been through made her doubt.

That's why I waited, no matter how badly I wanted to say it. I waited for her to be ready. Because I'd do anything for her.

I love her so much that it hurts when we're not together. I will do everything in my power to protect, love, and care for her.

I'd lay down my life if I had to.

I'd die if it got her to live.

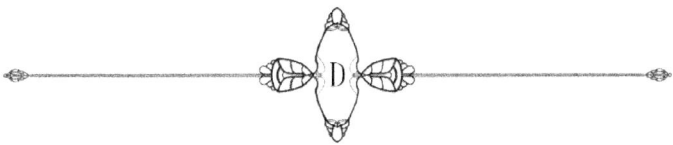

Nate and I walked back to the castle, hand in hand, my new sword strapped to my back and our bracelets touching.

It's accurate to say things got emotional. I don't know why, but I always get emotional when he does something sweet. And when he did this, I just broke.

He's always too sweet for me, and I really need to think of a way to repay him. Because he might keep saying that I'm enough, but it doesn't sit right with me.

When all of this is over, I'm taking him on a trip or something.

Because I will not attempt to make any weapons. I think I'd lose fingers if I did.

Yet, just sitting here, reading a book with him leaning on the railing of our balcony, reading too, makes me understand how him just being here can be more than enough.

When we came back to my room, I kept walking to the balcony. Apparently, Nate stopped in front of my giant bookcases and picked two copies of the same book. I didn't even know I had two of that one. He dropped one in my lap, made his way to the railing and started reading it himself. "The cover and title seemed promising, so why not read it together?" he said, glancing back at me.

And now we're here, sitting and reading for about two hours now. Both of us are halfway through the book and it is a good book, I have to admit. I didn't expect to like it this much.

Nate is going to have to pick what book I read more often, if he can pick out the best ones like this.

I flip to the next page and the first line reads:

'Pain either changes or breaks you, and I'll be damned if I let it break me.'

And that is a sentence that will stay with me for all of time.

I might be in pain, whether it is still grief or something else. I will not let it break me. Nothing can break me unless I let it.

So no more crying, tears can be shed when everything is over.

But when I flip to the next page, I find a small note.

A fourth sliver.

I close the book with a loud thud, making Nate peer over his shoulder at me. I wave him off before reading the note.

~

Hold on, Dawn. I need you to hold on, little droplet.
I need you to find me.
Just like when we were little, playing hide-and-seek.

~

I completely fall silent as the sliver slips from my fingers and lands in my lap.

There is only one person who could've sent this one. Just one.

But I can't think of a way that would fit with everything else they've done.

Nate's voice suddenly rings through my head. *What is on that paper you're holding? You've gone completely still.*

I look up to find him still reading. *It's something I just need to figure out on my own, I think.*

Okay. His answer fades away slowly. Not believing a word of what I said.

Moments pass as I stare at the paper in my lap until I pick up the book and start reading again.

Then Nate shuts his book loudly and gazes over the garden. "Are you nervous?"

He's talking about the final trial, which I told him about on the way here. No one seems to be able to figure out what's going to happen there.

Me, the dome, and one final step before I receive my full powers.

"Of course I'm nervous." I drag a hand through my hair and look up at him. "I have no idea what to expect. No possible preparations that could help me. So I'm not nervous about the trial itself, just about going in unprepared."

"You already know what I want to say," he muses.

"I know. I can only do my best and prepare as I usually do. No need to remind me." I rub my hands roughly down my face.

"Nice to know you listen to me." Nate shoots me a wink before turning his gaze to the flowers curling around the banister next to him.

I let my magic wrap around the leaves and stems. Then let them grow and reach Nate, wrapping one tiny stem around his finger, with a flower sprouting from the tip.

"This one is beautiful," he says, gently stroking the leaves with his thumb.

"The person that sent it thinks the same." I grin at him.

He uncoils the stem and flower from his finger, careful not to break it, and comes to stand beside me, leaning against the door. "I think you're prepared enough for it all. You have the weapons, you have the magic, the only thing missing is that confidence you have every time you fight yet lose when things get too tough." He sinks into a squat. "You know you can do it all. You just need to believe it."

I lay my head on his knee. "That confidence will come once I step into the dome. Now I can still fuss about everything."

His hand lands on my head, and he digs his fingers into my hair. "Do you have anything you want to do before we go to dinner?"

My finger traces circles on his knee. "I want to check in on Yuno and her new partner. I haven't seen her in a couple of days and I'm curious about what her partner thinks of me now. Our first encounter wasn't the most successful."

"I don't even want to know." He chuckles. "Let's see if this time is more successful."

We both arm ourselves as usual. It has become second nature to do so, and head out. I take Lio and Nate takes his horse, Bronze.

We reach the clearing in half an hour and tie the horses to a sturdy branch.

"We'll be right back." I scratch Lio's head and hand him an apple. He swallows it in seconds before moving to the grass at our feet.

Nate grabs my hand as we walk towards Yuno's den and the male that is most likely with her. Let's hope he's at least more friendly than last time.

The waterfall is still peacefully moving next to us as we stop a couple meters from the hole. Nate lets go and sits down on a tree stump at the edge of the water, looking at the fish beneath the surface. I walk to the entrance of the den instead and squat down. No red eyes meet me this time. I see yellow ones.

"Hello, Yuno," I whisper.

A few sniffs sound from inside, and I shuffle back, giving her space to come out. She comes waddling out, her tummy bigger than last week. Bigger on either side of her.

"You—You're—" I stammer, not believing it yet.

Then red eyes come into view behind her. No snarl this time as he walks to Yuno's side and sits down.

"You two have been busy, haven't you?" I gesture to both of them.

The male licks Yuno's face affectionately.

Gendril pregnancies go faster than ours. They last between two and four months. They can have a litter consisting of around six pups. What colors the pups will have, of course, depends on the parents. Here, I already know those pups will be beautiful.

"I have a question," I say, and Yuno cocks her head to the side. "Can you show me what his name is?"

She reaches forward and touches my nose with hers, before she walks to a nearby tree and picks up a fallen branch. Then she carves letters into the earth in front of us.

"*O-N-Y-X.*" I read and say out loud, "Onyx?"

The male's ears perk up at the name and he trots over. Onyx plants himself in front of me and gives me a questioning look. He probably hasn't heard that name in a long while.

I raise my hand in front of him, letting him sniff it. "Nice to meet you, Onyx. I'm Dawn." I incline my head to where Nate is monitoring us. "And that is Nate."

He sniffs and then directs his focus to Yuno and her belly. I smile at both of them. Yuno lays next to me and curls her tail around my leg. Onyx follows suit and curls around her.

Nate eventually leaves his stump and sits on my free side. My hand drags through Yuno's fur as Nate's hand rubs circles over my thigh.

"Why don't we leave those lovebirds alone and head back to the clearing?" he says.

I nod and say goodbye to Onyx and Yuno, who just nuzzle closer together as I get up.

When we reach the clearing, we find Bronze and Lio dozing off. Their heads slightly swaying in the wind.

"I think that's a sign we'll have to train for a bit." Nate nudges me.

I grumble in agreement and walk further onto the bare plain, only grass and an occasional flower beneath my feet.

Nate unsheathes his sword and stabs it into the earth beside him. "No weapons. Just magic. I have some things I want to try out today."

I follow suit, stabbing my sword in the ground. "I have one thing I want to test with you. Or rather, on you."

"Oh, really?" one eyebrow perks up.

"Not in that way," I say as I point the palm of my hand at Nate's feet. "Try to see if you can counter whatever I'm going to do before it reaches you."

He nods but doesn't notice I had already started while we were talking.

I've been tweaking the earth bonds I used on Madion and Jade for a while now. Making sure I don't leave any cracks, no soft spots, nothing that could break them. And I think I've got quite the structure in place now. This final test is to see how it holds up against someone with magic more of my caliber.

Not that Madion and Jade are not powerful.

Oh no, they are a force to be reckoned with and can lay waste to a small army in minutes. I wouldn't want to go against them on a day that I'm not at my best.

As the earth slowly reaches for his wrists, I keep my eyes locked with his. Does he not feel me using my magic? Or is he waiting for the last second to stop me?

I clench my fist and let the earth snatch both his wrists and circle around them. Yet Nate does not look surprised as he's wrenched to his knees.

You know I felt that coming from a mile away, right? he muses between us.

I squat down. *Try to get out of them then.*

He tugs at the bonds first, but they won't budge.

Of course, they won't. Nate glances at me as I see the magic flowing from his hands. It wraps around the pillars rising from the ground, which are attached to Nate's wrists, and starts poking. Searching for any weaknesses that may be present.

You're not going to find anything, I drawl, a satisfied smirk on my face as I walk towards him.

I kneel before him as he leans forward as far as he can. "Now what?" he asks.

"You still haven't broken free. So nothing is happening yet," I say, leaning closer so that our noses almost touch.

"Cruel," he whispers, a smile tugging at the corner of his mouth.

I playfully kiss his nose before pulling away and leaning back on my hands. "Not cruel, just showing you that my magic is stronger."

Nate lets out a hearty laugh. "You might be stronger, but it doesn't make you smarter."

"Free yourself then. I'm waiting," I provoke him.

Just let him try. See if he's smarter or stronger than me.

His magic flares and wraps around both bonds, slowly crushing them. But they won't break. I made sure my magic lingered behind in the core to push against anything hitting from the outside.

"Not going to work," I mumble, my gaze directed at the sky.

Nate grumbles, but keeps pushing, prodding, and assessing. To keep him even more distracted, I let the distance between his wrists and the ground shorten. Trying to get him on his back.

And he does. One second of not paying attention and he's down. His wrists pinned to his side. He lets out a grunt as he hits the ground, heaving out a deep breath. "Fine," he mumbles. "You win."

"I didn't see you as a quitter," I say as I move closer to him on hands and knees

I lay down beside him, my hand finding his. However, I don't free him yet.

"Are you going to let me go or am I to lie here for a while?" he says, annoyance clearly nagging him.

I squeeze his hand. "You'll be free momentarily."

I close my eyes and drift off, listening to the birds, the wind, everything that makes a sound. And it's peaceful.

My mate by my side, not a worry on my head as we lay here. Nothing is going to happen at that trial. I can complete it and free the final piece of my magic.

When Nate clears his throat after a moment, I crack one eye open to look at him. "Yes?"

He tries to move his bound hands in emphasis. "You know, I'm still kind of stuck."

I let go of his hand and sit on top of him, legs on either side of his waist. "You indeed are."

"Are you going to let me go?" he asks.

"For the right price."

"And what would that price be?"

I lean closer. "A kiss."

My lips touch his, my hands go to his face and my magic lets go. Seconds later, one hand wraps around my waist and the other lands at the back of my neck, tugging me closer.

"You're still very cruel," he whispers.

I laugh. "So are you."

Suddenly, he wraps his legs around me and flips me over. Now hanging over me, he chuckles. "When have I ever been cruel to you?"

I poke my finger into his sternum. "Right now."

He drops low, his face only inches from mine now. "And why is that?"

"Because I was expecting a proper kiss by now." I give him a light peck.

His legs straddle mine, stopping them from moving. He then pins my hands beside my head. "The roles are reversed now."

"Oh, really." I jerk my knee up, which doesn't go off without a hitch, and hit him right where it hurts. "I didn't think so."

Nate rolls off me and grunts in pain. "Now you're definitely cruel."

I laugh until he moves a bit again, then he puts on his attack.

The rest of the afternoon is playing around, magic practice, and just spending time together before the day after tomorrow comes.

Where, unfortunately, a lot can happen.

CHAPTER 33

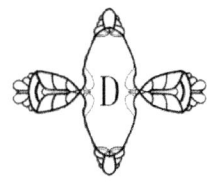

And just like that, two days pass.
And I wake the morning of the defining trial.
Jade dropped off my clothes yesterday morning. Madion came in the afternoon to talk some strategies through, but they both left quickly when they noticed my nerves rising.

Nate and I went to bed early, but I couldn't catch my sleep. I know I kept him awake all night, but he didn't say a word and just held me tighter. Eventually, I managed to drift off, but every second of sleep was filled with nightmares.

My parents, Leanne tormenting me, people dying. It did not help with the fear for today.

Nate doesn't let me leave the bed this morning, we're just laying here now. Several pillows, including Nate's arm, propped under my head, his other arm draped over my stomach, occasionally rubbing over the small scar that was left behind.

We don't say a word, nothing. The silence keeping us both calm.

"I think we might have to get out now. The trial is starting in—" I squint my eyes to look at the clock. "Two hours."

He gives me one more kiss on my neck. "Okay. Go take a shower. I'll go when you're done."

I twist around and place a light peck on his lips. "I won't be long."

Untangled and completely naked, I step under the shower. The water running down my back calms the muscles in its wake, but it doesn't relax as deep as I want it to.

When today is over, I'm just going to lie somewhere and breathe. Breathe, to let it all wash away for a moment.

I don't care who joins me and who doesn't. It matters that my mind and body can have peace for once.

After my shower, I turn the water off, wrap myself in a towel, and walk into the bedroom. Nate puts another kiss on my cheek before stepping into the bathroom and closing the door behind him.

I walk to my side of the bed, where I laid out my clothes, next to my weapons. Jade's handmade suit, sturdy boots, the enhanced sword Nate gave me, several daggers, including the one I got for my birthday from everyone, and my necklace.

The moon necklace from my mom, representing mates, always staying together. Mates doing everything in their power to free and protect the other.

If someone ever dares to hurt Nate again, they won't live to see the sun rise another day. I can promise him and everyone that.

I slip into my suit, put my shoes on my feet and sheathe a couple of daggers.

Nate comes out a couple minutes later, his wet hair hanging limp over his forehead. He pulls open the chest at the end of my bed.

We moved quite a lot of his clothing and stuff over here when we got back from the mountains. He didn't want to wait any longer after what happened and, to be honest, neither did I.

When he's got his clothes on, I take a deep breath. "Nate?"

He zips up his pants and looks up. "Yes?"

"Come with me for a moment, please." I walk to the balcony, my necklace still in my hand.

He eyes me suspiciously but follows me out.

I lean against the banister and toy with my necklace, with the crystals inside of the tiny cage.

Nate leans beside me and puts his arm behind me on the banister. "What is it?"

I lift the necklace to his face. "Can you hold on to this for me? Until I get out of that arena."

"Why?" He holds his hand out and I let the moon touch his hand.

"Because I don't want anything to happen to it." I let go of the chain. "And I remember what you said about the necklace, so I hope you'll keep it safe for me."

"I'll keep you both safe." Nate clenches his fist around the moon pendant. "No matter what."

My head drops against his chest. "I love you."

His head comes on top of mine. "I love you more."

"Together till the end." I look up at him.

With his unwavering focus on me, he whispers, "Or no end at all."

We lean on each other for a while until someone knocks on the door. Jake and Adrian enter, in their armor, swords at their sides.

"Are you ready?" Nate asks.

"Yes." I grab his chin and kiss him, putting every emotion I'm feeling into it. His hand comes at the small of my back and presses every part of my body against his.

After a moment, I put one final peck on his lips before heading over to my guards. "Let's go."

The door is opened before me and I'm on my way to the all deciding final trial.

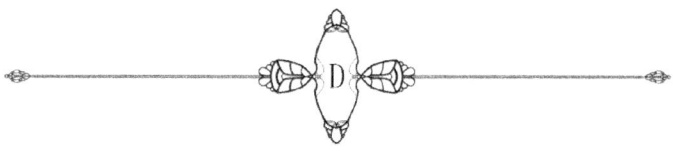

Jade is waiting for us at the side entrance of the dome, yet I see no one entering the arena through the grand entrance. Will no one come to watch?

I just keep walking. It's something I can think of later.

Yet when we close in on Jade, I can see the nerves basically radiating off of her.

Nate sees it too, and we pick up our pace.

I take her hands as soon as we reach her. "What happened?"

"Nothing happened," she says. "I just can't find Madion anywhere. She left this morning, saying she needed to run an errand, but she hasn't returned yet."

Nate glances at me. I nod to him, and he immediately turns to Jake and Adrian.

"We'll find her, don't worry," I mutter as she wraps her arms around my waist. "You know she'll always come back to you."

I hold her tight until Nate taps on my shoulder, saying, "Adrian is staying here with you. Jake is coming with Jade and I to find Madion."

"You heard that?" I say to Jade.

She nods and lets go. Nate takes my hand as Jade walks over to Jake.

"I'll be back as soon as possible," he says, his other hand cupping my cheek.

I slightly lean into his touch. "I know you will."

"You'll pass all of this." He kisses my forehead. "And when you do, we'll celebrate and relax in any way you want."

With a smile, I nod. "I'd like that. Now go find her."

Nate gives me a final warm smile before turning on his heels and following Jade and Jake.

I turn to find Adrian holding out a dagger to me.

"What's this for?" I ask as he presses the dagger into my hand.

He curls my fingers around it. "This dagger saved my life multiple times over the years. I hope it can keep you safe too from whatever you'll have to face."

I pull him into a hug. "Thank you. I know it will."

"Shall we head for the entrance? I think it's time." Adrian tightens his grip on me one more time before letting go. "You got this."

I don't know why, but it's nice to know that I have someone, someone I call my brother, in my corner whenever I need him.

"Let's get going."

Side by side, we walk to the entrance.

But dread curls in my stomach after a few steps. It's too quiet.

However, when we round the corner, we find the priest in the middle of the dome. Casually waiting for me to arrive.

Yet no bowl with the silvery liquid, nor a table are with him.

"Stay here. This is my fight," I order Adrian as I palm his dagger. "Wait for the rest."

He gives me a firm nod. "Please, be careful."

I nod in return before walking onto the sand. My dagger hidden behind my back, ready to strike when necessary.

Carefully, I make my way to the priest. He only stares at me. Not a word comes from him.

A few steps away, I notice him not even breathing. He's like a statue and I stop in my tracks. I throw the dagger at him, and he dissipates before my eyes. The next dagger is already in my hand as I turn to look at Adrian.

He's not where I just left him. I don't see him anymore.

And not a sound comes from anywhere. It is dead silent.

I make a full circle, taking in my surroundings, but no one is near.

I'm all alone.

Dawn! Nate suddenly yells through my head. *Get out of there now! It's a trap.*

What? I whirl back around to the entrance to find Nate, Madion and Jade running into the arena with several guards on their tail.

Behind you, he says, before the three of them are tackled to the ground.

I'm yanked back as a hand wraps around my throat.

I come face to face with Leanne. "Oh, Dawn. You stuck your nose in business you shouldn't have mingled with."

I claw at her arm. But in my rage, I don't notice her hand on my chest at first.

"Sleep tight," she whispers, releasing a burst of energy into my heart.

My vision blacks out and the last thing I hear is a muffled scream coming from behind me before I hit the ground.

CHAPTER 34

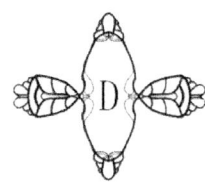

I come to with a pounding headache and my chest feeling like it's on fire.

My thoughts are hazy as I try to figure out what happened.

And then it hits me.

It was a trap.

Nate, Madion, and Jade ran into the arena with an armada of guards behind them. Before they could reach me, they were all tackled to the ground and tied up.

I remember the hairs on my neck stood up, and I whirled around to find Leanne standing behind me. One hand around my neck, the other flat against my chest, hovering over my heart. Both hands humming with the magic that was waiting beneath her skin.

She mumbled words I can't remember as she lowered her face to meet my eyes. I had put both of my hands around the arm that held my neck, not bothering about the hand on my chest.

But that was all I could do, before she had pushed that humming magic into my heart and body, making me seize up before passing out.

And now I'm here.

I try to bring my hand to my head, but I can't move it. Neither of my hands move as I tug on the bonds that keep them in place.

My arms are spread wide, both wrists clasped in shackles, attached to what I think are long chains that go straight into the wall. I'm on my knees, on a cold metal plate. Shackles around my ankles. My knees scraped open, I feel them throbbing. Probably from dragging me wherever I am now. And my chest still feels like it's burning. I tug on my chains once more before opening my eyes.

I'm only met by darkness.

I squint my eyes to slits, but still can't see a thing.

With a grunt of discomfort and pain, I try to shake off the pounding headache.

Until I suddenly pick up the breathing in front of me. I slowly back away as far as I can, but stop when I feel the faint stroke of someone's magic over my skin.

Nate's magic.

Easy. We're here. You'll be okay, he reassures me.

I try to talk, but only slurred words escape.

They gagged you.

I noticed. They blindfolded me too, didn't they?

Yes.

How is everybody looking?

They knocked Jade out. She's slowly coming to. Madion is awake, but a bit slow, he says, leaving himself out.

And what about you? I ask, my worry rising for his state.

I hear him take a deep breath as a wince sounds from someone else.

"Is she awake?" Madion mumbles, sounding very slurred.

"Just now," Nate answers. "You can share whatever you found."

Madion clears her throat. "I took the summons for the trial to the priest." A deep breath. "It didn't sit right with me."

And what did you find?

"What did you find?" Nate asks for me.

"He never sent those summons. He said he didn't write them yet because he wanted to give you another week to heal up," she says. "So my guess was Leanne had them delivered to set all of this up. The moment the priest said it hadn't come from him, I ran, trying to stop you from entering that arena, but I was too late."

A dull thud sounds from her direction. She must've let her head fall back against the wall. Disappointed in herself.

It's not her fault, I say to Nate as I pull on the chains again.

Is Leanne going to be that much of a coward and just leave us here for hours?

My biggest problem right now is that I can't do anything if she enters. I can't fight her, I can't see her, I can't talk. She rendered me completely defenseless and at her mercy.

All because I didn't see through one of her many lies.

Speaking of, I hear the bolt of the door click open. Heels sound on the stone floors and stop right in front of me.

Here we go, I whisper to Nate.

I love you, he breathes.

I love you more.

I lift my head to where I think Leanne must be standing now. A hand comes around my neck and undoes the knot of the blindfold. It drops to the floor, and I look directly into the eyes of the traitor.

"Ah, there are those beautifully gold decorated eyes," Leanne muses. "I'm still confused why people never wondered how you got them. Why it never got you thinking about people being honest to you."

I know they should've been silver. So what is she playing at?

As she steps aside, I take in the full damage she has already done to my friends. All three of them are sitting on the floor, with their hands shackled to the wall above them.

Madion has a nasty wound at her temple, her eyes only half opened. Jade is slightly leaning against Madion, but isn't conscious, even though I don't see any blood that would indicate trauma.

Then my eyes fall on Nate, who is looking sympathetically at me. His arms are burned, several thin chains wrapped around them. They used his most precious element against him to make him compliant.

The exact same picture is in front of me as I saw at the second trial.

I have seen all of this.

Nate, I mutter between us, his eyes staying fully focused on mine.

Dawn, I'm okay. It's already healing, he counters, giving me a faint smile.

I let my head drop, and that's when I see what is causing my own pain.

My chest is burned, pieces of my shirt dangling by a thread. And I'm not healing. It feels as if something is stopping it, some darkness woven through it.

Darkness that is not mine.

Leanne grips my chin. "Everything will be just fine, as long as you listen to me. Understood?"

I just glare at her, not that I can actually say anything back.

"You can't talk back, of course. Allow me." She pulls the gag out of my mouth and lets it dangle around my neck. "See, now we can talk."

"Why would I want to talk to you?" I sneer.

"Oh, because we have a lot to discuss." She plucks a bit of dirt from under her nail. "Or shall I say uncover?"

"What are you talking about?" I grind out.

She's playing. She's playing a dirty little game with all of us.

"Let's start at the beginning, shall we?" She circles me. "The first trial. Before that, we had been monitoring each other, and we were at each other's throats so much that the council decided to take matters into their own hands. Now you can't truly believe those idiots came up with these all on their own." She taps my wrist. "Let alone finding someone who could make them."

Leanne stops right behind me. I don't glance back. I just keep my eyes focused on Nate. To keep me grounded.

"So, you went to Vergus, threatened him and had him make these?" I pull on the chains.

She squeezes my shoulders. "You could see it like that, yes."

In the corner of my eye, I see Jade slowly opening her eyes. Madion notices at the same time and grabs her hand. They both fall silent, talking to each other through their bond.

Madion glances at me after a moment and gives me a faint smile.

Everything will be okay. We'll get out of this.

"But unfortunately, they didn't use them in the right places," Leanne continues. "So I took it upon myself, as you've probably figured out, and used them to my advantage." She puts one hand on each of my wrists and leans down to bring her face right next to mine. "And how much it turned out to be perfect."

"It gave me the opportunity to undermine you." She sweeps her hand in front of me, indicating all the soldiers present in the small room. "And get them closer."

That's when I look at them, really look at the soldiers. At their armor, their shoes, even their swords. They don't match the Iluniel soldiers. The swords don't have the normal indication of someone's element.

And these swords have black hilts.

Railon.

She got them inside the kingdom.

"How did no one notice them?" I nod towards the soldiers.

"Ah." She walks further around me. "They actually blended in quite nicely. No one noticed them at the ball, no one even noticed them outside the dome just now.

"But that's beside the point. Your first trial. How I was hoping you would just trip and fall. Just so we could've avoided all of this. But you got your mother's determination, I'll give you that. No matter how much I broke your defenses down, you crawled back up. Even killed two shadow hounds, without life-threatening injuries. I was slightly impressed." She chuckles as she moves onto the next thing. "Luckily, you slipped soon after, giving me a reason to lock you up again. I had hoped that collar would've caused more of a reaction, though, but you came out fine as usual."

"You've got a funny definition of the word 'fine'," I snap at her.

She looks over her shoulder. "Fine, but breaking on the inside, is that better?"

I don't respond to that.

"Well, you survived the first trial. And I knew I couldn't do anything to you during the second trial. No one could interfere, otherwise they would die, and I was not planning on dying before you did."

"How heartwarming," I mutter.

Leanne ignores it and continues. "I knew locking you up the night before would do much more harm than anything else I could think of. Seeing you flinch the moment you saw the shackles was almost satisfactory. However, you survived again. No matter what horrible things you saw, you had a big enough heart and soul to get through it."

"I bet that annoyed you, didn't it?" I playfully say.

Let her snap.

I want to see the real person who hides behind those eyes.

And she does.

Her hand finds my throat and squeezes, pulling me close to her face. "I could kill you right here, right now. Don't forget that."

"Loud and clear," I choke out.

Leanne lets go and wipes her hands on her pants. I breathe in deeply as Nate looks at me with concern.

"Next big happening," she says as she leans against the wall between Jade and Nate. "The ball. Our dance together was the perfect place for me to take a good look at your soul. I was looking for something, something inside you. And I found it, while you didn't even notice it was there. You still don't. When I looked into your soul, I found the one little clue that told me a grand plan had worked and that we could move forward with it."

"Who is 'we'?" I ask her.

What grand plan could have anything to do with me, or my soul?

"Patience, Dawn. We're getting there." Leanne pushes off the wall and stands in front of me again. "During that ball, something even more shocking happened."

She turns and crouches before Nate, who gives her a death stare in return. "My little sister found her mate. And it just so happened to be the one person you had been hoping for years to be the one, hadn't you?"

As she rises, I notice the faint darkness swirling around her heels. Like whiffs of smoke coming from a fire. It curls all the way up her legs and around her waist.

That darkness. It looks and feels the same as the one stopping the healing of my chest. That same darkness that is woven in my chest and seems to spread across the whole room. Yet nobody notices except me.

"I saw another opportunity arise that night. The amount of love that came from you was sickening for me but blinding for you all the same. I could use his anger to protect you against him and hurt you with it." She grips Nate's chin and wrenches it up to make him look at her. I pull on the chains as hard as I can, but they won't budge.

"Didn't I always say mistakes get you killed, or in this case, hurt? You decided it was a good idea to enter my office that morning, giving me another reason to lock you up. I was hoping Nate would come to me for answers, but he didn't. He went to those two." She throws a glare in Madion's and Jade's direction. "That part crumbled, but luckily, I had other plans set in motion already. One that happened about a week ago."

She pushes Nate's head aside as she takes a few steps back, standing next to me overlooking my friends. "The third trial had already helped me so much. Taking your friends, using them as bait for the wolf. It was beautiful to watch. However, that final wolf was supposed to kill you, but once again, your pure soul was willing to sacrifice itself to save these three."

Without her seeing, I smile faintly at them. They keep their faces blank, but I see the sparkle in their eyes.

"And it gave me more insight into how to break you. These people mean so much to you that if I was to kill you right now and they would walk away unharmed, you'd be happy." She glances over her shoulder at me.

I just stare back, let her do her story. I want to hear every single detail about how she screwed me over and tried to get me killed.

"And then those foolish men that tortured and almost killed you," she says as she crouches in front of me and jabs her finger into my thigh. I clench my teeth, keeping my hiss of pain in. "They did quite the number on you. And it was pretty annoying to see you come out of your tent the next morning, when I had tried my best to pick out the best men for the job. But they enjoyed it too much, took their time and that's what cost them their lives." She looks at Madion. "Killed at the hands of one of Iluniel's most brutal soldiers."

She's in front of Madion in seconds. "When you need to be, you are ruthless, swift, and lethal. Yet with the two remaining men, you took your time. Why?"

Madion's emerald eyes seem to darken. "Because they deserved it, just like you deserve whatever pathetic death comes your way."

Leanne swiftly punches Madion in the face. "Oh, how I'm just itching to take those shackles off you, just to let you show me how awful you can be."

Madion leans her head back against the wall, stopping a possible nose bleed and smirks. "Then do it. Let's see who will be the last one standing."

They stare at each other for another moment, rage coursing through both of them.

Madion has always been efficient, to put it nicely. It can get bloody, but she most of the time, she tends to keep it clean and collected. Which is why hearing that she took her time with those men very surprising. I had expected her to just slit their throats and be done with it.

"Maybe some other time. I have a story to finish with my dear sister."

Leanne walks around me and puts her hands on my wrists again. Leaning her chin on my shoulder, she says, "During that dreadful night, you could've saved them. I know you could. I was there. If you had just taken that one step inside, you could've distracted the killer, given mom and dad a window to disarm them and be done with it. They would still be here if it hadn't been for your cowardice."

"You could've chosen to not kill them, either. But instead, you stood there, you looked them in the eyes and stabbed them in the heart with no remorse. What did they ever do to you?" My voice slightly wobbles. "We had everything. And you took it away. You said you loved them."

"I never said I loved them. Have you ever heard me say that word in the past five years?" She makes me think as she steps away.

And the answer to her question is no. She hasn't used the word love, or even like, the past years. The first person to say it to me again was Nate.

Those slivers I received couldn't possibly have been hers. But they all came from the same person. And the letter, the words little one and little droplet. Leanne called me by both nicknames when we were younger.

But that night, every single name and moment we had was cut short. Leanne became cold and distant way too quickly.

It was unnatural.

So unnatural that I wouldn't have believed it if I hadn't been living through it these years.

"You used to say it. You used to say it every day to me, and I said it back every day. So what made you decide to ruin the happiness we had?" I yell at her, tears threatening to fall at my outburst. "You had no right to take it all away. Nothing had ever pushed you in the direction of killing them."

Her face is now so close to mine that our foreheads almost touch. I let my magic seep out as much as it can with these shackles. Which is not much, but I felt that these were the first pair ever made. They aren't fully sealed.

And if Leanne wants to see my soul that badly, then I want to know what lurks beneath her skin, too.

"If I wanted to, I could kill every single person in this room with the snap of my fingers. Even those friends of yours. No matter how powerful your mate or you might be, you wouldn't be able to stop me," she scoffs at me.

Good, keep talking. I need more time to unknowingly look at your soul, sister.

I stop hearing her as my magic plunges deep into her chest, down to its core. And if I hadn't been chained up, I would've stumbled to my knees at the sight.

Her soul—her soul is completely and utterly black. No light, not one speck of light in it.

My magic closes in and lightly pokes it. This does not feel like Leanne's magic. Even if it hadn't turned this dark, you would always recognize someone by their magic signature. No matter how much the person changed.

"That day in my office, you found something," she says, snapping my magic and my focus. "You read the letters on my desk. Do you really think I left those there by accident? Everything in my way of doing things had purpose, the purpose of bending you so far you'd break."

She flicks her wrist, revealing the bloodied dagger I discovered that day. "You found this."

The blood of our parents covering the blade from tip to hilt. You can barely see the Alk itself.

"If you had just stepped into that room, if you had just used your magic to take this blade from the killer, dear mommy and daddy would still be here." Leanne drums her fingers over the blade. Yet it does not hurt her.

She should be hurt by it.

Her fingertips should be burned.

She lets the dagger tip forward against my sternum. "I never took the time to clean it after I got it. I didn't deem it worthy of my time." She drags it down, leaving a long red streak over my chest. "I had one last purpose for it. One you'll find out soon enough."

Biting back the pain, I say, "What made you do it? Give me one good explanation, because right now you're talking to give yourself more time."

She swipes the dagger across my cheek. Leaving a stinging pain in its wake.

Chains in front of me rustle. When I look, I find Nate hanging forward as far as he can. "Get away from her," he snaps.

Leanne barely gives him attention. She just snaps her fingers, and a guard moves in on Nate. I pull on my shackles as he punches Nate in the face, before moving on to punch him in the stomach. Nate doubles over and sucks in deep breaths.

Leanne looks over her shoulder. "I suggest you keep your mouth shut when we are talking." She digs the tip of the dagger into my thigh, right in the still healing scar. "Unless you want me to use this dagger earlier than planned."

Now I get angry, with an underlying pain coating my voice. "Leanne, this is between you and me, as sisters. Leave him alone and we can talk."

She lets out a faint chuckle. "Oh, I have to admit, I always had to keep myself from smiling whenever you called me sister."

Before I can ask her anything, she has the dagger against my throat, the metal biting into my skin.

"Why do you even still have it? It only makes you look more like the killer," I say, careful not to move.

Leanne pushes slightly, causing a whimper to escape my throat. "Because I wanted to use it one last time." She moves the dagger to my heart. "Right there."

That's when my mind starts racing.

At everything, she just laid bare.

Her intentions to get rid of me at every single trial.

Her plans to use Nate against me by hurting him.

Her plan to pay men to torture and kill me, and then being disappointed when I walked out of my tent that morning.

Her intentions with the dagger still hovering over my heart.

Everything. Everything made me doubt these past years.

She had always smiled when I called her sister, but it was never a warm smile. It was a smile that was hiding something.

And she is right. She never said she loved me in the past five years.

Everything changed that night.

And so did she, more than should be possible.

Which brings my mind back to that very night.

The time she was unaccounted for, from running away on my left, to emerging again on my right. To not killing me but having no hesitation with our parents.

The slivers calling me little droplet and little one.

Leanne calls me that.

It hits me.

The slivers coated in her magic. The black heart of the person in front of me that does not feel like her at all.

The woman in front of me is not my sister.

She can't be.

She can't be Leanne.

I know she isn't. She wouldn't completely turn on me in one night.

The woman in front of me stops talking when she sees me spacing out.

"You killed Anna, didn't you?" I mutter, catching her off guard.

She rises to her feet. The darkness that is not Leanne's still curling around her ankles, now reaching me. "Little Anna saw things she wasn't supposed to see." She taps her nails on the blade. "So she paid for it with her life, taking the secrets to the watery grave you gave her."

My rage rises.

The secret that no one was supposed to figure out got her killed.

"You killed her because she figured out the truth that night." I pull on the chains with my full might. The bolts in the wall groan under the pressure. "The truth I just figured out, too," I sneer at her.

The chains creak as I keep pulling, channeling every bit of magic I can muster into my muscles.

The unknown woman just looks at me. "Sister, calm down."

I look up, showing the anger inside me in my eyes. "Just stop. I know you're not my sister. You're not Leanne."

I see the rest look at me with disbelief.

Disbelief that only grows when the woman responds, "I might not be Leanne."

She pauses for a moment. "But I am still your sister."

CHAPTER 35

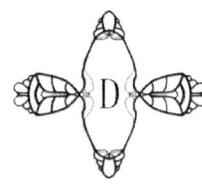

"She finally figured it out." She chuckles, hiding the dagger back up her sleeve. "It only took her five years."

I let myself sag back, all my strength suddenly gone.

Leanne has been gone for five years. I don't know if she's still alive or met the same fate as our parents.

No, she has to be alive. She's the one that has been sending me those slivers.

Then my apparent other sister steps back, closes her eyes and takes a deep breath.

The darkness climbs up her legs, curls around her chest and arms, weaves itself through her hair. Turning everything in its path black.

As it recedes, black has replaced white hair. Blue eyes, circled with silver, are traded for black, circled with gold.

"I was getting tired of this ugly blonde and white hair, anyway," she says as she pulls her braid loose. Then her eyes fall on me. "Hello sister. My name is Madelena, pleasure to meet you."

"How?" I breathe.

She crouches in front of me again. "Did you not pay attention during your history classes? There are people that can shape shift in the north."

I lean forward. "I couldn't really finish all of my lessons because you killed the man that was teaching me."

"Is that what you think?" She laughs. "Oh, I didn't kill them, Dawn. That was still Leanne."

My breath catches in my throat. "She would never do that."

And I can't get that breath down. The room feels like it's closing in on me. The chains constricting me even more.

Dawn, look at me, Nate's soothing voice rings through my head. *Look at me.*

I look past my apparent sister, into Nate's eyes. *I see you.*

And I see you. Now breathe, breathe for me. He sucks in a deep breath himself. *Just focus on me. Everything will be okay.*

I breathe in. *It won't be and you know it.*

A faint smile spreads across both our faces. *Even though things won't be okay, we'll face it together,* he whispers before directing his attention to the woman in front of us.

I take one quick look at Jade and Madion to see their faces set in rage and disbelief. Madion gives me a nod before looking at Madelena's back.

"Well, maybe she didn't do it out of her own free will, but she was still the one to wield the dagger," Madelena says, putting her hand on my cheek.

My attention snaps to her. "What the hell are you talking about?"

"The night of your seventeenth birthday, Leanne went to meet up with you before the ball, right?"

"She did."

"Well, right after that little chat you had, you were supposed to go outside to get some fresh air, as usual. Since you always needed a little breather before such a big event. Yet it was Leanne that came out instead of you." Madelena wipes a stray tear from my cheek. "You were supposed to carry the blade that night. You were supposed to end all three of them and then stab it into your own heart.

"It would give me the opportunity to take your place and rule this kingdom. But a better plan arose when Leanne stumbled into me. I would be queen, with no one in my way."

She rises. "But this so-called family of yours has too big of a heart. All of them. Your parents barely fought when they were on their knees. Leanne could barely fight me when I took control. The dread and panic in her eyes as they fogged over, completely in my control, will be something I'll never forget. But the only time she fought me was when she was sucking the air out of your lungs. Only then was she able to run instead of killing you. Your big sister loved you so much that even under my influence, she couldn't kill her little sister.

"Over time, I didn't mind you surviving that night. I found my fun in tormenting you every day. As you know, it started with mere stumbles and threats. But when you started getting more agitated, the fun really began. Then I overheard the council talking about ways to control us, to keep us in line. That's when my idea for these came." She taps my wrist again. "And then locking you in that dark dungeon. I consider that my biggest accomplishment. Just slowly, oh so slowly, seeing you crack and shatter."

"You bitch," Nate sneers. His chains groaning under the pressure he's putting on them.

Easy, Nate, I mutter to him. *I got this, trust me.*

"How did you take control of her?" I ask Madelena.

She's in front of me in the blink of an eye, with one needle made of darkness inches from my temple. "One precise attack right there. And you'd do my bidding for as long as I saw fit."

"Then why did you not use it on me?" I see Nate struggle slightly at the words. "If you saw me as that much of an inconvenience?"

Madelena pokes my temple with the darkness, but doesn't push through. "As I already said, playing with your prey is much more fun than leashing it immediately."

"But I did do it with Leanne. The outcome would just be too valuable to let her walk away and wait for you. So, she went in with the dagger, cornered your parents and killed them. And when she neglected to kill you, she ran. But I caught her just outside the doors and sent her off." She reveals. "I walked inside, as Leanne, and found you. You know how everything went from there."

"If you sent her away, how did you get the dagger?"

"She happily handed it to me right before we knocked her out and whisked her away," Madelena muses.

"Where is she?" I feel my magic rising to the surface, even though these chains are holding it back.

"Safely locked away in her lonely tower." Her smile widens. "In Railon."

"I'll kill you for that," I sneer. "For everything you've done."

Her finger under my chin lifts my face to hers. "Oh honey, wait until I tell you the biggest secret of all. You already knew Leanne killed them, no change there, but you don't know why someone even sent me here in the first place." Madelena searches for something in my eyes as she says, "Someone wanted revenge. Revenge on your parents for taking something that was his. His little creation."

"And who might he be? Because I haven't heard any name," I retort.

I try to keep myself in check, but as she keeps talking and talking, without giving me an actual answer.

"For the whole story, we need to go back in time. Somewhere at the end of The Great War. A war your parents finished, according to their story. At the end, all three kingdoms had suffered great losses. Soldiers, families, friends, all dead. Even that one camp, that one camp that killed so many men, women and children." She gestures to Nate. "Including his parents and brother."

The room falls in silence.

Nate had a brother—

"What brother are you talking about?" Nate asks, sadness washing over him.

Madelena gazes at him for a moment as Nate looks up at her. "Oh, this is almost sad."

She kneels in front of him. "He doesn't even remember his older brother. Well, it doesn't matter. Sweet Amel is gone either way." She puts her hands on Nate's knees. "Pity I had to burn his tent down. He would've loved to see his baby brother find his mate. And unfortunately, nobody buried him, since his body couldn't be recovered after I burned it to cinders."

Nate shoots forward, the chains around his arms nearly snapping under the strain. Madelena only leans forward, looking straight at him. "And what are you going to do about it?"

Hold on to that memory, Nate whispers. *Your friend's name was Amel, and he went to that same camp.*

Your brother was my friend, I whisper back.

"But that camp happened long after he set his plan in motion." She lets go of his knees and turns around to me. "Did dear Ricon ever tell you what happened halfway through the war?"

"He never got to that point," I snap.

"Then he also didn't tell you that your mother went missing for a few months. Or rather, taken from her bed in the middle of the night," she states. "She was brought to Railon, to my father. He thought, with his powers and your mothers, he could make his own weapon. Capable of leading both Railon and Iluniel if necessary."

She lets out a long sigh. "So he took her to bed, every night. Until one morning, Ricon, thinking he was some valiant knight, came rushing through the front doors and took her back."

"So this man raped my mom, and for what? To make some all-powerful weapon, from what I've heard, he didn't succeed," I mutter, carefully keeping my anger contained.

"Your mother got home safe and eight months later you came." She smiles. "But Ricon was not the father. He was not the one that conceived you." Now she outright laughs. "Your family had been lying to your face for seventeen years, until they died, taking the secret with them to the grave. And even after your true eye color came out, you didn't question things for a second. So let me ask you. Did our father's little experiment fail?"

She falls silent, only a wicked smirk on her face.

"No, it did not." She grabs my chin and wrenches my face up. "Because his little experiment is right in front of me. An experiment I'd call a failure, but father thought you could still be broken and molded again."

She pushes my face away and rocks back on her heels. "Now, who is this mysterious father?"

Her eyes bore deep into mine. "The eyes are the window to someone's soul, don't you think? And since you are pretty smart, you should be able to figure out who would benefit most from making you, just to torment Ricon."

Dawn, Nate starts, trying to keep me grounded.

But the ground was just ripped away from underneath me. Ricon is not my dad. Mom was raped by a man who wanted to 'make' me and use me as a weapon.

I should've thought more about my eyes, because these eyes only belong to one man.

"You figured it out, didn't you?" Madelena muses. "Draven, king of Railon, our father, set one of his greatest plans in motion two decades ago."

She rises to her feet. "And the only part of his plan that is left is getting you home."

I don't know what to answer. I just stare at the floor, trying to process everything.

My whole life—my whole life has been a lie. Dad, or Ricon, lied to me.

Why?

To protect me?

To protect mom from the traumatic experience?

How did she really feel all these years, knowing I was forced on her?

Did she secretly hate me, keep her distance at certain times on purpose?

Dawn, don't let yourself get swallowed by those thoughts. Ricon and Rowena are your parents. They loved you. Don't let this wrench tell you any different.

I force myself to focus again before I look at my sister.

"It seems father put more of his darkness in you than I thought. I can almost feel it filling this room, trying to choke the air out of me."

She claps her hands. The guards perk up with their hands going to their swords. "Now why don't we move somewhere more comfortable for what's happening next?"

She flicks the dagger from her sleeve into her palm and walks over to Nate. We all struggle as she slowly approaches him.

Madelena grabs Nate's hair, yanks his head back, and presses the blade to his throat.

"Get your hands off of him right now." I pull on my chains, leaning forward as far as they let me.

"One moment, sister. We're going to unshackle all of you." She motions to a guard close to Madion. He levels his sword at her heart. "Those two will keep quiet. I know they will. As for you." She presses the dagger so hard it draws blood. "One wrong move and you can say goodbye to him."

My fists clench and unclench. She can't hurt him, not because of my disobedience.

I sag all the way down, my hands go limp in the shackles.

You're not getting hurt because of me, I mumble to him.

And I don't want you getting hurt because of me. I love you.

I love you, inside and outside. No matter what, he says, his eyes solely focused on me.

I take a deep breath. Just listen to what she says. Everything will be fine.

She motions two guards to unshackle me. They free my ankles, then another shackle opens and my hand drops to the floor, soon after the other follows. Leaving me on hands and knees, trembling all over.

"I suggest you keep all that bottled up power in," she says.

I glance up at her, heaving and sweating from the massive strain building inside me.

The soldiers grab me underneath the armpits and pull me up. My arms are wrenched back by another and tied together. Others have already dragged Jade and Madion from the floor, and Madelena frees Nate, leaving the additional chains around his arms.

Madelena points at me. "She goes first."

The soldiers grab my upper arms and move us to the door. It's pulled open, and we leave the room. To wherever Madelena wants us to be.

My arms are kept tight behind me as we walk into the dark hallway. I have no idea where we are right now. It almost looks like we're in the old crypts residing beneath the castle.

But as we round the corner, a servant stands in the middle of the hallway, which means these are not the crypts.

Her gaze darts over all of us, until it lands on Madelena, and then on me.

Run, I mouth. But she's frozen from fear.

"Get rid of her," Madelena orders from behind me.

A soldier makes his way from the back and closes in on the servant, yet she does not move.

"Run!" I shout at her.

She snaps out of her daze and turns around, but the soldier is already there. He grabs her by the throat and runs his sword straight through her.

She drops to the floor and gazes at me as she releases her final breath.

"No," I whimper.

But I have no time to dwell as the soldiers tighten their grip on me and start walking again.

We reach a room at the end of the hall, one of the soldiers holding me lets go and opens the door.

Revealing an even bigger room.

And as I survey the room, I start to struggle.

A thick pole with bindings stands in the middle. A pole used for whippings. Another table filled with all kinds of instruments for torture sits against the back wall.

I plant my feet against the floor. I can't do this again.

My feet stay in place until I hear a bark of pain behind me.

Nate.

I turn my head to find him leaning against the wall, a large gash running down his upper arm. Madelena raises one finger and moves it from side to side. "Tut tut, you know where the next cut will be." She raises the dagger to Nate's neck again. "Right there."

He gives her a sideways look before smiling at me. *Just keep walking. We're all in this together and we'll come out together.*

I give him a nod and let the soldiers drag me into the room.

"We can all see where Dawn is supposed to go," Madelena muses from behind me. I look to the left wall and immediately know what she means.

She had the metal plate from the dungeons moved here, shackles for both my wrists and ankles, and her favorite, the collar.

"She can go over there, her mate can go here, as can Jade." She pats the wall to our right. "And that leaves dear Madion to start in the middle."

"No!" Jade shouts as Madion is pushed to the pole. "Please," she begs.

But none of us get the chance to struggle or do anything as we're led to our places.

I'm slammed onto my knees and a hiss of pain escapes me. My hands and feet are restrained. Then Madelena squats in front of me. She picks up the collar and stares into my eyes.

"What?" I ask, tugging harshly on the chains.

"Nothing." She sweeps my hair to the side. "I was hoping to see the defeat in your eyes already. But it'll be there when I'm done."

The collar snaps around my neck, and she steps away. I tip my chin up, steadily breathing as the ring starts constricting me. Yet my magic keeps pushing, searching for a way to come out.

Nate and Jade are shackled with chains that lead to the floor as Madion is pushed to her knees before the pole. Her arms are pulled around it and shackled to the wood.

She's breathing very slowly, centering herself to minimize the pain. A soldier behind her is already toying with the whip in his hands. Another palms his dagger and cuts open the back of Madion's shirt. Showcasing the wounds I stitched close myself a couple of years ago.

Two thicker ones run down her back and several smaller ones are scattered around them.

Madion catches my line of sight and gives me a faint smile. "Do you think you can stitch me up again when this is all over?"

"Of course," I whisper, trying to hold back my tears.

The emotions coursing through all of us, we're all trying to keep it together at the sight of someone we love getting hurt.

They're getting hurt because of me.

Madelena stands behind Madion and scans her back. "Are you not afraid?"

Madion chuckles. "I've done this before. For two weeks. Whips, knives or anything else don't scare me that easily anymore."

Madelena thinks on it for a moment, not quite understanding what Madion is playing at.

But it soon dawns on her. "Ah, that's right." She crouches down to look at Jade, and I see Madion pull on her restraints in response. "I read the report on your trip to Yedel. You were sent to talk about armies and alliances." Her hand shoots out and grabs Jade's face, squeezing it. "But you came back bloodied and mated instead."

"Get your hands off her," Madion sneers at Madelena.

Madelena raises a hand and the whip flies.

Madion arches in pain as it hits her back. They don't even give her time to recover as it flies again. My gaze goes to the quiet sobs coming from Jade. Her eyes are planted on Madion's back, the red streaks now covering the white scars.

They've been through this already. It shouldn't have to happen again.

"Jade, close your eyes," Madion says softly. "Please, close your eyes for me and just listen to my voice."

The whip flies twice in a row and Madion sucks in a sharp breath, causing Jade to start trembling as the tears stream down her face. Another lash and Jade wrenches her eyes closed.

"Remember when you took me to that waterfall? Where you dared me to climb all the way to the top. And then you pushed me off the ledge when we got there." The whip flies again. "I screamed all the way down and landed belly first in the water. You just climbed down afterwards and laughed at me." Madion takes a deep breath right as the whip goes for her back. "Promise me you'll take me there again, no matter what," she grinds out.

Jade slowly opens her eyes to find Madion looking over her shoulder at her, with a soft smile on her face.

Jade sobs, "I promise."

"Good, I love you," Madion whispers.

"I love you too."

"How sweet." Madelena holds up her hand to stop the soldier whipping Madion. "See what you're doing Dawn? That all of this is your fault."

Madion looks up at me, heaving in breaths, clenching her trembling fists. She looks me in the eye, telling me none of this is my fault.

"They have to go through this all over again because they're friends with you. You all care too much about each other and that's what will be your deaths in the end." Madelena walks over to me.

"How is any of this my fault when you are the one that put us here?" I pull on the chains around my wrists.

"Because you should've seen that caring for these people, loving them, will get them hurt or killed." She grabs the chain connected to the collar and pulls me forward. "Everybody that ever loves you dies. Your parents. Your friends. Your mate. And when I'm done here, Leanne. Everybody dies. And you'll be left all alone. Never to be accepted anywhere else again. Your hair is truly Iluniel, but it's the eyes that matter. Those eyes that show you're from Railon.

"An experiment like you will be thrown out by both kingdoms when they find out who, or rather what, you are. Nothing more than a weapon, a rather failed one, if you ask me."

She pushes away the chain, making me slam the back of my head into the wall. "Continue," she orders as she stands next to Jade instead.

And the whip keeps going. Two, three, six, ten times. Until Madion can barely keep her eyes open. She sags against the pole, breathing heavily, blood coating her whole back and seeping into her shirt and pants.

"I think she's done for now." Madelena observes.

Two soldiers close in on Madion. One frees her hands, the other catches her before she drops to the floor. They drag her over to Jade and let her fall to the ground. She lets out a groan of pain but reaches for Jade.

Jade latches on to her hand as if Madion would vanish into thin air if she let go.

"Shh, I'm okay," Madion whispers.

Seconds later, she closes her eyes and holds onto Jade for dear life.

Madelena gestures for them. "Now, since those two are occupied, and I want to let you watch something that will break you, sister. I think it's Nate's turn."

Three soldiers move in on him. Two hold his arms tight, the third unshackles him. They haul him to his feet and drag him to the whipping.

But they're careful, maybe even afraid of him.

My breathing stops as he falls to his knees and Madelena kneels before the restraints on the other side of the pole.

Nate catches my eye. *Dawn, breathe. I can handle whatever I need to if it means we get out of here. So breathe, don't pass out. I need those beautiful eyes of yours to keep me going.*

"Please, just stop this," I yell at my sister. "Just stop. Torture me, hurt me, kill me for all I care, just leave them alone!"

"How tempting torturing you even more sounds." She snaps one shackle shut around Nate's wrist. "This will be more satisfaction for me." The other snaps around his other wrist.

Madelena's eyes fall on Nate's bracelets. She fidgets with a bead before twisting his wrist around to see the locking mechanism. Nate lets out a hiss of pain in response.

"What pretty things. I noticed you have matching ones, Dawn." She unlocks it and throws it to the floor. Then she twists his other wrist around and takes that bracelet off, too.

She rises to her feet when the sound of a fire lighting up fills the room. A second whip is pulled from a sack, a whip with iron tips.

They let it hang over the fire, heating the tips until they're burning red.

I pull on my chains. I pull with everything I've got.

She can't do that. She already hurt Madion in ways I don't want her to be hurt. Madion gave me everything, and when it mattered, I couldn't even protect her.

The chains groan as I try to rip them from the wall. I couldn't help Madion, no matter how much I wanted to, but I'll be damned if she hurts someone else I love.

As I feel the chains giving me more and more way, something else wraps around my throat.

I'm slammed against the wall as Madelena's darkness encloses around my neck and cuts off my breathing.

"You know, at that ball, I was looking for that kernel father left in you." She pushes harder. The bricks behind me crack. "And it turns out that it's bigger than expected. You just never found it, because you do not dare go into those dark parts of your soul." She lets me take a breath before pushing me back again, very harshly, almost splitting the back of my head open. "The dark scars that reside there. Scars are where you draw your power from, magic or not."

She walks over to the table and yanks the whip from the soldier's hand.

Scars hurt, but they tell your story. Whether they're visible or not, they show what you survived. Madelena is right, my scars are my strength.

And I'm going to use them.

As she raises the whip, ready to shred Nate's back, I plunge into my soul. Past the last remaining layer, past the core, into the darkness below.

Draven, even his name makes me sick, left me a part of his power. Somewhere deep inside me is a kernel of his immense strength.

He uses it for awful things, but I need to use it to save the people I love.

I spread a wide web of my magic across the dark plane beneath my soul.

Then it bumps into something.

One small kernel lives at the dark bottom of my soul.

I let my magic rip into it, but it won't open. It just stays closed.

Please, give me this strength. I don't need it for myself. I don't even want it, but I need it for others.

Give me strength.

I cut into it again, and a small tear opens, leaking darkness into my soul.

As Madelena lets the whip fly, I rip it open further.

And explode into darkness.

CHAPTER 36

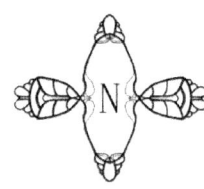

The room fills with darkness as Dawn lets everything out she has hidden inside of her.

Tendrils shoot out, hitting several soldiers square in the chest.

The remaining ones are slammed against the walls and crumple to the floor, including Madelena.

The whip only grazes my back, leaving what feels like a light burn, before it flies to the wall, too.

Everybody is out cold, except for the four of us. Somehow, she didn't hit any of us.

What she did hit were our shackles. They all disintegrated, and the remains are floating to the ground.

However, my hands stay tied around the pole. The shackles dissolved, but the ropes stayed.

Then a blinding light erupts from Dawn, and I squeeze my eyes closed.

She screams in pain.

Fighting within herself.

Dark fighting light. No one has ever existed with both inside of them.

She needs help, or it'll rip her apart from the inside out.

"Dawn!" I try to shout over her screaming. "Dawn, listen to me."

She doesn't respond.

And I feel her magic fighting within her.

Dawn, please listen to me, I say into her head. Into her soul. *Don't fight it. Just let it flow together, let it do what it needs to.*

It hurts so much, I don't want any of it, she whispers back, pain rushing through her whole body.

I let my magic gather around her, just like at the ball, just like the second trial. And I push, very slowly, trying to calm her.

I don't want it to take over, she whimpers. *I don't want to be like him.*

You won't be like him. I know you, and I know you'll use all of this for good. I know you can.

Pushing harder, I guide her magic slowly back into her.

And eventually she takes over the final bit, breathing through it as her magic recedes. The light and darkness vanish back into her soul, revealing Dawn on her knees, heaving in her breaths and shaking heavily.

"Dawn," I whisper. "Look at me."

She lifts her head. Her eyes are bloodshot from the tears and screaming. She sucks in a deep breath and steadily lets it out.

Her hands wrap around the chains at her ankles and crush them. Then she tears through the ones around her wrists. Last, she puts both hands around the collar and rips it off.

Completely freeing herself.

She crawls over to me and tries to untie the ropes at my wrists. But her hands are trembling so hard, it's impossible.

I grip her hands with my fingers. "That man has a dagger in his boot. Use that."

Dawn crawls over to the soldier and pulls it out. Her hands are still shaking so much that she nicks my palm with the dagger before cutting through the rope.

Dawn immediately drops the dagger and stumbles back.

I shake the ropes off and pull her to me, close to my chest, and dig my fingers into her hair. "It's okay, you didn't hurt me."

"W—we need to get out of here," she stammers out.

"We will." I bring her face to mine. "Together."

She slams her lips onto mine. A kiss filled with desperation, as if she might never have the chance again. I return it just as greedy and press her tighter against me.

"I love you so much. It hurts," she whispers.

"Together till the end, or no end at all, remember?" I whisper before pulling her back in for another kiss.

But we break off as we hear a soft groan behind us.

We turn and find that Jade has pulled Madion closer to her. Madion's head now lays in her lap as she gently strokes her hair. And Madion's back is bleeding heavily, blood drips on the floor.

"Oh heavens," Dawn gasps as she rushes forward.

I quickly grab my bracelets and the dagger and shove them in my pocket before joining them.

"Jade, I'm okay," Madion mumbles, but the pain seeps through her voice.

"You're not. We need to get you out of here," Jade says with tears still streaming down her face.

Madion lifts a trembling hand to Jade's face. "We'll be okay."

Jade leans into her touch and lets out a deep sigh. "We will."

Slowly, we turn Madion over to her belly. Then I grab her arms and lift her to her feet.

Jade immediately goes to her side and wraps an arm around Madion's waist, making sure to avoid the open wounds. I stand on her other side as Dawn steps in front of us.

"Ready?" she asks, shooting a last glance at her unconscious sister in the corner.

Madion tries to get her feet underneath her, but sags right through them. I let her lean on Jade to grab my earlier discarded jacket from the floor.

Dawn and I get it on Madion, protecting her back with it. Then I slide my arm under her knees and lift her in my arms.

She winces slightly, but quickly settles down. "Thank you," she says as she closes her eyes.

"Don't thank me." I direct my attention to Dawn and Jade. "You two walk upfront, I'll follow."

They both nod. Dawn goes first, then Jade and lastly, I leave the room. Glancing back one last time to make sure Madelena is out cold, before following them.

The hallway is still as dark as it was when we got here. Just as dark as when they dragged an unconscious Dawn to her shackles, how they gagged her and pulled her limp body up. They didn't know how much I was holding back not to kill all of them right on the spot.

But I knew that if I made one wrong move, I'd have signed our death sentences.

We pass the room we were in first and I can already see the staircase up in the distance.

But suddenly something shoots out from behind me. A dark tendril rushing for Dawn.

"Dawn!" I shout.

She turns right as it wraps around her throat and squeezes. Her eyelids droop within seconds. The darkness yanks her to the right, straight into the stone wall. Her head collides with it, and she slumps to the floor. Blood runs down her temple from where her skull made contact with the wall.

I step forward, but a sword lands on my shoulder, faintly touching my neck. "One more step and you're both dead," Madelena says from right behind me. She leans closer and sneers, "Did you really think her tiny outburst was enough to bring me down?"

At the snap of her fingers, soldiers emerge from all sides. From behind, from the front and from the sides. All of them with their hands on their swords, ready to strike if we dare step out of line.

"Put her down," Madelena says with a tick against my neck from her sword.

Madion lets out a groan as I carefully put her back on her feet. I don't let go of her waist though, it's the only thing holding her upright at the moment.

"Take Dawn to the arena. If she wakes up before I get there, knock her out again," Madelena orders from behind me.

Two guards walk to Dawn's limp body. Each of them grips an arm and starts dragging her away.

I want to punch both of them so hard for touching her.

But I can't do anything.

I'd be dead before I landed a blow.

"And there she goes again," Madelena whispers in my ear. "Out of your reach."

I stay silent, not giving her the satisfaction of seeing every emotion coursing through my body.

"Very well. I'll leave you with my friends while I have a chat with my little sister." She steps away, her sword vanishing from my neck. "Let's hope you're all as powerful as everybody says."

She slowly retreats down the hall and calls out over her shoulder, "You'll need it."

Then she rounds the corner to do whatever she has planned for Dawn.

We need to go after her as quickly as possible, because if those two start fighting each other, they might bring the whole arena down with them.

Madion steps out of my grip. She sways slightly, but when she takes a deep breath and releases it, she looks like she's no longer in pain. That battle instinct coming to the surface.

"Do you think you can fight?" I mumble to her.

She glances at me. "I could take on these soldiers with one hand tied behind my back. I got this."

Jade and her summon their magic, letting it gather around them and in their hands, creating swords from air and fire.

I palm the dagger I took from the soldier earlier and fill my other hand with magic.

"We need to take these bastards out quickly," I say. My magic is reeling beneath my skin at the thought of what might happen while I'm fighting here.

"Agreed," Jade says with the same lethal calm as Madion.

This is going to be a massacre if they get into it.

"Easy, you two. We need to do this quick and clean," I mutter to them.

They both look over their shoulder at me and it's Jade who says, "We'll be quick. The clean part might be loosely applied, though."

And that's all they say before throwing themselves into the closest soldier.

I whirl around and take on the two behind me.

They look me over, see my wrists, feel my magic, and take one step back.

If they want to see a monster.

I'll give them a monster.

I throw the dagger at one and grip the other by the throat with my magic. The dagger is deflected, but I let the tangled-up soldier clash with him.

They both crumple to the floor, unconscious.

Three other men have already taken their places by the time I retrieve the dagger.

My sword would come in handy right now, but I'll have to work with what I have.

Let's finally put this magic to good use.

I shove water down one's throat, burn the hand of the other and slam the third into the ground with a wall of air.

They go down, but several more soldiers are already coming around the corner.

I dare glance back once. Jade and Madion are mowing all the men down, but they're slowing, especially Madion with her injuries. And even more soldiers swarm the hallway.

A hand lands on my shoulder and yanks me back. I land awkwardly on my spine, letting out a groan of discomfort.

But I shake it off immediately when I see a sword coming toward my head.

I roll out of the way, narrowly missing the blade, and jump back on my feet.

My fist connects with his face, rendering him unconscious immediately. As he slumps to the floor, another soldier wraps his arm around my neck and pushes down.

I went through this twice in the past weeks, not again. I throw my hands against his arm and spin out of his reach.

My back slams into another man behind me, who takes me down with him to the ground.

I stab the dagger in his thigh as I get up and rush forward to collide with the other man.

But I don't see the third soldier coming from behind. His sword slashes across my thigh and I go down.

I barely catch myself, and take in a sharp breath.

Expecting another stabbing somewhere, but the soldiers sound in distress before they go silent.

The sound of their bodies dropping to the floor comes from behind me.

A shadow looms over me, ready to make the final blow.

But it does not come.

I look over my shoulder and don't find a soldier. Instead, a blonde-haired male looks me over. "Need some help?"

He extends his hand and I say, "You have no idea how happy I am to see you, Adrian."

I take his hand and let him haul me upright. Then I lean against the wall as my thigh bleeds heavily. Adrian crouches down and takes a small kit from his pocket.

Giving me time to survey what's happening around us. Jake and Vergus are holding off soldiers to our left. And to our right, Jade and Madion look stronger than ever with the swords they no doubt got from Vergus just now. They fight as one. The mating bond connecting everything between them.

A sharp pain shoots through my leg. I look down to find Adrian stitching up the gash.

"Talk to me, Nate," he says with his focus fully on my leg. "What's going on? The four of you went into the arena and didn't come out. Then the whole castle and arena were locked down. Jade's unit had to break down the front doors to get in."

Adrian looks around the hallway, searching for something, or someone. "Where is Dawn?"

I drop my head back against the wall. "Madelena has her."

"Who?"

"Oh, right. Leanne hasn't been in Iluniel for five years. It was Dawn's psychotic half-sister." Adrian gives me a confused look. "We'll explain everything later. Right now, we need to get to the arena and help Dawn."

"We will," he mutters as he knots the final thread. Then he quickly wraps a bandage around my leg, protecting the stitches and healing wound.

Adrian unsheathes a second sword, my sword, and hands it to me. "Let's clear the way."

I join Jade and Madion, and Adrian joins the other two men.

And we fight. We fight so we can all get out of here alive.

CHAPTER 37

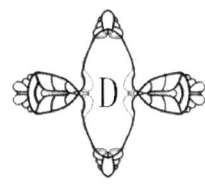

I slowly open my eyes, feeling blood dripping down my temple and a pounding headache beneath the skin. I'm laying on my stomach, cheek on the cold stone floor.

Madelena slammed me into a wall, knocking me out. Just to have me dragged all the way over here.

The arena.

Where it began and where it will end.

I lift my head to find the entire dome swarming with soldiers. Every single exit and entrance are occupied. The soldiers are lined up in two circles around me and Madelena. An inner defense against us and an outer defense against anybody that might interrupt Madelena's plans with me.

The witch herself is standing a couple meters away, a smug smile on her face. Seemingly thinking she already won.

She most certainly did not, neither will she ever.

I push myself into a sitting position, bracing my hands on the floor behind me to make sure I don't fall over because of this headache.

Madelena looks up and smirks when she sees me in my sorry state. "Finally awake."

"You slamming me into a wall didn't really help, you know," I counter.

She lets out a laugh. "Glad you've still got a sense of humor when everything is against you."

I just shrug and slowly push myself to my feet. My vision slightly sways, but it vanishes quickly. I focus back on my sister as she unsheathes a sword.

My sword.

The sword Nate made for me not long ago.

"He is quite skilled in the art of weapon making, I have to admit," she says as she drums her fingers down the blade, "You're lucky to have him make your weapons. They will not break easily."

The sword comes flying my way and lands at my feet. I look up at Madelena, who has already pulled out her own sword.

"Pick it up," she orders as she lets the Alk dagger slide out of her sleeve into her free hand.

I snatch my sword up and immediately let the lingering magic Nate left behind in it fill me, calm me down.

"Why won't you just let me kill you?" She points the dagger at me. "I'll make it quick and even spare your friends."

I push my magic into the sword. The lines glowing beneath my palm and across the blade. "You're not getting rid of me that easily."

In the blink of an eye, our swords meet. A burst of energy releases from mine and Madelena skids back from the impact.

She now forms a barrier of her own around her sword, ready to slam into mine.

The blades meet, but we're both ready this time.

Barely sliding back before meeting again.

The dagger comes towards my neck, but I deflect it with my sword and drive my elbow into her face.

Just like Nate taught me after he did it with Madion.

Madelena staggers back, blood dripping down her nose.

The rage in her eyes grows, and so does the darkness surrounding her. Slithering around her arms, her chest, and through her hair.

I do the same.

I will that darkness from my soul to come out. Gathering in my palms, around my wrists, up my arms. Tracing every single line that runs there. Turning silver to black.

We both hit at the same time. Darkness slamming into darkness.

The whole arena shakes at the collision.

Even though I just released this power from its cage, it is evenly matched with hers.

I push harder and she retreats, but slams right back and I'm forced to take a step back.

Then we both pull back for a second and slam the full might we gathered into each other.

An explosion of darkness and dust spreads across the dome as our swords meet. Soldiers disappear in it.

The walls shudder and groan under the pressure and we stare at each other.

Until we're both spent and stumble back.

Madelena heaves in deep breaths, as do I. But she manages to say, "We are equals, sister. Equal in power, yet you lack the strength to put behind it. You'll never beat me."

"You are not my equal, nor will you ever be," I snap back, pumping every bit of anger I'm feeling into my words. "No one, but my friends can call themselves my equals."

"And where are those friends now?" she taunts. "I don't see them anywhere."

"Oh, they're coming. And when they get here, you're going to wish you hadn't tormented us all these years."

She snarls as she draws the dagger, leaving her sword at her side, and charges again.

I knock the dagger aside, but she doesn't let go of it. She swirls around and puts it away, no doubt for later purposes.

Madelena pulls her sword and meets mine with it. We clash, but neither of us backs down.

In the corner of my eye, I see several soldiers closing in on us. Either to push us closer together, or to try something else.

But the moment I pay too much attention to the soldiers, Madelena seizes her chance.

Her foot rams into my abdomen, sending me flying into a few soldiers who immediately circle me.

Madelena takes a few steps back, sheathing her weapons, and chuckles. "Have fun with them, sister."

All eight soldiers draw their swords as I jump to my feet. My own sword is back in my hand within seconds.

The first one charges, and I fight.

I fight for my life.

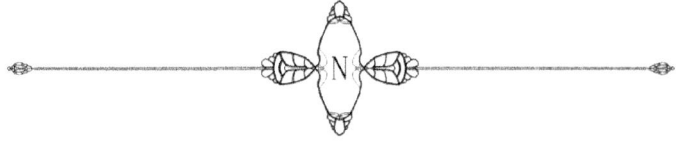

"That was Dawn," I heave out as Madion puts down the last soldier on our side.

The earthquake we felt moments ago filled the air with their magic. Dawn and Madelena's.

"She needs help. If they're swinging around those amounts of magic, one of them will run out before the other," Madion says as she flicks blood off her sword. "Somebody needs to get there. Now."

I take a deep breath and dislike what I say next. "You two go to her. I'll make my way through the soldiers here and be right behind you."

They eye me warily, knowing that I'd rather run like hell to get to her. But I need to make sure they have a clear path, so they can help Dawn first. The two of them by her side will give them all more time until we have the forces to take the Railon soldiers out.

"Go," I say, my voice slightly cracking.

They both embrace me, their arms tight around my waist as we make a silent promise.

We're getting out of here together. No one left behind.

The hug breaks and Madion and Jade rush down the hall, their goal to be next to Dawn.

Adrian, Jake and Vergus are still fighting off the last ones in this hall when I can already hear the stampede of the next soldiers coming.

We need to move.

I muster my magic to come out and let it hang around me. Ready to blow these men to pieces.

"Get down!" I shout before releasing it upon them.

They don't hesitate and Jake, Vergus and Adrian drop to the floor as my power smashes every single person in its path to the ground. They don't survive the blast. Swords disintegrated, chests caved in.

The three men gape back at me, as the power I unleashed becomes apparent to them.

"We need to get out. Now," I say to them, utterly calm. "Let's go."

I turn on my heels and hear them get on their feet and fall into line behind me.

We round several corners and pass multiple hallways when Dawn's voice rings through my head. *Nate, please tell me you can hear me.*

I pick up my pace. *I'm here. I'm on my way, Dawn, hold on.*

I'm not going to last for much longer, Nate, she whispers back.

Dawn, Jade and Madion are almost with you and I'm right behind. Please, hold on for a bit longer, I plead to her as I round another corner. Where I'm now facing a hallway crowded with dozens of soldiers. *I'm coming, Dawn. We're facing this together, even when we're not side by side.*

I'll hold on, she answers.

And my heart cracks at the amount of fear and pain in her voice.

I'm coming, love. I'm coming, is the last thing I whisper before throwing myself at the first soldiers, only a small part of what's standing between me and my mate.

So I fight. I fight for my life and hers.

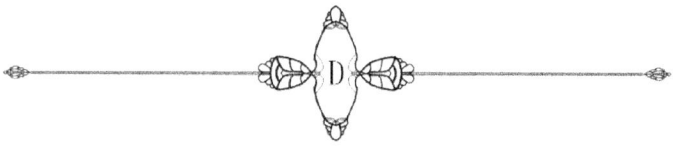

Five soldiers are down when I'm shaking on my legs to finish off the final three. This has taken a harder toll on me than it should have.

Madelena still stands at a distance, hands in her pockets, watching me crumble down.

I'm not giving her the satisfaction. If she wants me dead that badly, she can come do it herself.

Nate's words still ring in my head as two soldiers at once go down in my wake.

He's coming. He'll be here for anything. I won't be alone for much longer.

The final soldier lunges for me, but I step out of the way. He stumbles forward and I slam my fist into his neck, causing him to collapse to the floor and not get up again.

I point my bloodied sword at Madelena. "Come fight me yourself, you coward."

A wicked smile spreads across her face. "Gladly."

She unsheathes the dagger and her sword and charges up. The darkness already swirling up her legs, strengthening them.

I let my magic flow together in response, darkness and light, and strengthen myself with it. Around my legs, my arms, my chest.

Our swords clash, and the impact vibrates through every stone in the arena. Several crack and shatter, but nothing collapses.

"You know," Madelena starts as she brings her sword down upon me, "your mother named you Dawn, hoping you'd bring peace, a new beginning, to all kingdoms. That you would bring hope."

"And how would you know that?" I ask as I push her back.

"Your mother talked in her sleep during her stay in Railon," she muses as she pushes back with everything she mustered around her legs. "She had nightmare after nightmare, because she was terrified you were going to turn out just like father."

I slam back into her with ever more force, sending her stumbling back.

"Don't talk about her, don't talk about what horrible things he did to her," I sneer. "She didn't deserve any of it."

"She didn't indeed, but it wasn't about her," my sister says as she sprints at me in a blur and tackles me to the ground. Her sword rests on my throat as she leans over me. "It was all about you." She puts the tip of the dagger against my sternum. "And what is now inside of you. Father realized he needed you at home. Where he could train you, train those powers you've had locked away ever since you were born in this pretty castle."

She drags the dagger further down to my abdomen. "He wants you back. But I'd rather be done with it." She leans down to whisper in my ear, "Right now."

The dagger plunges into my abdomen.

And I scream in pain.

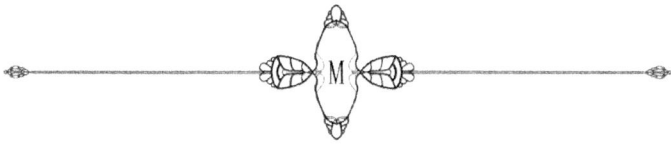

Jade and I sprint down the halls towards the front doors. But my back is slowing me down. I ran with the same injuries six years ago, and I could do it then to save my own life.

I'll be damned if it stops me from saving Dawn's life this time.

The first time I was whipped was by Jade's hands.

Her father forced her to bestow five lashes for sneaking out at night to see me. She thought she had friends she could trust within their organization. But at the sight of money, they all betrayed her.

However, that chapter is behind us. We got out, we're together. Now we need to make sure Dawn and Nate stay together.

Six guards come at us when we're in the hall leading to the front doors. I take the three on the right, burning them to a crisp. Jade chokes the other three until they drop to the floor. Dead or unconscious, I don't care anymore at this point.

The doors slam open from a distance with a powerful blast of air from me. Clearing the way for us to the arena.

But outside, another twenty soldiers have gathered, all ready to stop us from going any further.

"Meet me in the middle?" Jade mutters, a murderous gleam in her eyes.

"Meet me in the middle," I whisper back.

With a kiss to her temple, we break apart and close in on either side. And from the terrified looks on some soldiers, I notice that this is not the most well-trained unit.

These men are barely soldiers. Some can't even hold their shield right, I say to Jade, who is on the other side of the group now.

All the more fun to see them cower in fear when we come by, she answers before unleashing herself, magic and steel, upon her first victim.

I follow suit and together we bring down every single one of them.

Carving our way to a friend who desperately needs our help.

CHAPTER 38

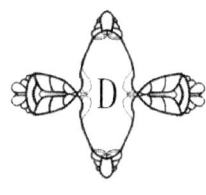

Madelena gets off me, and I immediately grab the hilt of the dagger.

My magic wraps around the blade on the inside, but there is nothing to be done.

I'm going to bleed out.

"Three down. One more to go before your entire line is eradicated," Madelena states as she sheathes her sword.

Nate, I whisper to my mate. *I'm not going to make it.*

His answer takes a moment. *Yes, you are. You're not going to die.*

I might, because I'm not going to be able to hold on for much longer. I take a deep breath as I feel the tears gathering in my eyes. *I love you Nate. With everything I am, I love you.*

Don't you dare, Dawn. Don't you dare say goodbye, he snaps, but there is desperation underneath it. Pure desperation for me not making it.

I slowly push myself into a sitting position, firmly holding the dagger in place. *Remember when we first met? I think I've been hoping that you'd be by my side from that moment on until the very end. And you are. I didn't care that day whether there was a mating bond or not. I cared about you, just you being there. And you were. Every step I took out of the darkness, every step you took out of that darkness, we were there together.* I suck in another sharp breath as I brace myself to stand up. *I love you, Nate. For every single thing you've ever done for me.*

A tear streams down my face as Nate's answer follows. *I love you too, Dawn. The moment you stepped into the forge that day, the moment you stepped into my life, it got brighter. No one makes my day light up as you do when I look into your eyes.* Pain seeps between us as he continues, *No one makes me feel as happy as you do when you hold my hand. No one gave me the gift of love like you did.* More tears roll over my cheeks and slide down my neck. *So please, Dawn, I beg you. Hold on. Don't let go. Don't leave me, please.*

Madelena's smile widens as she sees the amount of effort I'm using to get up.

But I do it. I get on my feet, the sword in my hand fully charged.

She has to die. I can't leave her here with everybody I love.

It almost sounds like Nate heard my plan when he whispers, *We said together till the end, or no end at all, Dawn. You were the first to even say it. Please, please don't let this be the end.*

I take a step forward, closer to my sister. *It's not the end, because I love you, Nate, and that love will never end,* I whisper, my voice breaking. *And death is never a goodbye. I will see you again, just not in this world.*

This is what the third trial prepared me for. I had to be ready to leave everything and everyone I love behind to save them.

Because right now there is only one way this can end with everybody safe in the end.

If the cost of protecting my friends and killing her is my own life. I'll gladly pay it.

How important are the lives of your friends? The question of the priest once again rings through my head.

"More important than my own," I whisper to myself as I take two steps forward. One hand still cradling the dagger, the other gripping my fully charged sword.

Dawn, Nate begs me, *Don't. Please, there has to be something else we can do. Not like this. Please, not like this.*

I step in front of Madelena, who eyes me, not fully comprehending how I'm even standing.

Let me save you this time, Nate. Let me be the one to let you live your life.

I let go of the dagger. A searing pain launches through me at the movement. I rip my father's signet ring off her finger and put it in my pocket, hoping for somebody to find it later. *I love you, Nate. With every fiber of my being, I love you.*

I love you too, he whispers back.

Cracking my soul with the gentleness, yet overwhelming pain and sorrow in his words.

My left hand shoots out to Madelena's neck. Darkness sweeps around it quickly after.

"If you want to end me that badly, sister." I lean in and whisper in her ear, "Let me take you with me."

I love you, Nate. Never forget that, I repeat to him one last time.

Then I drive my sword into her heart, releasing every last drop of magic I have left.

And shatter our souls with it.

CHAPTER 39

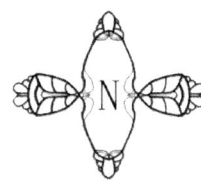

An explosion shakes the arena and everything around it the moment I stumble through the front doors.

I fall to my knees and scream out in agony as a blinding pain sears through me.

A pain that reaches the darkest corners of my mind and soul.

No, no. Please, no.

Dawn, I whisper in desperation.

Only to be met by a dark void, nothing on the other end of that bond.

"That came from the dome," Adrian mumbles in horror.

I lift my gaze to see pitch black smoke rising from it. Rising from where Dawn is supposed to be. I push myself back to my feet and rush down the stairs. Heading straight for the dome, Adrian, Jake and Vergus close behind.

Six soldiers rush towards us from both sides. I snap my fingers and all their necks snap simultaneously.

The three men behind me stop short, but I keep running.

I need to get to her.

The doors seem to be ripped from their hinges when I reach the entrance. I run inside, dodging bodies here and there.

And as I sprint through the dark halls of the arena, they feel endless.

They feel endless as I try to reach the dome.

The origin of the explosion.

I'm afraid to find out what happened there.

I felt her.

I think I felt her die.

But this can't be her end. Our end. Not like that.

I can't believe what Dawn just said was her goodbye. I won't believe it.

As I round the last corner, I slow down, seeing the devastation that has taken place. Numerous soldiers are lying motionless on the floor, several bleeding heavily from lethal wounds.

Large cracks cover the walls, stones have fallen to the ground and the building might very well collapse soon.

But then my eyes fall to the one thing I feared to see. The very dagger that killed her parents protruding from her abdomen.

I come to a halt a few steps away from Madion and Jade. The former gripping a hand, which is decorated with silver swirls, from the fingertips all the way down to the shoulder, a bracelet hanging loosely around the wrist.

The latter just stands there, looking at who the hand belongs to.

When Madion turns her head to me, I drop to my knees. Tears are streaming down her face as she looks at me and shakes her head.

"No," I whisper.

We promised each other. Together till the end, or no end at all.

And as a final confirmation my greatest nightmare became reality, Madion mutters, "She's gone."

FOUR THREADS OF FATE

FOUR THREADS OF FATE

WHAT HAPPENS NEXT?

FIND OUT THIS DECEMBER IN THE SEQUEL
TO FOUR THREADS OF FATE.

Printed in Great Britain
by Amazon